Jane Yardley was brought up in an Essex village but went to university in London, where she has lived ever since. She has a PhD from Charing Cross Hospital Medical School and works on medical projects around the globe. Much of her life is therefore spent on aeroplanes and in hotel rooms, and this prompted her to get to work on her first novel. In common with her central character Annie, she has synaesthesia – 'hearing' music in colour.

Acclaim for *Painting Ruby Tuesday*:

'When a rash of murders startles the modest Essex village of Muningstock in 1965, the local police can't seem to crack the case. This is because ten-year-old Annie Craddock keeps inadvertently stumbling through, removing or vomiting over the evidence. An emotional mass of red hair, lanky physique and vivid imagination, Annie normally spends her summer holidays larking about with her best pal Babette, playing the piano with the dazzling charismatic Mrs Clitheroe who shares her love of music . . . (they both see music as colours), and hurling herself adoringly on Ollie the rag-and-bone man's dog. When things go frighteningly awry . . . Annie finds herself questioned by the police and wrong-footed at every turn.

The story is told in the first person by the present-day Annie, whose imminent move to New York with her husband has stirred up ghosts from her past. The highly original tale moves between past and present, told with humour and poignancy by a hugely likeable heroine. Yardley effortlessly evokes the confusion and egotism of childhood . . . Now, as an adult, [Annie] finally realises the truth behind the events of that summer . . . This is an entertaining and compelling read filled with rounded, memorable characters, and both darkly funny and moving' *Time Out*

PAINTING
RUBY TUESDAY

Jane Yardley

BLACK SWAN

PAINTING RUBY TUESDAY
A BLACK SWAN BOOK: 0 552 77101 5

Originally published in Great Britain by Doubleday,
a division of Transworld Publishers

PRINTING HISTORY
Doubleday edition published 2003
Black Swan edition published 2004

3 5 7 9 10 8 6 4 2

Set in 11/12pt Melior by
Falcon Oast Graphic Art Ltd.

Black Swan Books are published by Transworld Publishers,
61–63 Uxbridge Road, London W5 5SA,
a division of The Random House Group Ltd,
in Australia by Random House Australia (Pty) Ltd,
20 Alfred Street, Milsons Point, Sydney, NSW 2061, Australia,
in New Zealand by Random House New Zealand Ltd,
18 Poland Road, Glenfield, Auckland 10, New Zealand
and in South Africa by Random House (Pty) Ltd,
Endulini, 5a Jubilee Road, Parktown 2193, South Africa.

Printed and bound in Great Britain by
Cox & Wyman Ltd, Reading, Berkshire.

Papers used by Transworld Publishers are natural, recyclable products
made from wood grown in sustainable forests. The manufacturing
processes conform to the environmental regulations of the
country of origin.

To the memory of three men – my uncle Alf,
my headmaster Mr Glyn Jeffreys,
and Richard Murphy, my friend.

ACKNOWLEDGEMENTS

A surprising number of people have had a hand in writing this novel. First, Helen Corner of Cornerstones, without whom it might never have got beyond the first draft. I must also thank Norman Price of Manuscript Appraisals for excellent advice exactly when it was needed. Veronique Baxter at David Higham is the best agent and friend a new writer could have; thanks also to my publisher Diana Beaumont and everyone at Transworld, and my friend Paul Abrahams (who is not a singing teacher), without whom there would be no central character to the story.

Much of this book was written on planes and in hotel rooms around the world, and I owe a debt of gratitude to everyone who helped to make this bizarre life sufficiently comfortable that I could write a novel in it. Most of all, Adela Tramson at Virgin Atlantic for treating me like a VIP, and to everyone at the Villa Belmonte, Cape Town, particularly Tabea and Cliff Jacobs, Lovet Robinson, Este Laurence, Solly, Joseph, Annamarie, Milly, Yolisa and Catherine, for providing me with a home from home.

1

When I was ten and our humdrum Essex village was convulsed by a series of murders, I worked myself up into a fever, afraid that the police had me down as a suspect. Well, of course they didn't – I was no more of a hooligan than the average ten-year-old daughter of respectable parents, and mine were so respectable that they ran our village school; it wasn't likely that I would suddenly go berserk with a meat-axe, even taking into account what elders everywhere had been warning for years about the influence of rock 'n' roll. Besides which, one of the victims had always been a friend to me; she taught me how to hula, and do the twist, and play boogie-woogie on the piano. So no, the CID did not suspect me of killing anybody, least of all our lovely neighbour Mrs Clitheroe. They only suspected me of breaking and entering, theft, tampering with evidence, and conspiring to pervert the course of justice. Which I couldn't really quibble with.

Unusually for an Essex story, this one begins and ends with New York. In that same summer of 1965, my

9

father, who had never been further west than Cardigan Bay, managed to get himself invited to New York to present the mayor with a scale model of the Empire State Building made out of matchboxes. Seven thousand, five hundred and seventy-four of them, standing three and a half feet high, pasted over with crêpe paper and painted; all done by my classmates and me during that summer term. New York was host to the latest World's Fair, and my father must have convinced the mayor that a matchbox model of the Empire State was what the event had been lacking. The smell of spent matches always takes me back to it, and 'Ticket to Ride', which played incessantly on every transistor radio. Years later, when my friends started to produce babies, a whole new world of squeezable toys and plastic teats drove my memory back to Cow Gum bottles, and squashing the rubbery mouth hard down onto desks and tables until glue seeped through its clotted lips.

My father was a short, bumptious, 'go for it' sort of man, and the cane he carried under his arm during school hours lent him a touch of the sergeant major. On the day he flew to New York, my mother and I went up to London airport with him in the car, singing and playing word games around the airline BOAC: Better on a Camel, Beware of Angharad Cradock. That's me, and in my father's accent it evokes Welsh castles and close harmonies suspended like skeins of mist, high above the waterfalls of Betws-y-Coed. Unfortunately, from most people's mouths it's all phlegm and rasping, so I mostly answer to Annie or even Aggie, which I don't enjoy, but it's better than being flecked with spittle.

Our in-car singing was always based on my father's repertoire of hymns and campfire songs. As a concession to my own taste we also sang 'Yesterday' – the only pop song he ever approved of – while numbers by groups with names like the Zombies would be vetoed out of hand, not to mention my proposal, just the once, to entertain everyone with some Roger Daltry, with me innocently piping, 'Why don't you all f . . . f . . . f . . . fade away.'

This is a family adventure, all for one and one for all – that is, until we reach the departure lounge, where the shared treat is suddenly traduced to a game with a solo player and two spectators. We have met one of the great dividers of caste: the gulf between those who have tickets to ride and those who don't.

London airport crepitates with loudspeaker announcements: Rome, Hong Kong, Anchorage. These are magical litanies, but the authority of the announcers is charged with the same casual rejection as the overhead sign: *Passengers Only Beyond This Point*. For the first time in my life I have no rank; it is nothing to these people that I am the headmaster's daughter.

We eventually take leave of my father after a lively twenty minutes at the BOAC desk for special cargo, with Dad waving his correspondence of the last three months with both Mayor Robert F. Wagner and the chairman of the airline. I long to follow him through Passport Control; until now, New York City was just a symbol of my father's new status as international traveller. Suddenly I can see the skyline, the neon, the raucous, synthetic illumination like the world's largest fairground carousel, and I yearn to ride it.

All the way home I rain questions on my mother about air hostesses, and how old must I be?, until she snaps at me to pipe down. But I can't; I am feverish with faraway places, I fizz with a self-wounding excitement.

And now I am married to a native New Yorker, and we visit the Empire State on a trip from our home in London. We stand at the lookout on the eighty-sixth floor and I marvel at the quality of New York light: the

November air is glacial, the East River shivering glass; sun slices down the avenues like a sabre. I love this city with a child's love of magic; this has never stopped being the wonderland my father flew off to in a jet plane in 1965. My husband Alan always welcomes the opportunity to instruct; he's confidently spouting facts and figures that conflict with my open guidebook, whose pages are slapping in the same wind that blows at Alan's hair. This is cut to make the most of his waves of cornfield blond. He is a good-looking man, and conscious of it.

It is Halloween and the stores on Fifth Avenue have ghouls and gore in their window displays – amputated limbs drizzled with blood. I flinch, even after all these years; not many ten-year-olds have watched a severed hand fly out of a caravan window, let alone walked halfway home without noticing that the gold ring that came spinning off one of its dead fingers was now wedged in her shoe. My 1965 was peppered and salted with the grotesque, and it still flaps with loose ends. The unsolved murders gape in my mind like a wound; the sense that I let Mrs Clitheroe down, that without me to play merry havoc with their inquiries, the police would have solved the crimes. It's something to do with being here in New York, this guilt, it has been seeping out of me ever since our plane touched down. I always did associate New York with Jenny Clitheroe: during that fevered summer of Dad's Empire State building (Dad, who I also let down in the end), she used to tell me fabulous tales of this city, paint pictures in words, in music. New York reeks of her.

This is far from being our first trip, but this time we're here because Alan has been offered a job, a career move that will not only bring him back to the States, but also give him the resonant title of President and Chief Executive. It is unthinkable that he will turn this down, but we walk and walk, mile on mile, and Alan discourses on whether or not we should leave London. He lists upsides and downsides in solemn tones and the language of macroeconomics, and reprimands me for not paying attention: this is our future; use it or lose it; life is not a dress rehearsal. But unlike Alan, I know about dress rehearsals, and the similarity is striking – muddle and mayhem, the occasional catastrophe, and the near-religious faith that everything will be all right in the end.

THE PAST

2

Our house was square, brick, semi-detached, and built about the same time that I was – the mid-1950s. When I was a babe in arms we moved into one half and into the other came a commercial traveller who had left Dagenham for the countryside. His name was Frank Lucas and he had a family – his wife Irene, and their daughter Babette who was exactly my age, and with whom I grew up. Frank, who was 'Uncle Frank' for twenty years, worked for Imperial Tobacco. He would light up cigarettes in shops like Marks & Spencer with prohibitive notices on the walls. When, inevitably, the manager was called, Uncle Frank would remonstrate along the lines that he didn't go around telling people not to buy their underpants from Marks & Spencer, so he didn't see why they should tell their customers not to smoke tobacco. This was quite an eye-opener to the daughter of a non-smoking, teetotal headmaster who would never transgress the rules on a shop wall in all his born days.

Muningstock in Essex was still a village when I was

brought up in it. A lot of our neighbours were new-comers like the Lucases, from Dagenham or the East End, though there were some older families with proper Essex accents, and a number of Romanies or travellers whose children didn't come to school much in spite of my father's crusade, and who were not called Romanies or travellers by anyone except him – they were called gypsies, or more usually 'gyppos', and they were widely distrusted.

I never had a sister or a brother, but I had Babette next door. When we were both seven, her brother Craig was born. The night of his birth she slept round at our house. When Uncle Frank got home from the hospital, a joyful man, he called to her through the cavity wall. Babette hammered on it and hollered back at him, to the horror of my mother, who foresaw fist prints on her floribunda wallpaper. Then, in 1965, when we were ten, Auntie Rene had another baby girl, Amanda.

My colouring is the same as my father's – wiry red hair, pale eyes, and the sensitive, itchy skin that some-times goes with them. When relatives tried to comfort me over school jibes about carrots and ginger, they would tell me how ladies with hair like mine often mature into auburn, which is beautiful. But Babette was *born* auburn. She was petite (I've always been long and skinny), with a head of shining conker-coloured curls, and dark eyes beneath a velvet veil of lashes. Speaking of which, she was also the brown-eyed daughter of two blue-eyed parents, which was to be the cause of a very acrimonious dispute with her biology teacher when they got on to genetics. But back in 1965, Babette was in the same class as I was in our village school and it was her steady fingers that stuck the final matchstick on the top of the radio mast, which Mayor Robert F. Wagner sent spinning into oblivion as he reached out to shake my father's hand.

*　　*　　*

'My daddy's in New York!'

Babette carried on eating her sandwiches; she was becoming familiar with these non sequitur outbursts about America. Our two companions stared at me for a bit, and then glanced at each other.

'So?'

'So nothing. Only that's where the Beatles are, too. It's where Shea Stadium is. I bet you saw that on television.'

'Your dad one of the Beatles, then?'

We were sitting on bales of straw between a damp ditch choked with stinging nettles and a pea field. All week I had been coming here with Auntie Rene and Babette (and Craig and baby Amanda). We picked the peapods into bags that we emptied into a sack, the weight of which determined our wages. Babette and I worked together and split the profits.

'Of course he isn't one of the Beatles. But he could meet them. He might, while he's there.'

'Oh leave it out, you silly bugger. We know your dad – he's headmaster of Muningstock primary school. I bet the Beatles want to meet a teacher from a titchy kids' school, I *don't* reckon.'

The friend sniggered something into her ear, which I suspected, with growing dread, was an insult to my father – I thought she said something about short-arse and fatso. If they'd been our age, mine and Babette's, no doubt this would have escalated until I was in tears, but these were big girls, teenagers from the local secondary modern school, and they were past the days of child-baiting. The first girl abandoned me and the Beatles for Babette.

'Your mum's a hairdresser, i'nt she?'

'Used to. She stopped when she had my sister.'

'She's pretty, your mum.'

'*She's* pretty, an' all,' said the second girl, indicating Babette, of course. The other one jabbed an index finger at us in rhythm: 'She's pretty, she's not. She's brainy, she's not.'

'You don't know – perhaps Babette'll grow up just as brainy,' said the first.

And perhaps I'll grow up just as pretty. It was a neat response, but of course I wouldn't come out with it. There was no expression for 'street cred' in 1965, but I knew that's what I lacked – no currency with which to negotiate in the pea fields, where even my father's proximity to Shea Stadium was laughable.

So why was I putting myself through this? Now the New York preparations were over, I was at a loose end, and having someone to be with (i.e. Babette) meant more to me than getting my own way. And a week's work would earn enough money to buy at least three singles from the Top Ten. It was like love; living without them was like physical pain.

One of the girls was talking. 'See that boy over there. That sloppy joe he's wearing, that's American. My boyfriend's sister's friend brought one back from Disneyland. See, lots of people go to America.'

'That boy over there' was sprawled across a straw bale. He was about three years my senior, and might well have been American himself on the evidence that he was wearing a sneer worthy of Elvis. Babette, who was occasionally sensitive to my humiliations, suggested that we finish our sandwiches and go off for a wander, but we only got a few yards before being lassoed back by Auntie Rene. We were well-drilled citizens in the police state that is childhood.

When we returned to the pea fields the following day, I saw the boy again – same sloppy joe (grubbier), same bale of straw, but this time I went up to him. I went thundering up to him. He and a smaller boy were hunkered down over a springer spaniel; they were laughing and the dog was crying.

'Stop it! I'll tell Sir! I'll tell Mr Cradock!' Playground tactics. But what earthly use were they here?

'Get off us, you stupid fathead!'

I was flailing at them, all arms and legs. My elbow caught Sloppy Joe in one eye. The spaniel scampered off to freedom, yelping.

'Fucking moron! Get her off!'

'Oy! Oy! Oy!' There was an adult yelping now. The commotion brought several of them, including the boy's mother – not Sloppy Joe, the other one.

'They were hurting a dog! They were being cruel to it!'

'We weren't hurting the dog, stupid! It had a stone stuck in its paw. We were helping it.'

'*What* dog?' demanded the mother.

'It's run off, now. 'Cos of her – screaming her stupid head off!'

Other grown-up voices joined us. 'Break it up, the pair of you! I'd wallop her if she was mine!'

'That's my neighbour's little girl.' (Auntie Rene.) 'She makes more noise than my Amanda!'

I was yanked out of the scrum, Auntie Rene's fingers like a vice around my bony upper arm. 'You've had your chips, madam. I'm not bringing you again.'

'They were being cruel to a dog! I heard it crying.'

'They were *helping* the dog, you silly girl. Showing me up!'

'YOU'RE NOT FAIR!'

We often brought out the worst in each other. Babette was always an obedient child, and neither Craig nor Amanda was old enough yet to be judged. I suppose mine was the only juvenile rebellion she regularly had to contend with. Auntie Rene dragged me, boo-hooing, back to the peapods, back to Babette, who was conscientiously snapping green stems and filling her little bag in the teeth of the crisis going on around her.

'Now dry your eyes and do some work for once. What with your daydreaming, you don't pick anything near the amount Babette does. I should dock your wages, an' all!'

This wasn't the best way to pacify my tantrum, and no doubt I would have sobbed all afternoon had it not been for Babette; her presence always brought the boys round, and one of them stopped en route to have a humane word with me. His gist was that 'Rupert' really *had* been performing vital surgery on the farmer's dog. 'Rupert' was the farmer's nephew – a guest up at the house. He was a posh boy, not one of your yobbos or gyppos. Now those gypsies really *did* go in for cruelty to animals; did I know what they did to their horses once the poor old nags were past it?

With the air of someone lunging to rescue an endangered toddler, Babette attempted to drag me off. I was to go *right now* and apologize to this boy Rupert. If I didn't, he would probably tell his uncle, the farmer Mr Lawrence, about me and I'd never be allowed to come pea-picking again.

As a threat, this wasn't the most persuasive. By now I had no intention of going near a perishing pea field ever again in my life, and if every pea field in Essex were wiped out by locusts and biblical floods I'd be the happiest child in Muningstock. And the same applied to the sneering, swearing Rupert, no matter if he was the Dr Dolittle of springer spaniels. I'd never heard the word 'fucking' before, but I'd heard it now, and I'd know it when I heard it again.

The day wore on with its fitful August sunshine and smell of vegetation, and my socks got progressively dirtier from the dun-coloured soil. I stewed over the injustice of everything. There was some short-lived excitement when one of the toddlers fell in a ditch and swallowed the used condom he found lying in it. A large lady attired in crimplene slacks steamed across the field with the mysterious cry of 'Let me through, I'm St John's Ambulance!', shortly after which the child was upside down and projectile vomiting, which was certainly a diversion. Then there was a bigger one, when somebody trod on Mrs Maxwell.

She was a neighbour of ours, living in one of the crescent roads that developers were looping around Muningstock like kiss curls. Ostensibly, Mrs Maxwell worked in the pea fields for pocket money the same way that she worked evenings, selling cosmetics and toiletries door to door ('Avon calling!'), but in practice we were pretty sure that she'd never been in contact with any pea that wasn't tinned, and the fields merely provided a flat surface on which to top up her suntan. (Though whether the consequent effect could be called 'tanned' or 'mummified' was a matter of taste.) She did have a garden at home, but one of the lads who helped weigh our sacks (and who sometimes had to be shouted at quite loudly to get his attention away from the ins and outs of Mrs Maxwell's supine breathing bosom, which still managed to make its presence felt even when flat out under gravity) had told her the farmland was up an incline and therefore nearer the sun.

'I do need that extra something for my skin now that I've turned thirty,' I'd heard her say, which prompted Auntie Rene to ask whether she'd remembered to count the Saturdays and Sundays.

On this particular afternoon, stripped down to a slip as tight as a sausage skin and much the same colour, through which could be seen her exhausted roll-on girdle, Mrs Maxwell and her limbs blended so well with the soil that a stuttery teenage girl in spectacles strode right across the hillocks of her ribcage. It wasn't the accident itself that brought the pea fields to a standstill as dead as a dock strike; it was Mrs Maxwell's ringing accusations that this same girl had stolen a ten shilling note from her handbag while she was asleep.

Everyone in Muningstock knew Gina Maxwell of old. She took dislikes. It was already known that she nursed an antipathy towards this poor child, and the present accident was sufficient evidence as far as Mrs Maxwell was concerned to set the accused bang to rights. She pulled on a terylene dress and stood at the weighing machine, doing her figure no favours by setting it amongst the bulgy sacks, with a ten shilling note cocked between root-like fingers, screaming that its twin had disappeared from her purse into the hands of the unfortunate teenager.

'I never forget a face!' she was shouting into the bespectacled features of the wrong girl. 'I knew you was a villain soon as I set eyes on you.'

'Gina!' said Auntie Rene. 'You can't go around accusing people like this. You got no evidence.'

'I got my own eyes!'

'You said you was asleep. Now look, we all know how careless you are with that flippin' bag.'

'I was only dozing, and when I opened my eyes, there was her thieving fingers snapping the catch shut. You saw her kicking the breath out of me! What do you think that was about?'

'She tripped, Gina, on account of you being invisible. We've warned you before. It'll be a tractor one of these days . . .'

At this point, two of the farmer's men arrived to frog-march Mrs Maxwell off the premises, squealing like a pig shed, and I resolved not to be a pea-picker when I grew up, but to have a proper career. Preferably as an air hostess, flying between London and Idlewild airport, New York.

Of course, this incident drew everyone's attention away from my own shortcomings. Then there was a further upswing in my fortunes when one of the teenagers turned up her transistor radio from which Radio Caroline was belting out 'Satisfaction' by the Rolling Stones ('I Can't Get No').

I too had a transistor, though I wasn't allowed to take mine from the house. This was a birthday present, and it says something for parental love that although I learned a lot of words like 'cacophony' and 'corncrake', no-one subsequently locked it up or took an axe to it. Anyway, the afternoon would have proceeded with me as good as gold, if I hadn't caught sight of something shocking. Ready to take my bag along to empty it into our sack, I turned to Babette, my placid, feet-on-the-ground best friend, and discovered her in tears.

This wasn't slowing her down – the tiny fingers continued to flicker over the peapods, plucking and snapping – but she was indisputably having a cry. As I watched, she split open the pod and crammed the contents into her mouth. Comfort eating? I don't suppose I had seen Babette cry in public since before we started school, and I was not only shocked, I was embarrassed and ashamed on her behalf, as though she had started dribbling like a baby or pulled her knickers down.

'Babette?'

Nothing.

'Babette, what's the matter?'

'Go away. You're horrible.'

'I haven't done anything!'

A lot of succulent sniffing (Babette was a sniffy crier), but she wouldn't answer me. From behind a pea plant came even worse sounds of distress – Radio Caroline was now playing P. J. Proby, a sobbing singer in tight leather trousers that would one day inevitably split on stage mid-song. He had recently set the scene for this by recording the three hits 'Hold Me', 'Together', 'Somewhere'.

'Why won't you tell me what I've done?'

'Leave me alone!'

It might have carried on like this indefinitely, with no response except that I was horrible and she hated me (I already knew that Babette could sulk – it stunned me that anyone had the patience), but perhaps my side of the exchange was seeded with the threat of a banshee wail, because Babette eventually gave in.

'You wouldn't apologize to that boy! You hit him in the eye, and I bet we won't be able to come no more. I bet Mr Lawrence won't let my mum come pea-picking no more.'

Because of me? I couldn't absorb this. Nobody ever blamed an adult for an action of mine. Every action of mine rebounded on me directly and immediately like some moral boomerang.

'It's all right for you, Annie! Your mum and dad are well off and they've only got you. My mum can't do her hairdressing in the salon now we got Amanda, and we need the pea money.'

'Well, I need the pea money, too.'

'You only buy pop records with it! My mum and dad need Mum's money at home!'

This conversation was plummeting into the bizarre. Uncle Frank was demonstrably better off than my father; their house was always full of sweets and biscuits, which ours never was, and anyway, their house was bigger than ours – Auntie Rene's brother was converting the loft into another bedroom so the family could come to stay without Babette having to share with Craig, Amanda and her cousin. What is more, this conversion had dormer windows! Dormer windows were the last word in sophistication in Muningstock in 1965. I'd nagged my parents for so long about dormer windows that the subject was banned from the house.

'Your mummy and daddy don't *need* the pea money,

Babette. It's just for a bit extra, like Mrs Maxwell doing the Avon.'

'You don't know anythink, Annie Cradock! You think just because we wear clean clothes and don't go about smelling like gyppos, that we're all rich like you. There's lots of families at school that don't have much money, only you don't realize!'

I now felt wretched. Babette was my friend. There were plenty of times when I was in the doghouse and Babette was my only ally in the world. My scalp tingled and I felt a constriction in my throat.

'You know what grown-ups say, Babette: least said soonest mended.'

'But you hit him! "Least said soonest mended" doesn't work when you wallop someone!'

It began to dawn on me that I could be in genuine trouble over this assault. My only aim had been to rescue a crying dog from two kids who were boys and therefore psychopaths, but now everyone said the dog was all right. Well, I couldn't cope with another encounter with Rupert, but . . .

'Do you know what?'

'What?'

'If you come with me, I'll go and tell Mr Lawrence I'm sorry and it's not Auntie Rene's fault.'

'You don't know where he is.' We were country children; we knew that farmers aren't indoors during daylight hours.

'Mrs Lawrence, then. She'll be in the house.'

'She might not.'

'No, but she might.' And if so, I could tackle her, just about; it was other *children* I was terrified of. Eventually I negotiated it with Babette. We would go up to the house together. Babette would stand at the door in front of me, fully visible, and I would do all the talking. Horses for courses.

She and I threaded our way back through the

24

fragrant green aisles, through the pickers and their babies and their bags, and across the adjacent fields and the road, towards the farmhouse. August was always a mongrel time of the year in East Anglia, the trees a weary dark green, ditches and verges full of the dirty rust of dock weeds, fields under the plough, little colour except for willow-herb, deep pink in the hedges. Huge machines droned sluggishly up and down the fields, churning over the stubble.

A fine electricity of fear tickled the lining of my stomach, and as the house got nearer, P. J. Proby's song thumped through my brain like a dirge. But then we reached the paddock, and everything was horror and dismay because there was Rupert slouching in it.

He was alone, lolling against the wall, a picture of disaffection now the row had ejected him from the fields. Childhood is full of concepts that you can't properly enunciate because the vocabulary isn't there, and in the paddock I didn't have 'poetic justice'. True, I had recently gained 'fucking', but it would be some time yet before that came in handy. My dismay wasn't shared by Babette.

'Are you Rupert? Please don't get cross. I bought my friend. She wants to apologize.'

'What – her? She nearly had my eye out! Silly cow. Get her out of here.'

There was indeed a livid mark beneath his left eye, like a sty coming up, or a welt.

'She come to say she's sorry.'

'You're not allowed here. You're trespassing!' He hissed the sibilants at us. 'Pea-pickers aren't allowed in the house or grounds, because you're common and ignorant.'

'*I'm* not common and ignorant!' I retorted, the implications of which couldn't have been lost on Babette.

'She just said "I bought my friend". How much did she pay for you, then? Half a crown?'

25

He didn't have to spell it out; I was familiar with having my own English corrected day in and day out at home. But I wasn't common and ignorant.

'My daddy's in America with the mayor of New York!'

'So what? My father's a commissioning editor for the BBC. I've been out on location and watched them making *Z Cars*.'

'*Z Cars*!'

Everyone in Great Britain watched *Z Cars*. It was police realism, it was new, it was now. It was certainly a higher bid than Mayor Robert F. Wagner.

'The TV cameras weigh more than thirty stone each, and they run on fifty feet of cables.'

'Have you met Bert Lynch and "Fancy" Smith?'

'Those aren't their real names, you spastic, they're actors! I've got their autographs. I've met loads of famous people at the BBC.'

'Have you? Please tell us – who, who?'

But Rupert seemed hesitant about divulging any more, except technical information about TV cameras, for which, of course, Babette and I were a rotten audience. When cornered, he admitted to meeting one of the newsreaders.

Time was getting on and Babette was beginning to feel that our furlough was running out. 'We better go back to picking now. Annie and me only come to say sorry.'

We didn't know it, but Rupert had been banished from the house for strangling two ducks on the pond for a bet. Babette was therefore a welcome diversion with her risible grammar and heart-shaped face. He made an effort at keeping us.

'My father's well known right across the BBC. Everyone from *Z Cars* will be coming to our house for cocktails. And the actors from *77 Sunset Strip*.'

'I can't hang about, Annie. You shouldn't, neither.'

'*You shouldn't neither?!*' Rupert twisted his features into someone's notion of an East End wretch – one of Fagin's boys, perhaps, picking a pocket or two. Nevertheless, I suppose there was something about his *in loco parentis* corrections to our English that made me believe the rest of his statements – even that his father knew the stars of the American series *77 Sunset Strip* from the BBC, which would normally have struck me as dodgy logic. I watched Rupert as he watched Babette retreat across the road towards the pea fields.

'Can ordinary people go along and meet *Z Cars*, too?' I asked, as she disappeared.

'You mean people as ordinary as you? My father will fix it so you're never allowed at the BBC – you nearly had my eye out!'

I wanted to make it up to Rupert, but what did I have to offer him? (which sounded nauseatingly like 'The Little Drummer Boy', but I couldn't help it). I then invited further derision by volunteering to write Rupert a song at my piano which he could tell the *Z Cars* men he wrote himself. Apparently pianos were kids' stuff. And when I replied hotly that it took a lot of nerve to play in front of an audience, something I'd been doing since I was seven, I was treated to a lecture.

'That's not nerve! Nerve is when you break into someone's house while they're actually inside it and loot the place without them even seeing you, like I'm learning to do.'

'Are you? What for?'

'That's how they train secret agents.'

'James Bond doesn't do it!'

'He's not real, you fathead! It's how MI5 trains real ones. You have to oil the lock and hinges so you can sneak in by the back door while the stupid twats are watching *The Black and White Minstrel Show*. Or climb the drainpipe and break in through an upstairs window. You put Contac across the pane to hold the glass while you smash it – cuts the noise down and stops it shattering everywhere and slashing your own wrists. I know one boy did that. He severed an artery. The blood spurted out so high they were washing it off the guttering. Or you can use putty on the window pane once you get really good. I've done it when they're in bed, even – got in through the bedroom window while the deaf old buggers were in beddy-byes, and sneaked over to where they were snoring, close enough that I could've sliced their throats with the window glass if I'd wanted. You keep on until you've got nerves of steel.'

Rupert had insider knowledge because a friend at boarding school had a father in MI5, and the boys were part of a training programme every holiday. Each had to break into a stranger's house while the owner-occupier was *in situ*. When term restarted, they displayed their booty. I considered this, and it was flawed.

'I bet you just make it up. You all bring something in from home and pretend.'

But I was a cretin. There followed a long exposition on the rules of MI5 cat burglary; there were prohibited households, proscribed bounty, and intricate rituals, all finely honed by Rupert and his public school friends in their cold comfort dormitory and fantasy world.

'Anyway, you can't join MI5 because you're a girl and a spastic.'

I might be a girl but I was NOT a spastic, and I bet I'd make a perfectly good cat burglar, breaking into people's houses and looting them! I proclaimed this in my high, clear treble, with the vocal delivery that would one day knock 'em dead in the aisles. I was projecting splendidly across the paddock just as Auntie Rene arrived like Nemesis, and dragged me

28

bodily away. She was rigid with anger, and didn't speak a word to any of us all the way home, not even the wet and bawling Amanda.

3

The village of Muningstock. The walk from our house to our school was about a mile, half of it along a track between hedges and brambles, known as Rainbird Lane. This was a picturesque name, but the eponymous bird wasn't a peacock, it was a pub. My parents didn't go to pubs, but I was occasionally allowed there with Babette's family, to sit in the garden and drink lemonade. Uncle Frank would say at least once that he was off to see a man about a dog, yet he never let me go with him.

It was a magical garden, with a pergola of pink rambling roses, ye olde rustic seats, and a stone bird-bath inscribed with a verse: 'The kiss of the sun for pardon / The song of the birds for mirth / One is nearer God's heart in a garden / Than anywhere else on earth.' Babette and I both had fair-sized gardens at home, but they were distinctly unromantic. Hers featured a child's swing and a sandpit. My mother's garden was ruled into sharply rectilinear beds, and she favoured sober colours such as 'bleeding hearts' with their trailing fur as though we were growing our own flock wallpaper.

Rainbird Lane divided the old village from the new. The newer side had semi-detached houses like ours, an estate of council properties in utilitarian style, and some recent developments of chalet bungalows, lined up like Monopoly houses in roads named after the countryside they'd replaced – Hornbeam Lane and Coppice Crescent and Old Oak Avenue.

My father enjoyed a vicarious pride in these new homes, these spanking new designs for living in the 1960s. He would talk the builders into letting him inside, and would trot through the rooms seigneurially, running a hand over the gleaming stainless steel in the kitchen, flushing the lavatory . . .

'Progress is a wonderful thing, Annie-*fach*! Science. Engineering. The space age!'

I never knew much about his background near the Wrexham collieries, though my mother's occasional remarks hinted at outside privies and three to a bed.

On one occasion, he bounced home to fetch me, and persuaded the plumber to show me how the ballcock works in a cistern. Whether it was the functioning of lavatories or lavatorial functions, my father believed in plain speaking because knowledge is light. No doubt he deserved to have a daughter who would grow up to be a specialist in gastroenterology and could fix her own plumbing.

The older side of Muningstock had our school, St Matthew's church, the rectory and Muning Hall. This was a fine, no-nonsense Georgian house, the grounds of which were large enough to hold the Romanies' or travellers' camp without much noticing the encumbrance. The uncamped grounds were thrown open once a year for the church's summer fête. Muning Hall had a concert grand piano, elderly but still tottering gamely along. For the past few years I'd given a short recital – the first movement of the

Beethoven 'Moonlight' Sonata – priced a shilling a ticket.

This year, when the applause subsided ('Oh Mr Cradock, you must be so proud!'), the musical discussion slid into the arena of the Beatles, and whether it was right to give them the MBE. This was a controversial award from the Queen's recent Birthday Honours List; already, two venerable members of this long-gone empire had sent their own medals back to the Queen in disgust. Here at the fête, a village wag had set up a box with a sign reading 'Return Your MBEs Here', until the vicar had it removed on grounds of irreverence. In our round-piano discussion, there were those in favour of the Beatles and those against, but I was the only one to voice the opinion I'd heard at home – still in my upstage position on the piano stool – that their manager Brian Epstein had been ignored for the MBE because he was Jewish and homosexual, shortly after which the company started talking about something else.

My own manager was my father, organizing gigs and setting the price of tickets. He was also the one who kept tabs on my practising, dragging me back from pop song riffs to scales and arpeggios, for which I should have been more grateful, since the arpeggios helped me to play the riff from 'House of the Rising Sun'.

The nearest neighbours to have a piano were Jenny Clitheroe and her husband Leonard. They lived in one of the chalet bungalows in Bluebell Crescent, which looped euphoniously behind our house. Mrs Clitheroe would happily have been Auntie Jenny – 'I answer to anything feminine short of "Grandma",' she'd say in that lovely voice, smiling and smoky, like the wispy embers of a wood fire – but her husband put a stop to it. 'The words "Mr" and "Mrs" are in the English language for a reason, girlie. It's a matter of respect.'

Mr Clitheroe originated from Lancashire, appropriately enough. He was a chiropodist, and he was peculiar. I remember going there to tea one Sunday when I was small; he suddenly darted out of the room and returned carrying a plastic model skeleton of the foot.

'You think you're a clever chap, Cradock, but I'll wager you don't know there are twenty-six bones in the human foot!'

He also brought sheep's heads home from the butcher, whole, which his poor wife had to chop up with a cleaver to make brawn. Babette and I regarded this as one step short of cannibalism, though my father said it wasn't uncommon in the north. Well, it seemed sufficiently *un*common when you were sitting in your daddy's car next to Mr Clitheroe's at the traffic lights, with a sheep's head staring at you from a bag on his passenger seat.

Jenny Clitheroe was in her mid-thirties, and was the only grown-up Babette and I knew who wasn't square. She could do the twist right down to the carpet and back up again without toppling over, her blond pony-tail wagging like an excitable puppy, and she had a dazzling collection of pop records including every release by the Rolling Stones. Her husband blamed them for her migraines (he was also once heard to blame them for the Labour landslide).

Mrs Clitheroe's migraines could be terrible, and were signalled to the outside world such as Babette and me by the tight closure of all the curtains at the front of the bungalow during broad daylight. But when she wasn't prostrated, Jenny Clitheroe was a gentle creature with a liking for children, or at least a high pain threshold. When summer holiday boredom drove us to extremes and neither set of parents would allow us back in the house, Babette and I often gravitated to 16 Bluebell Crescent. Provided the front curtains weren't closed up against us, we would spend a couple of happy hours with Babette browsing through Mrs Clitheroe's family photograph album, an impressive collection from Edwardian days to the present, and me entertaining everyone with my keyboard prowess. Jenny Clitheroe, too, was a pianist, and unlike every other grown-up, she made proper sense when she talked to me about it. She could even talk about it in colour; we shared the peculiarity that we heard music as great colourful swathes, rich scarlet symphonies, soft verdant ballads. Not only music, we visualized all sorts of inappropriate things in colour – numbers, letters, days of the week – as though we both had our brains wrongly wired up. And so the two of us would chatter about whether the *Goldfinger* theme was green or purple, while Babette placidly leafed through the family album.

There was a stylish wooden clock above the fireplace, upon which Babette and I kept half an eye so that we were always completely gone before Mr Clitheroe came home for his dinner at one o'clock or his tea at six. Somehow, poring over the family photos or belting out R&B on the piano were equally impossible under the black button eyes of Mr Clitheroe.

My mother said that he wasn't peculiar really, they were just unhappily married, and that made for a strained atmosphere.

The next nearest piano as the crow flew belonged to the Frobishers: Horace and Doris. He had read Classics at King's College, Cambridge, but he was never quite the same after Burma, and now sold insurance for the Prudential company – he was our Man from the Pru. The Frobishers had previously lived for a short time in Dagenham (which is a long way from King's College), so they already knew many of Muningstock's other newcomers. Horace was plainly fond of the Lucases, even though Babette's dad made no bones about the fact that he couldn't stand the sight of either of them. I had once overheard him in the garden of the Rainbird with a new neighbour who'd asked whether the Frobishers had any children.

'No, they've never had kids. And looking at him and looking at her, I don't suppose they've had much of anything else, either.'

They were the sort who said 'pl*arst*ic'.

Horace and Doris were church people (something else he got after Burma), so Uncle Frank called them Hassock and Cassock. Despite his antipathy, Babette and I saw rather a lot of them because it was with the Frobishers that we went to Sunday school. This took no heed of conventional school terms because God never takes a holiday, and so every Sunday morning for years we were ironed into several layers of clothing and sent off in Uncle Horace's Morris Minor to the icy microclimate of the Norman church in Wittle Massey. This was a splendid piece of architecture, but it was infused summer and winter with its own damp chill, as though the warmth of the sun were short-circuited outside the lichened walls of the churchyard. In the depths of winter the heaters were turned on, with their single, angry, orange elements, fitted halfway up the columns of the soaring nave on the interesting principle that heat sinks.

The Frobishers ran the Sunday school between them, and no doubt they didn't do a bad job, but Babette and I were used to the Cradock method of learning, an educational technique fired by my father's white-heat-of-technology outlook on life. At the age of ten, every child in Muningstock knew basic trigonometry from having fun in the playground with mocked-up theodolites, and knew that computers were based on the binary system, from playing 'on/off' games with all of us lined up, flashing black or white flags. In the shadow of this, Babette and I spent nearly every Sunday morning of our childhood listening to Bible stories and singing watery post-war hymns, stiff with cold and boredom.

Hanging in the nave of the church was a reproduction of Holman Hunt's painting *The Light of the World*. The sight of Jesus's lamplit face amid the tumble of flowers invariably warmed my heart, complementing as it did my favourite poetic line about being nearer God's heart in a garden, and so reminding me of the pub. When I wasn't dreaming of sugary lemonade in the garden of the Rainbird, I was yearning for the day when I would be old enough to leave Sunday school. My ambition was to join the choir at St Matthew's, back in Muningstock. Among the advantages of this were that the building was heated, they sang proper hymns with those deep velvet chords and crimson-coloured cadences, and the choir not only sang descants, but *they were paid*.

It was on our way home from Sunday school, towards the end of my father's New York sojourn, that we heard about the first of the murders. Uncle Horace's Morris Minor was sedately turning a corner from one bland country lane into another when he sent it careening across the bank, the alternative being to mow down Mr Clitheroe, who was in the middle of the road waving his fists and hollering. Apparently some boys on bicycles had swept past close enough to make him dodge.

'So now you're walking in the middle of the road on a blind bend, Leonard, where it's safer?' suggested Auntie Doris, mildly. She was a tall, authoritative figure with a mass of black hair tamed into a fat, wobbly bun. By contrast, Uncle Horace was small and wiry, and was yet another Muningstock redhead. Shimmering through a refractive layer of Brylcreem, his hair was a thick cushion of coppery chestnut with a central parting, like the rump of a Grand National winner.

It was Jenny Clitheroe who answered. 'We're all a bit shaken this morning, Doris. By the news.' She looked across the car. 'Good morning, Horace. Hello, Babette, Annie.'

'News?'

'Murder!' Mr Clitheroe exclaimed with a further wave of his fist, as though now it was up there, he may as well put it to good use. 'Hasn't it reached you? A man knifed to death last night, here in Muningstock, by God, in't gypsy camp!' Occasional bits of eroded Lancastrian would creep into his speech whenever Mr Clitheroe was agitated or angry, which pretty well covered most of his transactions with Babette and me.

His wife made a protective gesture in our direction. 'Leonard, please.'

'What the hell d'you mean – *please*? Just telling 'em, aren't I? Over in that shambles they call a camp, back of Muning Hall, on Sir James's land! He should have evicted 'em before it ever came to this. Partly to blame with his lily-livered views, if you want my opinion. See what it leads to!'

Mrs Clitheroe turned to us again, speaking as softly as she could from the front passenger's window across to me in the back seat and Babette in the front. As often, Uncle Horace had Babette sitting on his knees pretending to drive (I had grown too big for this game). She perched there in her habitual serenity, apparently unstirred by the car's recent violent skittering off the road.

'You mustn't worry, girls,' Mrs Clitheroe told us both with a gentle smile. 'It was something between the travellers, an argument between two men on the camp. Nothing that will affect us.'

'Argument? It was simple burglary, Jenny. Theft and murder. He broke into one of the caravans while the owner was out, and was getting away with some valuables when another didicoi caught him at it, and got a knife between his ribs for his trouble.'

'Leonard, the girls might not want to hear all this.'

'You keep saying "he", Leonard,' Uncle Horace pointed out. 'Who are we talking about?'

'Didicois! Don't know them by name.'

'But is the killer caught? Is his identity known?'

'You can bet your life *they* know. But they're not telling the police, of course not. Gyppos are bigger liars than the Irish and Welsh!'

I saw his wife wince on behalf of the Cradock in the car.

'It all sounds dreadful,' said Horace.

'Professional job, the burglary, so the police reckon.'

'Wherever have you gathered all this forensic information, Leonard? I assumed you two were on your way home from matins at St Matthew's.'

'Where better?' There was a new edge to Jenny Clitheroe's voice. 'The porch is always a crucible of gossip. There's so much chitter-chatter and "Have you heard?" and "Well, I never!" goes on, I'm surprised the gargoyles haven't toppled out of the masonry from sheer boredom.'

'Gossip?' shouted her husband, incredulous. 'This is a bloody murder, woman!'

'So these good people have gathered, Leonard.'

'Why do you say it's a professional job?' asked Auntie Doris.

'Wasn't a smash-and-grab sort of thing. The thief lifted the pane out with a proper glass-cutter and putty. Knew what he was doing.'

Babette frowned, perhaps trying to remember where she'd recently heard talk of burglary linked with talk of putty. In fact, she'd heard it twice, once from her mother after the long walk home from Rupert's paddock, and once from me.

'Really, girls, there's nothing for you to worry about.' When Mrs Clitheroe was upset or concerned, her blue eyes darkened, and she had a habit of lifting the wavy blond hair of her pony-tail away from the back of her neck. 'You're safe as houses.'

'Bloody funny expression to choose when there's a murdering burglar about!' put in her husband.

At this point, another car rounded the bend. The driver wasn't quite so sanguine as Uncle Horace about being made to swerve towards the ditch; he lowered his window and shouted some short, economically worded abuse.

'I think,' said Auntie Doris drily, 'that we'd better deliver Angharad and Babette home before irrevocable damage is done to their spiritual welfare. We'll see you later, Jenny. Leonard.'

With that, Uncle Horace drove us home. The news had had a deleterious effect on his clutch control, and we bounced along Mountnessing Road like baby kangaroos. This was sufficiently entertaining to erase any sense of unease, and anyway, when the Frobishers dropped us off, we found Babette's cousin Lorraine in the front garden.

Lorraine was Auntie Rene's niece, daughter of Uncle Arthur the loft converter, a large, loud, hearty man, always happy to grab a passing child and piggyback it round the garden, with never the slightest attempt at improving its mind in the process. He was widowed young, and seemed to have reared a daughter without her particularly noticing any deprivation. As for Lorraine, she was a teenager, and in 1965 this was the highest attainment anybody could aspire to.

The three of us were folded into the half-carpentered corners of the half-finished roof-space, a wonderland of crannies and holes and hazards – there were entire stretches of flooring where a child's ill-placed foot could come crashing through the bedroom ceiling. The travellers and their troubles forgotten, I was fascinating my audience with imaginative tales involving me and the New York World's Fair, and when that audience grew restless, I switched to the St Matthew's choir, descants and all.

'Now, *that's* the way to get on, Annie,' said Lorraine, 'get paid for enjoying yourself. It's like me, see. You and singing, me and the boutique.'

The wages, I outlined, were sixpence for choir practice (Thursday evenings), a shilling for matins (routine Sundays), one shilling and sixpence for communion (the first Sunday of the month) or evensong (the last Sunday), and five shillings for a funeral. Even a barren month with no-one dead in it would bring me the wherewithal for a new record.

'*Funerals?!*' Lorraine's face puckered in distaste. 'Not weddings and christenings?'

'I expect there's those too. Only I've been to weddings and christenings before; I've never been to a funeral.'

'I shouldn't think so, neither! Anyway, I don't reckon you'll need the extra money. A little bird told me you was planning to become a burglar.'

A burglar.

'Don't, Lorraine.' This was Babette. 'There's been a terrible thing happened. One gyppo's burgled another one's place and killed a bloke what tried to stop him.'

'Yeah? When was this?'

'Last night. Round the travellers' camp.'

'Your mum never said.'

'Don't think she knows. We got it off of Mr Clitheroe on the way home from Sunday school.'

While Lorraine was making a face at the mention of this name, I was deliberating on the fact that she knew about my confrontation with Rupert. It seemed that Auntie Rene had distributed the story liberally across

40

her own family, though so far she hadn't told mine. When she'd delivered me home, it was with a pretty comprehensive report to my mother on the original fracas over the dog, and also my going AWOL and being found in the paddock, but my burgling ambitions weren't touched upon.

'Dogs again!' my mother had sighed. She was a primary school teacher; you develop a summary system of approximate justice, otherwise you could spend all day in a classroom establishing precisely who did what to whom. 'Cruelty to animals is a phase she's going through. It's over-excitement because of this American adventure of David's,' she had diagnosed. 'We've had no end of broken nights, haven't we, madam?'

I could see the words 'I'd give her over-excitement if she was mine' hovering over Auntie Rene's head in a cartoon bubble.

Now Babette was reassuring me. 'It weren't Rupert done this one, Annie, putty or no. You don't want to worry.'

'Rupert isn't good enough to use putty yet,' I explained to her. 'He holds the glass together with sticky-back plastic. But the burglar could have been one of his schoolfriends, doing the same training.'

'*Sticky-back plastic?*' queried Lorraine, fascinated. 'They giving out Blue Peter badges for burglary, or what?'

'No, honestly. He and the other boys use it to do cat burglaries because they're training to be secret service agents. It makes them have nerves of steel. They're learning how to oil locks and climb pipes.'

She gave me a look through lashes heavy with mascara. 'How old was this boy of yours?'

'I don't know. About thirteen, I suppose.'

'*Thirteen!?* And him and some other thirteen-year-olds are being trained up like flippin' James

Bond? I thought you was supposed to be brainy!'

'Annie, he *was* telling us some whoppers,' put in Babette. 'The stars from *77 Sunset Strip* don't really go round his house.'

Cornered, I tried to explain myself, but precision reasoning requires better verbal tools than I possessed; I knew no way to put across to her how Rupert couldn't have been making up the story as he went along because it was too internally consistent.

'But they might be training *themselves*, Lorraine. Perhaps there aren't any adults who know they're doing it, but it wasn't all fibbing. They have these rules to check they don't cheat.'

Lorraine chuckled happily at my innocence, but Babette didn't, she never laughed at trouble brewing.

'Mum's worried. She said it sounded like you was making a bet you could steal from somebody's house. And she thinks you might do it because you're highly strung and unpredictable.'

The intonation was Auntie Rene to a T.

I didn't want any of this; I wanted Lorraine to talk about her boyfriend Barry, and retell the story of how they met and had their first slow dance. The unseen, much-imagined Barry played a part in my bedtime daydreams, as I lay hugging the pillow. I also sensed that Lorraine's absorption in our childish affairs was wearing out; after all, she was sixteen, and was curled up in a dirty, half-converted loft with her hipster miniskirt and air of *noblesse oblige* chiefly because adoration radiated out of me so that I glowed like *The Light of the World*. On the other hand, there is only so much mileage to be had from the gaze of a bony ten-year-old, and I knew that I had to get in quick before we lost her to the grown-ups. They, incidentally, were still sitting at the kitchen table around the *disjecta membra* of a roast beef dinner, chatting and smoking, accompanied by Elvis Presley singing 'Crying in the

Chapel' continually until Uncle Arthur complained that it was doing his head in.

'How's Barry?' My standard question to Lorraine, always greeted with a coy little moue, and eventually a torrent of fascinating information. But not today. There was the briefest of pauses, while something happened to Lorraine's heavily painted eyes, as though an adjustment of sorts were being made.

'Barry? We don't want to talk about *him*. Barry's yesterday's news.'

I had no idea what this meant, and I had never knowingly observed a look like that on anybody's face before, but something about it cut me to the bone. I knew only one frame of reference.

'Do you mean it's like Roy Orbison's song about nobody loving you?'

Lorraine's reaction was startling; she stared at me as though I'd turned into one of Dr Who's Daleks.

'What did you just say?'

'It was top of the hit parade last summer. "It's Over",' I enunciated carefully. 'About being lonely and sad and nobody will ever watch rainbows with you ever again.'

At which, Lorraine unfolded herself from her nook and cranny, and left precipitately by the loft ladder. Babette watched her go.

'You didn't ought to of done that, Annie,' was all she said before following her.

4

'Mummy, can I go up the pub with Babette?'

'*To* the pub, Annie. And *may* I.'

'*May* I go *to* the pub with Babette?'

'Well, I don't know, dear. Did Irene specifically invite you?'

'No. Uncle Arthur specifically invited me.'

She was knitting my father a jumper in complicated Tudor grill-work that required concentration and a rigorous tally. My mother knitted for all three of us until I finally escaped from it by leaving home. I was nearly eight before I'd managed to persuade her, with the evidence that I'd scratched my skin raw, that *I could not wear wool*, after which I was forced instead into crackling cardigans knitted from Courtelle that made my hair stand on end and discharged itself as an electric shock every time I touched metal.

'Then I suppose you can go,' she told me. 'But I think we should give them a rest tomorrow, don't you, dear? Irene has enough on her plate looking after two men and four youngsters in her own family without having ours foisted on her. And it won't do you any harm to stay in on Tuesday, too, after we bring Daddy home from the airport.'

My mother had established with the Lucases that they were entirely free to refuse entry whenever my visit was inconvenient, and to dismiss me when the welcome had expired. These options were exercised occasionally, but looking back I wonder how much restraint was forced upon them by the circumstances. Both my parents were Babette's teachers, and in time they would be Craig's and Amanda's; perhaps it wasn't so easy to chuck the Cradocks' daughter out of the house. I was always aware that Auntie Rene's reports of my wrongdoing were delivered to my parents without much rancour, though I'd heard her being bad-tempered enough with other mums.

As for the murder, there was no doubt about it, although my mother was shocked at first in a 'surely not in Muningstock' sort of way, because it had happened to the travellers on their own territory, the crime had taken on a remoteness more like that of the Great Train Robbery. A terrible thing, but no-one we know, thank Heavens.

It was a warm, soft evening, and we were lucky to find an empty table in the Rainbird's rapidly filling garden. Babette and I sat together, her short legs swinging, my long ones scuffing the grass. Next to Babette was her dad, Uncle Frank, with Craig on his knees. Uncle Arthur, Lorraine and the Auntie Rene–Amanda combo sat opposite, on the other side of the splintery wooden table on which both women had laddered their stockings in the act of sitting down. The rustic seats in the garden of the Rainbird were the first furniture I ever saw that was built deliberately to be used outside, and the notion of outdoor furniture seemed as strange to me as if it were surreal.

As neighbours appeared and hailed us politely, Uncle Frank handed Craig back to the boy's mother, and wandered off to chat; throughout the evening we would hear 'Now that's just where you're wrong, if you don't mind me saying' float across from various tables, usually on the subject of cars.

Elsewhere, pub-goers were swapping holiday stories, and it was clear that for some it was the first proper summer holiday they'd ever taken. I heard a lot of talk of Butlins holiday camps, and a few tales from the more sophisticated, of bed and breakfasts and motoring up and down the coast. The murder was also being discussed, theories passing confidently from table to table. It was taken for granted that the killer was one of their own, another gyppo, and would soon be under lock and key. Best in the world, the British police. Not that our bobbies often have murder to contend with, England not being a violent sort of place. Not like America, for instance. Not like New York, where the streets are like the Wild West, and as for the police, they'd shoot you as soon as look at you . . .

'Excited about seeing your dad home Tuesday, Fanny Cradock?' enquired Uncle Arthur, rummaging through his packet of crisps to find the twist of blue paper with the salt in it. 'He must have been away, what, ten days now?'

'Don't call her that, Arthur,' responded Auntie Rene. 'She doesn't like it.'

This was true. No-one with a name like mine could avoid being nicknamed Fanny after the domineering television cook. While I had nothing against being named after a cook, bossy or otherwise, the boys at school lost no time in enlightening me about the more exotic meaning of 'fanny' in the British Isles, and the word rapidly became soaked in this association until it was so richly obscene that I could still blush to hear it as an adult. When I married my American

46

husband, to whom a fanny was nothing more intimate than a bottom, and he lightly referred to my bumbag as a 'fanny pack', we were left staring at each other across an ocean of misunderstanding.

Craig, with his child's gift for homing in on someone else's sores, started screeching 'Fanny Cradock! Fanny Cradock!' until his mother slapped him on the legs.

Still fascinated by the way Lorraine had run away when I'd talked about Roy Orbison, I was now staring at her as though she were the TV. She was vivacious enough most of the time, but occasionally the sunlight left her face. I wasn't the only one to notice; before his departure, Uncle Frank had asked Lorraine why she was sitting there with a face like a slapped weasel. It was Auntie Rene's reaction that prompted him to seek the company of the neighbours. Meanwhile, Arthur punctuated the general chat with little pats and hugs for his daughter, and even stuck his fingers into her packet of crisps to rummage on her behalf for the salt, although this elicited a teenager's response of simulated retching. He was a big man, with a different style of obesity from my father's, who was small, round and bouncy. Uncle Arthur's chest was as broad and solid as St Matthew's porch door.

Two lemonades later, and I needed to spend a penny. As this meant entering the licensed premises of the pub, which the law didn't strictly allow, we usually made the journey with Auntie Rene, who bustled us through the posher of the pub's two bars, one child in each hand. Tonight, however, with Frank's abrogation of fatherhood, she really didn't have a hand available, and it was Lorraine who was deputized to take Babette and me inside. Being a relative stranger, not apprised of local shibboleths, Lorraine turned left inside the pub door instead of right, and led us through the public bar instead of the saloon.

This was a place of lino and darts, and I'd never seen it before. Beer was cheaper by a penny ha'penny a pint than in the carpeted saloon, which glowed with a subtler light on the far side of the bar. There were a lot of cigarettes, mostly Woodbines, but until we surprised the clientele with our arrival, no women. I recognized the men. Among the population of Muningstock and its environs, the orthodox Romany men never frequented the Rainbird because in addition to its other ills it was a two-storey house, forbidden by the culture. But among the more liberal of the travellers were a few who regularly dropped into the public bar for a pint. Tonight there was no-one besides the travellers in there, though whether this was normal, or their community was being shunned by Muningstock in its time of trouble, I couldn't know.

I recognized an elderly man known to us – though probably not to his fellow travellers – as Old Ollie, who was our local rag and bone man. Every Wednesday in living memory, Old Ollie had come down our road with his horse and cart and his strange, consonant-free cry of 'U or ah! U or ah!', which my father explained was a corruption of 'any old iron', though only after he'd discovered that a boy at Sunday school had convinced us that it was short for 'up your arse'.

On the tobacco-coloured floor at his owner's feet was Old Ollie's dog, a matted half-breed that lay on the cold lino in a dishevelled flop. Here was an old friend. I dropped Lorraine's hand and swerved across the floor.

'Hello, Ollie, please may I cuddle your dog?'

'Oh, it's you. Wotcha, cock!'

And I was down on all fours planting a kiss on the dreadlocks of the dog's grubby old head, to which he responded by thumping his tail heavily on the lino and slobbering my face with a tongue that reeked of jellied eels and brown ale. Lorraine yanked me to my feet and dragged me through the door marked Ladies, with a grip that reminded me she was the same flesh and blood as Auntie Rene. She was still remonstrating as we re-emerged into the garden.

'I never seen anythink like it! Snogging a gyppo's dog! Serve you right if you catch rabies off of it!'

And suddenly, as though any argument about a dog were an invocation to conjure him out of thin air, there stood Rupert.

Lorraine, of course, didn't know Rupert from Adam, and although Babette did, she was endowed with an aristocratic ability to turn a blind eye to the unpleasant, whatever its provenance. She trotted past him, directing a look of lively interest towards a garden shed in the middle distance. Rupert, needless to say, recognized me in an instant. No doubt he also recognized the startled look in my eyes, and saw the opportunity for an excellent return on a small investment. The boy took one stride across my path, swooping as he did so to hiss in my ear, so that his breath tickled the hairs on my neck.

'It was my schoolfriend who killed that gypsy, the police have fucked up as usual. And you're next!'

Then, with one look to confirm that he'd achieved what the pop music business would call a 'hit', Rupert was gone.

Babette and Lorraine were already across the garden and sitting back at the table before anyone was aware of my tardiness. Naturally, it was Uncle Arthur who saw that something was wrong, and he didn't need to look twice; he was over the seat, and across to the pub door like an avenging deity.

'What's up, Annie? What is it?' And to Babette and his daughter, 'Oy, yous two! What happened?'

Of course, they had no idea that anything had happened, and stared at him, bemused.

'Has someone hurt 'er?' a passing father turned to enquire.

'That's what I'm trying to find out. Something's frightened the nipper.' Arthur hollered across the garden again, like a loudhailer. 'Yous two! Get your-selves over 'ere!'

They did as they were told, though looking utterly bewildered. Auntie Rene was gathering up the two infants and trying to attract the attention of her husband, who was in deep, beery argument with a train driver about the top speed of the Coronation Scot. My stammerings were unintelligible to Uncle Arthur, who didn't know the ins and outs, but between them Babette and Lorraine could unscramble my whimpered half-sentences and interpret for him: that boy from Annie's burglary lesson in the farmer's paddock, he had turned up here and threatened her with cold-blooded murder. They both looked randomly around for a sighting of Rupert, including Lorraine who'd never met him.

'What on earth's going on?' Auntie Rene had joined us with Amanda and Craig, both of them howling. Then Babette, who of all of us present should have been the least likely to turn drama queen, suddenly flung out an arm and shouted, 'That's him, there!'

This was enough for Uncle Arthur. He followed the direction of Babette's arm, which was outstretched and quivering like the Ghost of Christmas Yet to Come. It was therefore unfortunate that Babette had always been short-sighted, and that Uncle Arthur delivered the subsequent rollicking to a poor young lad of nervous disposition, who burst into tears and ran to his father, who was our local police constable, and was in professional conference with a known informer and a pint of Watney's Red Barrel.

In a vague sort of way, I understood that I had done nothing, and said little, yet here I was in the eye of a hurricane that was now wreaking such widespread havoc that even a policeman was caught up in it. The pub door opened behind me, and grown-ups began to push past in the peremptory way that adults reserve for inanimate objects and children. In sidestepping them I found myself once more beside Rupert. This time he clearly did not intend either to stop or to speak.

There's one thing about living in a house of round-the-clock education: occasionally you pick up something of real, practical use. My mother had made sure that I knew how to cope with the hazards of the world, including what to do if my nightie caught fire (roll up in a rug), or atomic war broke out (hide under the stairs), but also how to defend myself against assault, and I now realized, in a blaze of understanding so sudden it must have been divinely inspired, that this defence could also be used for attack. I took a half-step towards Rupert, and with a quick jerk of the leg, brought my right knee up into the soft flesh at the lower front of his jeans, in accordance with maternal instruction.

The breath left Rupert's chest first as a scream like a whistling kettle, and then, as he jackknifed, with a low, ghostly moan. Walking away across the Rainbird's garden to rejoin Uncle Arthur, it occurred to me that Craig's teddy bear made *exactly* the same moaning noise when you turned it on its head.

THE PRESENT

5

I am not a singing teacher. Singing teachers are mostly concerned with technique, like finding the head voice and chest voice; their advanced students can reach top C, sight-read, and know the precise value of a dotted crotchet. Singing teachers teach singers to hit the right notes. I am something called a vocal coach, and I'm surprisingly generous on the subject of right notes. What my students learn from me is how to put the song across – this is about characterization, how to act out the lyric, how to sing it believably – and how to audition, which in the case of West End musicals usually means auditioning before a casting director who's looking for a particular physical type and who wouldn't know a crotchet from a hatchet.

The premise of my work – and I suppose the fundamental tenet of my life – is that anyone can sing. Outside the so-called developed world are cultures that have no word for 'singer'. 'Are you a singer?' would make no more sense than 'Are you a breather?' Anyone can gain the confidence to raise their voice full-throated to Heaven in a song. Confidence is the key; it is the singer's (the breather's) most vital equipment.

There is no conventional training for my job; I came to it from many years of working with music in live performance. Much of this was with companies in rep in the provinces. Some was in West End theatres and on tour in Scandinavia, Hong Kong and Japan. But there were also a great many rooms over pubs in Soho, Manchester and Wigan. Wigan is where Paul Simon wrote his sad and lyrical song 'Homeward Bound' ('I wish I was . . .'), which is understandable when you've been there yourself. I've also heard that he wrote some of his early love songs for a girl at Brentwood High, not so far from my own Essex school, and at more or less the same time. But from then on, unfortunately, Paul Simon's career and mine diverged.

My earliest London venue was a strip club in Brewer Street, Soho. Their previous piano player (a composer and therefore strapped for cash) was sacked after the girls complained that it was impossible to perform a convincing striptease to the waltzes of Johann Strauss. I took over the job one grubby afternoon, and quickly developed a sympathy with the strippers. Unfortunately, the clientele hated me. I was visible, I was female and I was clothed. Now, a *naked* female pianist would be a different matter. But my fiancé put his foot down.

To my friends I was a creditable, struggling musician, and to my mother when I got her on her own, but in my father's eyes I was unemployed and clearly unemployable. I was also in with the wrong company; I was marrying an artist named Daniel, a wonderful, huge, hot-headed, hopeless, disorganized genius. At this time, he was working on a sculpture he described as a three-dimensional depiction of the Rolling Stones' song 'Ruby Tuesday' as an externalized

53

sensory synthesis. Somehow this failed to impress my father.

Daniel's first face-to-face meeting with my parents was at a terrible tea, where he spent an hour explaining conceptual art while Dad's face took on a look of fixed indignation that I'd only previously seen on a disgruntled Persian cat. His only private comment to me was to ask whether Daniel's hair, modelled on David Bowie's, had been cut with a knife and fork.

'Mum, he has to understand that this is my life.'

'You could try seeing things from your father's point of view.'

'I thought Dad admired genius. Well, Daniel's a genius!'

'Yes, dear. You keep telling us.'

'What with my father and Daniel's mother, sometimes we feel like the Montagues and Capulets!'

'But, Annie, you must see that you were doing perfectly well at medical school until Daniel came along, and now you're an out-of-work songwriter.'

I had not been doing well at medical school, I was useless and hated it – I regularly threw up outside the dissection room, practically *any* profession would have been more suitable. And in her heart Mum, though not Dad, had always known it.

Daniel's mother went a step further. When she learned that he was marrying 'out', she sent the rabbi round with a heavy mob. They turned up at the rented lean-to that Daniel shared with two painters and heckled him with 'Your beloved father not cold in his grave!' Apparently, the nude model took it all without flinching.

My own father was wrong about me being unemployable – there's always work for a keyboard player. I did a lot of one night stand-ins for bands of all denominations (good money, rotten hours), played bar piano at the Inn on the Park (good money, rotten

54

hours), and did a bit of fringe theatre (rotten money, rotten hours). I also picked up some work playing the piano at West End auditions. They were a nightmare, but one day I would base a career on what they taught me.

A leggy young woman in ballet pumps, who was after the lead role of the erotic Gypsy Rose Lee, sang 'I Love a Piano', and to prove her point, began to caress the keyboard while I was trying to play it. She then performed a series of ballerina's *pliés*, legs bent outwards, with unmistakable looks at the director as her thighs parted. When she reached the high kicks we had to stop; the first cracked me on the funny bone, and the second caught the music, sending it flapping into the empty orchestra pit.

'Well?' she demanded of me, hands on hips. 'Aren't you going to go down and fetch it?'

Of course, most auditioning hopefuls were on their best behaviour; many didn't realize I was only a jobbing pianist and took me for an extra piece of the casting team they had to impress, while others were so nervous they took me for an extra piece of the piano. What shocked me was the way performers with real talent scuppered their own chances. Totally impossible songs remained perennially popular. For just one example, 'Over the Rainbow' jumps an entire octave between the first two notes, so unless you're Judy Garland the scene will probably go:

Singer – 'Some WHERE—'

Director – 'Thank you. Next!'

And the first morning, we heard the same song from *Jesus Christ Superstar* so many times that when we broke for lunch the casting director shouted, 'If anyone in this room *does* know how to love him, for Chrissake get out there and tell 'em before I top myself!'

Anyway, it taught me my future trade, though at the time I hoped I had a career ahead packing out the

Hammersmith Odeon with one-woman shows as a singer-songwriter.

Around that time, I met a director who needed original music for a production of Ford's Elizabethan tale of lust, incest and revenge, *'Tis Pity She's a Whore*. I still had a lot to learn, like not panicking when the director says, 'Can you write something that sounds like that clump of trees?' or 'What the show needs is a cross between Liberace and the Sex Pistols.' In the end I didn't come up with any punk-by-candelabra, but I wrote a strong, bluesey number for the scene where Giovanni comes on, waving his dagger about, with his pregnant sister's heart skewered on it. The macabre sequel was that I suddenly had a reputation for writing gory music. I was actually in demand from directors of low-budget films with scenes of extreme violence and insufficient cash – or perhaps taste – to run to a more accomplished composer.

Obviously, film work involves watching the damn things – over and over again with a stopwatch, in fact – and unfortunately I have a phobia, a horror of Horror, dating from the murders of the summer of 1965. But Daniel found a way around it. Time and again he sat through these creations and recorded them on audiotape. He would then overdub the worst sequences with his own narrative, featuring the Flintstones: '. . . now here comes Barney creeping round the door and *flickety-flick!* goes the knife blade, but *look out!* Wilma's got hold of the power-saw and WATCH THAT TOMATO SAUCE SPURT!'

The bizarre joint venture paid the rent for a while, until one day I heard about snuff movies, in a pub in the Portobello Road, and never wrote anything like that again. As Daniel explained to one hard-nosed director, 'The day Annie throws up over the synthesizer, I'm the one who'll have to clean between the keys.'

In time, I progressed to be a musical director in rep and learned another lesson; when the orchestra arrives they bring an entire new dimension to rehearsals, which throws the actors, so the show falls to pieces, and there's total panic. Of course, it's clear to everybody that the production was fine until the musicians buggered it up, so this crisis is entirely the fault of the M.D. Perhaps this never happened to Leonard Bernstein on *West Side Story* (though I would require witnesses), but it happens to all the rest of us, on every show, always.

I also wrote a musical of my own around this time, with the strange title *Cruising with Miss Swan and Mr Lilliput*. Just me and two actors fresh from RADA, we took it to Hong Kong and Japan, though we refused to change the name Lilliput, despite local agonies at the box-office window.

By 1990 I was thirty-five, and unlikely ever to sell out a major venue or win an Academy Award for Best Musical Score. I was now teaching a couple of mornings a week at one of the London drama schools, and loving it. I also began to take private students. And so, over the years, I became a full-time teacher who occasionally takes a commission, and not a composer manqué who only teaches to make ends meet.

My marriage to Daniel came apart in a terrible seismic upheaval after just six years. Two highly strung people. To be fair, my father never gloated, but I was on guard against it, and stayed away from home for far too long. Daniel went through a bad time with drugs for a few years, but eventually found his feet and married again – a lovely young woman from Bradford with family roots in Pakistan. A Muslim. The only smile I raised throughout the entire tragedy was from picturing Daniel's mother when she copped the news of that one.

And then, when I was forty, I met Alan, an American

doctor working over here for a drug company – an MD of the sort my father approved of. Ambitious, earnest, a man a million miles from my Daniel, though not a million miles from my dad. Almost the first words Dad said to my future husband were 'This singing that Angharad does – it isn't a profession. Can you talk some sense into her?'

6

New York. In the East 50s Alan finds a waterfall. At first, I take the sparkling light effects to be a result of the low morning sun, a retinal after-image or migraine aura. In front of us is dazzle; ginkgo trees point their long arms in silhouette, and silhouette men sweep the fan-shaped leaves from the sidewalk. But the waterfall isn't a visual aberration; Alan and I sit in the paved garden with asters and impatiens, watching the cascading water and drinking hot coffee bought from a kiosk nearby. Right across town, the smell of coffee soaks into Manhattan's skin, percolates from the pores of New Yorkers, softens the chill in the air.

Eight in the morning, and the city is full of dogs. Owners gather in the railed gardens; joggers run with Pomeranians; professional dog-walkers stroll past us with pedigree canine assortments on seven leads, sleek, aristocratic and smelling of the poodle parlour. I try to picture our own dog trotting among them, a scruffy Battersea Dogs' Home mongrel. Knowing Alan, he'll probably have him shaved and painted up as a Dalmatian.

Yesterday we paid a visit to Alan's Aunt Margo, who lives in a roomy apartment on the Upper East Side, where she sits beside Alan with a thin, liver-spotted hand lying across his sleeve, and talks urgently of soaring property prices and politics, convinced that from the other side of the Atlantic, we have no access to this information. Aunt Margo is delighted when Alan tells her – prematurely, I feel – that we are moving to the States. Her principal reaction is relief that her nephew will be out of the asphyxiating London fogs before they choke him to an early death.

We have been through this before. Alan, deeply submerged in the squashy cushions of her couch, looks surprisingly at home in this draylon palace, with its velvety chairs and deep-deep-pile carpet swirled by the vacuum cleaner. The fabrics muffle sound, but strangely they also seem to muffle the light, so that her apartment contrives to be sunless and stale in spite of the broad windows and effluvium of furniture polish. Only the walls are free of this touchy-feely material, and they are covered instead with sepia photographs of the dead. Admittedly these people weren't dead when their picture was taken; Aunt Margo buys the pictures from New York's equivalent of bric-a-brac shops, and now owns a gallery of dislocated countenances without a scrap of biography attached to them. The sepia coloration resembles tobacco stain; these faces are smoked, dead as kippers.

It would be difficult to design a home further removed from the crisp, daylit Scandinavian lines that Alan sought so uncompromisingly for our own. It is Alan who is house-proud, not me; I could live happily in student squalor, stepping over dirty plates and having to search for the phone when it rings – and for a long time after the end of my marriage to Daniel, I did.

*   *   *

At home we give parties, fifty people, eighty people.
At 4 a.m. Alan shoos them out of the house by the John
F. Kennedy method – 'I don't know about you folks,
but I'm going to bed.' He sets the first dishwasher load
going, throws the empty bottles into bin-liners, *outside*, so they can reek on the other side of the wall, and
we fall into bed. But after a short sleep I creep out
again, moving stealthily through our open-plan space,
just to gaze at my favourite still life: chairs and sofas
displaced into social clusters, collages of left-over food
and smeared plates, twinkling olives and tomato pips,
fish scales and trembling heaps of fruit, with all the
colour and disorder of a Mediterranean market.
Shortly, Alan will be nagged awake by dirty crockery,
and will sweep through the house obliterating all trace
of foreign occupation. In this way we make a good fit
– I create and Alan clears up the mess, a pairing that
brings to mind comments from Auntie Rene about my
childhood games with Babette.

Alan *likes* physical work, hoovering and hammering, creating order out of chaos. At our local theatre,
where I sometimes do sound design, Alan helps with
set construction. But I notice that he is happiest with
*de*construction, the 'get-outs': an entire set to be dismantled and tidily distributed around the theatre in
the appropriate stores and workshops before the next
production gets in at lunchtime, by a production team
unslept and hung over from the end of show party.
Alan is in his element – up and down ladders wielding whizzy drills, carrying steel decking and lethal
scaff poles, lining up all the screws in order of size.
And I can remember one get-out when he didn't tell
the stage manager there was a more efficient way to
do it.

In Aunt Margo's stuffy opulence, Alan resettles

himself in the billowing red plush, and explains about the London fogs.

'It all went away with clean air legislation, Aunt Margo.'

'Well!' she humphs. 'I'd say that's about time too!'

'No, ma'am, this was way back in the Sixties,' he tells her, as he does on every visit and every phone call.

'My mother told me about the fogs,' I add, wasting my breath. Aunt Margo scarcely acknowledges my presence. 'She said they were the colour of pea soup and seeped in under the door. But not in my time.'

We had true fogs in Essex, though, where the low-lying lands were occasionally suffocated under the sort of cold-boiling, winter-white fogs that Magwitch appeared out of in *Great Expectations*.

'Coal dust,' Alan is saying, a tad pompously. 'Particulate smog. Not a natural phenomenon.' On the word 'natural', he wiggles his fingers in the air to indicate quotation marks.

'Well, I thank the Lord, Alan, that you'll be clean away from them!'

Gershwin had told the world that we have foggy days in London town. Who can blame Aunt Margo for not accepting our word above his?

Perhaps this mental reference to Gershwin wasn't a good idea, this allusion to songs of love. Stuck here in this stupefying apartment, I'm sluiced by a wave of sexual longing, and can't trust myself to speak or look across at my husband. I'm in trouble; back in London, I've fallen head over heels in love with somebody else, a man of imagination and wit, a man who has never wiggled his fingers in the air for quotation marks. It is early in the affair, most of my lies are by omission still, but nevertheless it's strange how my conscience is less troubled by this than by older sins; how it is the latter that plague me here in New York, where the Empire State conjures my dead father whose heart I broke by abandoning medical school, and dead Jenny Clitheroe, whose husky voice I can still hear describing the light of a New York afternoon late in the fall, its canyons of steel shining like a suit of armour, the razor-sharp criss-cross of these gridded streets glinting like switchblades, snicker-snack. Alan and I had driven out to New Jersey the previous day, something for his work, and I'd watched the Manhattan skyline recede and reappear in our rear window like a portrait on the wall where the eyes follow you. Now I turn away from the London fog discussion which is gyrating endlessly above Aunt Margo's soft furnishings, and seek out her phone directories. Back in 1965, Mrs Clitheroe had a cousin here, a GI bride who had married a Brooklyn man. His name was Hoffenstander.

To my surprise, the New York phone book has no fewer than seven entries for Hoffenstander. I'm not the sort of woman who carries anything practical like a pen and paper, and I don't want to draw Aunt Margo's attention by borrowing any, so I quickly commit all seven to memory, phone numbers and addresses. This is a party trick of mine, which seems to be related to that sensory aberration with which I colour numbers, letters, days of the week, and music. They call it synaesthesia, a synthesis of the senses, and I'm not alone, all kinds of clever people have had it: Nabokov, Hockney, Messiaen. He wrote music for accompaniment with coloured lights. Nobody points out that so did Liberace. Not surprisingly, this can be confusing – Gershwin's 'A Foggy Day' sounds more like Manhattan than London to me because of its cappuccino colours, so pungent I can virtually *taste* the song; my eyes smart with the onslaught of its coffee breath. My idiosyncrasies are something else not to draw attention to: at Columbia University, a few miles uptown, Alan knows a neurologist who does research into this condition. There's a real danger Alan will sell me to him.

*　*　*

Back in the East 50s we find Irving Berlin's house, now improbably a consular building of the Grand Duchy of Luxembourg. It is round the corner from Irving Berlin that the trouble begins. We are on Beekman Place, overlooking the cold, blue sheet of the East River, and I'm caught by a sign that says 'Sotheby's'. I see that the house for sale has a theatrical history: a round plaque tells us that this was home to the actress and director who brought *The Barretts of Wimpole Street* to Broadway. I ask Alan jokingly if we can put in a bid for the house. And speaking of somewhere to live, how about an apartment in the Dakota Building, where John Lennon lived and died. And now Alan points out – *not* jokingly – that we won't live in Manhattan at all, we will live in the suburbs. Westchester. Family houses with daylight in the windows and good-sized yards.

'But if we don't live in the city, how will I teach?'

'What's the problem? We commute into Manhattan along with millions of other people, you to Broadway, me to my biotech.'

'But I don't have a job with a drama school here. Even in London where I'm established, most of my time is spent teaching private students in my own home. Here it makes sense to do that full time.'

'Sure.'

'But if we live outside the city, I can't expect to get the students.'

'Well – this is something we need to discuss.'

'We *are* discussing it. This is me, now, discussing it.'

'Look, Annie,' says Alan gingerly, who dreads this sort of mood in a public place, who has learned the hard way that crowded streets don't inhibit me one jot, who knows that I can burst like a New York fire hydrant, 'instead of reacting this way, like it's a problem, maybe you should see it as a challenge and an opportunity.'

I have no idea whether my husband genuinely has something in mind, or he's forgotten until now that I'm a teacher, and is improvising fast.

'What opportunity is that, Alan?'

'A career move.'

'Oh yes?'

'Into working full time as a composer.'

'Ah.'

So he's not improvising. This is an oft-played theme. Once every couple of years or so I get a commission – bits and pieces for a TV production company, music for corporate videos, that sort of thing. They pay way beyond anything I'll ever earn as a teacher. Therefore, in Alan's opinion, I should do it full time. QED.

'Alan, even in London, where I'm known . . .'

'You just said that.'

'. . . I'm never going to survive on commissions, because it's an overcrowded field.' But I have been here before, and I know where it gets me.

'Annie, all it takes is a "can do" attitude.'

'And I happen to love teaching, Alan. I don't actually want to be alone in a studio fourteen hours a day trying to write for tone-deaf clients, when what they really want is to steal the theme from the latest Hollywood blockbuster. I *love* the interaction with students, and the variety, and the exhilaration when they get it right and the music soars to the heavens!'

'But that's in London. We belong to a species that survives by adaptation.'

Or by coercion, I think. I stamp away from Alan, reciting Hoffenstander phone numbers on the edge of my breath like a kind of mantra, their colours taking shape in the glassy air, swimming like blobs of oil in a lava lamp. A passing dog-walker glances at me. 'Hoffenstander!' I snap back. His Afghan hound flops down onto the sidewalk as though pole-axed.

'Just tell me, Alan. *Why* can't we live in Manhattan?'

'Have you looked around you? This isn't London. This isn't Ealing, Annie, a small town with a green common and two parks at the end of the Central Line. This is one hundred per cent city, all day and all night, with wailing police sirens. I was born and raised here, but I was younger then. I'm not starting over now.'

I do look around me. Leafy streets. Narrow town houses with bevelled glass in their mahogany doors. I've even found a Palladian dormer window! I can picture myself here, among all the other European borrowings, the Venetian palaces and Viennese cafés that I can see in these brownstone façades, right across the city, rich and poor. I can picture myself here with none of that ominous sinking of the heart that accompanies every thought about Alan's suburbs.

'Well, pardon me,' I say crossly, 'but I thought Manhattan had a park even bigger than Ealing's.'

When you are in love with somebody else, it is all too easy to see your husband's every action as that of a tyrant; it was all too easy to see our move to America as non-viable. My beloved New York that I'd had under my skin since I was ten. This would not do. I wandered back to the Grand Duchy of Luxembourg, and gazed at the little plaque in the hope of deriving some balm from the sight of Irving Berlin's name up there on the wall.

'Anyway, Annie,' says Alan, 'you don't teach them how to audition on Broadway. They just stand up and talk to the casting director about their tits and ass.'

I stared at him, and then realized that this was a scene from the musical *A Chorus Line*. It was therefore a joke, and as Alan didn't often crack jokes, this could be taken as a peace offering.

7

'Hello?'

'Oh, hello. I'm sorry to bother you, but I'm trying to trace a Mrs Mabel Hoffenstander, who came to New York from England many years ago.'

'Maybelle Hoffenstander?' His isn't a Brooklyn voice, I think, but perhaps my ideas about New York accents are out of date. But *Maybelle*?

'Um. Perhaps,' I reply.

'Oh, well now. I'm real sorry, but Mrs Hoffenstander deceased, two, three months back.'

'Oh.'

'This is her nephew. Well, her great-nephew.'

'Then I'm sorry I bothered you.'

'Maybe I can help at all?'

'That's kind of you, but to tell you the truth, I haven't a very coherent purpose for phoning in the first place. She and I never met, but I was very fond of a relative of hers at home in England.'

'Oh, yeah, you said just now Aunt Maybelle came from England. I never knew that.'

'Really? Possibly we're not talking about the same

person. I always believed she was just plain Mabel, not . . .'

'I just never got to know her well is all. My partner and I've been living out in California. So it's England you're calling from? Wow, you sound like you're in the next room!'

'Actually, I'm in Manhattan.'

'Yeah? This your first trip?'

'No. I've been here many times.'

He might have asked why in that case I've never tried before to contact this relative of someone I was so fond of, instead of waiting until she was dead. But he doesn't.

'The lady I'm enquiring about would have been something like seventy-five years old.'

'Sounds about right. Aunt Maybelle was pretty senior, I know that.'

From the moment he answered the phone, I've been aware of noises, a mewing or mewling sound. It could be anything from a murmuring baby to the whirr of some mechanical apparatus. Now I am disconcerted by champing noises, the sort of thing that makes you picture saliva drooling over gnashed teeth.

'GEORGE!' he bawls into the phone. 'GET OFF OF THAT, YOU MANIAC!' The crash of furniture falling, then 'Pardon me?'

'I didn't speak,' I reply, startled.

'George, get down! Get . . .!!' And into the mouth-piece, 'Excuse me.'

The phone clatters in my ear. The noises now escalate to a complete furore of roaring and yelping. The ripping of cloth. Other sound effects that resemble bludgeoning and the squeals of a cornered animal. To me, hanging on the other end of the telephone line, the scene veers between the hilarious and the intolerable – innocent slapstick like Tom and Jerry, or something unspeakable from the annals of the RSPCA. When he comes back on the line, his composure is, I am thankful to notice, shaken.

'Hey, I apologize for that. Aunt Maybelle's dog. He hasn't behaved right since she passed on.'

A tired 'woof' accompanies this statement. So the dog hadn't been cudgelled to death while I listened on the end of a phone.

'My partner and I only moved into this house last month, and he ain't gotten used to it yet. The dog, I mean.'

'I see.'

'Could be he's not forgotten the sale. My partner's in the antique business, arranged the house clearance. He figures the dog remembers him toting Aunt Maybelle's stuff out of the house. I guess he concluded we burglarized the place.'

'Indeed.'

'My partner belongs to the Humane Society, so I can't bring myself to have him destroyed. The dog, I mean.'

On cue, there comes a whimper. Then rustling, and a human murmur about doggy chocs.

'But we gotta find a way to keep him out of this room. I mean, if you could see what we're doing to the place, you wouldn't recognize it from before, I guarantee. The stuff that old lady kept! Scrapbooks, picture books, all junk I thought, but my partner got a hundred bucks a piece from a dealer off Bleeker! Can you believe it? We're going for oriental eclectic. My partner's travelled. Bali, Java, Japan. The dog already ate the kabukiprints. We are *so* pissed!'

I've kept our own dog out of Alan's study by Mongolian throat-singing at him whenever he sneaks in, but this might be a difficult thing to teach over the phone.

'So, we're gonna give it a go with Dr Lipschitz,' he

continues. 'He's a canine psychiatrist, got an office on Madison.'

'Dr Lipschitz. Right.'

'I'm real sorry about Aunt Maybelle deceasing before you could meet with her again.'

'Thank you.'

'You're welcome. Bye-bye!'

The phone goes dead in my ear, but I don't put the receiver down; I continue to hold it for some time, just sitting there, looking at it.

THE PAST

8

Monday. Tomorrow my father would be home from New York, and I'd been banned by my mother from going next door until after we'd brought him back from London airport, 'to give Irene a couple of days' break'. Forbidden to seek Babette in her own home, my best course of action now was to scour Muningstock for her. Deprived of my company, she would be out there somewhere, getting somebody else's. I would start with Mrs Clitheroe. So would Babette.

In addition to the piano and the photograph album for entertainment at 16 Bluebell Crescent, there was also Jenny Clitheroe herself, telling us tales of New York in burnished images derived from wanderlust, wide reading, and letters from the cousin who had married an American and moved to Brooklyn. Mrs Clitheroe was a beguiling raconteuse. New York, she would tell us, was built on granite studded with semi-precious stones. In various places across Manhattan, such as Central Park, great outcrops of this bejewelled granite had heaved themselves out of the earth, as though the bones of the city were showing through its skin.

She would talk about a city of chic women and summer heat, surging crowds shimmering on the sidewalks, the roads silver as mirrors; white steam billowing from manhole covers like theatrical mist in a pantomime. She told us how their subway system wove its vinous tendrils above and below ground over three hundred miles of track, with station names that resonated like trains in a tunnel – Hoyt-Schermerhorn, Bedford-Nostrand, Myrtle-Willoughby. There was even an Essex Street at the heart of the Lower East Side, with its air of London's Whitechapel – rasping accents and remnant ends. She would talk about the sun like a copper ball over the Hudson River, sinking fast into the New Jersey shore, and about Central Park on a summer's evening, with a westering sun and a warm, mothy twilight.

Breakfast was over, and I turned into Bluebell Crescent as its men were leaving for work. In the village as a whole, fewer than half the households owned a car, but in new developments like Bluebell Crescent most families did, and this morning I was just in time for the daily driveway shuffle, the poorly choreographed edgings and nudgings, the Muningstock morning gavotte. As I reached the Clitheroes' bungalow, two of their neighbours in identical VW Beetles were cautiously manoeuvring in reverse out of facing driveways; slowly, and with infinite care, they drove slap bang backwards into each other like a comedy routine. It was quite a pretty sound – prang, tinkle-tinkle. An inspired timpanist could make something of that. Heads popped out of drivers' windows with shouts of 'Why don't you look where you're going!', heads popped back in again, and drivers' doors swung open, all in comic synchronization.

By now I was halfway up the Clitheroes' path and I realized I'd made a mistake – Mr Clitheroe had not yet left on his chiropody rounds. He was indoors, shouting at his wife.

'I've said no, and I mean no!'

'But you're not making sense!'

'Sense doesn't come into it.'

'You're telling me! Look – I'd still be here in the mornings when you left, and home again before you—'

'I'm not having people say I can't support my—'

'Leonard, at least *try* to imagine being stuck in Bluebell Crescent all day every day. *Please*. I am bored out of—'

'Spoilt! That's your trouble. Always been your trouble – spoilt!'

I left them to it. Presumably, this was something I would understand when I grew up: why a man spent half his time grumbling at his wife for spending money, and the other half forbidding her to earn any.

In the meantime, my search for company directed me to look for Babette at the house of Melena Watson, a classmate of ours who lived a mile away, at the other end of Rainbird Lane. Our road, Mountnessing Road, had open woods along one side all the way up to the pub and houses along the other. You only had to walk for five minutes off the road to be in surroundings that brought to mind tales of Central European woodcutters. Even on the built-up side there was no pavement, but a broad band of greensward binding every front garden to the tarmac. Uncle Horace, in a flight of fancy after Sunday school, had once likened this lawned sweep to the Cambridge 'Backs', an imaginative feat that required Mountnessing Road to flow as the River Cam, along which Uncle Horace presumably punted dreamily in his Morris Minor.

Bungalows were the most popular style of dwelling in Muningstock, and pebbledash the most popular facing for them, particularly grey pebbledash, which the rain then dribbled on, year in, year out, until the weathered façades were the colour of the Thames estuary on a wet bank holiday afternoon. Turning into Rainbird Lane, I passed the Mortons' place, a ramshackle collation of outbuildings, apparently without any inbuildings, on whose pockmarked concrete drive shone an E-type Jaguar. Babette and I often saw Mr Morton as we trotted home from school, a chamois in his hand. There was a Mrs Morton, too, whom Babette and I also ran into sometimes, trudging along the road from the bus stop, dragging the week's shopping while her husband industriously buffed the E-type.

It was another fine late-summer day, the morning air sweet as apple juice, the sky cloudless but for a high cirrus, blown by some unfelt stratospheric wind into feathery lace. The same wind had also nibbled the vapour trail from a recently passed jet, tickling its edges into a sort of twist, like a cable stitch, so that the entire sky looked like something ambitious knitted by my mother. The twined vapour trail fascinated me; I was daunted by the thought of the flight path that must have moulded it, barrelling across the heavens in a long, leisurely loop the loop. I contemplated my father in a similar corkscrew mid-Atlantic, and my insides contracted with a pang. It was the same pang I'd felt at London airport. Envy.

'Hello, Annie. You looking for Melena? You just missed her. She got the bus into Wittle Massey with Babette. You must've walked past the bus stop.'

I'd not only walked past the bus stop, I'd actually walked past the bus.

'Do you know where they've gone to, Mrs Watson?'

'You mean in Wittle? No notion, love. Sorry.'

Even if she'd known, there wasn't another bus for

an hour, and they could have been and gone by then.

'Thank you anyway, Mrs Watson.'

I turned forlornly away and down the garden path flanked with its shining daffodils. Not spring bulbs miraculously out of season, but plastic ones free with Daz washing powder; Mrs Watson did a lot of washing. The rag and bone man's cart was parked opposite, unattended. I looked up at the dog for solace. Having tramped all this way, I'd earned a cuddle.

'Excuse me, Mrs Watson. Do you know where Old Ollie is?'

'You again, Annie? Ollie's next door arguing about an old Frigidaire. I'd keep out of his way, if I was you, he's not well pleased. The vicar's new verger give him a hearth-rug, and Ollie says it's hopping!'

With this mysterious allusion she smiled a dismissal and shut the back door. Whatever it meant, anything to do with the church was bound to irritate Ollie. I thought of the pair of them last week, our vicar doing the rounds on his latest anti-smoking mission, giving out free tins of snuff as the healthier alternative.

'If the Good Lord had intended us to fill our lungs with cigarette smoke, old man,' he had declaimed to Ollie, who was halfway through a roll-up, 'he would never have created cancer!'

'And if the Good Lord 'ad intended us to fill our faces with snuff, old cock,' had come the response, 'e'd've stuck our noses on upside down!'

I wandered over to the cart. Ollie's dog was slumped on top of a pile of sacking, giving his own impersonation of a hearth-rug: head flat out, limbs splayed, eyes as glassy as a bearskin and exuding an air of unqualified doom. I swung myself up into the cart, an activity I was getting better at year by year, and then spent a happy interval rolling around in the back with the transmogrified dog. In the course of this, I vaguely registered a transient sense of resistance against my right foot, a resistance that gave way in a sudden, dramatic capitulation – somewhere between a rip and a crunch.

This would have to be investigated. Elbowing the dog sideways, I uncovered a handless clock, a doorless kitchen cabinet and an ambiguous porcelain bowl with a lot of unplumbed holes and an 'Armitage Shanks' signature squiggled across the cracked white china. And leaning against this was a picture that had once been *The Laughing Cavalier*, before I'd put my foot through him.

I knew the painting of course, which figured prominently in the 'Art' section of one of my encyclopedias, so it was the cause of some chagrin to realize that of all the rubbish and scrap I might have collided with, I'd managed to trash a Frans Hals.

The temptation to run away was strong, but in the end my Cradock training was stronger, plus the suspicion that Old Ollie might have trained his dog to bark out tip-offs, like Lassie. I checked it over, but the painting was clearly beyond repair, the hardboard ripped away from the frame, the glass webbed with cracks, and a lavishly frayed, foot-sized hole right through the cavalier's sumptuous hat. Nothing for him to laugh about.

I sat glumly in the cart awaiting Ollie, while the tearing sound hung about in my head like tinnitus or a bad conscience. I tried rehashing some of the abject apologies I'd had reason to compose over the years, while the dog, miffed and flummoxed by my air of abstraction, slumped back into its state of despondency. My own attention span wasn't much better than the dog's – it wasn't long before I was rummaging through the treasures around me.

Slung over the back of the cart was a thick polythene bag. A brief glimpse inside revealed a rolled hearth-rug of indeterminable pattern, encrusted in a generation of dirt, a small cloud of which came puffing out of the top of the bag as I unpeeled it. The words 'vicar's new verger' floated into my mind, but I couldn't place them.

Babette and I and Mrs Clitheroe had once helped Auntie Doris of Sunday school beat a carpet, after her elderly aunt died and left her one. She was really grateful; it didn't take much extrapolation to deduce that I could improve my position in Ollie's bad books by cleaning his filthy rug for him. Unfortunately, I didn't have a carpet-beater on me, but I could hold up the rug with one hand, and wallop it with something flat with the other. The most obvious candidate being what was left of *The Laughing Cavalier*.

I tugged at the rug, which grudgingly emerged from its polythene. When the dog had stopped sneezing, I was able to edge him out of the way and spread the rug across the sacking at the back of the cart. I dragged the broken picture towards me, and grappled with it until I had an unwieldy rhomboid. It seemed to me that the cavalier's laugh didn't have quite so much swagger as I swiped the carpet with it.

The dog could have been useful at this game – by chewing some of the grime off the tassels, maybe, or licking grunge off the floral motifs. Instead, he wriggled forward on his belly, arf-arfing at me, his ears stiffly horizontal with quivering tips like rotary blades, as though any second they might airlift him off the cart and up into the fancy knitwear of the summer sky above Muningstock. Then the dog's behaviour suddenly changed. First, he seemed to flinch as though his entire skin were rippled with twinges, then he started gnawing lumps out of his own back, folded up like a switchblade.

There was something odd about my own skin – a freckling of small dark spots that I could have sworn were not my own. On closer scrutiny, they vanished.

One of the spots was a touch slower than the others, and I thought I saw it spring. At the same moment, the cart gave a furious lurch forward.

'Ollie? Ollie!'

Presumably, the heaped furniture completely hid me from his view. As soon as we moved I lost my footing, and was simultaneously drowned out by a loud and tinny fanfare. At Ollie's end of the cart church music gushed at distortion volume from a distressed transistor radio. He was singing 'Hallelujah, I'm a Bum' to the tune of 'What a Friend We Have in Jesus'. Even when I succeeded in scrambling to my feet, I couldn't make myself heard or climb over the furniture. The dog was still trying to dig a hole in his own coat, and there wasn't a lot I could do but wait until a householder on this side of Muningstock called Ollie to a stop. It was a pity he wouldn't be clopping past my own house, but he didn't take that route until Wednesday. I decided I may as well go back to my former activity, and picked up the hardboard. And so, Old Ollie's cart croaked along the Breeden Road, with me on the back batting at the fuming rug with *The Laughing Cavalier*, like some avant-garde performance art at a Surrealists' carnival.

After a while I noticed the looks I was getting from passers-by. Suppose they assumed that my parents had handed me over with the rubbish? Horrified, I slunk quietly down onto the sacking, and concentrated on rolling the rug into a decent cushion to act as a shock-absorber for my jolted bottom. Every now and then, a cluster of small russet specks would settle on my exposed skin and vanish like a mirage when I reached for them. Old Ollie, oblivious to the presence of such diverse stowaways on his normally unmolested cart, reset the transistor to Radio Luxembourg, and Muningstock was enlivened by his 'U or ah!' while a transatlantic voice sang jingles about Pepsodent toothpaste; apparently it got the yellow off your teeth. The dog, I noticed as he frantically nibbled his coat, could have done with some.

9

Ollie's horse plodded slowly towards Muning Hall, past the high Victorian gables of our school, empty and on hold for the summer, and on beyond the ribbon of houses. The fields were under the plough; birds wheeled and swooped noisily over the upturned earth. We left the road and clopped in at a gateway, and we were in the travellers' camp. Past a hollow tower of tractor tyres. Caravans and trailers. A rotting Hillman Minx up on bricks. On the perimeter of the camp nearest the road were assemblages of Muningstock's junk – exploded mattresses, unsprung armchairs and unplumbed sinks. I stared at a sculpture of rust-darkened metal – throttled exhaust piping, slumped girders, and something that resembled a tuba tied into a knot. The whole mound looked the way the Eiffel Tower might if a bomb had gone off and flattened it.

As the old horse slowed, and the cart dragged, and the dog bayed, I would have scrambled over to Ollie, but another traveller strode across to him first, rasping and agitated.

'What they sayin', Ollie?'

'Who?'

'The village! What they sayin' 'bout us?'

'I never arksed 'em.' Ollie turned his back on his interlocutor, and got down from the cart. He hadn't seen me.

'I din arks you if you arksed 'em! But you got ears, 'ntcha? Wass their community sayin' 'bout ours?'

Ollie led the horse forward, who seemed to think his day was done and shook at the bridle. 'They's ain't a community,' said Ollie.

The cart had come to a halt beside a compilation of pitted prams and buckled Bakelite, from the depths of which protruded, incredibly, an entire collection of pairs of false legs, all sticking out of the heap in ungainly Vs as though their owners were in there, flat on their backs and legs in the air.

'Now git! I'm busy,' concluded Ollie, and with this he started disengaging the cart from the horse.

All in all, it seemed an inopportune moment for confessing what I'd done to his Old Master. When the dog jumped off, I followed. Ollie's companion didn't *git* as requested, but stayed his ground in shuffling impatience. Oily smoke blew from some unseen chimney and split-levelled the air with a smutty black residue. We were only yards away from the harvesting, though I couldn't make out the fields through the layers of smoke, so there was something eerie about the thick texture of birdcalls crying out of an apparently empty sky.

I slipped back across the camp the way we'd come in, across the clay-coloured earth scored with tyre marks, while the stinging black soot wafted between the men and me. Over towards the gate, a child sat on the steps of a trailer and stared at me. Her little blouse and skirt were starchily clean despite the air quality, and she had on short, frilly socks that I admired, and on which subject I had fallen out with my mother, who declared that the rightful place for a short, frilly sock was on the ankle of a lamb chop. Faced with the girl's unadmiring stare, I rolled my own socks down, and fluffed them out a bit at the sides. Ahead of me, between lurking oil drums, was the flaky carcass of an elderly caravan. Voices issued from its open window, and continued after this was slammed shut. There seemed to be three men inside, one of whom was doing most of the talking.

'It's like this,' came a chirpy, conversational tone. 'Our guvnor don't like gyppos in general, and he don't like *joking* gyppos in particular. In't that right, Mickey?'

I heard a mumbled assent.

'And *very* disappointed 'e's gonna be. Our guvnor had a bit of business goin' with your mate. Your *late* mate,' he amended. 'The geezer whose luck run out. Him 'n' our guvnor 'ad somefing a bit special to the tune of a coupla grand. See, in 'is travels, your late mate got 'is hands on some high-class stuff, and I'm not talking paste. Sparklers. *Very* nice.'

There was a half-hearted interjection that the protagonist easily motored through. 'Our guvnor was lookin' forward to this bit a business, only along comes *anuvver* friend of yourn. Funny, this one ain't a gyppo, he's a Bow Bells man, only it don't stop 'im fetchin' up 'ere and burglin' bleedin' gypsy caravans.'

There was a low burble of response.

'An' bumpin' off bleedin' gyppos.'

The burble died.

'So along comes Burlington Bertie from Bow, an' it all goes to buggery. Oh yeah, I should of mentioned!' A loud tut, and the sound of hand slapping forehead. '*He's* popped his clogs an' all. We paid 'im a visit 'fore we come here, din we, Mickey? First thing thi smornin'.'

The protestations were louder this time, and were again overruled.

'You met Mickey, 'ave you? Machete Mickey, we call 'im, for reasons we both 'ope our little chat will mean we don't 'ave to go. Into,' he amended, with temporary slippage of confidence. 'An' do you know what your newly late mate told Mickey this mornin' before he cashed in 'is chips? 'E told us the *real* joker was *you*. 'E told us it's *you* what 'e's give the sparklers to on account of you being 'is fence.'

Like all children, I was frequently privy to adult conversations that were ninety per cent garbage, but seldom had I been exposed to such thorough drivel. Jokers and cashed chips and sparklers. Whatever was at the heart of their quarrel, there wasn't a game in the land that merited this barrage of heckling. I walked on in clucking disgust, but didn't get further than about ten feet before an explosion rendered me temporarily deaf. It took a few seconds before the pain resolved itself into something identifiable: pop music, issuing at ear-splitting volume from inside the same caravan, and obviously from equipment a great deal more powerful than the trannies and dear old Dansettes beloved of most of Muningstock. The volume and level of distortion were so great that even I didn't want to stay and listen to it. I walked on.

Suddenly the caravan window was wrenched open, and something came flying out – something pale and meaty, which thunked onto the ground thirty feet or so away from me. As it landed (and it appeared to twitch as it landed), an object spun away, small and solid like a bullet from a gun. It ricocheted off a cement-mixer and stung me smartly on the back of the calf.

My first thought was that the meaty lump was a joke-shop hand, part of the hilarious arsenal of the man with the mouth and the sparklers. Babette's little brother Craig had been given one by his Uncle Arthur, until it was confiscated by Auntie Rene after her husband slipped it onto her pillow one evening when she went upstairs for an early night. That was my first thought. My second didn't bear thinking about. I had once read a boys' comic strip featuring a mad professor and foreign spies who sliced his hand off at the wrist. '*Th-wack!!*' read the caption. *Th-wack!!*

Music continued to blare from the caravan at eardrum-perforating volume. I stared across at the rubbery thing lying there, its bounce deadened now, its fluttery agitation silent. Joke-shop tomato sauce trickled deviously from the messy bits. *Th-wack!!*

I walked out of the gate and down the road and through the field and across to Rainbird Lane. I didn't run; I knew that I'd frighten myself if I ran. Fear was something yellow and clotted on the edge of my vision. Fear was the colour of sick. If I turned around, I would panic, though I was panicking anyway, prickles of it inside me, sharp as a blade. I chewed at my fingernails, tore at them, tearing nail from nail-bed. *Th-wack!!*

As I route-marched homewards, my skin set up its own bid for attention, with unexplained twinges and sudden, uncontrollable itching. My right calf still stung from whatever missile had hit it in the travellers' yard. I found out just what this was in Rainbird Lane, when white-hot pain seared through my sole and I collapsed. It was a thick, gold ring, a man's signet ring, which must first have lodged in the side of my shoe, then worked its way down, and was now stabbing at the tender pink heart of my foot. I wriggled the ring back out, tore off my sock, blew as best I could on the livid pink flower that was developing before my eyes like a Polaroid, and then examined the weapon that had assaulted me.

Inset was a chip of diamond. Valuable, then. I didn't have a pocket, so instead I tucked the ring into the sock of my uninjured foot, rolled the sock around it, and with a lot of pushing and shoving wove a hair grip through the material underneath, fashioning a sort of pocket. On recommencing my walk, the weight of the ring caused this sock-pocket to wag, and the ring to knock rhythmically at my ankle bone like a woodpecker. My Cradock's sense of duty wouldn't let me fling the damn thing across the field and have done with it – this was so evidently a costly piece of jewellery – but the obvious alternative, to carry it home *holding it in my own hand* made me want to throw up at the thought. *Th-wack!!*

Into Rainbird Lane, past the pub with its birdbath poetry, into Mountnessing Road. *I want my mummy.* The sentiment came whistling out of the hedgerows. *I want a cuddle.* I passed the council estate. *I want someone to tell me everything's all right.* The cottage with the E-type Jag. The Cambridge Backs. The woods along one side of the road. *I want someone to listen to me.* I stopped short, doubled back on myself away from our house, and was up Bluebell Crescent, ringing Mrs Clitheroe's doorbell.

'Annie!'
  'Mrs Clitheroe, may I talk to you, please?'
  'Of course you may! Come in, sweetheart, come in!'
  She was a vision in blue – denim jeans low on the hips, and a cotton T-shirt that intensified the ocean blue of her eyes. Her long, fair hair was loose and wavy today, not in its usual pony-tail.
  'Come into the sitting room.'
  The Clitheroes' front door opened into a T-shaped hall, with the bedroom and bathroom on either side of the upstroke, and the sitting room and kitchen opening off the crossbar. The entrance was dark once the door was shut, but this was an inviting dark, not the muggy obscurity of most people's houses. When we

reached the sitting room, Mrs Clitheroe sat me down in a capacious armchair (low and leather), and knelt in front of it.

'What is it, my love? What's happened?'

'Mrs Clitheroe.' I swallowed convulsively and my chest hiccuped; that *really* hurt, hot pain through my ribs like heartburn. 'Mrs Clitheroe, do grown-ups buy things for themselves from joke shops?'

Her eyes wavered at the unexpectedness of the question.

'Joke shops?' she repeated uncertainly, and then when I didn't expand on it, 'Well, I suppose they might, Annie. What sort of things exactly?'

'I mean . . .' I dug my bitten nails into my palms. They hurt, too; the nail-beds were bleeding. 'Uncle Frank played a joke on Auntie Rene with one, but that doesn't count because Uncle Arthur'd already bought it for Craig. And I'm scared *this* one wasn't make-believe.'

'This one, Annie? This what?'

'This chopped-off hand that flew out of a caravan window in the travellers' camp just now.'

Th-wack!! My lips trembled and hot tears dribbled onto my cheeks. Mrs Clitheroe was completely still for a moment. I saw my own fear reflect in her face, then dissolve. I saw her lips move tentatively, but the words, if words had been intended, died on her. Eventually she repeated, 'In the travellers' camp just now?'

'Old Ollie took me. He didn't know I was on the cart, it was an accident. So when we got there I sort of jumped down and went away, only these men were having an argy-bargy in a caravan. And one of them kept saying he wanted something from the other one, and calling him names, and then I couldn't hear because they put the Kinks on so loud I went deaf, and this' (*Th-wack!!*) 'this cut-off hand flew out of the window. So I wandered off home.'

86

'Yes,' said Mrs Clitheroe, after a lengthy pause. 'So would I have done, Annie.'

I gave her a résumé of the monologist's sarcasm as best I could, to which she listened with a deepening frown.

'These men,' she said at last, 'did they say "hello" when they saw you?'

'They didn't see me. They never knew I was outside.'

The ring! I had forgotten all about it. I now grappled with my sock, the cotton of which was badly scarred from the hair grip, now missing. There was nothing inside the sock but me.

'Oh, Mrs Clitheroe, I've gone and lost it! When that hand flew out of the caravan window, a ring hit me on the leg and I found it stuck in my shoe. It's a gold one – somebody will want it back!' I ransacked unlikely things – my other sock, both feet, the floral folds of my summer frock. 'Oh, Mrs Clitheroe!'

At this, I burst into tears. Jenny Clitheroe gathered me up and squashed me against her. Her fair hair tickled me, and I smelled eau de cologne, its violet-coloured scent permeating my distress like an infusion. She was speaking urgently.

'Listen to me, Annie! I'm *glad* you've lost the ring, whatever it was. Really glad! And I don't want you to worry and wonder about that joke-shop hand. These are grown-up men and they're big enough to sort themselves out without little girls worrying about it for them or keeping track of their gold rings. Do you understand me?'

'Yes, Mrs Clitheroe.'

'I expect they gave him a bit of a scare, and he's handed the sparklers over, and that's the end of it.'

She was so *beautiful* – even more so than usual through the soft focus of my brimming eyes, her own dark with concern. This wasn't like my admiration of

Lorraine, which was aspirational. Lorraine worked in a boutique, spent her income on clothes and pop records, and slow-danced with handsome boyfriends at discotheques. Lorraine had a way of walking that suggested a line of young men behind her carrying hat-boxes and a poodle. Mrs Clitheroe was something else: she was goodness; she was my entire repertoire of song lyrics, old and new; she was the Beatles' Michelle and *West Side Story*'s Maria, and Alexander's Ragtime Band. In the swimmy darkness of her glass-fronted cabinets, I could see my own plain little face reflected back at me.

'Anyway,' she was saying, gently releasing me from the embrace I'd tunnelled into. She handed me a tissue that had been tucked up her own sleeve and I trumpeted into that. 'If you hadn't come round here, I would have come to see you. I've found another wonderful painting, Annie, that you and I can set to music.' She made for her bookshelves, full of warm Penguin-paperback orange. 'The painting's about New York.' Mrs Clitheroe slid a thick tome from the shelf. 'Here we go,' and we were looking at a glossily repro-duced abstract painting, all lines and squares.

'The painter was Dutch,' she told me. 'You know about Holland, don't you, how the people are reclaim-ing land from the sea, and the whole country is flat. Well, he was famous for painting coloured rectangles in patterns a bit like the patchwork of fields in his homeland. Then he went to live in New York. Of course, the city doesn't have fields, but you know how the streets are on a grid system? That sort of suited his style.'

We looked together at the picture, which was indeed a grid of sorts, a geometric arrangement, all rectangles and right angles. The artist had painted it in yellow, red and blue on a lot of white space, and had then broken up the gridlines with small squares and a scattering of larger ones. With its irregularities and primary colours on vibrant white, it looked as though somebody had jazzed up one of those electrical pictures my father tried to teach me about. Circuit diagrams.

'He named it *Broadway Boogie-Woogie*,' Mrs Clitheroe told me, so 'jazzed up' was right, 'and that composition with its broken lines and shining colours is the painter's way of depicting the music and bustle and flickering neon lights.'

'What was he called?'

'His name was Piet Mondrian. He was a dapper little man, and we can imagine him working in his orderly studio all day long, and then when night fell, off he went to the streets and jazz clubs of Manhattan.'

The jazz clubs of Manhattan. I felt the Zs twang and zing. I tasted the city, and my brain tingled. I'd heard about nightclubs from Mrs Clitheroe's New York cameos. And she was right about the neon lights; look at that picture for long enough and it would start to pulsate.

'Did he hear boogie-woogie music in these colours, then?' I asked.

'I don't think he really heard music in colour, Annie,' she explained. 'But his mind was so fertile, so creative, that he could *imagine* hearing it in colour. Shall we play some, and see what we think?'

Mrs Clitheroe sat herself down on one edge of the stool before her Bechstein upright piano, and directed me to perch next to her. Her left hand began to strum a fast-tempo arpeggiation in F sharp: *one and two and three and four and one and two and three and four and* . . .

'You know about jazz bands, don't you? You know how a double bass sounds?'

'A bit like this.'

'Exactly. In boogie-woogie, the pianist supplied his

89

own bass line – I suppose sometimes the band couldn't afford a double-bass player. Self-sufficient, sort of thing. So that's what the left hand's doing – very full and fast. The right takes the melody and improvisation.'

With this, she was off, the light touch of her fingers rippling in the bass, while her right wrought from the treble a melody line I recognized.

I gave a squeal of delight. ' "Roll Over, Beethoven",' I said happily, remembering that Babette's dad called it 'Sod off, Ludwig.'

'Now,' she called to me across the swelling music, 'to me, that sounds yellow, no doubt about it. But just suppose . . .'

The melody veered off now, into something that had no collaterals in rock and roll, this was a jazz born of midnight and liquor and cigarettes, its syncopations falling into the tune and subverting it. In my own mind, or whatever organ I heard colours with, this was a great, luminous mint-green piece of music. Though green wasn't one of the painter's colours, he and I seemed to agree that the music was urban, full of the grit and granite of Mrs Clitheroe's conjured sidewalks, the relentless rhythms of Manhattan's purposefulness, its forward-thrusting drive like a masonry drill. My luminescent green was electrified light; it was traffic-light green.

'What colours do you hear there?' she called to me across the music.

'It sounds green to me.' I felt apologetic about it.

'OK, let's see if I can modulate it to bring you some others.'

Her Broadway boogie-woogie slid bluely into the relative minor key. 'Now?' she asked.

'Bluer!' I laughed back at her. 'It's going blue!'

'Magic!' cried Mrs Clitheroe, her hands dancing on the keyboard. 'Now let's *really* roll Beethoven over!'

It took a moment to register with me what she had done. Her left hand continued to flutter its up-and-down runs, while her right irreverently vamped the opening of the Fifth Symphony. The contours of Beethoven's transfigured architecture loomed at me in uncompromising shades of red.

'It's red!' I cried out, all unadulterated joy now, metamorphosed like Old Ollie's dog. 'Redder and redder!'

Our boogie-woogie Beethoven hung in the air in streaks of red, like tail lights in a long exposure photograph of nocturnal city traffic.

'Can you picture other jazz instruments joining in? Think of brass. Try to imagine tenor sax, and the slow, sensuous slide of the trombone!'

Mondrian's shining lines skyrocketed into the music, yellow as taxis. My imagined trombone bent them and stroked them. Gravelly saxophones growled around the seedy stage door lights of 42nd Street. I could taste the greasy heat of an August night, and the tangy blue atmosphere of Mondrian's nightclub, tobacco-flavoured dust hanging in the air, backlit by the flash of neon signs, their blue light leaking past the bouncers at the door.

'Knock knock,' said a man's voice just inside Mrs Clitheroe's French windows. 'Are we interrupting something?'

It was Horace and Doris Frobisher of Sunday school.

10

I wanted to holler at them. I wanted to scream 'Get out! Leave us alone!' I wanted to call Rupert over to swear the air blue. It's possible that I would have done all these things, but as Horace and Doris marched confidently in from the garden – blazer and flannels, twin-set and pearls, against whose bracing Englishness the jazz clubs of Manhattan dissolved as though neutralized with air-freshener – Babette was revealed, strolling in behind them.

'Melena Watson and me's been looking all over for you,' she told me in a cheery scold. 'Hello, Mrs Clitheroe.'

'Hello, Babette.'

'I say, Jenny, there's a formidably strong smell of dog in this room.'

'Hello, Horace. Hello, Doris. Annie and I have been listening to some Mondrian.'

'I beg your pardon?' queried Horace.

'The painter, dear,' explained his wife. 'This is Jenny, remember. Presumably she's been knocking out a few bars of abstract expressionism on the Bechstein.'

The flippancy of this remark, and its undertow of assumptions, caught me like a cold squirt from a water-pistol. Rudely, I swivelled back round to face the keyboard. Uncle Horace was talking – asking Mrs Clitheroe what colour Monday was, presumably because it happened to be Monday today.

'Gold,' was the prompt reply. 'The same colour as the number six!'

Personally I saw Monday as powder blue like the number four, but I knew better than to make statements like this out loud. People backed away. People made 'loony' gestures when they thought you weren't looking. Or sometimes even when they knew you were.

'Actually,' continued Uncle Horace, 'I don't know what I'm being so jovial about. There's been some more rather awful news. That's what we're doing here.'

'Oh?'

He addressed the stiff, inflexible huff that was my back. 'We would rather spare your feelings, Angharad, but you see, little Babette already knows, so it would be hypocritical of me to pretend that you wouldn't hear it anyway.'

'Whatever is this, Horace?' Mrs Clitheroe asked.

'There's been another murder, I'm desperately sorry to say. Apparently related to Saturday's. A revenge killing, the police think.'

'Revenge killing,' repeated Doris with an air of wonder, shaking the heavy black bun of her hair. 'Makes one think of Al Capone. Violin cases with bullet holes. But surely not in Muningstock.'

'Doris and I have decided to set up a collection for the children. Both the murdered men left young families.'

'Annie?' said Mrs Clitheroe. I was shivering. As

soon as the Frobishers had burst in to bugger up our boogie-woogie, she had left the piano stool. She now knelt down and wrapped me in her arms.

'When was this, Horace? When was he found?'

'Well, I don't know exactly.'

'Today? Yesterday? When?'

'Oh today, today.'

'Where, then? In Muningstock? The travellers' camp again?'

'Jenny, dear,' interposed Auntie Doris gently, 'you must give Horace a chance, and he'll tell you.'

'Yes. Well, it's a bit complicated, but it seems likely that today's man was himself the killer from Saturday night, you know, the one who burgled the traveller's caravan and killed the occupant. PC Harris – you see, we walked into each other, I had some business next door to the police house – PC Harris says he wasn't actually one of Muningstock's travellers at all, but a known East End crook. Heaven knows what he was up to here, but anyway, his crookery is over for good, poor chap: he was found in his own caravan parked halfway between here and Wittle. Still in his pyjamas.'

'You hear that, Annie? Not at the travellers' camp. It's nothing to do with what you saw.'

'What Annie *saw*?' questioned Auntie Doris.

'Just a misunderstanding. Something completely un-related gave Annie a fright earlier today. Do you understand, Annie?'

'Yes, Mrs Clitheroe.'

'Truly?'

'I think so.'

'Good.'

She gave me a squeeze that winded me and wrung out a wheezy moan like organ bellows, and kissed the top of my head. Horace and Doris continued to stand about wearing expressions of good-natured puzzle-ment. Babette was seated tranquilly in the leather chair, absorbed in the photograph album to which she had helped herself from the sideboard, as we were accustomed to do. By her elbow were the ornaments that we loved: a flamenco lady that a friend had brought Mrs Clitheroe all the way from Spain on something called a package holiday, and two spaniels modelled in Staffordshire pottery that were not really Mrs Clitheroe's taste, we knew, but had belonged to her mother. They were my taste, however. I loved them almost as much as the piano. It was Babette's voice that now piped up in the hiatus.

'If you're going house to house collecting money for the gyppos, you better try mine whilst Uncle Arthur's still there. Him and Lorraine are leaving tomorrow, and I don't reckon your chances with my dad.'

There was a general clearing of throats. Babette closed the photograph album, and applied her attention to her patent leather sandals, slowly rotating each ankle in turn, the better to admire them. 'If you want to talk more about the murders and things, Annie and me can go off.'

Auntie Doris looked as though she were about to demur, but Horace spoke across her. 'Well, that's a very generous offer, little Babette. I think it would be preferable if you left us to it. Do you mind, Angharad?'

I didn't answer. I didn't move from the piano stool either.

'C'mon, Annie,' said Babette. 'Let's go over the woods.'

'Are you sure that's all right?' Mrs Clitheroe's eyes searched mine. 'You won't go off and worry?'

But I was too choked to do anything other than shake my head. Babette hopped out of the chair, and filed the photograph album neatly back in the sideboard. I disengaged myself from the piano stool with the exaggerated slowness of an underwater swimmer, and dragged myself to the door. With a bit of luck, the smell of burning martyr would go some way towards counteracting the heady pong of dog, which Uncle Horace was again enquiring about as I left.

'Why did you have to drag us off like that?' I demanded irritably, as we left Bluebell Crescent and turned into Mountnessing Road. Behind us, one of the neighbours was kneeling in the road with a brush and dustpan, sweeping up a spangle of tiny cubes of orange glass. This morning's prang.

'You didn't want all the gory details on another gyppo snuffing it, did you?'

'Yes,' I answered. 'I did.'

'Well, they wouldn't of, Annie. Not with us there. They'd've kept shtum.'

We seemed to have forgotten the woods, and were wandering up the road towards the Rainbird and the council estate.

'Aren't you going to ask what all that was about, with me and Mrs Clitheroe?'

Babette's unruffled detachment could be quite difficult to live with on occasions.

'You was in the travellers' camp. I know already.'

'No you don't! You can't! You can't know!'

Babette sighed. 'Melena Watson's mum see you on the back of Old Ollie's rag and bone cart, clopping down Breeden Road towards Sir James's place.'

'So? So? You still don't know what it was about!'

Babette considered the data available to her. 'I suppose you was telling Mrs Clitheroe all about it, and when Uncle Horace come round and said another bloke'd been done in, you got scared, in case you'd been there when it happened.'

I might actually have taken a swing at her if I hadn't been arrested by a maddening itch around the ankle that siphoned off my entire attention. Scratching, I remembered: that gold ring with the diamond chip – it had wriggled against this same ankle bone while I was following Mrs Clitheroe through her hall. Therefore I must have dropped it in the bungalow.

'Babette, do you know what?'

'What?'

'I've left something behind in Mrs Clitheroe's. I've got to go back.'

Babette eyed me dubiously. 'You're just trying to do a bit of nosy-parkering about the murders.'

I stomped off, grumbling and huffing like a grampus. Somewhere in the vicinity a radio was playing Max Bygraves, the singalong entertainer from Rotherhithe. 'You Need Hands,' sang Max happily. 'You Need Hands.'

It seemed that I'd left the Clitheroes' front door open on my way out, as I discovered on my way back in. From the hall, I heard a door on my right-hand side click shut. Somebody going into Mrs Clitheroe's bathroom. I crossed to the sitting-room door and heard the voice of Uncle Horace.

'Jenny.'

But it wasn't a casual statement of her name. Something was out of kilter. I didn't call or carry on through the door into the sitting room.

'How are you, really, Jen? How are – things?'

'Things? Ah well. Not good.'

'I worry about you.'

'I know. Bless you for it.'

My position was somewhere to the left of the sitting-room door. Uncle Horace moved into my line of vision.

'Jen.'

She reached out a hand and touched him lightly on the arm. 'What is it, Horace? There's something wrong, isn't there? I mean, something new.'

'Yes, my dear. We have to talk.'

Distantly, behind me, was the tinkle of falling water. At Horace's tragic expression, Jenny Clitheroe made an impatient gesture, and her voice broke out of its previously constrained tones. 'If you're going to put a stop to our affair,' she told him, clear and steady, 'I'd be grateful if you'd just tell me. I'm not sure you're actually *capable* of stopping it, Horace, but if you intend to start trying, I need to know.'

'*Jenny!*'

Silence.

'Oh God, I'm sorry. Forgive me, I'm beside myself. You can't begin to know.'

'Of course I know.' And then, 'Jen — are you all right?'

This was a different tone of question, businesslike, directed at the fact that Mrs Clitheroe's right arm was twitching. She scratched at it jerkily with her left.

'I'm so sorry,' she said, with a teary laugh. 'To add to my woes, I seem to have been bitten by something. Ouch! Another one, dammit! I'm so sorry. All right, it's stopped now. So we need to have a talk, do we? Must we?'

'Jenny, I know you well enough to recognize a change in the air.' A pause. 'I think you're making plans to leave Leonard.'

No response.

'And I know what you want, my dear, in your heart of hearts.'

Still no response.

'I'm so sorry, but you have to understand, my primary concern is Doris. She's still my wife.'

I had a pretty full view of the room and the high tension between its occupants, but was concentrating so hard on the two of them that I hadn't noticed the third figure. Lolling against the doorjamb of the open French window, the suntanned fingers of one hand tweaking at the straps digging into her brown, adipose shoulders while the other hand twiddled with the green-tipped strands of her scratchy yellow hair, was Mrs Maxwell, sunbather from the pea fields.

'Pardon me, if I'm in the way.'

Stunned nothingness. They just stood there, taut as coiled springs.

'I only popped over to show Jenny our soap-on-a-ropes. I'd best call back when it's more convenient, eh? When you're not so . . . busy.'

A smile thinned Mrs Maxwell's lips and her eyes glittered. Mine watched her melt back around the side of the house. There was still no sound or movement from the occupants of the room. Behind me, the lavatory flushed. Any moment now Auntie Doris would return. I had no place here. I was through the hall and out of the front door.

'Did you find it then, whatever it was you dropped?'

Babette was sitting on the low wall outside the bungalow, cleaning the sole of one of her glossy sandals with a handkerchief. I saw smears of blue. I hadn't known you could step in anything that was blue.

'Babette, did you see Mrs Maxwell come out of the bungalow?'

'Course I did. Just now, you mean?'

'Do you want to know something funny peculiar?'

'What?'

It wasn't so easy to tell. At my insistence, we moved away from number sixteen, but suddenly I found myself profoundly reluctant to recount the conversation between Mrs Clitheroe and Uncle Horace. I was also aware that something was going on inside me that was at least as extraordinary as the scene I'd just witnessed. My reaction had been instantaneous and raw, as though I'd been skinned. Jealousy. I was profoundly and humiliatingly jealous. I couldn't bring myself to tell Babette more than the solitary hard fact that Mrs Clitheroe wanted to leave Mr Clitheroe.

'Well, you would do, wouldn't you?' responded Babette with a shrug.

'Yes, but,' I continued, 'that isn't the half of it. Uncle Horace and her looked up and there was Mrs Maxwell leaning on the French windows and sort of smiling as if she knew something. And they saw her and went funny.'

'D'you mean Mrs Maxwell heard?'

'Don't know if she did or not.'

'If she heard, she'll tell him,' decided Babette. 'She'll tell everybody. She's a spiteful piece.'

'Thick and spiteful your mummy says.'

'And when he finds out he'll kill her.'

In the unifying warmth of our shared concern, my former resentment dispersed.

'Babette?'

'What?'

'You know when I was in the travellers' camp.'

'Yeah?'

'I saw this chopped-off hand come flying out of a caravan window.'

Babette blinked a couple of times. 'Yeah?' she repeated at last.

'Babette?'

'What?'

'Do you think grown-up men would have a joke-shop hand?'

Having access to a very slim collection of facts on which to hang a theory, Babette decided to take us down the path most likely to keep the peace.

'They got heaps of scrap and stuff up the travellers' camp – you never know *what* might come flying out of one of their caravan windows.'

There was sense in this.

'We gave Old Ollie my nanna's meat-safe,' she

pondered, 'so you're lucky it was only a hand come flying at you.'

'Ouch!' I cried, suddenly, like Mrs Clitheroe. A tiny *ping!* behind my knees, urgently itching. The clouds of doubt that had been scudding across Babette's symmetrical features vanished, and her eyes bulged. She was pointing at my arm with a look of scandalized horror.

'What? What?' I demanded, panic-stricken, half expecting to see dead men's fingers sprouting from the parts of me that had touched that blighted ring.

'*It's a flea!!*' cried Babette, hopping about in illustration.

'Where? Where?'

'Stand still. Don't move!'

Her delicate fingers darted at me like a reptile's tongue and plucked at my arm.

'Ow!'

I watched as she rubbed her thumb and forefinger together, and then apparently jammed her fingernail into her own thumb. I heard an infinitesimal *crack!*

'Got it!'

'It' was a dark fleck, ciliated by a tiny fuzz of legs, two of which dangled like stray cottons from a hem. I had never seen a flea before. I honestly don't think I'd really known what a flea *was*.

'But where could it have come from?'

'Annie Cradock, I don't know what to do with you! You bin up the gyppos' camp! Where d'you *think* it come from?'

I caught a fleeting image of Mrs Watson alluding to a hopping rug, but it was impossible to focus beyond the drubbing I was getting from Babette.

'Flea-ridden! Your mum'll go spare. She'll make you sleep in the garden shed!'

There was something in this. Flea-ridden. You had to admit, the words had a certain ring to them.

'What am I going to do, then?'

'Wait here. I'm going to fetch Lorraine.'

And with this, Babette strode officiously away, leaving me on the greensward, frantically examining my limbs for more of the things. I pounced on a particularly huge-looking flea, and pinched it to death between thumb and fingernail as Babette had done, only to find that it was one of my own freckles. The pain as I turned it into a blood blister was staggering.

Lorraine was brisk.

'Now then. The thing about fleas is, you can't pick 'em off. They jump.'

'Babette picked one off.'

'Yeah? Well, either Babette can sit there all day picking them off of you like one of them monkeys at the zoo . . .'

'No,' said Babette.

'Or we drown the buggers.'

'How do we do that?' I asked, interested.

'We hose you down.'

'Sorry?'

'Babette, you know where to turn on the garden tap for the hose, yeah?' Lorraine spoke with the efficiency of a chief constable calling for water cannon. And to me: 'Look, we can't put you in the bath, you'll infest the whole flippin' house.'

I did not go like a lamb. One logical objection after another fluted from my lips. For a start, I couldn't go near Babette's dad's garden hose because I was banned from being a nuisance to Auntie Rene until Tuesday.

'She's not in,' Lorraine told us. 'She's round the postman's wife's doing a Twink home perm. Spect they're nattering about the postal strike and hysterectomies.'

Yes, but my mother would go berserk if I came home wearing soaking wet clothes.

'You can borrow my hipster skirt and skinny top.'

In the end, it was the promise of Lorraine's gorgeous clothes, plus the real dilemma of how to get fleas past the radar traps of my mother's domestic vigilance, that had me standing on the clover clumps of Uncle Frank's back lawn, while Lorraine, who looked oddly as though she were used to this sort of thing, picked up the serpentine hose by its business end, and aimed the metallic eye at my midriff.

When the jet slammed into my middle it was like belly-flopping off a very high diving board. I folded up like a deckchair, making keening noises that even Old Ollie's dog would have been ashamed of. Scrambling upright, I hopped along the flower beds and was halfway up Auntie Rene's trellis when my mother's voice cut across the air. The feral screams of her only child must have reached her maternal antennae.

'Angharad?'

My mother's best classroom voice carried across the fence like a siren. I froze. Lorraine froze. Babette turned the water off at the tap. The hose flopped, impotent and crestfallen, to the ground.

'Angharad!'

She was up against the privet hedge. I flattened myself along the trellis, sprawled like an espalier fruit tree. If pressed, my mother was capable of hacking her way through jungles. Her advance caused agitation to ripple outwards from the privets, until Auntie Rene's side of the fence was adither with nodding foliage. Eventually the rustling ceased, and our back door closed irresolutely.

'She's not doing it no more, Lorraine!' Babette faced her cousin square on, hands on hips, in full mutiny. 'Look at her!' she demanded, waving an arm in my direction, like an evangelical preacher directing the congregation's attention to tonight's sinner. 'She look happy to you? She look like she wants to carry on like this? Look at her head hanging down! Look at the hump on her!'

'Yeah, I suppose she don't look too clever!' conceded Lorraine. 'Babette, go and run some hot water into your mum's washing-up bowl. We'll put her frock in it.'

But Babette had resigned her commission. 'You run it yourself!'

'I should've known it'd be me did all the flippin' work!' And with the injured air of one already worn to a frazzle from hosing down the neighbours, Lorraine flounced as best she could across the gloopy clay to slam herself in through the back door to the kitchen.

I emerged from Babette's bedroom in Lorraine's clothes, my hair nit-combed into a vast frizz like the halo of some harried Renaissance angel. We surveyed the garden. Much of Uncle Frank's lawn was waterlogged, choking the trampled faces of what had formerly been a bed of smiling pansies. I looked worriedly at Babette.

'All we got to do,' she reasoned, 'is say my dad forgot to turn the hose off properly. Mum'll always believe Dad forgot to finish off a job.'

We picked the still-dripping frock out of Craig's sandpit, and set off next door to tell my mother a tale about how I'd fallen into Melena Watson's paddling pool.

THE PRESENT

11

Home again. London. We've been back a month.

'You're in a line-up of hookers in a seedy New York nightclub,' I'm saying to the milky-complexioned daughter of a Conservative MP. 'All stale air and over-priced liquor. A hot August night. Every one of you is bored *senseless*. That's how *Sweet Charity* opens. Unfortunately, for an audition you do have to keep the song true to the original context, and in this case it's prostitution and torpor.'

'But perhaps the casting team won't know where the song comes from. I mean, it isn't as though it's *Sweet Charity* I'm auditioning for.'

'Believe me, the casting team will know where every show song comes from.'

She takes it very well, very gracefully, considering she'd bounced in here aglitter with plans to give them 'Big Spender' oomphed to the nines, herself frocked up like a gay icon. I've never enjoyed the 'no you can't' side of coaching, which is a pity, as I've got a bit of a day of it ahead. Meanwhile, I try to conjure an

105

atmosphere of sleaze in the clinical surroundings of my studio. I need to do something about that top-of-the-milk look of hers. Like curdle it. OK, we'll start with a bit of torpor. I get her stripped off and into our sauna upstairs. Somewhat to her surprise.

The sauna is one of Alan's recent additions to the house, and now that we're likely to sell, he keeps arguing with the estate agent about the value it's added to the property.

'But not for a family home, sir – think of the hazard to toddlers. And not everyone would trust their teenagers in a dark, warm room behind closed doors.'

'There's a glass panel set into the door! You can look through it and see what's going on inside. It's been all the rage for years.'

'What, voyeurism?'

I leave my student dripping in the wooded gloom, and invade Alan's study. I'm after his collected colour supplements and pharmaceutical industry magazines (filed chronologically, subfiled alphabetically). I rummage for images of bloated men in late middle age or elderly emaciation. Wrinkles and jowls. I accidentally clunk into Alan's desk and shake his sleeping PC, which whirrs back to life. It's unlike him to leave it logged on with a document open, but he has, the protocol for a new clinical drug trial. In the instant of its revivification on the computer screen, I wonder how I would feel if this document were something else. I don't know what, a love letter, evidence of an affair. And in the space of those milliseconds, I know that my feeling wouldn't be one of relief. I'd be hurt and angry. I'd be jealous.

The spellchecker facility has squiggled little red lines under his text; Alan can never type the word 'patients' correctly, an unfortunate failing in his line of work. Patinets. Pastiens. Pstielnts. Moved to be helpful, I click the mouse to make the corrections, and the spellchecker offers me 'panties' and 'pestilence'. And they're too good to resist.

In the sauna, I rejoin my melting student. I hold up one glossy middle-aged man after another under the dim wall-light. There is a nasty moment when the politician in last Sunday's *Telegraph* turns out to be her godfather, but otherwise the pantheon has its desired effect.

'Oh *yuck*!' she cries, unconsciously crossing her wet legs. 'Oh, gross!'

'Now,' I instruct her, 'sing "Big Spender" in here, like this, to them!'

My last student of the day is a female vocalist who has hired the Canal Café for a short season of cabaret. I used to wonder how she could afford this sort of thing until one day she arrived still in her workaday clothes, which included a black leather basque and jackboots. Big spender, indeed.

We are just getting into the swing of things when a worry begins to niggle at me. Something about her choice of numbers. Then I have it – by a filthy co-incidence, another student of mine is also singing cabaret, and her selection is nearly identical. Popular songs, all of them, fashionable today, but it's still a bloody awful fluke. She'd do herself no favours with this, so most of her show must be chucked in the bin a fortnight away from opening night.

There's a lot of anguish in any standard repertoire of ballads, and no doubt this has taken its toll on her, but anyway, she goes totally berserk. When I judge that it's safe for me to leave the studio (i.e. when she starts weeping, and therefore can't throw so readily), I walk back across our courtyard garden to the house, to check on the turkey. Ealing this may be, but in our house it's Thanksgiving. Benny, my mongrel, who has an inadequate grasp of the duties of a house dog, slinks out of the studio after me, with a 'Phew, what was that about?' look in his limpid eyes.

I can hear the turkey spitting in the oven, and the kitchen smells to me of all my Christmases. Alan was in his forties and married to me before he had turkey for Christmas. It is interesting that our frames of reference are so often different; my past was Christmas dinners and *Dr Who*'s Daleks and *Top of the Pops* and carnival queens; his, Thanksgiving and Dr Seuss and homecoming queens and high school proms. We say 'You remember when . . . ?' and find that the other doesn't. We have rock 'n' roll in common, of course, but even with something as apparently ubiquitous as the Beatles, the ground is unsafe. For example, over here 'Yesterday' was only ever an album track, whereas in the USA, it was released as a single in 1965, a piece of information that reminds me of our honeymoon. I lost twenty dollars in a bet.

Alan has promised the chairman of the biotech company a decision by the end of the month. We don't actually know when the United States would allow me in; my husband has to file a petition with the embassy in Grosvenor Square, which then goes to somewhere in New Hampshire and can take months. My vocabulary has now been enriched with terms like 'Family Sponsored Immigration', plus the imaginative convolutions of American foul language, which Alan lets rip with every line of every form he has to complete.

Tonight, we have people coming to dinner. Alan prides himself on his Thanksgiving pumpkin pie; he views the preparation of food as a mark of social status, so it is a disappointment to him that I've never managed to present my fashionable mangetout and sprout tops *al dente* rather than at the bipoles of raw or mush, and that past turkeys have shown a tendency to emerge from the oven desiccated. I get distracted and forget. Now cakes I can keep track of because I decorate them, which reclassifies them as *art*, so they get my respect. There on our kitchen table is this year's: a mass of light fruit-cake sculpted into the shape of other wives' turkeys, life-sized, its plump little marzipan legs holding a tiny stars and stripes flag, the whole gleaming in golden rolled icing. Last year, I'd piped 'The Star-Spangled Banner' in icing sugar across a drape of theatre muslin – tune and lyrics, like sheet music. This year's offering has the line 'O my America! My new-found-land' piped across the turkey's sugary flesh in a swirl of red, white and blue.

It is only now that I stop to think. Alan won't know where the quotation comes from, I guarantee it, but our guests might. This is the trouble with having your sub-conscious continually heave with thoughts of sex: it even gets into your cakes. John Donne's elegy 'To his Mistris Going to Bed':

> Licence my roaving hands, and let them go,
> Before, behind, between, above, below,
> O my America! My new-found-land.

A thanksgiving indeed. Oh well, it's too late now. Irrelevantly, I notice that my piped quotation starts at the breast and finishes at the end you'd normally stuff.

I think of my marriage to Daniel, whose life has been one long rebellion against the 'I cook therefore I am' philosophy of his Jewish mother. Oh what acres of bacon sandwiches there were, what yards of sausage rolls washed down with milky tea. And what other gastronomic rubbish we happily survived on: jars of pickled onions, hamburgers from the Wimpy in Notting Hill Gate, Vesta curries out of a packet and eaten off paper plates while lying together in the bath with the water going cold. Daniel, the size of a heavy-weight boxer, with a hand full of soggy toast and

109

tinned spaghetti, his toes wiggled around the hot tap, reading me articles on the relationship between art and language, out of which we conceived three-dimensional structures animated with lyrics that David Bowie had himself put together by chopping words out of newspapers and scrambling them, like the Dadaists. Above us on the tiled wall was a Magritte print from which bowler-hatted Belgians rained ineluctably into our bathtub.

My marriage to Alan is under even worse strain now. Something else happened in New York and we're pretending that it didn't. Nothing to do with Daniel – an entirely different escapade of mine. And I'm just not up to facing the consequences.

Benny and I leave the two turkeys to themselves (gladly on Benny's part, as he thinks the one in the oven is spitting at him), and return to my student. I sit with her at the piano in the afterglow of her tantrum, holding mugs of coffee on which we ritualistically warm our hands. Above our heads, through the sky-light, colour bleeds from the half-hearted dusk of the afternoon. The studio is strewn with her sheet music. Where she threw it at the walls with all the strength of her whipping arm behind it, some is still caught up there, hanging precariously from my amps and book-shelves and speakers like mad black and white bats. One of my synthesizers is wearing a sort of dunce's cap at a rakish angle. Every now and then, a song sheet slips from its perch on a shelf and crackles to the ground, frightening the wits out of Benny.

'What fantastic photos!'

She is looking up at the only decoration in the studio – a panel of photographic enlargements the size of a window.

'I've never taken them in before – look at that one in front of a fountain! The way the light plays on the water and the spray on the people's faces.'

'Central Park. I wish I could take the credit,' I tell her, 'but the photographer was Daniel Woolf.'

'Cool! Does that mean you paid a fortune for it?'

'Believe it or not, at the time those pictures were taken, I was married to Daniel Woolf.'

She looks so completely flabbergasted that I laugh.

'He wasn't well known then,' I assure her. 'We both thought of ourselves as struggling artists.'

For a while, we just sit quietly, looking at the faces on the wall.

'The girl in front of that fountain reminds me of someone.'

'Yes? Probably Mandy Lucas.' I get a puzzled look and have to prompt her. 'The actress?'

'Yes. Of course.'

'That's her sister, Babette. I'm sorry to keep dropping names like this, but I was brought up with the Lucas family – they were our next-door neighbours in Essex.'

But Essex girls are not in the same class as famous artists; in fact it is evident that Amanda has actually lost me some of the kudos I'd earned with Daniel. I have not come so very far from the paddock and the pea fields.

'Who's the other picture?'

'That's my father. I suppose I should say was my father, because he died. That's when I had Daniel's portrait of him enlarged and mounted.'

'I'm sorry. Was it an accident?'

'Cancer. Five years ago.'

I don't usually talk about my father to my students. On the other hand, I don't usually have them hurling things at my sound equipment. There's nothing quite like terminal cancer to knock some sense into a performing artist in a paddy.

I look up again at my father's energy and drive, caught for ever in Daniel's magical *punctum temporis*, and for a moment I'm washed by that age-old astonishment that the image still survives when the original has perished. However, I must return us to the cabaret; it is Thanksgiving and Alan will be home shortly to start on his pumpkin pie.

'So,' I say, 'what are you going to sing instead?'

While she's responding to this with a lot of high-drama hopelessness, I have a flashback – I see her centre-stage in my studio in mid-tantrum: raw, magnificent, and yelling obscenities. This is a singer put on earth to belt out sex, angst and misery. In which case the composer is obvious.

'Can you sing in French?'

'You kidding? I've got a punter who pays me a hundred quid for a wank while I stand to attention singing the "Marseillaise".'

'Ah. Right. Good.' I open one of my untidy cupboards and riffle through the tumbling sheet music, looking for some Jacques Brel. My student plants a foot on a runaway sheet.

'This one's in French,' she tells me, 'though God knows what it means.'

'Who's it by?'

'Serge Gainsbourg: *"La Plus Belle Fille du Monde N'arrive Pas à la Cheville du Cul-de-Jatte"*.'

I translate distractedly, still searching for Brel. '"The world's most beautiful girl doesn't match up to an amputee's ankle-stump." Something like that.'

'*Yeah?*' She swings round with the first sign of animation since her tantrum. 'Let's give it a try. In my line, who knows when it might come in handy!'

12

'Oh I woke up this morning,' wails Daniel, clobbering the piano keyboard in the closest he can manage to a blues riff. 'I woke up yesterday, too. Poom-pa poom-pa poom-pa poom-pa poooooom . . .'

And *I* wake up. There is only a split second in which I assume that I've fallen asleep in my tame present and woken in 1975; through plate-glass I can see Tower Bridge at an arty angle and the cold, agitated waters of the Thames. I am in bed in a converted warehouse somewhere around Butler's Wharf, all exposed brickwork and vases of twisted willow. And yes, I have just been to bed with my ex-husband.

When Daniel used to sing this in 1975, he was doing it in our rented Notting Hill pigsty that we shared with an R&B singer called Black Willie. Daniel succeeded in winding him up with this particular twelve-bar parody at least once a week.

'If I wake up tomorrow,' concludes Daniel, now at full throttle, 'it'll be three days . . . pa-poom . . . in a row.'

I wriggle upright, squash a pillow behind my back. The sheets slide slimily around me. My God, are they *satin*? The shape of the bedding beside me is eloquent of Daniel – the twisted imprint of his huge head, the throttled duvet. Sculpture of a sculptor. Odd how my heart turns over even before I've consciously registered what I'm looking at, like being caught unawares by an emotive phrase of music. My feelings tumble out of control like an unstrung rock-climber down a precipice.

Seeing the energy articulated in the bedding, I give a thought to those of my students who are New Agers and believe that people and events leave their energy behind them in houses, saturating the walls with their miseries, their terrors, the convulsions of their joy. I also give a thought to the time, and the whereabouts of the apartment's owners, from whom Daniel has apparently borrowed a key. It will be a while yet before I give a thought to my husband.

Daniel has borrowed the key 'to take a shower between ordeals'. Not such terrible ordeals, really – just a private view of his 'Retrospective' at the Hayward Gallery. Daniel does the celebrity host rather ingenuously, all warmth and wit, booming his jokes, padding along the gallery on those enormous feet to seek out and bear-hug the next guest.

He had started inviting me to the private views after I married Alan. By this time, it was generally assumed that our smoulders had gone out, and nobody worried about us, except Babette.

'Well,' she'd said the first time, holding my glossy invitation, 'do you think it's sensible, Annie?'

'Sensible?' I'd repeated, not understanding.

And now it's late afternoon in the leafless Docklands, and none of it is sensible any more. Not in any way, whatsoever.

How has it happened? It is the day before my trip to

New York. I agreed to join Daniel for lunch 'before the hordes arrived' at one of his shows. His wife was at home with a chicken-poxed seven-year-old. We fell into each other's arms in the taxi.

And why has it happened? Because Alan was riding roughshod across my career, my preferences, my feelings, my life. But perhaps it's all too easy to blame Alan. It happened because it was bound to happen, some day or other, sooner or later, given Daniel and given me. At least, that's the best I could come up with to explain myself to Babette.

His clothes sprawl on the floor, untouched since we fell into bed, another sculpture, the contused limbs caught by the artist in mid-thrash. It is possible that he has previously deposited another set of clothes in the walk-in closet and has already changed while I slept. But it is equally possible that he is sitting out there at the Steinway concert grand in the midst of all this millionaire minimalism, stark naked.

'I HOPE I HAVEN'T WOKEN YOU!' hollers Daniel, launching into 'Chopsticks'. 'I HOPE YOU'RE NOT LYING AWAKE WORRYING ABOUT WHETHER I'M GASPING FOR A CUP OF TEA!'

I slip from the bed, and I'm with him on the piano stool before he's got to the end of 'My Old Man's a Dustman' in the style of Pavarotti. Nobody bursts in waving their homeowner's Yale and spluttering. We're still naked at the piano when the first trays of white wine are being set out in the Hayward, and black cabs are debouching celebrities onto the cold, concrete kerbs of Concert Hall Approach.

THE PAST

13

'There riz . . . a house . . . in New Orlinz . . . They call the raaaasin sun . . . AN IT'S BIN . . .'

'Annie! Daddy and I can't hear ourselves think! Either practise properly or leave the piano alone!'

My parents' remarks about the piano often had this anthropomorphic touch – leave it alone, give it a break, let it rest – as though the instrument were alive and tormented like Mr Lawrence's spaniel.

'You've got Grade 5 exams next term and I haven't heard you play a single one of the set pieces.'

But rather than slog through these, none of which featured a house of ill repute, I decided to rejoin Daddy, who hadn't stopped talking since we picked him up from London airport.

His return was a joyful occasion, not least because somewhere over the Atlantic at thirty-three thousand feet he had decided that we could have a loft conversion with dormer windows. My mother's reaction to this was distinctly more subdued than my own, and later I heard her asking him why in Heaven's name we needed a room in the roof. The reply was unintelligible.

We hadn't heard a word while he was away, not so much as a postcard, because our post office had gone on strike. This was one of the things you heard adults grumbling about up and down Muningstock. It was all right to post things into the pillar boxes, apparently, but they were being stockpiled somewhere until the GPO agreed to fork out some money. The husband of Mrs Maxwell (sunbather and eavesdropper), worked at the post office. He was a nice man, surprisingly, and he promised to have a ferret through the massed correspondence and fish out anything he noticed with my name on it.

Daddy didn't arrive home empty-handed. For my mother there was a porcelain plate decorated with a gilded picture of the Empire State Building. This was not the only place it featured; there were glossy press photographs of Daddy at the World's Fair with mayor and matchbox model, all of which would still be up on the walls when I left home for medical school. Meanwhile, for me there were: an American dollar bill in a glass frame, a copy of an American poem called *Hiawatha* by Henry Wadsworth Longfellow, and a pamphlet about the Statue of Liberty.

'Just listen to this, Annie-*fach*,' announced my Welsh father, holding it at arm's length and clearing his throat. ' "Give me your tired, your poor, your huddled masses yearning to breathe free!" ', that 'yearning' pronounced dark as a Wrexham slate roof. He made a convincing Lady in the Harbour, glowering under heavy brows, looking tubby and pregnant.

The New York World's Fair, located somewhere called Flushing Meadows, was the largest exposition ever held anywhere in the world. It took up one full square mile, with one hundred and fifty-six pavilions worth a *billion* dollars. The dominant visual symbol was a terrestrial globe constructed from 900,000 pounds of stainless steel, miraculously balanced on a tiny V. Numbers unfolded in the air around my father, multiplying, replicating. There was a big top with the world's largest suspension roof – 50,000 square feet. There was a scale model of all 835,000 of New York's buildings, set out across a space 100 by 180 feet. I asked him whether all this made our matchbox model look a bit puny, but he didn't reply.

Over the past few weeks I had learned a lot about jet lag; its manifestations were portrayed to me in a way other families might warn darkly about premenstrual tension, yet Daddy was full of beans. He didn't even seem sleep-deprived from spending the night on a plane. He chatted away about skyscrapers, the food (my father was particularly taken with the 'diners' gleaming in chrome – he liked anything clean-looking), and about Mayor Robert F. Wagner who, it turned out, wasn't a *Vah*gner after all, he was a *Waggna*.

For me, the most stunning of all the exhibits I heard about was an entire home built underneath the ground, with proper rooms and furniture, pretend daylight, and even pretend weather, and a sort of 'dial-a-view', so you could choose your own landscape to be projected onto the retaining walls. This was an atomic fallout shelter designed with full mod. cons for all the family. Apparently the theme of the fair was world peace.

Babette came round at teatime. My mother set an extra place for her, and Daddy talked about America while we all ate toast and Marmite and home-made rock cakes, except that he waved his about a lot to add emphasis to the narrative. He was a great hand-waver was my father, and would stand in classrooms drawing pictures in the air as he spoke, like an extravagant new sign language for the deaf, made even more ungainly by the fact that his left arm was shorter than his right and wouldn't straighten – the legacy of a bad break in his teens. As for the two murders in his village, Daddy was naturally upset by the news. But it was difficult to ignore the signs that he also felt a bit upstaged.

It was my mother who noticed that Babette was subdued. 'Is anything the matter?' she asked, interrupting a story about a newspaper vendor who'd told Daddy that he'd grown tired of being one of the many John Smiths of this world, and had changed his name to Seven-eighths Euphonium Jones. 'You seem a little out of sorts.'

'Well, Lorraine's poorly, and everybody's getting ever so upset about it.'

'Upset about it?' repeated my mother, picturing fatal illness.

'Uncle Arthur told Mum, and I heard them going on and on.'

'Oh dear. Do they know what's the matter?'

'Yes, they know what's the matter. Lorraine's up the duff. Pregnant,' she added for clarity.

This stopped my parents in mid-Marmite. There must have been a good minute in which nobody said anything, a phenomenon without wont in the Cradock household. My father coughed quietly on the crumbs of his toast.

'Well,' said my mother eventually, 'how very worrying for everyone.'

Babette explained that Lorraine and Uncle Arthur had just left for Canvey Island for a bit of a holiday; she'd heard Uncle Arthur saying that he'd stand by his daughter in her hour of need. It all sounded smashing, and it was just my luck to have been at London airport. I watched my parents make desultory attempts to ask pertinent questions, but fail to think of any.

119

When she'd finished her toast, Babette asked whether I would come next door, where there was something important she wanted to show me. Strictly, I was still under my mother's ban, but she agreed that I could follow Babette provided I finished my tea first. Perhaps she felt that the disorder in the Lucas household had now gone beyond my power to make matters worse.

After Babette left, and I sat at the table gobbling down toast and rock cakes with my cheeks bulging like a hamster, my parents were able to elucidate their thoughts. That boyfriend of Lorraine's, Barry, he really mustn't be allowed to get away scot-free, was the gist of their contention. He must face his responsibilities. He had been man enough to cause the trouble in the first place, he must now be man enough to take the consequences.

'Barry's *not* her boyfriend any more,' I explained, through a mouthful of cake. 'It's over, like Roy Orbison.'

'Under the circumstances, dear, it isn't over at all,' my father pointed out curtly. 'On the contrary, it has just begun.'

'But what's Barry got to do with it?' I asked.

My mother gave an exasperated tut. 'You know how babies are made, Annie! We explained it to you. *That's* what Barry has to do with it, dear.'

I didn't reply, and my father followed this up. 'You do remember, don't you, Angharad? I know you're a dream-boat, but even you can't have forgotten the facts of life once they've been spelled out!'

This sounded suspiciously like the dreaded jet lag to me, and the quicker I got out of here the better. I shovelled down the last of my tea, and got up from the table.

'Of *course* I know all that,' I assured them both. 'You told me.'

120

'Well then!'

'It's just, I thought that was only what you did when the normal way didn't work. I'm off round Babette's now. Bye.'

I believe my statement was followed by a supplementary question from the table, but I was already out of the door.

A concrete path ran immediately in front of our pair of semi-detached houses, uninterrupted by my mother's privet hedge. As I whipped along it to the Lucases', I saw that Babette was in her own front garden, waiting for me.

'I thought you was never coming!'

'What's up?'

She drew me away from the windows of their front room, and spoke in a whisper. 'Me and Lorraine, we was talking about Rupert.'

Oh no! Here we were with some truly sumptuous happenings for once, not to mention an entirely new perspective on my hero Barry – the contemplation of which gave me a strange, hot, prickly feeling – and now I was being dragged back to Rupert. It was as though I were haunted.

'All the grown-ups started going on and on and Lorraine couldn't stand it, and me and her was going to come round and see you, but you'd all gone off to the airport, so we went round Mrs Clitheroe's instead.'

So I had missed out on that as well. At this point, unaccountably, Babette's head started to twitch. She didn't look ill otherwise, except for this series of galvanic jerks, and I was wondering whether I should rescue her tongue to prevent her from choking on it, when her thumb also started jerking and I realized that she was beckoning to me. I was to follow her across the lawn to the crab-apple tree, which was surrounded by Auntie Rene's thorny shrubs. As I did so, Babette slipped behind them and

121

seemed to be fiddling behind the gatepost. I would never have been allowed to fiddle behind ours, as they supported my mother's wrought-iron gates, and wrought iron was to my mother what dormer windows were to me. When Babette emerged, it was with a heavy package partly wrapped in a paper bag. This parcel she pushed into my arms, all the while casting looks about her as though she expected spies to be lurking behind my mother's privets. I started to peek inside.

'*Don't open it here!*' she hissed.

But I had. 'It's Mrs Clitheroe's photograph album,' I announced in surprise.

'Annie Cradock!' cried Babette. 'Will you keep your voice down!'

'It's Mrs Clitheroe's photograph album,' I repeated in a stage whisper.

'It's to show you,' explained Babette.

'Why?'

'Lorraine stole it.' Lorraine stole it.

'Lorraine *stole* it? Why?'

'We was trying to show you that anybody can steal anythink!' And because I didn't look immediately enlightened, 'So you'd know Rupert was telling whoppers!'

'Oh.' I looked down at the album. It was a large and heavy book, bound in olive-green Moroccan goatskin, with endpapers luxuriantly marbled in reds and gold. The word 'Photographs' was tooled into the front, within elaborate borders picked out in more gold. The whole volume looked like my piano teacher's tomes of orchestral scores, and smelled of posh shoe shops. In fact, if paradise had a library, it probably smelled like Mrs Clitheroe's photograph album.

'How did Lorraine steal it?'

Babette shrugged. 'We was looking through the album like I always do, and then when we went to go she pretended to put it back in the sideboard, but really she shoved it up inside her sloppy joe, and sort of walked out of Mrs Clitheroe's sideways.'

This was a lot to take in.

'So Mrs Clitheroe knew you two had the photo album last?'

'What do you mean, "last"?'

'Well, it was you who had it before it stopped being there.'

I got my second tut of the evening.

'She won't know it's gone! Mrs Clitheroe never looks at them pictures no more because they make her feel old. You heard her say.'

I wasn't convinced. Mrs Clitheroe's actual sentiments, provoked by pictures of her late family, were: 'You never feel completely grown up, girls, until you lose your parents. And if you're already grown up, that's when you start to feel old.' Besides which, she used the album to tuck little mementoes into, like pressed flowers from a walk in the bluebell woods, or thank you notes from friends' children. The more I thought about it, the more it seemed to me that Mrs Clitheroe was in and out of that album all the time.

'Look, we haven't stolen it to keep. You and me can go round again tomorrow and you can put it back.'

'Me?'

'Well, *I* can't hide it under my clothes, can I? Look at the size of me!'

I wasn't the Cradocks' daughter for nothing. I would get to the bottom of this.

'Lorraine wanted to steal this for me because of Rupert?' I probed.

'Oh Annie, sometimes you're so slow on the uptake. Look. Anybody can nick anythink, you don't have to break in like a burglar. All them things Rupert was telling you, it was all porkies, all that stuff about training to be secret service agents and showing each other at school what they've pinched!'

123

'So?'

'So, it's *all* lies and he's never broken in nobody's house, and it wasn't him and his friend did the murders, so he isn't going to break into yours, neither!'

'I—'

'So he ain't gonna do you in!'

I looked at the exasperation twisting Babette's pretty features out of alignment.

'Thanks, Babette. That's kind of you and Lorraine.' But all I could really think was that Rupert should redefine the word 'nerve', because *real* nerve is stealing something when the owner will know perfectly well it was you that did it.

'Can't we go round to Mrs Clitheroe's now, and put it back?'

'What, with Mr Clitheroe there? Pull yourself together, Annie.'

And so it was agreed that tomorrow morning we would turn up at the bungalow in Bluebell Crescent — me, with a large stolen photograph album stuffed up my jumper — and somehow I would replace this in Mrs Clitheroe's sideboard, right under her nose. I had had better nights.

14

Wednesday morning. I'd seen shoplifters on television; one woman had a vast coat with huge secret pockets inside it big enough to take a photograph album. In the absence of such a useful garment, I planned to hang a string shopping bag round my neck with Mrs Clitheroe's album inside, and to hide the bag from view underneath a man-sized jumper, on the assumption that in a family that housed more man-sized jumpers than you could shake a stick at, this would be an easy attainment. Once again I had underestimated the power of mothers to put the kibosh on the best-laid plans.

'Mummy, can I borrow one of Daddy's jumpers?'

'*May* I, Annie.'

'*May* I, Mummy?'

'One of Daddy's? Certainly not.'

Language always took precedence over content; if I'd ever stated that I wanted to go out murdering old ladies if only I was big enough, they would have made me recast the statement in the subjunctive rather than pick up the phone and call a child psychologist.

At least I had got my hands on a string bag, pilfered from the glory-hole under the stairs. I now needed a way to bypass Auntie Rene, who had 'kibosh' as a middle name, and borrow a jumper from Uncle Frank.

Luckily Babette came round as soon as she had finished breakfast, sparing me the need to negotiate with my mother, or, worse still, my father, who was grumpy and irritable and loudly reminding everyone at eight in the morning that it was only three in the morning in New York, and his internal clock hadn't adjusted yet.

'Mum's just said she's doing a shampoo and set for Mrs Clitheroe tomorrow morning in their kitchen.'

That did it: we had to return the album to its rightful owner today, unless we wanted to risk it under the bloodhound nose of Auntie Rene.

'I need a big jumper. Do you think we can borrow one of your daddy's?'

'How big?'

'What do you mean?'

'Uncle Arthur left his washing for Mum to do when they went off for Canvey. She found it in the basket this morning and went mental. I saw a jumper.'

And so it was that Babette and I were walking up Bluebell Crescent, me wearing a heavily laden string bag and a vast woolly garment that reached to my knees. The jumper was softer and less itchy than any of ours, Uncle Arthur's benign presence having presumably calmed the very fibres.

The string-bag-round-the-neck idea had worked extremely well in theory, and while I was waiting stationary by the gatepost, but as I began to walk along, the mechanics of the system were subtly altered, and the project began to show its defects. To a more competent engineer, these defects would have been apparent at the drawing board stage. The thin string handles cut into my skin, burning a terrible red halter most of the way round my neck. What is more, even the gentlest walking pace caused the weighted bag to swing. I had effectively devised a method for slowly sawing off my own head.

Strangely, when I stopped and prised the instrument of torture out of the flesh into which it had eaten, far from easing, the pain flared so sharply that tears coursed from my eyes and all the hairs stood up on my arms. When I put a hand gingerly under a pigtail, the fingers came away sticky with blood.

'Babette, do you know what?'

'What?'

'I'm going home to change into my trews.'

'What – *now*??'

'I'll have to put the photo album down the front of them. This bag's killing me.'

I persuaded her to return to the gatepost and re-stash our increasing number of stolen items while I nipped home to perform a quick change into trousers. When I eventually re-emerged into Bluebell Crescent with one of the leather corners of the photograph album rammed down my knickers, the pain in my neck was still shocking; it was cold and yellow, like acid biting through alloy.

'Babette?'

'What?'

'Wouldn't it be better to go along with Auntie Rene tomorrow, and put it back when they're hairdressing?'

'What – you and me walk up here with my mum and a stolen photo album? She'd wheedle it out of you. She'd go barmy!'

True. So we continued our trundle along the road until we reached number sixteen, and turned in at the gate. Not for long. Across the bedroom and bathroom windows that punctuated the red brick at the front of the bungalow, Mrs Clitheroe's curtains were drawn tight shut. We knew what this meant – migraine. And no entry whatsoever.

'Oh *no*!' wailed Babette.

'Shhhh!'

Mrs Clitheroe herself had never talked much about her migraines ('Let's just say they even stop me listening to music'), but Auntie Doris had a sister who was a martyr to them, and apparently it was like someone wrapping your brain up in barbed wire while flashing lights into one of your eyes and drilling a hole through it. We backed away from the gate rather sharply.

We might have stood there on the pavement all day, staring at the uncompromising blankness of the blinded windows, had not the photograph album, which was unbalanced by my latest posture, levered itself out of my trews, and landed on its back on the concrete in an ungainly somersault. In the act of tipping itself out of the trousers, one corner of the album had gouged a deep scratch into the flesh of my abdomen. I scooped the book off the pavement, and we scuttled away.

'What we gonna do?' wailed Babette, casting wild glances at the silent, watchful bungalows of Bluebell Crescent.

'P'raps Mrs Clitheroe won't still have her migraine this afternoon. Auntie Doris's sister's migraines don't last all day.'

'Yes they do,' corrected Babette gloomily. 'Auntie Doris's sister's migraines last up to three days at a certain time of the month.'

I, too, remembered her saying this, so on a brainwave I suggested we pop round to Auntie Doris's and ask whether she knew what time of the month that was. This earned me a withering look from Babette.

'Don't you know anythink, Annie Cradock?'

We walked back to the house in silence. Babette

tucked herself under the thorns and crab-apples, hid the album again, and slithered back out.

'My mum'll do for us!' she said, and then (rather belatedly, I thought), 'I'll kill Lorraine and her clever ideas, up the duff or not.'

Next, we had to return Uncle Arthur's jumper to the washing basket. Babette went first, and I was to follow a few seconds behind unless I heard anything to stop me. I did. I heard Babette's arrival hailed by *both* our mothers, asking variously where was Annie and where was Arthur's cashmere sweater that Sir James had given him up at Muning Hall? There was nothing for it but to slink around the side of the house, and stand quaking until one of them noticed me. It was Auntie Rene. I struggled desperately to be free of the jumper before she finished bearing down on me, with the result that it became hopelessly tangled, and in pulling one of the sleeves inside out, I managed to get its cashmere cuff down my throat. I was doubled up, choking, with the garment over my head while the remaining sleeve waved about like the trunk of an enraged elephant. Suddenly, Auntie Rene's grip tore through the soft fibres, and a full set of lacquered fingernails gleamed in front of my face.

'That's worth twenty-five guineas!' she snapped. 'Sir James give it him as a thank-you for building them greenhouses!', and she whipped the jumper off my head and through the air with such speed it hummed. 'I'm sorry, Myrtle, but I can't cope with the pair of them together.'

'Home, young lady, this instant!' My mother. We left to the sound of slapped legs, and an atypically unfeminine howl from Babette.

It was my misfortune to have a father at home as well as a mother, and for the next half hour I suffered the 'Whatever will become of her?' fate of all only-children caught in misdemeanour. This lament stopped strangely in mid-sentence, like a needle snatched off a gramophone record.

'What on earth is that on your hand?' My mother marched forward and grabbed me. 'It is! It's blood!' they told each other.

When at last I stopped dodging the hands, and allowed my parents to raise my hair and look, there was a second interlude of silence broken by Daddy stating in an awed voice that I had been garrotted from behind. They didn't ask any further questions; I was bundled into the car, and taken off to the casualty department of Epping General Hospital. On our way there, a light rain began to dapple the windscreen, and presumably Babette's garden, the gatepost and Mrs Clitheroe's photographic album with the exquisitely tooled leather cover and her family's history in pictures since the First World War.

If only the circumstances had been different, I could have enjoyed being a celebrity at the hospital, not to mention the novelty of hearing my parents say 'I've no idea', which they did repeatedly to a variety of people, some of whom seemed to carry a lot of clout.

'Was it a boy who did this, dearie?' I was asked by one of the nurses.

'No, it was just a game. I was pretending to be a donkey.'

'A what, love?'

'A beast of burden.'

And to my parents: 'This friend, Babette, does she have a spiteful streak?'

I tried to picture Babette with a garrotte in her hands and murder in her heart, and it occurred to me that with the difference in our heights, she would have to do it *en pointe*.

Eventually I was allowed home, but not until my

wounds had been painted with something yellow and smelly which stung, and had been bandaged and stitched in two places with wiry thread that protruded from both sides of my neck like a soft toy model of Frankenstein's monster. If this hadn't cleared up before school restarted, I would have to run away from home.

Once we got outside, I tried to make myself more comfortable by wriggling, which exposed the deep, purple graze across my tummy. My parents looked at it in shock. I heard Mummy say rapidly, 'I can treat her at home with Zam-Buk', and when Daddy started to argue, 'You saw the way they looked at us, Dai; if we walk back in there with another injury, those nurses will call the police.'

And so we went home.

The sight of their only child being swabbed, painted and stitched, seemed to have chastened my parents, and instead of resuming the tirade against my theft of Uncle Arthur's cashmere, they allowed me the run of the house. Daddy turned to music to cheer himself up. He was a Beethoven *da-da-da-DA* man, but he was every bit as happy listening to 'Colonel Bogey' or anything by Souza. Today we had the 'Triumphal March' from Verdi's *Aida*. It was about the ancient Egyptians. I had a book. I had another on the ancient Romans too, both of them bought by my father to remedy the influence of the robust British comedy film *Carry on Cleo* on my understanding of history. The Romans wore garments called togas, and there was easily room enough to hide photograph albums under them. You could fashion a convincing toga out of a couple of bed-sheets. And if anyone in Bluebell Crescent queried it, I was a Roman emperor, I was Caesar, I was Mark Antony, I was mad, potty Caligula who murdered his sister and appointed his horse to the Senate. That should shut them up.

At least they'd be grateful that I was quiet – the day Babette and I were Vestal Virgins, our dialogue from *Carry on Cleo* elicited complaints.

My mother's airing cupboard was a place of warmth, heaped-high sheets, and the mellifluous smell of comfort. Threadbare or iron-burned sheets were legitimate loot for dressing up, unlike the curtains and tights we'd filched for Batman and Robin (Babette was Robin). With the aid of a couple of safety pins, I looked like a reasonable facsimile of a Roman, albeit a decapitated Roman whose head had been sewn back on. Five minutes later, the photograph album and I were on our way to Bluebell Crescent.

Mrs Clitheroe's curtains were still drawn. The usual practice of Auntie Doris's sister when attacked by migraine, was to crawl into the safety of her bedroom and cover her head in a blanket to stop the daylight getting in. I knew which of the front rooms was the Clitheroes' bedroom, in which the lady of the house was presumably lying deaf and blind in her blanket. On the other side of the front door was the bathroom. Although the curtains were closed, the window was not only open, but in fact the frame looked damaged in a way that stopped it closing, a fact that I had already noticed on the earlier visit with Babette.

'U or ah! U or ah!' The cry came tearing through the air at me, accompanied by the drag of cart wheels and the slow clop of an elderly horse. Of course, it was Wednesday. Old Ollie. He and his horse lumbered unhurriedly down Bluebell Crescent, past number sixteen, on their way to Babette's and my road. I could see a television set lying in the cart, an ironing board, a moose's head, a mangle, and a tailor's dummy, on the outsized bosom of which was perched Old Ollie's old dog, nose twitching in the air.

'Wotcha, cock!'

'Hello, Ollie.'

132

'Thought you'd be up the church 'aving a chortle.'

'It's Wednesday, Ollie.'

'Don't make no difference. There's a couple getting wed.'

There now. If only I were in the St Matthew's choir, that would be five shillings towards Sonnie & Cher's 'I Got You, Babe'.

'Hats? I ain't seen fevvers like it since the 'orses at King George's funeral!'

'Doesn't sound very with-it, Ollie.'

'Donkey's years old. Mothy, the lot of 'em. Let them things on me cart, and me dog 'ould go bald. Mind you,' he added, 'might be a good thing. Some scumbag's give him fleas!'

From somewhere at the back of the horse there issued deep rumblings, like an approaching catastrophe. His enormous dusty ears swivelled as though trying to place the sound.

'So that get-up of yourn's all the rage, is it?'

I glanced down, having forgotten I was wearing a sheet. 'I'm a Roman, Ollie.'

'Ah. They stuff books up their frocks, do they, Romans?'

I smiled wanly.

'Giddy-up!' and without a goodbye, he and the old horse loped off down Bluebell Crescent towards Mountnessing Road.

I looked around me; luckily there was no-one about to have witnessed this incriminating exchange. I nipped across the Clitheroes' front yard, and hopped onto a tub of geraniums under the window ledge. By the evidence of scratch marks on the ground, this had recently been dragged across the concrete to its present position, which was lucky for me. I chucked my sandals through the open window first and then, sure-footed as any of Rupert's cat burglars, I followed the sandals over the sill.

I went in backwards, with a knee on the window sill, left foot in the basin, right foot dangling in mid-air. Whatever agency had bent the window frame had also cracked the glass, and as I swung round to face the bathroom, the photograph album whacked the pane, and the window instantly smashed to smithereens.

There was a noise like a hundred greenhouses shattering. They must have heard it in Brentwood. My body convulsed with the shock, and then sagged, and my right leg slipped into free fall. Something cold slithered across my foot and pain screamed through the ankle, which was now both wet and trapped. I'd jammed it down the lavatory. The photograph album, meanwhile, glided out from under my sheet and thumped onto the bathroom floor.

Amazingly, no-one came running to investigate, not even Mrs Clitheroe. Auntie Doris's martyred sister must be right about the efficacy of the head blankets. By levering myself back up, I eventually had one foot on terra firma again, and was able to step out of the lavatory. That was when I looked down and saw a nasty iridescence of yellows and globular brown in the bowl, and a wet tissue clinging to the inside of my bare toes like a soft marine creature finding a home in the rocks. Appalled, I managed to wash it off and flush the lavatory, by which time my clandestine entrance had made at least twice as much noise as if I'd stayed outside, safe and dry, and simply flung the photograph album through the bathroom window from the far side of Bluebell Crescent, together with the moose and the mangle from Old Ollie's cart.

The bathroom door wasn't quite shut. By peeking through the gap, I had a view of the cross-bar of the T-shaped hall, which showed me the doors to the sitting room and bedroom. The bedroom door was shut. Clearly Mrs Clitheroe hadn't stirred. I crept into the sitting room.

It was in a tremendous muddle. Babette and I had once before seen the bungalow in a mess, accidentally turning up before Mr Clitheroe left for work, and we heard him shouting at his wife. And he was known to chuck things around; on one famous occasion the song 'Does Your Mother Come from Ireland?' started up on the wireless, and he shouted 'Does she hell as like!' and hurled the radio across the room. But this time he must have been in a *real* mood; the contents of drawers were strewn everywhere, the table lamp lolled across the coffee table, our coveted flamenco lady lay spread-eagled on the floor, and my beloved pottery spaniels were smashed, broken at the neck, their poor heads lying where they'd rolled under the table.

Messy splodges of red suggested to me the cause of the marital row – my father occasionally cut himself shaving and infuriated Mummy by smearing blood across her bathroom towels. But *these* blood splodges were huge.

Mrs Clitheroe's modish wooden clock had been knocked out of kilter. It said the time was one o'clock; at one o'clock Mr Clitheroe came home for his dinner, and although there was clearly no dinner to be had from a prostrated, blind, deaf, migrainous wife, the man might not yet know this. The man clearly *didn't* yet know this, as I could hear his key turn in the front door. I flung open the French windows to the back garden, and was outside, round the house and flitting up Bluebell Crescent like the Woman in White. I didn't even hear Mr Clitheroe shut the front door. And I was still clasping the photograph album, which I'd forgotten all about.

15

I am Hiawatha. Using the settee and a travel blanket, I have constructed a makeshift wigwam, and I'm trying to sit cross-legged inside it, but my right ankle is still swollen and sore where I jammed it down Mrs Clitheroe's lavatory. I am composing my own story, in which Hiawatha is the Indian who famously sells Manhattan island to the white man for twenty-four dollars, when I hear a knock at the back door, and then Auntie Rene. Of course, this is so commonplace that my mind anticipates the sequel and half-consciously plays through the familiar bright chatter as though it were a soundtrack in my head. But this evening the greeting is muffled and there's no chatter; after answering the door, my mother steps outside and closes it behind her. After a while, she comes in and calls my father. They whisper together, and then *he* goes outside. I wouldn't normally bother to listen, but the last time I heard Auntie Rene's voice was when she was slapping Babette and tearing clothes off me, so perhaps I am sensitized.

It was a long time before any of them came back into the house, but eventually my parents did. I watched them through the sliver of light where the edges of the travel blanket didn't meet. They came in together, and paused at the threshold of the room, together. This was very odd and I was suddenly, unaccountably, dreadfully, frightened.

'Angharad?' and after a bit, 'Annie!'

'I'm in the wigwam.'

'Come out please, dear.'

I did, forgetting about the ankle, which caused pain to scorch through my foot. They sat me down on the settee, between the two of them, which meant that the only way I could follow the discourse was to swivel my stitched head around like that thing on a submarine.

'Annie, we know how fond you are of Mrs Clitheroe; we know she has always been kind to you and Babette.'

With this, I was now so frightened that I could not properly understand the words. I heard 'Mrs Clitheroe', and knew that the photograph album would follow, and the bathroom window (and presumably the lavatory bowl), and then the police. The police did follow – my father was talking about detectives at Leonard and Jenny's, and somehow this was directly related to Old Ollie with his horse and cart.

It seemed to me absolutely horrid that Old Ollie had handed me over to the police. I'd always liked him – he had a horse and a knotty old dog, and he lumbered around Muningstock crying 'Up your arse!', which no-one else had ever dared to do. Tears ran down my face.

'Mr Clitheroe has gone to stay at a bed and breakfast in Ongar for the time being,' my mother was saying. 'There will be policemen around the neighbourhood for a little while.'

137

'They might want to interview the local children to find out if any of you witnessed anything with a bearing on the crime.'

'What Daddy means is that one of you might have seen or heard someone coming into Bluebell Crescent or leaving it around dinnertime, including Ollie.'

'If they ask, you must tell the detectives anything that you are sure of, and you've no need to be afraid, because they are here to help the village. But you mustn't invent anything or embellish a story.'

'You really mustn't, Annie. I know how clever your imagination can be, but you mustn't exercise it this time, no matter what the dramatic potential. Mrs Clitheroe wouldn't want you to.'

'Because this is serious, darling. This is murder.'

I was not a stupid child. Probably I was above the average intelligence for Muningstock. But my preconceived ideas had run so nearly parallel with reality that I had to stumble a long way down my separate road before I realized the truth. Mrs Clitheroe had been murdered. This was a different nightmare, but it wasn't a better one.

'What did you just say Old Ollie said?'

'Ollie? We don't know what he said, dear. It was Mrs Maxwell – she saw him entering the house.'

'What house?'

'The Clitheroes' bungalow, Annie. Gina Maxwell saw Ollie breaking into number sixteen.'

'Or so she says now,' qualified my father, always judicious. 'She didn't report any burglary at the time, only after the body was found.'

'Don't say "the body", please, Dai.'

'I'm sorry, Myrtle, my dear. Until after Jenny Clitheroe was found.'

'I want Babette.'

There was a pause in the cross-talk.

138

'May I go round to Auntie Rene's, please?'

I actually got up, and was ready to leave the house at a vigorous sprint, but my father placed a restraining hand on my shoulder.

'Better not at the moment, Annie-*fach*; apparently Babette has taken the news rather badly. Irene says she's really quite distressed.'

Yes, I bet she was. All this talk of detectives, and 'bearing on the crime' – the first opportunity Babette got, she'd have been out to their gatepost to check on the stolen album. But when I'd fled from Mrs Clitheroe's, I'd found it easier to hide it in our garden shed than struggle with Auntie Rene's prickly shrubs. Babette would have found nothing behind the gatepost but a paper bag. I doubted whether 'quite distressed' would cover her response.

'Yes but,' I ventured, 'we always went to Mrs Clitheroe's together, so Babette might want to cry on my shoulder.'

This was weak, I knew, but I was thinking on my feet.

'I'm sorry, Annie. Tomorrow perhaps.'

'I want to go round now.'

'No.'

'Why not?'

'Because we already asked Irene and she said "No".'

Oh.

They *always* have to know better than we do. Even when they haven't a clue what's going on between us, they still have to know better. I sat back down, and tried to subdue the thoughts scratching around in my head. The only way was to escape to the garden, where I might be able to talk to Babette via our secret communication lines.

'May I go and play outside, please?'

Again, Mummy and Daddy were flummoxed. I suppose they had come into the room steeling themselves, ready for grief and weeping, anxious to offer parental comfort, and here I was, wanting only Babette.

'Annie, wouldn't you like to talk to us about what's happened?'

'If you don't mind,' I told them, with downcast eyes and an improvised sniff, 'I'd rather go into the garden and remember poor Mrs Clitheroe.' Which, of course, swung it for me. I knew that something about this wasn't quite right. True, I was horribly worried about my best friend, quaking next door, but mine wasn't much of a response to the news that a dear friend had just met a violent death.

Our garden. There was a low wall on the boundary between their house and ours, sandwiched between a privet hedge (my mother) and a chicken-wire fence partially clothed in convolvulus (Auntie Rene). Uncle Frank once described this arrangement as the belt, braces and safety-pin school of thought on keeping the neighbours out. He wasn't right; I could scramble onto this wall, with the double advantage of being invisible from the ground floor of both houses, but in clear view of Babette's bedroom.

Had I been the one who was 'quite distressed' and 'taking it badly', I would have been demanding company and attention, but Babette's usual response to trauma was 'I'm gonna bed!' followed by a slammed door.

I dodged around the privets, clambered painfully onto the wall, and peered upwards through the chicken wire towards the shadowy interior of Babette's bedroom. There was only a glimmering dimness, so I resorted to the time-honoured tradition of a handful of small stones chucked at the bedroom window.

'Annie!' The glass slid back, and Babette leaned out. She was in her nightie.

140

'Annie, you know what? The photo album's gone! There's been police sniffing about – they must've took it!'

'No.'

'*Yes!* I reckon I'm for it, Annie. I reckon they'll have me down the station.'

It was borne in on me that she'd been crying. Babette's tears were rare, but memorable for inducing virulent catarrh that was a distinctive shade of green. In the scientific environment of my family, I once asked why some people had green snot. My father promised that we'd discuss it after the Frobishers had finished their tea, but we never did.

'Babette, *I* took it. Listen, I took it away.'

'You? WHY?!'

'I thought you was told to leave Babette alone.' It was Uncle Frank. He had a way of standing and looking that reminded me of spivvy crooks on the television, a man-of-the-world, know-where-the-body's-buried look, his air of caginess enhanced by the cigarette perched in the side of the mouth.

'What I thought, Annie, was that Auntie Irene told your mummy and daddy that Babette wasn't to be bothered tonight.'

I heard the window sliding shut above me; Babette ducking out of trouble. Before it closed I took a deep breath, like for the top notes of 'House of the Rising Sun'.

'I'LL LEAVE A MESSAGE YOU-KNOW-WHERE!'

'Pack that in!' He tamped the cigarette out, and picked at the paper threads that had stuck to the side of his lip. I crept over to the far edge of the wall, where he could talk to me through the chicken wire. When he spoke again, the tone was low, steady, and reasonable.

'Babette's been upset, Annie.'

'So am I upset, Uncle Frank,' I said, trying to keep my own voice steady. 'About Mrs Clitheroe.'

'Yeah, but it's not the same thing. I bet your mummy and daddy broke it to you nicely, didn't they? Sat you down on the settee, and told you in words that wouldn't give you the willies.'

I looked up again at the bedroom window, but there was nothing except the watery shift of shadows.

'You see, that weren't how Babette got told. Gina Maxwell come running round, screaming blue murder. Before your Auntie Irene could stop her, she'd said we wasn't safe in our beds with all these killers on the loose.'

'I heard it too, Uncle Frank. I heard about Mrs Clitheroe being killed, and I knew there were other murders, so it's the same thing.'

'No, Annie. Mrs Maxwell talked about things you wouldn't want to hear.'

Tears tickled my throat.

'It weren't a nice thing for Rene to hear, never mind Babette. So you see, Annie, she's had a worse time than what you have, and she don't want to see you tonight.'

'Babette did want to see me, Uncle Frank. She wanted me to tell her something, it was important.'

'Well now. The way I see it, what's important to you isn't always important to anybody else. It's like all them fancy games you get up to, they're what *you* choose, not her. I'd say her wishes don't get much of a look in. Now you go back indoors, Annie, and your Auntie Irene will let you know when Babette's all right to come back out to play.' He turned on his heel, and made a move towards the back door.

'There isn't a murderer on the loose!' I called after him, scrabbling to score a point and lessen the humiliation. 'Mrs Maxwell said it was Old Ollie, and the police have got him, so he's not loose.'

'Ollie!' Uncle Frank snorted. 'That silly tart couldn't identify an intruder. She'd need both hands and a searchlight to identify her own fanny.'

This at least was fair comment. And how come Mrs Maxwell always got into everything – had she been poking her sunburnt nose in other people's business again? Snooping on Mrs Clitheroe again? Anyway, I knew I deserved to win some territory with Uncle Frank, and made one last advance.

'Mummy and Daddy gave me the gory details, too!' I said, desperately struggling to remember. I could hear an echo of my father's level voice: 'Somebody hit her on the head, Annie-*fach*. That's always a dangerous thing to do, and she didn't survive the blow.'

'They told me Mrs Clitheroe had her head hit!' What else had they told me? 'They said she was murdered by someone hitting her head, so there. It's just as bad for me as Babette, Uncle Frank.'

'Yeah? Babette overheard Gina Maxwell say that the murderer smashed Jenny's skull to a pulp with a meat-axe. That what your mummy and daddy told you? She said Leonard come home for his dinner and found his wife lying by the front door in a pool of blood and brains.'

I was silent. Tears threatened to pour from my eyes.

'You go inside now, Annie. It's getting dark and we've all had a bit of a day.' And with that he walked back across the garden, skirting the sandpit, and disappeared into the house through the kitchen door. I heard it click open, thump shut, and then there was no-one outside but me.

I didn't go indoors myself. I sat down on the wall, well behind the dual screens of privet and bindweed. It was twenty past eight, and daylight was dwindling. The parabola of Bluebell Crescent would be seeded with small squares of tungsten light by now. There were white roses next door, and blue lupins that always glowed in the Lucases' darkling garden long after my mother's red flowers had turned black. It was my comfort, the garden, and I knew its waxing and waning colours, its ways, day or night. One is nearer God's heart. I crouched there on the wall and cried into the soft gloaming.

When my mother came out to get me, her usual perfunctory tone was modulated. I went indoors and several thoughts struck me out of nowhere, things I should have realized before. If Mr Clitheroe found his wife murdered at dinnertime, then all the while I was in her bathroom, Mrs Clitheroe was lying on the other side of the wall, with her head smashed to pieces. If their hall hadn't been T-shaped, it would have been me who found her. And obviously the person Mrs Maxwell saw breaking in wasn't Old Ollie at all. It was me.

16

One o'clock in the morning.

I'd taken a hot-water bottle to bed, craving this regressive pleasure. I then spent the first part of the night fathoms deep in sleep, with the hot rubber squashed for comfort around a swollen ankle that would have been better served by an ice pack. By one in the morning, my right foot was twice its normal size, and throbbing like rhythm and blues.

This sudden-onset elephantiasis of the foot completely baffled my parents, who insisted on stripping me out of my nightie and giving me the once-over to check whether any other bits had been sawn, gouged or pumped up.

It wasn't until two that my sluggish mental progress brought me up against the fact that if I'd been mistaken for Old Ollie, and he was therefore logically innocent, then the real murderer was logically still out there. The next realization (half past two) was that the real murderer might still have been in the bungalow when I arrived, and not only that, but (three in the morning) if he saw me, he might well assume that I had seen and recognized *him*, in which case he would now take action to silence me. Pool of blood and brains. Skull to a pulp with a meat-axe.

It was around this time that my mother reluctantly accepted that she wasn't going to get any more sleep either, so we went downstairs to the kitchen. Daddy had gone back to bed about half past one, even though I'd reminded him that it was still only half past eight at night in New York, so I couldn't see why he was asleep in the first place.

I sat in a kitchen chair with one foot propped on the table, swathed in a sock packed with ice cubes, and drinking Ovaltine. We would have been playing Monopoly if I'd had my way, but my mother got surprisingly cross when I tried to suggest it.

I didn't tell her what had happened. It was only when she wasn't there that I was really terrified of the murderer, more terrified than I was of telling her and my father that I'd taken up burglary. And of course when she wasn't there, she wasn't there to tell. Perhaps it was this Wittgensteinian dilemma that finally wore me out. Anyway, by five o'clock my mother was tucking me back into bed with an aspirin, and because the sun was not yet up, she left the bed-side lamp burning, with a handkerchief across Yogi Bear's beaming head to soften the light. At least this way she might get a couple of quiet hours before I was off again.

BABETTE,
    I TOOK THE YOU-KNOW-WHAT, IT WASN'T ANYBODY ELSE.
                    ANGHARAD

I decided that this couldn't incriminate either of us if it fell into constabular hands, and slipped the note behind the Lucases' gatepost. I also took away the now damp and tatty paper bag that Babette had originally wrapped the album in. I could make out something small and stiff inside it, which turned out to be a handful of photographs and a note that must have slipped from their moorings.

Back indoors with this lot down my knickers, I discovered Uncle Horace, without Doris for once. He was engaged in the activity known in Muningstock as 'jawing', in the course of which he collected his premiums for the Prudential.

Horace was slight and wiry, and at the moment was craning his neck to look up at my mother. This morning, his redhead's skin had a mottled hue like bruised fruit, and his eyes were pink. My mother looked pretty off colour too, I noticed. The conversation was about praying, but then, it often was.

'However painful, Myrtle, I must pray for the soul of Jenny's killer.'

'David and I prayed last night, Horace.'

'Is Angharad disturbed by it all?'

'Extremely, and none of us has had much sleep in consequence.'

'I popped in to see Irene yesterday evening, and little Babette was very agitated. She seemed most troubled by the idea of the police in their front garden.'

'Yes, their imaginations work overtime.'

I ducked out of the house once more and was down the drive, taking care not to clang my mother's precious wrought-iron gates. But instead of turning left for Babette or Bluebell Crescent, I turned right. I had to know what Mrs Maxwell had said about this intruder, but I needed to find out in a way that wouldn't actually present Mrs Maxwell with that intruder in flesh and blood to jog her memory. I would ask Auntie Doris while she was alone. On her own, she'd be less likely to bring praying into it.

147

*   *   *

Horace and Doris Frobisher lived in a bungalow set back in a jungly garden that darkened the windows and presumably kept the air from ventilating properly, because their indoors always smelled of cooked cabbage. The roofline had an odd architectural feature of four towering chimneys, one on each corner, so that Uncle Frank, ever on the lookout for something to ridicule, said the bungalow looked like a double bed upside down.

The overall impression was of a vegetable gloom. I got halfway along the winding, weedy path, with the hulking bulk of rhododendrons lowering on my right and the hominoid shapes of conifers twitching ahead of me, and I stopped. I knew this path with its friendly shrubs; it was absurd to get the heebie-jeebies. But I was learning a lesson about the nature of fear: it wasn't merely that I couldn't carry on going forwards; I couldn't turn round and retreat either. I sat down abruptly on the crumbling concrete and wriggled in reverse until my back was up against the larchlap fence. Of course, if there were an axe murderer lurking about, this turned me into a sitting duck. But I could cope with anything now that he couldn't creep up behind me.

This wasn't the first time a visit had been abandoned; Babette and I occasionally trotted into the Frobishers' garden and then crept out again un-announced. Horace and Doris sometimes played oratorios on the piano and sang. From our recce position twenty feet and a wall away, we would catch a bovine groundswell beneath a soprano noise like a car with belt squeal. Babette and I never got quite so bored that we wanted to meet *that* at close range.

Time passed. This wasn't much of a way to spend a morning. Larchlap is not comfortable against the back, and the earth was damp and wormy. There was no way to guess how long before Uncle Horace would finish jawing with my mother and come to my rescue. I fished in my clothes for Mrs Clitheroe's loose photographs. A more suitable home than my knickers would have to be found for these — such as back inside her album in our garden shed. There were four pictures, black and white. They showed women in tight-waisted A-line skirts and skimpy jumpers that clung to their busts, sitting on the grass or perched on fences, with a breeze blowing their perms about and breathing at their petticoats. On the back of one was a lightly pencilled legend: 'Henderson's Sliding Doors Picnic, August Bank Holiday, 1955'. The sight of Mrs Clitheroe gave me a jolt. She was younger than I ever knew her, and of course she looked silly because of the old-fashioned clothes, but her face and attitude were different, too; they were rather like Lorraine always looked before this last time. Sort of . . . happy.

There was also a folded sheet of paper on which someone had pasted a picture. It was predominantly banana yellow, with a broad block of colour across the top left-hand corner, and a lot of blotches on the right. I noticed a line of print, upside down. I turned the paper the other way up. There was a broad block of colour across the bottom right-hand corner and a lot of blotches on the left. The legend read 'Kandinsky (1866–1944). *Impression III (Concert)*, 1911.' Concert? Light dawned. The splodges were people round a grand piano!

I turned to the back of the sheet, and found it covered with small, neat notes in green ink. I recognized the hand from other notes tucked into Mrs Clitheroe's album and remembered her saying 'When girls reach their teens, they develop affectations. Green ink was one of mine.'

Despite this, it was pretty to read:

Notes copied from 'Colour and Form' by F. G.
Grünwald, borrowed from Mr B.

From the time of Wagner onwards, artists and
musicians were seeking a synthesis of music and
visual art. This was particularly important to the
Symbolists. [NB, I think these were a group of
French writers including Baudelaire. Must look up
Baudelaire.]
    The painter Kandinsky was deeply influenced
by his personal experiences of synaesthesia. [NB,
this means a synthesis of different senses, such as
seeing music in colour, like me!] Another major
influence on Kandinsky was the composer
Schoenberg, who was moving away from
traditional harmonies in favour of atonal music
and dissonance. [NB, must look up Schoenberg.]
Kandinsky saw direct parallels between this
musical revolution and the movement of art away
from figurative painting towards the abstract. He
first came across Schoenberg at a concert in
Munich on New Year's Day, 1911. Kandinsky's
painting '*Impression III (Concert)*' is his attempt to
paint his experience of hearing Schoenberg for the
first time.
    [NB, Kandinsky heard trumpets as yellow (like
me!), the cello as blue (like me!!), and violins as
green (NOT like me!!!)]

Like me, though. Green violins. Sounded good to
me.
I studied the picture again, the banana-coloured
music coming from the piano. I knew about
dissonance from Mrs Clitheroe, and the more I thought
about it, the more I liked the idea. *I* could do that. I sat
and pondered the production of a really serious
dissonance that might come out in this Kandinsky

man's yucky shade of yellow. Both hands flat out and perhaps one foot on the keyboard. Except there was no chance that Auntie Rene would put up with the sound of that coming at her through the wall, so I'd have to try it round at Mrs Clitheroe's.

I pulled myself up. Of course I knew that Mrs Clitheroe was murdered yesterday. Of course I did. But until now, I hadn't properly understood that it meant she was dead.

The enormity howled into my head and wailed through my stick-thin bones, and my frame shook. I sat appalled. Mrs Clitheroe's hand-writing danced across the page with its free-flowing curls like her pony-tail, like the elegant arch of her hands on the piano keys. That smoky-grey voice followed the words as they skipped along. *He heard trumpets as yellow*, I heard her say. *Think of blue cellos, Annie, think of green violins!* In my own dimpled hand with its bitten nails, the paper trembled.

I watched the word *violins* dissolve in front of my eyes, spreading outwards in a green ripple, like a melt of every violin concerto, a liquefaction of sweeping strings. 'Schoenberg' followed, and 'synthesis', and 'New Year's Day'. Panicking, unaware that these were my own tears splashing the paper, I tried to blot it with the material of my dress until the skirt was dyed green and there was barely a legible word on the page. When a masculine voice hollered six feet away from me, I jerked into the air as though someone had plugged me into the mains.

'Doris!'

'Don't shout at me, I'm here,' was the mild reply. She was coming round the corner of the bungalow with a Tupperware dish, her dark hair studiously bunned, a pinny over her summer frock. 'I was about to put your sandwiches in the car for you.'

They were both on the path, close enough to see me.

151

I would have announced myself, but I was crying, and as I tried to speak, my chest gave an involuntary hiccup that took the words with it. A stray slant of sunlight caught the Brylcreem of Uncle Horace's copper-coloured hair. It looked as though his head were melting.

'Good! I've saved you a journey,' he replied. His voice dropped, and they both turned away so that I couldn't make out what he was saying until 'Gina was at home.'

'And?'

There was something else I couldn't catch, followed by, 'I couldn't budge her. She insists it was Ollie she saw climbing through the window. According to Gina she was looking out for him because she had something for the cart.'

'Oh yes?'

'An old iron, appropriately enough. She says she's prepared to swear it was him before God or a jury, whichever comes the sooner.'

'Blasphemy.'

'Not strictly, I suppose. Anyway, blasphemy isn't the crime at issue. She *says* the police found corroborative evidence in Jenny's sitting room.'

'Gina Maxwell used the term "corroborative evidence", did she?'

'Well, no, what she actually said was "That thieving old gyppo even left a gold ring behind him, and the coppers identified it from the camp." '

'I don't understand.'

'Neither do I, not entirely. The police found a signet ring, apparently, which Leonard said wasn't theirs, and then the police traced it to another of the travellers. They told Leonard, who told Gina. Don't ask me how that incriminates Ollie in particular, but in Gina's mind he's as good as convicted. Nothing will budge her now.'

'A signet ring? I don't believe a word of it.'

'No. Anyway, the police are trying to get other witnesses to the intruder.'

'In Bluebell Crescent? Fat chance. You know what Jenny always said: the Early Bird satellite could plummet to earth in Bluebell Crescent and no-one would notice.'

'It's the school holidays, remember, and children play up and down that road. The police intend to interview all the local youngsters; I sincerely hope they don't go upsetting Babette. While I was at Myrtle's, a CID man turned up hoping to talk to Angharad, but she had disappeared off somewhere.'

'As per usual.'

For a while, my reaction to this statement blotted out my surroundings, and when I caught the conversation again it had gone somewhere I couldn't follow.

'. . . suspicious circumstances, Doris. The loss adjusters are brought in for cases a good deal less fishy than this.'

'I'm not concerned about whether they pay out! I mean, please God the swine doesn't get a single penny. But this is evidence for the CID. I think you ought to tell them about him taking out a policy on her life.'

'Believe me, there's no need. The police check up as a matter of routine in any murder investigation. And the beneficiary falls under suspicion automatically.'

'Well, I just hope you're right.'

'But, Doris, I can't believe he did this dreadful thing for the money.'

'Neither can I. But I believe that once he'd made up his mind to kill her, he decided to make a bob or two on the side while he was about it. These other murders just nudged him into action. He banked on the police mistaking this one for another botched burglary.'

'Which it looks as though they have.'

I'd sort of noticed that Auntie Doris's voice was a bit

153

gravelly. Now she dabbed at her eyes with a disintegrating Kleenex. Horace, who was starting to look even worse around the eyes than she did, threw out his hands in a gesture of hopelessness.

'If you're right, then this crime was premeditated as far back as six months ago. Think of what we're saying here! That the man had murder in his heart and mind when I was round there giving advice about the premiums? Please God, no.'

'Why not? That's the trouble with evil – it splashes its muck over everybody.'

They had moved down the path towards the gate. Uncle Horace stopped, and touched his wife's arm.

'Are we so sure? Suppose we're speaking like this about an innocent man. I'm not comfortable judging my fellows like this.'

'Aren't you? I am. I loved Jenny Clitheroe. I wish they'd hang him.'

'Doris – charity!'

'I wish they'd hang him!' she said again, and left her husband standing on the path, looking lost and unhappy.

A little ignorance might have stood me in better stead here, but unfortunately I knew what a policy was, because they were part of the warp and weft of Muningstock School – policies on books, and sweets, and the education of Romanies or travellers. Apparently Old Ollie had a policy on Mrs Clitheroe. I was to spend a long time ransacking this for some sort of meaning.

Uncle Horace had gone – I heard the growl of his car drawing out of the drive. Auntie Doris was re-tuning her radio indoors. I loved Jenny Clitheroe – I wish they'd hang him. During my musings in the small hours of last night I had failed to work out the final logical syllogism: the police believed Old Ollie was the intruder. The police believed the intruder was the killer. In truth, I was the intruder. Would the police . . . ?

I wish they'd hang *her*?

Clambering to my feet I wrenched the sprain and yowled. Unheard, I limped pathetically back down the Frobishers' garden path. As I turned out of their gate, there appeared a smudge of black in a landscape that was normally expressed in greens and earth colours. As my eyes refocused, I could see that it was a black vehicle, which had turned up in our front drive. Of course it couldn't be a Black Maria, although they were much on my mind. Approaching as fast as I could hobble, I now recognized the car, and it wasn't much more welcome than a Black Maria. There, with an air of complacency that said it all, stood the highly polished Ford Consul of my Uncle Norman, my mother's sister Marjorie, and my gruesome twelve-year-old cousin Dorothea. It never rains but it pours.

17

'Of course you knew, Annie. You've known for weeks. You forgot.'

'But what have they come *for*?'

'Don't be silly, dear. They haven't come for anything. Dorothea's your cousin.'

'Well, when are they going home?'

Not for some time, by the look of my bedroom. A row of corduroy trews, extra large, hung in the wardrobe, and jodhpurs (unaccountably), and a starch-stiff Girl Guide uniform. There were eleven Mars bars on the dressing table plus a *Crackerjack* pencil and a Swiss army knife. By the bed was a bassoon. It was like some random assortment of objects used for a memory game. Cuddly toy? Yes, that too. On my quilted counterpane was a Bri-nylon poodle that would unzip, according to unhappy memory, to disgorge a pair of baby-doll pyjamas in pinkly beribboned broderie anglaise, extra large. To someone who would be sharing a bed with these dimensions, they had a significance greater than merely looking a fright in baby-doll pyjamas. As though all this were not enough, Dorothea invariably kept me awake at night by snoring. I tackled her about this once. She said of course she didn't *snore*, it was a kind of nocturnal bassoon practice.

'So where's our Annie, then? Not coming to give her uncle a hug?'

'Angharad, come down at once. Don't be so rude.'

'They prefer being upstairs, Myrtle. Monkeys like to be high.'

I changed into a clean dress, tucking my ink-stained cotton at the very bottom of Mummy's laundry basket where it would dye the towels green, and started reluctantly for the stairs. Then, as slowly as I could manage, I presented myself to the waiting Uncle Norman.

'Well, well, well!' he cried. 'You've got more bandages on than an Egyptian mummy!'

My own mummy had wrapped my neck in a chiffon scarf to hide the stitches, and had bandaged the ankle after breakfast. She knew a lot about nursing and health; it was she who'd explained to me that what Uncle Norman had was called halitosis.

'Hello, Annie.' Auntie Marjorie.

'Hello, Aggie.' Dorothea. 'Want to see my new darts?'

'I have done. They're stuck in my Ringo poster.'

'Angharad, don't be so unwelcoming! Take your cousin upstairs and have a look at what she's brought with her.'

And so I limped back up, accompanied by the galumphing Dorothea, while Uncle Norman continued to chortle about monkeys.

Into my bedroom, Dorothea strode ahead as though she owned the place. 'Hey, Aggie! Bloody fab, or what? *Three murders!* Most times, this place is a total boring dump.' She sat down heavily on the bed, and the

157

picture on the wall above slumped sideways on its wire. 'Have they taken the dead body away yet from yesterday's one?'

'I don't know, Dorothea, I expect so.'

'Did the killer chop her head right off or just bash it?'

'I think he only bashed it. I . . . I'm not sure.'

Smashing her skull to a pulp. Did that mean Mrs Clitheroe's head was no longer . . . or what? Pool of blood and brains. I wish they'd hang him.

'And I earwigged on Uncle Dai talking to Dad, and he said the first one was killed by a knife wound, and the second one by a hatchet in the guts. Is that right?'

'Um. I don't know where the wounds were, Dorothea.' *Th-wack!!*

I noticed that my picture frame had developed a bright sticker, like a boil, plumb in the middle. The picture was the Lord's Prayer, illuminated in sumptuous purples and golds, like a page from the Lindisfarne bible. It now read 'Thy Kingdom come, Thy Will be done in Earth as it is in Pratt's Bottom Pony Club.'

Pictures in purple. Like one of Mrs Clitheroe's verbal paintings – the purple light of evening in New York after a fall of rain, when the setting sun lights the rain clouds, reflecting wet blue and indigo in the canyons of glass and steel. It occurred to me that I associated New York with Mrs Clitheroe more than with my father who had actually been there. How odd. I knew the music that would play in my head the day I finally stepped out along Fifth Avenue: it would be smoky-grey and husky, her colours and cadences, while the rhythms of the city traffic thrummed in the bass.

'Come on then, slow coach!' Dorothea was on her feet.

'What? Where?'

'We're going to look at the house that the latest corpse was clobbered in, of course!'

'*No!*'

'Why? What's the matter?'

I thought fast. 'They'll never let us.'

'They will if we don't ask. You know the saying – what the eye doesn't see, the other person doesn't grieve about.'

This seemed to be an inherited trait. Uncle Norman was always saying things like 'a leap in time saves nine', and talking about Dusty Springboard, or the Strolling Stones.

'I mean, I don't think the police will let us up Bluebell Crescent, Dorothea.'

'Don't be silly, people still live up there, don't they? The ones who aren't dead.'

She was out of the bedroom, and barrelling down the stairs again, whistling 'The Sun Has Got His Hat On'. I remembered Uncle Frank's words about Babette: 'I'd say her wishes don't get much of a look in.' Perhaps God had set Dorothea on me to serve me right. Her family did a lot of visiting, they were always out and about, so perhaps it wasn't just me, and she had been put on earth to do the rounds of the self-centred.

As with Babette, it was impossible to miss the attraction Dorothea held for the boys, who presumably saw in her ample proportions some of the beauty of the bountiful Pam in John Betjeman's poem – his sexy, mountainous sports girl, all thighs and hairy forearms, slashing at tennis balls and swiping the rhodo-dendrons. On the other hand, if Betjeman's Pam smoked Embassy Number Six and said 'bugger' and 'sod', the poem failed to give this a mention.

Out through the front door (nobody questioned us), and there was Babette trotting towards us on the path. For a fleeting moment my misery was pierced by a ray of sunlight. Unfortunately, at the sight of Dorothea,

Babette skidded to a stop, spun on her heel, and vanished. It was like watching Jerry catch sight of Tom. I was just giving a hopeless cry in Babette's direction, when a different sort of cry, professional and brittle, reached us from the gate.

There were two of them, of whom one – a woman – was in uniform. It was the man who spoke.

'Hello there! I may be wrong, but I think one of you must be called Angharad.'

'Yes, that's me. Pleased to meet you.'

The policeman held out his hand. I intervened between it and Dorothea.

'She's only being funny. *I'm* Angharad. This is my cousin, Dorothea.'

There followed a lot of arch comments and heavy policemen's jokes, and I slipped into a kind of suspended animation while the man introduced himself as Detective Inspector Lilliput, and his colleague as WPC Swan. He was about six foot, rather young to be so utterly bald, and freckled like a plover's egg. They'd called earlier for a chat with my mum, he said, but missed me because I was out somewhere having an adventure. They could see that I was about to go off on another one, but they would be tickled pink if we could have a little chat. I suppose I said something in response; we passed around the side of our house to the kitchen door, with Dorothea whispering 'Tickled pink?!' and miming throwing up.

From the way the police were welcomed back by my mother, we gathered that the earlier visit must have been quite some little chat. She enquired with a solicitous air whether her directions to Billericay had been adequate, and already knew how many sugars as she poured their cups of tea.

'That's an unusual name you have, Mr Lilliput.'

'You're not wrong, Mrs Cradock. And there's an interesting story behind it.'

'Oh?'

'Yes indeed.' He took a sip of his tea.

We were in the front room. My wigwam had reverted to its component parts, of which the tartan rug was back in the car and the settee had the two police officers on it. My mother and Auntie Marjorie took the armchairs, Dorothea obliterated the pouffe, and I had the carpet. Uncle Norman and my father were up in the loft with a steel rule and some buckets, so we weren't expecting them back in a hurry. I could hear them – clanks and slow creakings as though some chain-rattling ghost were wandering about overhead. DI Lilliput's voice droned on.

'. . . so it turned out easier for people to call them after the French town they'd come from, and they became the Lille family. Unfortunately, with my grandmother being a heavy smoker, it wasn't long before they were calling her "Fag-Ash Lille" . . .'

It crossed my mind that it was a crying shame Uncle Norman wasn't here, as this was exactly the sort of thing he *would* consider an interesting story.

'Annie, dear, Mr Lilliput is talking to you.'

I gave a jolt. 'I'm sorry.'

'I was wondering if it was all right for me to ask a few questions?'

'Um? Yes. I suppose.'

My mother rested a hand on my shoulder as a gesture of support, though I assumed it was a clamp to stop me skedaddling.

'I was talking to your mum earlier today, so I know you already understand that something bad happened to your neighbour, Mrs Clitheroe.'

'She was murdered with a meat-axe.'

'That's right, Annie, she was murdered with a meat-axe. Now, in order to put everything to rights, the police need to understand a bit more about life in Bluebell Crescent. All right? All right if I ask questions?'

161

'Yes. All right.'

'Did you know Mrs Clitheroe well?'

'Sort of.'

'Oh Annie! You were great friends.'

'Were you, Annie?'

'Well, but she was a grown-up.'

'I see. Did you ever go round to her house?'

'Sometimes.'

'How often would that be?'

'Not very much.'

'Annie! The police only want to build up a picture, dear. Ever since she was old enough to toddle off, Mr Lilliput, Angharad's been round to Jenny Clitheroe's at least once a week all through every school holiday.'

'Once a week, Annie?'

'Only in the holidays.'

'It's the holidays now, isn't it?'

'Yes.'

'Yes. When did you last see her?'

Monday. The gold ring. Babette! Had he already spoken to Babette? No, he couldn't have, or he wouldn't be asking whether I ever went round to Mrs Clitheroe's.

'Not for ages.'

'No? Why was that?'

'We just didn't.' An inspiration. 'We've been pea-picking instead. Mrs Clitheroe doesn't go up the pea fields.'

' "We" means you and Babette Lucas, does it?'

A pause. 'Yes.'

'Good. So you've been pea-picking a lot lately?'

'Sort of.'

'But not today.'

'No.'

'Nor yesterday.'

'No.'

'Angharad went to the farm with the Lucases a few

162

times last week, Mr Lilliput. On a couple of other days recently, we have been up to London airport for my husband. Otherwise, she and Babette have been under everybody's feet all of this summer holiday.'

'Thank you, Mrs Cradock, that's very useful. I always say kiddies are excellent witnesses in some ways, but we're always grateful for a helping hand from mum or dad.' He reached inside his jacket. 'Mind if I smoke?'

'No, of course. We don't, but most of our visitors do.'

'Pipe all right?'

'Certainly. I'll open a window.'

He took from his pocket a decorous utensil of wood polished to a high patina. His face was turned in profile, light filtering through the net curtains onto his dome. His was a lean face, the cheekbones high, the nose aquiline. I watched while he took a pouch of St Bruno tobacco from another pocket, and tamped it into the pipe. The crackle of a match being struck, and the tobacco's opulent fragrance was replaced by the sulphurous odour of Swan Vestas, mucky yellow like Schoenberg. Like fear. He sucked and puffed, and dropped the match into the ashtray my mother placed at his sleeve.

'So you and Babette usually went round to see Mrs Clitheroe at least once a week?'

'About that.'

'Last week?'

'No.'

'This week?'

'No, not this week.'

'Had you quarrelled with the lady? Had she told you off about something?'

'No!'

'Oh, I'm sure they hadn't, Mr Lilliput. Angharad is very sensitive and easily upset. I would have known if there had been trouble with Jenny.'

'Sensitive. I see. I only wondered, because in the normal way of things, Annie would be in the Clitheroes' lounge playing the piano about once a week, but suddenly she's gone quiet, as it were.'

Who had told him? *Who?*

'Migraine! Mrs Clitheroe had a migraine. We weren't allowed in.'

'She told you she had a migraine?'

'No, we never saw her.'

'So how did you know?'

'Her windows were drawn.'

'Come again?'

'I mean her curtains. She always shut them when she wasn't well and that meant we weren't supposed to knock.'

'When were the curtains drawn?'

I paused. 'Yesterday,' I mumbled.

'I see. So you went round to Mrs Clitheroe's house yesterday.'

'Mmm.'

'What time would that be?'

'Ever so early. About breakfast time.'

'With Babette?'

'Mmm.'

'So you went up Bluebell Crescent together, intending to visit Mrs Clitheroe at number sixteen. And then what?'

'Nothing. We just went away again.'

'Where did you go next?'

'Nowhere.'

'Irene and I were looking for you, if you remember, Annie. You both made yourselves scarce.' And to DI Lilliput, 'The reason my daughter is being reticent, is that she and Babette were naughty girls yesterday; they took an expensive cashmere sweater from Mrs Lucas's laundry basket without permission, to play at dressing up, if you please.'

164

'Oh dearie me. Well now. What do you think of that, WPC Swan?'

'I suppose we can let it go this once, sir.'

I had forgotten she was part of this. I saw now that she looked a bit like Lorraine – there was a smile in her voice and her blond hair shone, but the uniform skirt was over her knees. It seemed cruel of the police to make the girls wear grotty clothes. A loud *clink* startled me, but it was only DI Lilliput resting his pipe in my mother's cut-glass ashtray.

'Who dressed up in this borrowed jumper, then, you or Babette?'

'I did.'

'About what time?'

'I can help you there, Inspector. Mrs Lucas came round here, very angry, about an hour after breakfast, say nine o'clock, so the children must have smuggled the sweater out when they left the house shortly before that.'

'So,' he continued to me, 'you were taking it with you to Mrs Clitheroe's.'

'Erm.'

'Yes?'

'Yes . . . no.'

'Let's leave that for a moment, see if the memory comes back later. So far then, we have you going up to Mrs Clitheroe's bungalow at 8.45 yesterday morning, maybe dressed up in a man's oversized jumper, and when you get there, the curtains are shut. Shortly after that you're taken to hospital to have those cuts on your neck treated. That right? You got them from playing at being an overladen donkey.'

This time I didn't even mumble a reply.

'When you were in Bluebell Crescent after breakfast, was anyone else about?'

'No.'

'Sure?'

'There wasn't anybody anywhere. We were all on our own.'

'So you noticed that particularly. Interesting. Were all the windows shut, as well as the curtains?'

'Don't know.'

'Try to think, Annie. It would really help me out. Do you know which window is the bathroom?'

'No.'

'Really? But I'm sure you've been to the toilet sometimes whilst visiting the Clitheroes, haven't you?'

'I suppose so.'

'OK, Annie, let's try a diagram.' He reached for an inside pocket this time, and retrieved a notebook with a stubby pencil. 'Now, I'm no Leonardo da Vinci, but for the sake of argument, let's say this is the front of the bungalow.'

He scribbled with the pencil, scratch, scratch, scratch, and showed me. It was the front elevation of 16 Bluebell Crescent – fascia, guttering, architrave – for all I knew, the thing might have been to scale.

'Which of those windows is the bathroom?'

'That one.'

'That's right. And the other one is . . . ?'

'Mrs Clitheroe's bedroom.'

'Exactly. Now then. As you stood in front of them, was either window open?'

'Yes.'

'Which?'

'The bathroom.'

'I see. And was it still open yesterday dinnertime?'

'Yes. No! I wasn't there yesterday dinnertime!'

'Then let's go back to the morning. There's a tub of flowers in the front yard. Do you remember where it was?'

'It was under the window. Like someone had pulled it there.'

166

'Which window?'

'The bathroom.'

'Thank you. You're really helping me now. And the front door, was that shut?'

'Yes.'

'Was there anything funny about the letterbox?'

'I don't know. I never saw.'

'Try to remember the door, there's a good girl.'

'I couldn't see the letterbox properly, because the newspaper was stuck in it.'

'Ah yes, the *Wittle Chronicle*. That paperboy wasn't a happy lad. The newsagent had an emergency, and didn't get to his shop until eleven o'clock, Annie. It was gone midday, Annie, before the boy could finish delivering them in Bluebell Crescent.' Lilliput pocketed the notebook. 'By the way, have you seen this before?'

It was between his fingers like a conjuring trick, a black and white photograph: 'Henderson's Sliding Doors Picnic, August Bank Holiday, 1955'.

Nausea washed across me, and I tasted something hot and sick at the back of my throat. The thud of my heart echoed and frightened me. Nothing made sense – I knew where I'd put those photos, and I don't care how good a conjurer he was, if he'd put his hand up my knickers then surely my mother would have noticed, even if I didn't.

'Is that a photograph, Mr Lilliput?'

'Take a look, Mrs Cradock. I can't hand it over, because of fingerprints, but you're welcome to see. And there's writing on the back.'

She got up from the armchair and he flicked the photo over between his fingers with all the dexterity of a card sharp.

'"August Bank Holiday, 1955",' read my mother. 'Ten years ago. The year you were born, Annie.' And then, 'Oh Jenny. Poor dear Jenny.'

No-one said anything for a while. My mother eventually broke the silence. 'Is that photo important in some way, Mr Lilliput?'

'There are some loose ends to be tied up, and one of them relates to Mrs Clitheroe's album of photographs – something missing from the scene of crime. I found this snapshot outside somewhere.' He waved a hand in a gesture evoking limitless horizons, and with the other hand slipped the picture back into a plastic bag.

'Annie might be able to help you there; she's thumbed through Jenny's photographs hundreds of times, and she has a good memory.'

'At the moment, Mrs Cradock, there's just one thing I want Annie to remember for me. Shall we have a go?'

I suppose I nodded.

'You've told me the bathroom window was open, with the tub of flowers underneath, looking like someone had dragged it across the yard to climb onto. And you couldn't see the letterbox because of the newspaper. I want you to think hard, Annie. In the morning when you were outside the bungalow with Babette – are you sure that tub of flowers was under the window *then*?'

'Yes.'

'Are you certain?'

'I saw it there.'

'But was that in the *morning*, not dinnertime? Please think carefully.'

'Why don't you ask Babette if you don't believe me?'

'Annie! Don't talk to Mr Lilliput like that!'

But he answered me directly as though she hadn't interrupted. 'I've already asked her, Annie. Babette remembers all the details of your Monday morning visit, but she never noticed any tub of flowers, or an open window, or a busted frame.'

'Well, it was open and busted, Mr Lilliput.'

'When Babette was with you?'

'Mmm.'

My mother started to speak, but he raised his hand like traffic duty, and she subsided. DI Lilliput looked at me so long and hard that I seriously began to fear that he had alien powers, and was reading my thoughts, getting in through my eyes. Eventually he smiled in a resigned sort of way, shook his head, and said quietly to the air, 'If only the Lucas girl remembered.' Then he carefully tucked away the notebook, and the pencil, and picked up his pipe.

'Mrs Cradock, I must thank you for your time and patience.'

'You're very welcome to any help we can give you, Mr Lilliput. Any help at all.'

'Will you hang him?' asked Dorothea.

Even her mother jumped. We'd forgotten her. I am willing to bet that this was the first occasion in Dorothea's life that anyone ever forgot she was in the same room.

'They told us at school that hanging's going to be whatsit, abolished. But they haven't yet, so will you still be able to hang him?'

There was now only one thing in the world that I wanted, and I wanted it desperately. It was for the police to get out of our house and leave me alone. I would still have Dorothea to contend with and that was awful enough, but the presence of Mr Lilliput with his X-ray vision and supernatural tricks was wearing away at me like pumice stone. I would rather have put that perishing string bag back on again and walk up Bluebell Crescent with it carving through my neck like cheese wire than carry on being subjected to that flat, colourless voice, which always meant something different from what it was saying. At this moment it was saying to Dorothea, 'That's not for

169

us to decide, miss. Parliament's on holiday at the moment. You ask them when they get back.' Lilliput smiled at Auntie Marjorie.

As he and WPC Swan finally got to their feet, I was appalled to hear my father and Uncle Norman pounding down the staircase to prolong the social leave-taking and delay the departure of the police from my life. Apparently they had all met earlier. Uncle Norman greeted DI Lilliput with a jovial remark about the Essex Regiment, some insider's pleasantry from the war. My father, who wasn't in the war on account of his manky arm, cut across this exclusive banter.

'I hope our Angharad's been useful to you, Detective Inspector. She's a bit of a dream-boat, but very bright. A certainty for the eleven-plus exam next year.'

This was a side-swipe at Uncle Norman, Dorothea having failed hers. WPC Swan flashed us one of her smiles. 'So what are you going to be when you grow up, Annie?'

'An air hostess,' replied my mother when I didn't. 'That's this week. Usually, it's a pop singer.'

'Nonsense!' replied my father. 'She's going to be a doctor, aren't you, Angharad?'

'I'm going to be a doctor,' I parroted. They were inching towards the door. My misery was palpable now; I could hear it, I could smell it – the colour and taste of vinegar.

'Very useful that will be, Dai,' chipped in Uncle Norman. 'She can do something for that disability of yours.'

'No need for it, thank you, Norman. I've never asked for anyone else's help yet.'

'But she's your daughter, Dai. I mean, you don't pay a dog and bark yourself, do you?'

There was the briefest hesitation in everybody's step, but as this statement was inarguable, nobody

170

tried. At last the company moved across the threshold and into the hall, and I managed to get myself out of the room, and escaped into the back garden without actually running.

18

As the cheery goodbyes withdrew to the garden gate, and the police wandered off in the direction of Chipping Ongar, I legged it round to Babette's. I'd forgotten it was dinnertime; Auntie Rene was spooning baby food into Amanda, and Craig was spooning egg yolk into a Tonka toy, but Babette wasn't there. Apparently, with the onset of Dorothea, she'd gone round to Melena Watson's. To walk there I had to cross the entrance to Bluebell Crescent. I was the sort of child who pestered her parents to take her on the ghost train at the fairground and then had nightmares for a week. The same perverse impulse now drew my footsteps, in spite of me, towards number sixteen.

The Clitheroes' bathroom window was boarded up. This shocked me somehow, perhaps by giving solid validity to events I was still hoping against hope to wake up from. Their dustbin stood where it had always stood, in the front yard. One irritable Saturday afternoon, Mr Clitheroe had erected a semicircle of arch-shaped fence panels around it, to conceal from the world the distasteful sight of a domestic dustbin. Now, on the low wall in front of one of these arches, stood a jar of dahlias.

Only Mrs Maxwell's husband Percy grew dahlias. He won prizes. Babette and I knew him slightly, which was probably the only way you could know him unless you were a tuber. He did shift work at the post office when they weren't on strike, an occupation allowing a gardener an excellent quotient of daylight hours, particularly if he didn't waste them on any crackpot activity like getting some sleep. Uncle Frank said that Percy Maxwell 'wasn't all there', but Babette and I always got a welcoming smile above his Dutch hoe and Danish Blue teeth as we sailed past on roller-skates or loitered outside number sixteen, hoping Mrs Clitheroe would come out.

No matter how 'not all there' Mr Maxwell might be, the one thing he could keep track of was his own dahlias, so their presence here – plumb in the middle of an arch, for all the world like an allusion to flower arrangements in a church window – must be a tribute to his lost neighbour. He had brought Mrs Clitheroe flowers. Why hadn't I?

Another thing I didn't expect was a uniformed policeman. He appeared around the side of number sixteen, not our local PC, one of Mr Lilliput's lot perhaps. In fleeing from him, I careened into Mrs Maxwell, who was coming up the road with a light shopping bag.

'Oh,' she said, as my head disappeared into her bosom. 'You looked like you was running away from that policeman. You frightening our kids?' She shot the words across at him, prising me out of her cleavage. 'Shame on you!'

Whenever Gina Maxwell laughed, her blond hair, back-combed into a high bouffant, wagged stiffly above her blackened eyebrows. I hadn't seen her since she was propped up against Mrs Clitheroe's French window, snooping. Now Babette's words about Mr Clitheroe slammed into my memory. I had just told her about Mrs Maxwell overhearing the tête-à-tête between Mrs Clitheroe and Uncle Horace. 'She'll tell him. And when he finds out he'll kill her.'

Mrs Maxwell was holding my head at arm's length to stop it burrowing into her breasts again. I heard my own voice. Like my footsteps, it seemed to have developed a will of its own.

'Mrs Maxwell. May I ask you something?'

'It's Agatha, isn't it?'

'Angharad, Mrs Maxwell.'

'Is it about the Avon, Agatha?'

'No, it's about the murders.' My voice caught in the middle of the word. What a soft word. Mur-ders. It had a mellow, blue sound like sad jazz. Mrs Maxwell didn't seem to think so. She recoiled.

'No, lovey. I got a rollicking off of Frank Lucas yesterday for talking to kids. Anyone would think they'd been interfered with, the way he carried on!'

She turned away from me, and tip-tapped across the road, her tiny, high-arched feet squashed into a pair of mules. Her garden was a riot of dahlias, flamboyant heads and fleshy stems. Mrs Maxwell's own head and fleshy stem bounced up the crazy-paving path, and the flowers trembled gently in her wake. Percy must be at one of those strike meetings the grown-ups talked about. It seemed pointless to me being on strike in the first place if you still had to go in.

Mrs Maxwell had already forgotten me, I could tell by the perplexed look when I called out her name again. 'Mrs Maxwell! Please!'

She sighed. 'I suppose you better come in then.' Her left hand already had a cigarette burning in it as her right was turning the key.

* * *

174

Off the sunless kitchen was a room with one wall entirely covered by an enormous matt photograph of the seaside – ice-cream van, a pier, donkeys.

'Like it, dear?' Mrs Maxwell asked me.

'It's smashing!'

'Thought you'd like it.' She left me there while she put the kettle on and slung her shopping around the kitchen.

The bungalow was kippered with the smoke of long-dead cigarettes. Its furniture wore a soft aura of mohair at cat level, even though the cats (Mr Maxwell's) were even longer dead. Our roads had been unkind to Percy. There was a story that when the latest went under the wheels of a Sunbeam Rapier, his wife wouldn't let him keep the dead animal in the house overnight, so the cat got a decent burial in the pitch dark. With macabre inevitability, Mr Maxwell dug up the neutered tom that had been run over the previous September. Conscientious gardener that he was, he gave his pet a good stir, and mulched him back in with a fork.

Mrs Maxwell's mules came slip-slopping back from the kitchen. 'I'm a bit busy, Agatha, so what did you want to ask me about?'

'It's Angharad, Mrs Maxwell.'

'What is, dear?' She had brought with her a steaming cup of Nescafé and a bulging handbag. She was fishing in it. Rummaging. The coffee slopped in.

'Mrs Maxwell, I used to visit Mrs Clitheroe a lot. With my best friend Babette Lucas.'

'Oh yes. Frank's little girl.'

'The thing is.' But I stopped. The thing was what? *Please tell me whether your description of the intruder could have sounded to Mr Lilliput like me dressed up in a sheet?*

'I really hope the person who killed her gets sent to prison. Only nobody will tell me who it was, but they say you might've seen him.'

'It was that old gyppo, lovey. The rag and bone man. Saw him climbing in Jenny's bathroom window yesterday dinnertime.'

'What did you tell the police he was wearing, Mrs Maxwell?'

'Eh? You can't trust 'em, dear. They're not like us. Ask anyone.'

'Yes, but what did you tell the police he was wearing, Mrs Maxwell?'

She wasn't listening. She was tipping her engorged bag upside down and shaking it over the sideboard.

'Please, Mrs Maxwell?'

Out tumbled litter like a landfill site, and from deep in the lining came a sticky detritus fleeced over with fluff and now wetted into a slurry by the coffee-wash. It was – I decided from an overheated brain desperate for a song – a slurry with a fringe on top.

'Only, you see,' I persevered, 'I was talking to Mr Lilliput. Would you tell me what you told him about the intruder?'

'Frightened you, have they, dear, all these killings? Getting like America, isn't it? New York. Just think how *I* feel! My Percy's forbidden me to go further than the Handy Stores without a male escort.'

She preened herself, her bust puffing up like a parrot, though from what we all knew of her Percy, he was about as forbidding as a wet jelly.

'But, Mrs Maxwell, what I'd really like is you to tell me what Mr Lilliput knows.'

'I'm not in cahoots with the police, lovey. I've only talked to the bloke once.'

'Yes, but can you tell me the words you said, about what you saw?'

'How d'you mean?'

'Well, *I* saw Old Ollie in Bluebell Crescent yesterday too, so you and I could check with one another, so please can you tell me what you told Mr Lilliput you thought he was wearing when you thought you saw him going in the bathroom window?' Fissures were appearing in my syntax, I could tell. '*Please*, Mrs Maxwell. *Please*.'

A man's voice answered me. 'If you're talking about that thieving didicoi,' it said, 'then according to Gina he was wearing a long white shirt, like a smock. Like the yokel he is.'

It was Leonard Clitheroe. The cup in Mrs Maxwell's hand shook. Coffee splashed her cigarette, which crackled like a bush fire.

'You frightened the bloody life out of me, Len! What you doing, creeping about? And knowing my nerves are all to pieces on account of the flippin' gyppos!'

'I've brought these back,' he replied without apology. 'Tell Percy thank you from me, will you? The police have finished with my safety razor. Christ knows what the idiots wanted it for. Any road, they've given it me back.' He was holding a shaving brush and an open razor folded back into its bone handle.

'Well then, give 'em here.' She peered myopically at the objects in his hand. 'What's that other thing?'

'Shaving brush. Time you got glasses, Gina.'

As she took them from his hands, Mr Clitheroe's eyes never left me.

'Len, this is Agatha. She's all hot and bothered.'

'So I see.'

He was a narrow man, and oddly stiff at the joints. The black button eyes were watching me. When I'd told my mother about Lorraine's broken heart, she'd said that when someone is grieving, you must be nice to them. Yet there was nothing about Mr Clitheroe's demeanour to invite sympathy, or suggest he was a man grieving for a beloved spouse. He looked exactly the same as he did when hollering at her from the pavement, or indoors casting his shadow across a pile of records that were actually mine, not his wife's:

'Thrown more money away on pop, have you? Time you learned the value of a penny, Jenny,' a remark that had somehow never prompted either me or Babette to point out that he was a poet and didn't know it.

'You back home, then?' Mrs Maxwell was asking him.

'Christ, no! It's still lousy with the rozzers. I'm in a stuffy B&B in Ongar. The landlady even rations the bloody bath water.' And then, to me: 'So, you were outside my place yesterday.'

'I was only talking about it, Mr Clitheroe, because of being sorry about *Mrs* Clitheroe.'

'Funny, isn't it, Len? Fancy her taking it up like this.'

'Fancy. Who were you with? Old Ollie?'

'No!'

'So where d'you see him?'

'I didn't.'

'What do you mean, "didn't"? I just heard you tell Gina.'

'It was only at breakfast time.'

'What was?'

'Now then, Len. Don't you go upsetting yourself, it can't be good for you.'

To give emphasis to this advice, she pointed at him with the razor, dong, dong, dong. On the second nod it flew open – a three-inch blade that would have been familiar to Sweeney Todd, glinting like an overripe fish in the gloomy interior of the smelly room.

'Put that down, Gina, before you decapitate someone.' He turned back to me. '*What* was only at breakfast time?'

'I was. But only on the outside, and anyway, we went away again.'

'Who's we?'

'Only Babette Lucas and me.'

'Lucas. She's that other girlie who's always coming

round for Jenny's photos. Has DI Lilliput interviewed you?'

'Yes, Mr Clitheroe.'

'Mention Jenny's photos, did he?'

'Photos, Mr Clitheroe?'

'Speak English, don't you? Not deaf, are you? You and that other lass have always got your noses in 'em.'

'What you talking about, Len?'

'Picture album of Jenny's. It's been stolen.'

'I can't see what Ollie would want with anything like that,' Mrs Maxwell reasoned. 'Couldn't sell it, could he?'

'Police have got evidence of two break-ins, and Lilliput's found photos floating about that he says don't fit with the gyppos.'

Gina Maxwell was still waving the open razor around. 'Well,' she concluded, 'if you're staying, Len, which it looks like, you won't mind me getting on. I've got to sort out my Flesh Tones from my Juicy Peaches, and Percy'll be home from his meeting any flippin' minute.'

With this, she slip-slapped out through the hall door. If her remark was meant to be pointed, it was wasted on Mr Clitheroe, who showed no signs of budging.

'You and that Lucas lass came round at breakfast time?'

'Yes, Mr Clitheroe.'

'But I heard you tell Gina you saw the rag and bone man.'

'Well, I *think* it was him.'

'He had a horse and cart with him, girlie, so I reckon you'd have noticed.'

I was silent.

'Don't mess me about, lassie, I'm not a patient man! Someone was in my lounge yesterday, frigging around with that photo album, and I want a word with them!

179

I want to know if they saw something they weren't meant to, and I want to know what they've told the police. Now, was it you, or wasn't it?'

We heard the back door open, and a call that might have been 'Gina, I'm home' with the vowels left out. Good old Mr Maxwell! Thank you, postal strike! Bless you, every judge who ever awarded Percy Maxwell first prize at a flower show to send him hurrying back to his little garden in Bluebell Crescent. Mr Clitheroe didn't seem to share my enthusiasm.

'Bloody Nora!' he shouted, and slammed his fist against the wall, seriously denting the straw hat of a trotting donkey. Out. I must get . . . Scooting past Mr Clitheroe, I had a full frontal view of Mrs Maxwell's sideboard. The handbag slime had dribbled right down the doors now. If my mother caught sight of my surroundings over this last half hour, she'd slosh me down with Dettol.

I couldn't run, but hobbled until I was clear of Bluebell Crescent, then limped slowly up Rainbird Lane towards Melena Watson and, please God, Babette. I found Mrs Watson in the plate-glass brightness of her kitchen, beside the bubbling cauldron of a twin-tub washing machine.

'Hello, Annie. You looking for Melena? You just missed her. She got the bus into Wittle Massey with Babette.'

Again?! Mrs Watson prodded her tongs into the fizzing water, from which shirts were apparently trying to escape in great bubbles of material.

'Thank you anyway, Mrs Watson.' As I said goodbye, she was striking at a particularly energetic garment that was twisting itself around the tongs.

The trivialities of other people's lives. I found Mrs Watson's preoccupations nearly intolerable. Even worse was the distant lilt of other children's uncaring voices, and passers-by in the Breeden Road, who walked along whistling as though it were an ordinary day. I was aware of a sickening envy that encompassed absolutely everybody in the wide world who wasn't worried half to death.

It was in this merry mood, in which it's unlikely that Uncle Horace's Jesus would have wanted me for a sunbeam, that I emerged from Rainbird Lane and ran slap bang into Dorothea. Conscientious Girl Guide that she was, she had tracked me. I suddenly knew that if she showed me a compass or map, I'd shove them up her nose. She didn't. Instead she fell into step beside me, wordless for once, and as soon as we were out of sight of the pub, she took out her packet of Embassy Number Six and lit a cigarette. There was always a tacit agreement that when Dorothea was smoking, we would loiter somewhere safely away from prying eyes, on the grounds that if she were caught, my parents would lecture her comatose, and jovial Uncle Norman would flay the hide off her. So I didn't argue when she slipped across the ditch and into the wood.

We sat on the peaty floor for a while, in the deep shade of summer leaves, and I peeled acorns to pieces and watched Dorothea, plump and dignified as a Chinese Buddha, smoking her cigarette. It always struck me that she was better at this than most grownups; she never got the paper stuck to her lower lip like Uncle Frank, or accidentally knocked a shower of sparks from the end that melted her nylons like Auntie Rene, or waved it about like Mrs Maxwell, setting her hair on fire. Dorothea sat cross-legged, supple as a bendy doll, and breathed out pretty little grey rings that wobbled upwards, and expanded, then vanished into the canopy. As soon as this exercise came to an end, she ground the butt carefully into the soil, and turned to me.

'You were scared shitless by that slaphead police-man,' she announced.

'No I wasn't, Dorothea,' I replied eventually. 'It's only because of missing Mrs Clitheroe, now she's dead.'

'Shitless,' she repeated. 'You know something about those murders you're not telling the police. You're hiding vital clues.'

I was up and flouncing out of the woods but she grabbed my arm and held it.

'Don't be a twerp, Aggie! I'm not going to snitch on you to that twat detective and his moon-faced girlfriend.'

'She's not his girlfriend!' I objected.

'Not much, she isn't,' responded my cousin. 'She had one eye up his trouser leg all the time they were in your front room. Sit down!' she demanded. 'Anyway, if you go back home now, you've got to tell Auntie Myrtle why you went all funny when Lilliput was talking about that bathroom window. *Now* what are you doing?'

I was checking my knickers, astounded that I'd actually forgotten to until now. Two photographs. Two. First thing this morning there had been four and a soggy green paper; had I walked about Muningstock shedding them from under my petticoat to be picked up by the police? And by Mr Clitheroe in Mrs Maxwell's bungalow?

'Pull that skirt down, girl!' But when she saw what it was I'd retrieved, she shut up, and we stood together in silence. Of course, Dorothea had had a good look at the photograph DI Lilliput was displaying in our front room like prize jam at a fête, talking about fingerprints and something missing from the scene of the crime, Mrs Cradock. (Fingerprints! Would he come back for mine, or had he already collected them by stealth?) The two photos we were scrutinizing now were siblings to his picnic picture.

'Well, fuck a duck!' said Dorothea admiringly and unwrapped herself a Mars bar.

My story was surprisingly easy to tell. I stumbled over the somewhat misguided rationale for Lorraine stealing the album in the first place, but Dorothea didn't have a problem with that. What she couldn't get her mind around was why I felt guilty about Old Ollie. It wasn't my fault, she said, if this Mrs Maxwell couldn't spot the difference between me and some old gyppo. No, I should just sit tight.

'But Mr Lilliput knows anyway, Dorothea. He knows I was in Mrs Clitheroe's on Monday, which is when the gold ring got dropped, *and* he knows about yesterday. If I admit it was dinnertime and give the album back, at least it'll make him stop blaming Ollie.'

'Why would he believe this Mrs Maxwell anyway? She sounds a scatty old mare.'

'She's not old. But she swears it was Ollie. She'll swear it in front of God or a jury, whichever comes the sooner.'

'You've got to look after number one, Aggie. Look, if Lilliput comes back to get you for it, don't say anything about that gyppo's ring. You don't want him running you in for *two* murders. As for the photo album, tell him a tale. Tell him you broke into the bungalow in the morning. You gave Babette the slip while she thought you were getting changed into your trews. Then, when you busted the window, you got scared and just ran off without putting the album back. Tell him you only walked up Bluebell Crescent at dinnertime to see if anyone had boarded it up yet.'

'Daddy'll kill me.'

'True. But at least Lilliput can't say you killed Mrs Clitheroe, because Mrs Clitheroe was murdered at dinnertime!'

The thought dawned on both of us that we were

batting this incriminating evidence about *alto voce* in an open wood, fifty yards from a council estate, and a pub with a garden overflowing with midday drinkers.

'Any road,' she continued, in more discreet tones, 'don't breathe a word to anybody else, you get me? Mum's the word.' And a thoroughly unnerving one, considering how mine would react when all this came out.

I reminded Dorothea that I would have to tell the truth to Babette. She already knew that the album had vanished from its hiding place behind her gatepost, so I'd have to explain why.

'You're mad!'

'I've got to, Dorothea.'

'You're mad. She'll tell.'

I flared up at this; Babette was my best friend, and we'd *never* snitch on each other. As Dorothea watched me ranting, a thoughtful look came into her eyes.

'If you tell her,' pointed out my cousin, 'you'll make her something called an "accessory", even though she didn't do anything. It would be like an accomplice.'

I considered this.

'And then Frank Lucas'll *really* kill you.'

We were quiet a moment, imagining Uncle Frank when the police came round with tales of Angharad Cradock making his daughter into something called an accessory.

'Now then,' concluded Dorothea, taking another Embassy Number Six from the dwindling packet. 'Why don't you try one of these? It'll help calm you down.'

THE PRESENT

19

My LAMDA graduate plants his feet solidly on the pine floor, shoulders back, and lets his rich baritone soar across my studio. He's a large lad, somehow made to look even larger by the skinhead cut he's wearing for a TV shoot tomorrow, in which he plays a football hooligan.

'Keep perfectly still,' I call across from the piano. 'And don't look severe, just serious. Focus somewhere over the heads of the casting team.'

We finish on a nicely sustained A natural, and then I do let him smile. We're working on a number to get him noticed among hundreds at an open audition; the song is 'I Enjoy Being a Girl'.

'Excellent!' I say. 'But remember you'll probably only be allowed sixteen bars, so don't hold anything back. Do you want to try the alternative one more time and choose?'

So we launch into 'I Feel Pretty'.

(1965. The garden of the Rainbird with Uncle Frank. Me tired, and losing the knack to distinguish between what was inside my head and what leaked out; unconsciously singing 'I Feel Pretty.' 'Oy!' demanded the leader of a group of rockers, slicking back his DA haircut, mirror in hand. 'She taking the piss?')

Teaching demands every ounce of your concentration and strength. So, just how are you expected to manage when every brain cell is screaming to be free to grapple with its dilemmas, its decisions, the crisis of its life? The decision 'Should I Stay or Should I Go?' But even if I do stay – can Daniel and I make a life together? This isn't *West Side Story*, I tell myself melodramatically, half my mind on my student; there's no 'somewhere' for us.

Half the night I'd lain awake. When I couldn't bear it any more, I'd slipped out of bed and told a half-awake Alan, murmuring next to his white-noise generator, that I couldn't sleep and would go for a drive. Into town along the Westway, I wanted the soothing cradle-sway of the rocking car. But after a few miles, the continual stop-start was an irritation, pointless robotic red lights holding power at empty junctions. I'd pulled up opposite Regent's Park, fled from the car and tramped along Portland Place under the ochrous, sodium-lit clouds of a hurrying sky.

I had it all to myself, just me and the robots, the lights silently blinking through their mindless sequence, controlling nothing. A sleety afternoon had given way to restless drizzle that was now a sort of damp fug, full of the smell of wet concrete and the city's jaundiced lights, sour yellows and greens like a fading bruise.

A dosser underneath a Georgian door-casing turned uncomfortably in his sleep. I would rather be him, I thought childishly. I could cope with *anybody's* life better than I'm coping with my own. I have absolutely no idea of what I'm going to do.

* * *

'New York, Annie? Now?'

'Alan's been offered a job.'

Silence.

'Darling, I'm married,' I remind him, meaning *you're* married. Meaning, even if I stay, what is there for us? Pain in Daniel's eyes; my own filling. You don't need the subtleties of great literature to sum this one up, all my life I've been listening to songs about it.

A passing car fizzed through a puddle and soaked my jeans.

At the end of the day, I try to walk myself into exhaustion, as I did in New York. Autumn had come late; the end of October and Central Park still rustled, the air full of leaves, the trees back-lit by a low, skirting sun which glowed through the maples and rimed the fancy ironwork with light, making silhouettes of the carriage lamps. I strode up and down the Mall, beneath the ribbed vaulting and delicate tracery of its overarching elm trees, and watched the Chinese wedding groups dotted right across the park. All around Bethesda fountain young women shivered in their dresses of soap-powder white like wounded water birds. And I thought the thoughts of everyone whose own marriage is on the rocks – please make a better job of it than I have.

I'd managed to mess up two. I thought of my wedding with Daniel – just Mum and a handful of friends, Babette looking spectacular in Indian cotton. Daniel read out the lyrics of 'The Prettiest Star', which David Bowie wrote for Angie, and I read 'Here, There and Everywhere', which Paul McCartney wrote for Jane Asher, never mind that the second relationship had blown spectacularly apart long ago and the first was floundering. Then, when I married Alan, he'd insisted on something more socially acceptable, and spent weeks fussing over details like a bride, though he failed to spot an error in the Order of Service where 'Angharad' had been written as 'And Gareth'. Alan And Gareth. I was sprawled helpless across the sofa shrieking, but Alan wasn't; he was on the phone with ice in his voice.

'Daniel, darling, I'm married.'

We're in that same apartment in Butler's Wharf. Spring now. Immigration visa arranged, everything organized. And nothing decided. As Daniel twists towards me, his bulky figure winds the designer sheets off my body like someone with a handle reeling them in.

'I'll find some way for us to be together, Annie. Trust me.'

Trust him. October 1976. The Yorkshire Moors. I have a gig in Ilkley, and we've driven here in my Citroën 2CV, my set of wheels essential for transporting the Fender Rhodes keyboard and making it to venues. Today I am also transporting a bigger instrument.

'Just *feel* that sense of space!' Daniel sweeps an arm at the tufty landscape under a very low sky that is getting ready to drench us. My St Mary's Hospital Medical School scarf is adrift around his neck, the trailing edge badly frayed – during one of Daniel's earlier orations, a sheep stood placidly behind him, nibbling the end.

'Tomorrow I'll make something of this landscape. Clay. Find a way to get the observer to interact, feel its energy beneath his fingernails!'

Tomorrow he's actually chiselling angels in Kensal Green cemetery to pay the rent, but never mind.

'Do you want to throw those wellies in the car boot?' I suggest, handing him the keys. I've no idea where Daniel got his hands on a pair of green Wellingtons, but all day he's been glancing downwards to admire them between bouts of declaiming about the moors, while I've tottered after him, my own feet staggering into hoof holes, high-heel traps lurking camouflaged behind clods of earth.

I still have one eye on that sky with its coddled grey. I don't want to get caught in a downpour on the moors even *inside* the car, the car being how it is. Now Daniel leans against the bonnet tugging his Wellington boots and socks off, the Citroën rocking like a rodeo. Joyfully wriggling his toes in a muddy tuft.

He opens the boot. Throws in the wellies. Throws the keys after them. Slams the boot. With the keys inside.

I look at him.

'Don't panic,' proclaims Daniel as inevitably it starts bucketing down. 'I'll get a brilliant idea any minute. Trust me.'

It is easy to make an affectionate farce of him in my memory: indulgently recalling his off-the-wall gregariousness; strangers he brought home for dinner that he'd met on the bus; parties where Daniel barged passionately into other people's discussions. 'But you *can't* think that!' he'd belabour them, his face puckered with sincerity. 'It's not a human *option* to think that!'

Daniel had no concept of privacy in a public setting. We'd be eating in a cosy trattoria and he would leave me in mid-sentence to join the conversation at a neighbouring table. No-one seemed to mind much. I sometimes did. For my twenty-third birthday he'd promised to teach me to skate at Streatham ice rink. When I'd clumped out from the changing room, dutifully booted and psyched up, I'd found him zipping round the rink conducting a party of teenagers who skittered at his heels, a terrifying human wall, fizzing adolescent testosterone on ice skates. Daniel was

189

sweeping along in an exaggerated Groucho Marx lope shouting 'Bend those knees, boys! Knees, knees, knees!'

'He doesn't half move, for a fat bloke,' I heard one of them pant as I shivered at the barrier, knowing it was where I'd spend the rest of the evening.

All too easy to remember our life together as a collection of these cameo eccentricities, and forget what he was like when we began to fall apart.

That dreadful summer of 1981 – unrelenting heat and something else in the air, pernicious. Riots in Toxteth, riots in Brixton. Daniel became jealous of the bass guitarist in my band, only I failed to recognize it. I would never have recognized it, because it was insane; I wouldn't have fancied the bass guitarist if he'd been the last man left on the planet and someone had spiked my drink with Spanish fly. Daniel started playing up to our new flatmate, a pretty German student called Ingrid. I didn't understand the game. Jealous myself, I decided to teach him a lesson; I went joylessly to bed with the bass guitarist.

Daniel was stunned, harrowed by sexual jealousy. I watched my panicky reassurances hang heavily from him like an ill-fitting garment tolerated out of love for the giver. In the wake of catastrophe, I discovered I was pregnant. I knew perfectly well this was Daniel's baby, but he was never entirely convinced. At three and a half months, I miscarried.

Despite my time at medical school, I was profoundly ignorant of what a fourteen-week miscarriage involves, so that horror was added to the dismay and pain. Traumatized and anaemic, I was a long time recovering, and no matter how hard Daniel tried to support me, there was no getting away from the fact that his paramount emotion was relief. The wedge was in; our marriage was splitting in two.

His style of speech changed when we were together, and became coated with a tragic Jewish sarcasm and family allusions that meant nothing to me. Any impetuous action of mine, and he'd claim to be reminded of someone called 'Maurice the meshuggeneh' or some disreputable cousin I'd never heard of who was thrown out of rabbinical school. Daniel suddenly had access to an entire private language most of which sounded like 'schlemozzle'. He was distancing me, the 'shiksa' from an English village where the nearest we'd ever come to Yiddish was the Andrews Sisters' version of *Bei Mir Bis Du Schein*', which everyone thought was 'My dear Mister Shane'. I was never certain whether Daniel knew why he was doing this to me.

'*Oi gevalt*, Annie!' he'd shouted in some pointless, late-night row, home from a pub or a party, both of us miserably drunk. 'It's like watching a mad tailor in a silk shop!'

'*A mad tailor in a silk shop?!*' I'd screamed back, out of my mind. 'You never used to talk like this. I need a translator. I'm a tourist in my own marriage!'

Worn down and desperate for a break, I fled. I went away on tour with my RADA friends. And when that was over, I didn't have the courage to go home.

And what of Alan? I was at an even lower ebb when we met; it was the morning my mother died. Alan did a clinic once a week at the Royal Marsden Hospital – after his UK company paid for him to requalify over here, they expected him to keep his hand in. For some reason, he was on the ward that day.

I'd sat most of the night at Mum's bedside with my father and Auntie Marjorie, amid the drip sets and other paraphernalia of terminal illness, listening to the terrible gentleness of her breathing punctuated by the nurses' crepe soles squeaking on the rubberized floor.

When it was over, Dad went home with Norman and Marjorie, but I stayed because I couldn't think what else to do, and couldn't remember where I'd parked. The dementia of exhaustion. Alan was just a white coat with an American voice who offered me a mug of coffee.

'You're a musician, right?' he suggested as we sat side by side on a broken sofa in the staff room. His hands were professionally manicured, I noticed, as they held the coffee mug. I put my own cup down and hid my fingers, the nails of which were bitten to the quick.

'Your mother said you write musical scores for movies. Sounds pretty good to me.'

'Well, no. I recently recorded something in a promotional video for a banking corporation, but that's a one-off. Principally I teach. My mother does know that. Did, I mean. She did know.' My voice caught, and he took over.

'I guess it's like my Aunt Margo, back in New York. I work in the pharmaceutical industry, but she insists I'm a brain surgeon.'

I managed a smile.

He talked on, and I half-listened, aware that his very self-assurance soothed. After all these weeks of trying to be in two places at once, and watching my mother's vibrant personality being crushed by the juggernauts of cancer and chemotherapy, it was a relief to delegate the responsibility for thinking to someone else.

When eventually I peeled myself away, he warned me that for a while I would miss the routine of visiting, and I should steel myself against an irrational nostalgia for the hospital itself, the rituals of parking, walking down the hall, greeting the nurses. I didn't tell him about me and hospitals. But when he phoned a few days later, I felt a profound comfort in the vigour and certainty I heard in his voice.

* * *

Well, since then I've also lost my father to cancer, and if I walk out on my second marriage, I will be very much alone, Daniel or no Daniel. Nevertheless, there was a long entr'acte between marriages when I survived well enough without another human being to lean on. I certainly can't say the same for Alan, who to my knowledge has never spent more than a short while without a partner in all his adult years. He acknowledges his dependence on others to provide him with a social life. A man who does not easily make his own friends, a misanthrope at heart, who has been known to lecture strangers about using cellular phones while his own is actually ringing, and who sometimes rewrites the 'Do Not Disturb' sign in hotels as 'Shut the Fuck Up', Alan has always invested in relationships that can provide what he lacks. He uses elaborate metaphors about plant-life and root systems to tell me how it is I who provides a life for him, through connections of my own.

Does Alan know about my affair? If I were him, I would. The first night, I'd come home from Butler's Wharf, Alan walked into the bathroom while I was showering, and instinctively, unmistakably, as *in flagrante delicto*, I covered myself up.

Walking, walking. Arguing with my head. The very thought of moving to the States exhausts me: the lawyers, the shipping agents, the embassy, the paperwork, the hours on hold on a phone, the hammering, sandbagging, weatherbeating, *scourge* of trying to organize a move from one country, to take up domicile in another. And so Alan and I talk selectively about the future in carefully mounted vignettes of concerts and restaurants and weekend trips – a tourist's schedule, as though we were planning a holiday.

New York. Aunt Margo's apartment again. I am on

my way back in from the kitchen, and she is address-ing Alan in the piercing whisper of the partially deaf.

'Just as soon as you have the date for coming home, you let me know; I'll move those packing crates out of your room, and get the decorators in, and a good king-size bed.'

'Well, that's real kind of you, Aunt Margo. We appreciate it. But we will have our own place, though, and I intend that it's ready pretty much as soon as we arrive.'

'Your own place! You have no idea of the price of property in this city! It's crazy money! And you don't even have real estate to sell.'

Alan tries to explain that he has a hefty piece of real estate somewhere called Ealing, the mortgage on which would keep her in Draylon for the rest of her life, but she is too busy painting word-pictures of Alan's imagined room, revamped red and lush like the auditorium of the Met or the Albert Hall.

'But probably we won't get a place in the city. Annie and I have agreed on Westchester,' he explains. 'We both like it quiet.'

'Annie?'

'Westchester.'

'But she won't want to live here – she's English, leave her there!'

Stamping along to Langham Place I find myself in front of Broadcasting House. Daniel again:

'You've *really* never heard the story?' He had been propped up in bed, his substantial back mangling a bank of satin pillows. 'Bloody marvellous, this! You know it was Eric Gill that the BBC commissioned as architect? Well, all the time he was working, the façade was kept sheeted up. Now, everyone knew he'd designed a statue of Prospero and Ariel for a niche at the top, but there was a rumour that Ariel was just a bit too naked for the heart of London.' Daniel peered over an imaginary pair of bifocals. ' "I mean to say, old chap, this isn't Florence or Rome, where you can't go a hundred yards without cracking your elbow on marble genitalia." So, being the BBC, they sent one of the directors up a ladder, still inside all the tarpaulins, with a tape measure in his hand. Then they held a board meeting and issued Gill with the directive to get up there and chisel precisely one inch off Ariel's penis!'

Convulsed, Daniel had come sliding down the bed from the slippy pillows like a polar bear down a chute, spilling our mugs of tea-bag tea across the high polish of the bedside table's walnut burr. Convulsed myself, I'd flopped on top of him. Tea had dribbled into his hair and mine.

Here in Langham Place in the small hours, the figure of a truncated Ariel glimmered dully amid the bleary haloes of the street lamps.

'Annie, please don't go and live in New York.'

Baby Please Don't Go. *Ne Me Quitte Pas.* If You Leave Me Now . . . round and round go my thoughts, revolving like vinyl, or the Windmills of Your Mind.

Night and Day.

THE PAST

20

There's a technique to sharing a bed with Dorothea. What you have to do is anchor some of the bedding down by hooking the toes of one foot around the sheet and wiggling the toes of the other around the blanket (it helps to have prehensile toes, though what you really need are suckers on your extremities, like a natterjack toad). Naturally, this doesn't combat Dorothea's snoring, not unless your toes are so thoroughly prehensile that you can wiggle them round her tonsils. At one o'clock in the morning, which appeared to be turning into a watershed for me, I was wide awake and bubbling with misery. Another hard day's night.

There was an image I couldn't get out of my head – Mrs Clitheroe's Staffordshire pottery spaniels, lying on her bloodstained carpet, decapitated, their necks severed, their poor little ears chipped. I thought of that room without her, ransacked by the police, her Bechstein upright piano unplayed, forlorn. I thought of the finicky hands of Mr Lilliput touching her Decca

196

stereo radiogram and LP records. Tears, hot and painful, seeped down my face onto the pillow I shared with Dorothea. As the distress took hold and accelerated, I felt my chest heave. If I made a noise, she would wake up and shout at me, and so, probably, would Mummy and Daddy.

I stumbled out of bed. Slippers, mine and my cousin's, toes pointing bedwards, having slid away from our upturned rosy feet while we knelt for bedtime prayers. '. . . And please help Mr Lilliput collect his evidence against the guilty. Don't open your eyes, Angharad, God's still watching.'

Feet into slippers. Must remember not to twist that right foot. TOO LATE. Twist, and shout. Being an invalid is like any other art, it takes some learning.

As I left the stairs and padded on slippered feet along the hall, the dam burst, and I blubbed loudly all the way to the kitchen. Stumbling through the door, I pulled the cord for the fluorescent striplight. It buzzed and flickered, but wouldn't light up properly, just a cold moon-glow seeping meanly from the buzzing tube. I pulled again. Off. And again. Still nothing but flicker and hum and dimness. Then I caught sight of the window.

The Venetian blinds were up and the dark garden glowered beyond them, my own reflection glimmering at me like a ghost. My breath caught in a violent hiccup and the tears dried in their ducts. It looked grainy and ambiguous, like a double exposure – was there something else superimposed? The very essence of fear stole through me, blinding all reason. It was the axe murderer coming for me, it was poor Mrs Clitheroe . . . I pulled frantically at the cord – on, off, on, off, on – *please* light up!

The dead of night, that's what people called it. I couldn't make out any human sounds outside or in; no snoring from upstairs, not a single speeding car on

Mountnessing Road, making for the open spaces and flattening cats.

'You'll Never Walk Alone,' I reminded myself through the panic. I tried to sing the song in my head, but after a couple of bars I lost Gerry and the Pacemakers to something far less sophisticated – the primeval rhythm of a heartbeat.

> The night closed in on little Ted,
> He wished he'd never left his bed.
> The ghostly path that wound ahead,
> The path which through the forest led,
> Would lead him somewhere worse instead –
> The graveyard with its buried dead.
> He heard them calling in his head,
> Its tenants wailing in his head,
> And closing in on little Ted.

A rhyme from a book Dorothea had found when we were little. She'd made me read it aloud although it terrified me, gave me nightmares.

'O God, our help in ages past' I sang under my breath, for protection. 'Our hope for years to come.' *The night closed in on little Ted, He wished he'd never left his bed.*

It wasn't working. Well, why should God pay attention to me? I pictured the grown-ups singing 'O God Our Help' round the war memorial with all the women of my mother's age quietly crying. They didn't belong to me, these petitions to the Almighty for safety; they were the prerogative of my elders with their Dunkirk and their doodle-bugs. Yet I desperately needed a hymn in my head if I was ever to move away from that petrifying window of blackness and its swimming images. Quite suddenly, the macabre heart-beat stopped. Something warm and rough was feeling its way through the cold chill in my brain, coming out of nowhere, as welcome as the snout of a friendly dog: *'I'm just a soul whose intentions are good / O Lord, please don't let me be misunderstood.'*

The voice of Eric Burdon from the Animals, one of my favourite groups. There was something weird about the arrival of this song, materializing fully formed inside my mind just when I needed it. Well, if God (our help in ages past) had started sending songs down, He knew what He was doing with this one. It was good; it was as good as I would get; it could have been my theme tune.

The fluorescent striplight died, extinguishing the eerie reflection in the window. I gave my nose a good blow on my nightie, and crept back up to bed, where I fell into a deep sleep, dreamless and untroubled.

Our garden shed smelled of grass cuttings and creosote, all of which were soon distributed freely about my clothing, including the scarf round my neck and the ribbons on my plaits. For choice, I've no doubt my mother would have subdued my hair by knitting it, but as next best thing she twined it daily into taut plaits, and snapped the ends into rubber bands that bit my fingers when I tried to pull them off. Babette, in candy stripes, formed a trim, cross-legged entity on a pile of torn tent (this had a chequered history via the local Cub pack), while Dorothea, by way of electing herself chairwoman, took the only actual chair, which was a deckchair.

A debate was raging.

'I'm *not* taking the photo album round mine,' Babette was reiterating stoutly to Dorothea. 'You don't know my mum. She'd find it.'

'I do know your mum.'

'Well then!'

I had been woken by my father, his face slowly impinging itself upon my consciousness. 'Come along

199

there, Annie-*fach*! Rise and shine, girl! You've overslept.'

Dorothea had been behind him, and behind Dorothea, Babette, who wasn't going to be bothered with preliminaries. 'That detective's on the prowl again,' was her opening remark the moment we heard my father's feet hit the staircase.

'Lilliput?'

'That's him. I was just wondering about that photo album.'

Auntie Rene had seen Lilliput out and about, therefore we could expect him round here again on a war footing. In fact, we had a plan for getting rid of the album, but this involved taking a bus into Brentwood after dinner, which left us with the logistical problem of finding a temporary hiding place for the rest of the morning that was accessible to us, but impenetrable to a determined policeman. Dorothea's suggestions were the most imaginative, and included sending Babette up a chimney with it, but in the end I pulled rank. My position in this inquiry was as Ollie's heir apparent; I was the one under threat of arrest, so surely I deserved the last word. Mrs Clitheroe's album was safer here than if we risked walking about with it.

While these negotiations were going on, Dorothea, who had never actually seen the legendary photograph album before, gave it her scrutiny. The pictures, the earliest of which were in sepia, weren't stuck in like albums I'd seen at my friends' houses, but were mounted by slipping the four corners into slits cut into the pages. The pages themselves were stiff, gilded at the edges and interleaved with protective paper called 'spider's web glassine', which was sheer magic. It was opalescent, it crackled, and the surface was crazed in a pattern that on closer inspection resolved into intricate webs, thinly scattered with spiders and an occasional fly.

Dorothea turned to an exterior shot bearing the legend 'Nell crowned Queen of the May, 1921'. And there was Nell, enthroned upstage centre on an improvised dais with a floral rug across it.

'She was Mrs Clitheroe's mum,' Babette informed us, who was better than I was at taking in what people said. Queen Nell smiled in the full bloom of youth, her cheeks dimpled in an expression familiar to Babette and me from Mrs Clitheroe. It seemed that her companions on the dais had a better grasp of the gravity of the situation, and gazed soberly towards the photographer in their daisy-chain tiaras and short, billowy white dresses, caught at the hips with a sash or a ruche.

Babette carefully turned the page with her handkerchief, the glassy glassine crackling like thin ice or an open fire. 'Mrs Clitheroe's mum's family was more posh than her dad's,' she continued, 'only they didn't mind her marrying him, 'cos there was seven daughters and there wasn't enough men to go round after they'd all got killed in the First World War. Nell was the oldest, and that's why she ended up with the album. Then she left it to Mrs Clitheroe.'

'Is Nell dead, then?' asked Dorothea.

'Long time ago.'

'I know lots of Nells and Nellies,' pondered Dorothea, 'and every one of them's dead.'

'Mrs Clitheroe's only living relative is her cousin,' I piped up. 'Mrs Hoffenstander in New York.'

'The next photo's Mrs Clitheroe's dad,' continued Babette. This was 'The Potter family at Dunton, Essex, 1924', a group picnicking in front of a bell tent, with low-strung barbed wire between them and the camera. A brightly smiling young man in shirt sleeves was identified as Mrs Clitheroe's father, Albert.

'Dunton was one of them "plotlands",' explained our resident modern historian. 'They was all over

201

Essex. People from places like Hackney what couldn't afford to buy their own place, paid a fiver for a piece of plotland and kept a tent on it. Or they come down weekends with bricks and cement and stuff, and built a proper home theirselves, bit by bit.'

New Yorkers too had their holiday homes, I explained. The city was so hot in summer that mothers and children fled to somewhere called Long Island, which was full of potato fields, leaving the men on their own in sweltering apartments with enormous fridges.

'My nanna had one at Canvey,' continued Babette as though I hadn't spoken.

'Is ·that where your Uncle Arthur's gone with Lorraine? Your nanna's plotland?'

'It's not there no more. After the war, someone said they was shanty towns and bulldozed the lot of 'em.'

Even Dorothea, whose natural tendencies were neofascist, railed at the injustice of this. 'But where'd all the poor people go then?' she demanded, incensed.

Babette gave one of her monster shrugs. 'Dunno,' she said, losing interest. 'Places like here, I suppose – Muningstock.'

'And this is supposed to be less of an eyesore?'

The plan that we had cooked up for the afternoon had the virtue, unique among all the plans we'd come up with, of simplicity. The Beatles' film *Help!* had recently been released, ready for the school holidays, and was showing in half the cinemas in the country, including the Breeden Empire and the Brentwood Odeon. We would tell our parents that we were catching the bus into Breeden, whereas we would actually catch the bus to Brentwood and would ditch the photograph album there. Brentwood was in exactly the opposite direction from Breeden, as previously confirmed by the Ordnance Survey map that Dorothea had picked up at some point in her career in para-military organizations. And so, for once, we had a calculated, predetermined *and* plausible alibi, yet it didn't even necessitate much of a lie, just a couple of misplaced consonants.

It was two o'clock when we left the house, with me carrying the photograph album disguised by wrapping it in my dressing gown of flower-sprigged Viyella. The bus arrived, and we settled ourselves on the top deck where Dorothea could smoke her cigarettes, and Babette and I could look out of the window and pretend we didn't know her.

As we pitched and rolled towards Brentwood, I felt my eyes closing. Two women behind me were talking about Mrs Clitheroe's murder. I knew I ought to listen, but my sleepy brain had problems following them.

'If the coppers've got the bloke that broke in, they won't be looking no further for the murderer. Stands to reason!'

Her companion made a snuffling noise like a pig. 'Well, if *I* was the police, I'd 'ave a good look closer to 'ome. You ever met that Leonard? Strewth!'

Next to me was some sort of pillow, Viyella – I could rest my lolling head on that. I was vaguely aware of Babette gently settling me across the seat and then slipping away to sit somewhere else. The voices behind me droned on, dipping like secrets.

'. . . because of my tubes.'

'Yeah, you said.'

'. . . legs in the air! And the doctor kept saying "relax"! If you could relax like that, you'd sit in the *pub* like that, wouldn't you?'

Nodding to the motion of the bus, I sank into spinning songs, down, down into seas of wine-dark music. And there was DI Lilliput. I could hear the swish of Percy Maxwell's cut-throat razor, which Lilliput was stropping. With horrible slowness he turned towards me. The bony face bore a lurid grin like a skeleton's. Then he slashed maniacally at the china-white throats of Mrs Clitheroe's Staffordshire pottery spaniels. Daleks crashed through the door squawking: 'Ex-ter-min-ate! Terminates here. Oy, are you listening?' The bus conductor was halfway up the stairs. 'I *said* everybody off!'

I stumbled to my feet, and wove drunkenly down the empty bus towards his unfriendly looking uniform and the metallic officialdom of that weighty ticket machine, clunking on his chest like a bandolier. The diesel engine throbbed, vibrating the seats. I looked helplessly beyond the windows. We were at Brentwood station. How? My tongue filled my mouth like a bath sponge, stupid with sleep.

'Oy! Wassat?' demanded the conductor. He stormed past me, and grabbed the bundle I'd been resting my head on. The photograph album. As he thrust it into my arms, I remembered not only who I was, but who I was with. Or should have been.

'Um, excuse me. There were two friends with me. A short, pretty one with auburn hair, and a sort of larger one.'

'Oh, with you, were they? If I'd known, I'd've chucked *you* off an' all.'

'*You threw them off the bus?!*'

Babette and I frequently watched conductors evicting children and teenagers on the Brentwood–Muningstock route; it was nothing unusual for the journey to grind to a standstill while the entire bus rang with protestations of innocence and threats of reprisal.

'I've nothing against kids smoking under age,' the conductor was declaiming, eyeing the stitches on my neck, 'but bumming cigarettes off of my passengers with menaces, that's another kettle of fish, and I'm not having it, not on my bus!'

Same old story, then. 'Where did you throw them off?' I asked nervously.

'Bentley,' he snapped back.

About four miles from here and another four from home. Babette stranded. Uncle Frank would, there could be no argument about it, slaughter me. I wobbled down the spiral stairs, clutching the parcel to my chest, with the conductor muttering at my back.

Station Road to the High Street was hill all the way. The slog seemed steeper today, on my own, but somewhere in the distance was the Odeon and the comfort of the Fab Four. Even in August the streets teemed on Fridays, because on Thursday afternoons Brentwood shut down like the Black Death. And speaking of the Black Death, there was Mrs Maxwell tittupping out of the tobacconist's, her plump calves with their wormy blue veins braced above the unfashionable stilettos, her face wearing a sneering smile as though she knew something to the detriment of everybody around her. Had she seen me? It would blow holes in the Breeden Empire alibi if she had.

There was a funeral parlour on my left, with its panels of glutinous black and bowls of pompous lilies. Dorothea once told me that in bad winters when all the old folks die off, the funeral parlours have to stack the bodies two or three to a shelf, so they get muddled up and you can never be sure whether it's your own granny you're burying or somebody else's. Mrs Clitheroe wasn't in here, though, stacked – I knew from Daddy that she was at one of the police places. Dorothea told me that sometimes people aren't really dead at all, it's a mistake and they wake up nailed inside a coffin buried six feet underground.

So, could they be sure Mrs Clitheroe was dead?

A thrill that was half hope, half terror, rang through my frame. I felt the weight of her photograph album in my arms. Skull to a pulp with a meat-axe. It wouldn't be nice to still be alive like that, would it? Pool of blood and brains. I plodded on.

When I passed the recessed doorway of the *Brentwood Review* and Mrs Clitheroe smiled out at me from a poster in the glass, I didn't know whether this was real or just the inside of my thoughts leaking out of my head again. 'Muningstock Mourns', it said. I knew the picture – the original was here under my arm. They'd chopped Leonard out of the photo, though. Muningstock Mourns. So it mattered to people here in town, too. This was astounding, like crystals in a kaleidoscope reshuffling to a different pattern. So I should be gratified. I wasn't though, I was jealous; I didn't want everyone else looking at her. I hugged Mrs Clitheroe inside her Viyella wrap, hugged her to myself.

Newsagents, tobacconists up and down the High Street, all carried posters with my lovely Mrs Clitheroe smiling at all and sundry. The *Gazette* had a different picture – Leonard standing next to her outside St Matthew's. That was the day of the church fête, when she'd done that thing to her Achilles tendon. Mrs Clitheroe and Leonard had posed patiently enough in front of the porch door, like at weddings. And then Mr Clitheroe went off to sort out the tombola and his wife suddenly fell down as though someone had shot her.

'*Ohhh!*' The cry had stopped everyone in their tracks. It was like a fox howling in the fields.

'Jen!' Mr Clitheroe had come crunching back across the gravel, a funny, leggy figure like a puppet, knees all over the place. 'Jen! What have you done?'

'Oh God, I don't know, Len.'

'Let me, girlie. Don't put your weight on it, lean on me. There we go.' And he had scooped her off the gravel into his thin arms. 'Come on, lass. Let's get you home.'

He had carried her all the way back from St Matthew's to Bluebell Crescent. The grounds around the church bustled with people getting the fête ready; they all watched with their mouths hanging open as Leonard lurched along like Boris Karloff in *The Mummy* with his wife in his arms, into the black shadow of the yew trees, and creakily out through the lich-gate, while Mrs Clitheroe made odd mewing sounds, half laughing, half crying.

She'd gone into Epping General after that, and had white bandages round her leg for ages. I remembered Auntie Rene's kitchen, with baby Amanda in Mrs Clitheroe's arms, and Craig drawing on her shoes with crayons.

'I can just see Frank carrying *me* home!' Auntie Rene had snorted. 'I suppose if my leg actually dropped off, he might push me home in a shopping trolley. Not that Frank would know a shopping trolley if it bit him. But still.'

'Oh, Leonard's in his element when anything like that happens – a damsel in distress. That's how he likes us, Irene, feminine and helpless. God, the poor man certainly drew the short straw with me! He's a ladies' man, you know, in the truest sense, he likes *female* females.'

Her head was bowed over baby Amanda, so she couldn't see the incredulous look that flickered across Auntie Rene's eyes.

'It's not all his fault, Irene,' continued Mrs Clitheroe. 'It's mine for marrying him. I shouldn't have married any man.'

'Oh look here, just because you want to go out to work doesn't mean you can't have a husband! At least it flippin' well shouldn't in this day and age!'

Mrs Clitheroe shook her head and smiled wistfully down at Amanda. 'Perhaps I should have had babies early, when we first married. Now it's too late.'

'What are you talking about? Thirty-five's no age!'

'It isn't that. It's just, well, the way things are between us . . .'

There was a strange edge to her voice. I watched Auntie Rene's eyebrows disappear into her hairline. Her voice dropped. 'Don't you . . . you know . . . ?' She twitched her head and mouthed something. It looked like *How's your father?* Mrs Clitheroe looked up at her over the baby. There was a long moment while the two women looked levelly at each other. When Auntie Rene spoke again, her voice was tinged with awe.

'You don't like it, do you? I don't just mean Leonard.'

Another long moment, and Mrs Clitheroe spoke on an intake of breath. 'Nightmare,' she said.

Auntie Rene opened her mouth to speak, but if this mysterious conversation had been going to take us anywhere I understood, the chance was lost for ever when Craig chose that moment to tug at the curtain, bringing the pelmet down.

Well, all these Brentwood people might have her photo in front of them, but they didn't know the other pictures, or Nell, or what Jenny had looked like as a schoolgirl in pigtails. Beneath the leather covers, Mrs Clitheroe's images flickered into a montage, all sparkling vivacity and the tinkle of piano keys. I tried to concentrate my thoughts on these instead of the newspaper ones that everyone could see. There was a picture of Leonard in Pilot Officer uniform, 1945, when he was twenty-four, because he was a lot older than Mrs Clitheroe. And next to that in the album, I pictured her wartime ration book. It had letters and numbers on it, I remembered. I bet I could even recall them, I was clever at that. It was a trick most people couldn't do, just me and Mrs Clitheroe, it was our trick.

Shoppers barged past me with her face all folded up under their arms. I remembered the letters CP followed by a long number that was a bit like 'Mr Tambourine Man' because it ended up all greeny gold. Yes, 7577. And it started with an unfriendly red. Thirty. That was it, CP 307577. I bet these Brentwood people didn't know Mrs Clitheroe's ration book number, so there!

An image of the Pilot Officer now appeared in my head.

'Well no, Leonard. I haven't seen Jenny all day.'

'Righty-ho. I'll be off.'

'But are you all right?'

He wasn't all right, even I could see that. The smile he gave my mother was sickly, just a tightening of his mouth across his face. Those funny sticklike limbs were juddering like an engine. 'I'm in the pink, thank you, Myrtle.'

'Well, I don't think so. Come in and sit down.'

When the knock had come at the back door, I'd been in the kitchen helping my mother wrap Easter eggs. Not last Easter, the one before. Mr Clitheroe hadn't noticed me. My mother led him by the elbow through the kitchen, and on into our front room. As they disappeared, she was chatting brightly, the way she did to difficult infants at school, truculent or crying for their mummies.

'I can't offer you a drink, Leonard, though I must say you look like a man who could do with one. What's up? Why the panic?'

'I should go to the police, Myrtle. Get those lazy twerps at the station earning their keep for once.'

'You can't report your wife to the police as though she were a runaway dog!'

'*Missing persons!* That's what it's for, and I'm entitled. I pay my rates.'

'Nonsense. Tell me why you're in this tizwas. Have you had a row, is that it? You've had a falling-out and Jenny's packed her things?'

I heard a sob.

'I see. Well, it's been building up, you can't deny it.'

'All her clothes have gone, Myrtle.'

'And her gramophone records, what about them?'

'No, I don't think so.'

'And she's left the piano behind, I take it. She hasn't dragged that away in a trunk? Well then. She'll be back. Sit tight.'

'Oh Christ.'

'That won't help, taking the Lord's name in vain. Come now, a good row clears the air.'

'No, Myrtle.' I heard raucous sobbing. This was horrible, yet I stayed put to hear it. Mrs Clitheroe had run away. Mrs Clitheroe had gone.

'Leonard,' said my mother in a new tone, 'you haven't done something silly, have you? You haven't *hit* Jenny.'

No response.

'*Leonard?*'

He scraped the words out. 'A man has a right to a wife. It's there in the Bible, Myrtle. And if she isn't. Well then. He's entitled to find comfort elsewhere.'

'Leonard Clitheroe, are you telling me that there's another woman? That Jenny's caught you out with a girlfriend?'

'It's in the scriptures! A man's right . . .'

'A man's right *fiddlesticks*! Well, no wonder you're in such a tizzy.'

I couldn't see them from the kitchen, but I could picture my mother, her lips crimped.

'She isn't a wife, Myrtle! I'm not one of your lily-livered she-men like those long-haired nancies in the pop charts . . .'

'You're not honeymooners, the pair of you. You can't expect a wife to be a handmaiden year in, year out. The lustre wears off. And you can sit there and tell me you actually raised your hand to her?'

There was another knock at the back door; Auntie Rene's shining head appeared in the kitchen. 'Myrtle? You wouldn't have Leonard here, by any chance?'

The man himself came scuttling through the door. 'What is it, Irene?'

'Oh! Well, your wife's in your front garden with a black eye, sitting on a suitcase. She forgot to take her front door key.'

He was out of the house.

'And if I was you,' shouted Auntie Rene at his retreating back, 'I'd keep my fists to myself in future! Wife-beaters are the lowest of the low, Len Clitheroe!'

'If you want that paper, it'll cost you fourp'nce,' snapped the newsagent. I withdrew my fingers, which had been leafing surreptitiously through the inside pages of the *Brentwood Review*. He turned to the lady next to me.

'Your *Woman's Own*, Mrs B?'

'And a *Gazette* please, Ronnie.'

The clink of coins, and she had Mrs Clitheroe tucked under her arm. A shopping bag full of tins bashed against my legs.

'Terrible thing, eh, Mrs B? Makes you wonder if there's more to it than meets the eye.'

'What, an inside job, you think?'

'That's what's being said by them as knew her. And him.'

I wandered disconsolately out of the shop, to run slap bang into the black and white of the Ursuline convent.

'Will you look where you're going?!' A hand reached towards me. My mother's survival tips didn't seem to encompass what to do when set upon by nuns. I lashed out with my elbows and took it on the lam up the High Street towards the Odeon, hugging Mrs Clitheroe to my chest, swaddled in my dressing gown, precious as a puppy. Misery was cold and sour, the colour of vinegar. Up to the box office window. *Help!* I read across the posters. I couldn't have put it better myself. Sitting cross-legged on the floor of the foyer was Babette, absently scratching an ankle.

21

'I never saw you in the High Street,' she complained.
'Where'd you get to?'

'Mrs Clitheroe's in all the newsagents,' I said, sinking, sick with relief, onto the floor beside her.
'Everybody's looking and reading. It's horrid, Babette.'
It was less horrid now, of course, though I was bothered by a vague sense of new unease, as though
something important were missing.

'Your flippin' cousin!' sniffed Babette.

Cousin! That was it. 'What have you done with her?'

'She thumbed a lift!'

'No!'

'Just stuck her thumb out, and when a bloke pulled
up, she got in. It must've been, what, an hour ago.'

'How far can a car go in an hour?'

Babette considered this. 'Speed he revved off at, I'd
say Southend at least.'

At least. What was further than Southend, I thought.
France? 'Good,' I said.

'You still got the album,' Babette pointed out.

'Mmm,' I admitted.

'Well, we can't dump it here in the foyer,' she reasoned. 'We'll get caught. And we can't get into the film without Dorothea.'

They'd banned children without an accompanying adult; Dorothea with her lipstick on could pass for thirty.

'Outside then?' I suggested.

'I s'pose. But I reckon you better get it ditched pretty sharpish, Annie. You aren't half pushing your luck, parading round Brentwood in broad daylight, waving a hefty piece of evidence about with the police after it.'

'Mmm. Babette?'

'What?'

'Oh, nothing.'

How to explain that my feelings about the album had changed? That, in the course of my progress down Brentwood High Street, it had stopped feeling like incriminating evidence and more like, well, like all I had left of Mrs Clitheroe. I thought again of the High Street shops, their recessed doorways and projecting, hatchet-faced windows, all plastered with her smile, and felt again the whiplash of my hectic jealousies.

'Babette.'

'*What?*'

'Nothing.'

She stared at me, and gave up. 'Come on, let's get going.'

But as she hopped to her feet, a complication struck me. 'Suppose we *do* need an alibi, like we planned?'

'Pretending we was at the Breeden Empire, you mean?'

'I might have to say what *Help!* was about.'

'Lorraine already told you, didn't she? That'll do if Lilliput puts the screws on you – he don't go to Beatles' films.'

'But I bet WPC Swan does.' I cast my mind back to

Lorraine. 'I think,' I began, 'she said it's all about a jewel.'

'Well then.'

'Yes. And . . .'

I tried to imagine the Beatles in Technicolor; visions came to me. 'There's a Dalek, and someone has a razor like Mr Maxwell's, then he hands it over to John and Paul and the dogs are killed. Two spaniels.'

Babette deliberated on this for a moment. 'I don't think the Beatles slit any dogs' throats in *Help!*,' she decided, 'or we'd have heard.'

Suddenly I sat down and started blubbing noisily, pouring out the accreted misery of days. Babette, who knew me too well to be startled, settled back down to wait patiently, without fidgeting. Someone in the queue went 'Sssssh!' at me, and she whipped round and shouted, 'You shush yourself!', which instantly silenced the entire foyer. Entwined couples by the sweet counter sprang apart. I saw one young man take his hand from under his girlfriend's skirt.

'What say,' suggested Babette, when I finally stopped sobbing, 'we have a look round Bon Marché?'

'Oh, *can* we?'

'Come on.'

'By the way,' I remembered, as we blinked into the daylight, 'how did you get here?'

Babette gave me a look. 'Caught the next bus, of course!' She took the Viyella parcel from my arms, presumably feeling that I wasn't up to coping with hooky packages.

My sense of oppression dispersed inside Bon Marché because the store was magic; instead of cash registers, money was sent whizzing back and forth in canisters on overhead wires that linked the shop assistants with the lone cashier, impounded in a cage at the back. On busy Fridays the ceiling was cross-hatched with cash cylinders hurtling across the store with a *zing!* on their whizzy wires.

'Oh yeah, I never told you,' mused Babette as we looked happily upwards.

'What?'

'About Rupert. He got done for shoplifting in here.'

'No!'

'Mum heard. He was caught Saturday, with his pockets full.'

I digested the information. 'I suppose that was him doing his thing for secret agent training.'

Babette gave a snort like Auntie Rene. 'Well, he's bloomin' useless at it. Some ladies from up the pea fields was in here when it happened. They told Mum he'd done himself up in disguise – one of them joke moustaches like Craig's got. Everyone in the shop was having a right old laugh at him, creeping about in a hairy moustache trying to pretend he was shopping, and nicking anything he could lay his hands on.'

'No!'

'Well, it didn't surprise me,' commented Babette with a shrug. 'I always thought he was a wanker.'

I knew the type of moustache she was talking about – it turned you into a cartoon Mexican bandit. You didn't go shopping in Bon Marché in it, you sang 'Speedy Gonzales' in it, and called everybody 'gringo'.

I was still absorbing this startling news bulletin when Babette suddenly hissed at me.

'Annie!'

'What?'

'It's Mr Clitheroe!'

I turned. Leonard Clitheroe was standing by a counter at the far end of the store – the gents' outfitters. He had with him the battered case he used for his chiropody things and was holding up to the light a necktie of jet black. I took a panic-stricken glance at his wife's album in Babette's arms.

'Let's make a run for it!'

'Hang about a sec,' said Babette, 'there's people watching him.'

I looked wildly around me. '*What* people?'

'Everybody!'

And then I saw that she was right. Every way I turned, there seemed to be a knot of women with their eyes on Leonard Clitheroe. Folded copies of the *Review* and *Gazette* twitched in their hands like Japanese fans. What was the matter with them?

'What's the matter with them?'

'Shhh! I'm trying to listen.'

Behind us: 'It's him, all right. Her hubby.'

A voice like a spitting cobra: 'Kitting himself out for her funeral, looks like.'

'Flippin' hypocrite.'

Over on our right, a matronly figure with a copy of the *Gazette*, her eyes glittering: 'Careful! He's turning round!'

With smiles stuck to their faces, the women pretended an interest in the umbrella stand. We watched Mr Clitheroe say something to the assistant, who nodded and made notes on a pad. To our left, more conspirators, oozing from behind a contorted plastic mannequin in a wilting tweed suit.

'Madge in Lingerie recognized him – he used to do her mum's corns. She said his wife was lovely, a real lady.'

'But it might not've been him that . . . you know. I mean, he looks ever so upset.'

'Pull the other one, it's got bells on!'

Sw-sw-sw-sw-sw-sw. It seemed to me that they were inching forwards, like the game of Granny's Footsteps, creeping up on Mr Clitheroe like oil trickling over the hardwood floor. Above our heads hurtled the magic canisters, their friction setting up whispers of their own. Sw-sw-sw-sw-sw-sw . . .

Like much of my experience of eavesdropping on adults, the women's repartee started off all right before plummeting into a swamp of tosh and twaddle. But I knew what it meant, because I could smell it – everywhere was the scent, the preternatural odour, of the hunt. Weary myself of being hunted, I felt an insane impulse to walk across the floor of Bon Marché towards this unlikely quarry, with his senescent suitcase and habitual short temper, and put my arms around him. I was seriously making a move in that direction when Babette's voice broke into my reverie.

'Annie, I been thinking. Can you throw a fit or somethink?'

'Fit?'

'You know. Do somethink noisy that will make everybody look in one place.'

'Do you mean create a diversion?'

'That's it, yeah.'

'Oh yes, I expect I can. Do you want it now?'

'When you're ready.' She shuffled the photograph album over to her right arm. Like everyone else's, her eyes were on Leonard.

'What you going to do, Babette?'

'Wait 'til you've got everybody turned round, then get that old case of Mr Clitheroe's open.'

'What for?'

'Drop the album in it. That won't half confuse Lilliput. That won't half get him going.'

I surveyed my surroundings. Within spitting distance was the stand of umbrellas. Within kicking distance. I shuffled a couple of paces away from the sw-sw-sw women, checking that no-one in the vicinity was looking my way (which wasn't likely considering what else was on offer for entertainment), and lifted my good foot. When the umbrellas went over, they'd knock the hat stand. That in turn should wallop everything off the counter. Domino effect. Out of the corner of my eye, I saw Babette slipping the Viyella off Mrs Clitheroe's photograph album. The foxed leather gave it a vulnerable air. Sumptuous Moroccan goatskin the colour of a Chopin *Nocturne*. The exquisitely tooled borders, the perfect scrolling of the word 'Photographs' picked out in gold, their beauty shone among the cheap newsprint, the crimplene women and stuffy black bombazine of the shop assistants, like a musk rose in a tub of free daffs from Daz. All around us were reproductions of Mrs Clitheroe's face in surreal replication, sticking variously up and down at random angles, poking out from under sleeves, out of fists, popping up from shopping bags, her inky smile smudged black, smeared . . .

'Babette!'

My voice came out louder than I intended. She snapped round.

'What?'

'I don't want to give it back,' I whispered frantically. 'I don't want to. I feel like it *is* her. Can't we find a way of keeping it? Hiding it? Can't we?'

Babette went quite still. My lips were trembling, my cry-baby lips, the tears welling yet again in my rheumy cry-baby's eyes. She sighed wearily.

'Come on, let's get you home. We'll ask Lorraine if she can look after it 'til the hoo-hah dies down.'

'Oh *can* we? *Can* we, Babette?'

' 'Course we can. Come on.'

We made off for the doors, Babette trailing my Viyella behind her, the photograph album still nude under her right arm. When she gave Mrs Clitheroe back to me, I dropped a kiss onto her covers.

'There's a number 260 due any minute,' reasoned Babette, indicating the bus stop. 'We'll be home by six.'

On its own, without the album inside it, my dressing gown looked oddly limp and incomplete, like an

219

old Mars bar wrapper or the discarded skin of some giant lizard. I suppose we were lucky to get out before anybody noticed it and assumed we'd been shoplifting in Ladies' Wear. Babette and I cast a final look through the doorway into Bon Marché. Leonard Clitheroe had turned away from the counter and was moving unsteadily between the shoppers. Crying.

22

While we'd been in Brentwood, Dorothea had arrived home in an Aston Martin driven, according to every female in Mountnessing Road, by a James Bond look-alike. He had explained that Dorothea had been stranded, after which the grown-ups had another of their powwows and came to a conclusion. Uncle Norman et al. were going home.

I was greeted with this news as I stepped over the threshold. A series of appalling events had darkened our village, and this was a particularly sorry time for all the youngsters who knew Mrs Clitheroe, but her death seemed to have affected Annie in a way that doctors would call 'morbid'. She had plainly been in a tizwas for days, and now her wild behaviour had got them all thrown off the bus. All in all, it was decided that Annie needed some peace and quiet. No-one could bring Mrs Clitheroe back, but it would be better for everybody if Annie stopped dwelling on it. Mummy would talk to all the neighbours to ask them not to discuss the murders in front of her. She was sure everyone would understand.

Dorothea didn't. 'But, Auntie Myrtle, *we* don't have to go. I won't talk about the murders to Aggie, honest, not even if she begs me. Wild horses couldn't talk me into it.'

'My dear, of course, we know we can trust you.'

My heart stopped.

'But you see, it will be easier to restore the status quo if there's just us, on our own.'

Upstairs in my bedroom, Dorothea, who had only unpacked yesterday, watched her mother refolding the clothes into a suitcase and restowing the bassoon.

'So now we've got *another* two hours in the car with Dad whistling "Paddy McGinty's Goat". Two days in a row!'

'We can try asking him not to, dear.'

'Well, I can't see why it's good for Aggie, me going away – I'm her best friend!'

Auntie Marjorie turned to me with a smile like those nurses in Epping General. 'You just want a rest after all that nasty business, don't you, Annie.'

Dorothea considered this the height of unreason. 'Well, if it was me, and there was something going on that everybody was talking about, and every time I walked up they stopped talking, I know how *I'd* feel,' she told us. 'I'd feel like ... like ...' Dorothea hesitated.

'Like a good cry?' I ventured.

'Beating them up?' supplied her mother, who knew her best.

'No! A leper,' decided my cousin, tucking her poodle nightdress case under her arm. 'I'd feel like a leper.'

The day of Jenny Clitheroe's funeral, there was a different feel to our village, an air of hushed bustle. Women donned smart, dark frocks, and ordered their children in muted tones to stop playing in the road. There were even some men around although it was a Tuesday. They put on dark shirts and jackets, or the better-off got into black suits and black ties with the acrid whiff of mothballs.

My parents had left early for St Matthew's, for what Uncle Frank called 'a ringside seat', and I sat in the Lucases' kitchen watching Auntie Rene look stunning, her blond hair set off by a black Mary Quant suit. She was brushing the three children, starting from the crowns of their heads and working downwards. Uncle Frank had set off for Romford and Imperial Tobacco, but Uncle Arthur and Lorraine were here, en route home after their week in Canvey. Babette was moody in dark-blue velvet, which she complained was too hot, and Lorraine looked like a pop singer in a black and white dress with appliqué daisies and white plastic boots that Mrs Clitheroe would have approved of. But I wouldn't look at Lorraine.

My mother had put me into purple nylon that squeaked, with floppy purple bows on my plaits, like a cross between Pollyanna and Crufts. Uncle Arthur, who had never met Jenny Clitheroe, had agreed to babysit me while everyone else went to her funeral.

Lorraine had accepted the photograph album from us, but hadn't kept it as she promised, she had sent it off to the police.

'You got to understand, Annie,' she had said, squatting down beside me as I was shaking with distress, 'it's evidence in a police case. We can't hang on to things like that, it isn't right. Murder's special, lovey. You got to give the police all the help they're after.'

'It was mine,' I mumbled, torment strangling my voice. 'You had no right!'

'It *wasn't* yours, Annie.' Very gently, she touched my hair. I recoiled.

Apparently Lorraine had posted it to the CID in an anonymous envelope, whatever one of those was. Even Babette had jumped on her. 'Well, that's no use, for a start! There's a postal strike on!'

But apparently Lorraine had taken her package into Breeden, and our strike didn't extend there. My dismay was further blackened by this evidence of a grown-up's ability to override our own efforts, to wipe out our enterprise. To bloody well know *everything*.

'I never even told it goodbye!' The words slipped from me like tears falling. 'It will think I just forgot about it!'

Lorraine frowned, baffled and concerned. 'Annie, it was just a book of photos. You don't say goodbye to things, they don't have feelings. It's not like somebody's dog.'

But I was choking. 'I never even said goodbye – she'll think I didn't love her!'

It was all I could say. I kept saying it. 'She'll think I didn't love her!'

Hearing so much unaccustomed traffic outside, and seeing the strange phenomenon of one family after another walking past the house, it was difficult to fight down the feeling that I was missing out on a party. A similar idea must have struck Babette.

'If there's cake or anythink, I'll hide some in a serviette and bring it back,' she whispered while her mother was polishing Craig.

Even so, by the time they had filed out and Auntie Rene had closed the front door, I was as forlorn as Cinderella. Eventually Muningstock's collective voices and footsteps ebbed away, and in the sinister silence that came seeping into the vacuum, Uncle Arthur tried to tempt me with treats.

'How about a game of Monopoly, Fanny Cradock?'
'No thank you, Uncle Arthur.'

'A game of cards, then.'

'No thank you, Uncle Arthur.'

'Rummy? You're a cracker at rummy.'

We played a hand or two of the rummy he'd taught us all one summer day on a trip to West Mersea, when Auntie Rene was pregnant with Amanda. The skies had opened, and we'd all sat crammed into the beach hut eating crisps and grizzling. Now, as then, he lost every hand, which was kind of him.

'We don't have to stay in here, you know, we can go next door to yours if you want, and play the old Joanna.'

'No thank you, Uncle Arthur.'

'I bet you've written some new songs, though. I'd really like to hear them.'

'I've gone right off the piano. I don't reckon I'm going to play it any more.'

There was something pernicious about this amount of quiet. I was never home in the week except for school holidays, and then there were always other children somewhere, retexturing the air with shouts and bicycle bells and the grating skid of rollerskates. This inhuman afternoon was more like being too ill to go to school; my inner landscape took on the introspection of sickness, the colour of fever and discomfort and tonsillitis. This impression was rubbed in by the sick-bed look of consternation that was coming off Uncle Arthur.

'When did you get the hump with the piano, then, Annie?'

'Don't know. Little while ago. I expect I've grown out of it.'

The silence was total. I didn't even have any music playing in my head. Since as far back as I could remember, I'd always had a song on the brain, and I knew how to exploit them for comfort when I was sad. For days now I'd been trying to catch hold of something warm and soothing, but the melodies kept trickling away from me, refusing to stick. It felt like a kind of rejection.

My itchy stitches had been removed at last, but I had broken out in a gauzy eczema that itched even worse, so I scratched it, against all adult advice. Had I been a dog, they'd have put one of those collars on me.

'Did you stop playing the piano after Mrs Clitheroe passed away?'

I didn't answer.

'It's not wrong to talk about her, Annie. Your mum and dad just don't want you dwelling on . . . you know . . . on the other thing.'

How could I tell him that I could hardly remember Mrs Clitheroe any more? When I thought of her, all I got were Mr Lilliput's accents and Auntie Doris's anger ('I wish they'd hang him!'), and fear I could actually taste, like sulphur, like Dorothea's cigarette. Uncle Arthur was telling me something about Lorraine.

'When she was a nipper, she used to talk to her mum,' he was saying. 'She'd sit up in bed with a pillow and tell her things, like what she got up to with her friends. Told her off, sometimes, too. She'd cry a bit, and tell her mum off for leaving us and going to Heaven.'

I nodded politely, but my entire skin prickled with embarrassment. To try to contact the dead was a sick and shameful thing. Our school had suffered a spate of Ouija boards some time back and I knew that it was unhealthy on every level. I now made a ham-fisted job of changing the subject.

'I used to talk to Mrs Clitheroe about music. I mean before. She liked the Stones.'

'The what, sweetheart?'

'The Rolling Stones. She liked them best.'

'*Did* she? Same as Lorraine, then.'

'Yes, that's right. She watched them on *Top of the*

Pops sometimes when Mr Clitheroe was out chiropodizing. She liked their single "Little Red Rooster". Do you know it?' I gave it to him. ' "I AM YOUR LITTLE RED ROOSTER, bam-bam-bam-bam, TOO LAME . . . TO CROW TODAY".'

'Yeah. Good one.'

'It's about a farmyard.'

' *'Course* it is.'

A few moments, and I had another go. 'And the Hollies, too. She liked their latest hit "I'm Alive".'

I shut up after that, and he offered me a game of draughts, but I couldn't be bothered. Besides, my mind kept meandering off to St Matthew's church. I had never been to a funeral. I had no idea what hymns you sang. My own favourite was 'Jerusalem', but Mrs Clitheroe's was 'The Day Thou Gavest Lord is Ended'; these had something in common – in both, the music glowed a deep blood-red, like a sanctuary lamp.

'And she likes red songs best.'

'What's that, sweetheart? *Red* songs?'

'Yes, because we both hear music in colour.'

'Oh, I get you.'

'But I bet you don't really. Mummy and Daddy don't believe me, they think I make it up, but Mrs Clitheroe's got it as well.'

'Got what?'

'We see things in colour that aren't. Not just music. Numbers. Letters. Days of the week. People's names. We're not exactly the same, though; Mrs Clitheroe thinks Wednesday is blue, but I see it green like the number seven, and she sees Monday and six as gold, but I see Monday as blue. But we both think "Ticket to Ride" is purple, and "Satisfaction" is the same shade of red as Tuesday.'

Uncle Arthur blinked at me, and my eloquence died away.

227

'The same shade of red as Tuesday,' he repeated, in tones no more encouraging than anyone else's had ever been, Mrs Clitheroe excepted. Perhaps there were only two of us in the world. Well, there was only one of us now.

'Show me,' said Uncle Arthur, placing Craig's papers and crayons on the table between us. 'Write the days of the week and things in their right colours.'

'Those are Craig's,' I objected. 'Auntie Rene will get really cross.'

'No she won't, Annie. Today's different.'

And so, with the promise of special dispensation, I sat in the Lucases' kitchen covering Craig's drawing paper with strident and greasy colours. Craig also had a tin of watercolour paints. If you use crayons first, the paint washes across the wax, leaving the gloss to shine against a pastel background.

After a while, Uncle Arthur asked me how I would paint Mrs Clitheroe, and although in terms of portraiture there wasn't a lot to choose between my ability and Craig's, I had a bash at this, and while he made a pot of tea, I produced a female figure with long, wavy hair and a glorious smile, in a glowing gown the colour of all Mrs Clitheroe's favourite songs.

'That's very nice, Annie,' he told me, when I laid the paintbrush down. 'And if you wanted to say your goodbyes to her, what way would you do it?'

'I don't know.'

'You could sing her something.'

' "The Day Thou Gavest Lord is Ended"?'

'Good idea,' he said. 'You have a think,' and he poured us both a cup of tea.

Somewhere in the back of my mind was half-imagined music – not a hymn, but rock 'n' roll, its waves of sound pumping in blood-red breakers, moving inexorably onwards – and that something seemed to have been born out of my painting. As I chased after it, I realized that Mrs Clitheroe had been both born and buried on a Tuesday, a day that was her favourite colour.

The song was beginning to glimmer, and it was about the colour of Tuesday; strangely enough it was also a song about goodbye.

'Ready then?' Uncle Arthur asked at length, and I sang 'Ruby Tuesday' to my picture of Mrs Clitheroe, and when the song came to an end, we went out to the garden and Uncle Arthur folded my picture into his handkerchief and put this into the earth at the far end, quite deep under Auntie Rene's red roses. Then I sang 'The Day Thou Gavest Lord is Ended', and recited the Lord's Prayer.

'That first one was a good song, Fanny Cradock!' Uncle Arthur told me when we came back indoors and he was washing his hands at the kitchen sink. Yes, I'd thought it was good, too.

The quiet that had lain over Muningstock for the afternoon was suddenly rippled with voices; people were coming back from the funeral.

Quickly then, and knowing he wouldn't laugh at me, I asked, 'Do you reckon it's sick or unhealthy if I believe Mrs Clitheroe got in touch with me while I was painting her?'

' 'Course it isn't, sweetheart. Why?'

I stopped. It was nonsense, this. I'd been hampering the police inquiry into her murder, and here I was, suggesting she'd just sent me a present. Yet this was the second time, there had been Eric Burdon when I'd frightened myself half to death on Thursday night. Was she saying she forgave me?

'I think,' I said, my confidence fast bleeding away, 'I think she might've given me that ruby-red song, to sing in my head.'

'Well, perhaps she did, too,' said Uncle Arthur. 'Mrs Clitheroe was very fond of you, I heard. So perhaps she sent you down a song from wherever she is now.'

Ruby Tuesday. 31 August 1965. Only another year and a bit before Mick Jagger and Keith Richards would get around to writing it.

The Present

23

And now for the terrible thing I did in New York. The day after Alan and I were in front of Irving Berlin's house narrowly averting a row, he'd had a medical conference to attend, which was Alan's official reason for being there (of course, his present employers didn't know about the offer from the other biotech company). The conference should have left me free, but instead Alan sent me off shopping with Aunt Margo, using a man's logic that the longer two incompatible people spend together, the better they will get along.

I loathe shopping at the best of times, and this was the worst sort of morning to dump me in a series of twilit interiors. The day glittered. In the glassy light, lemon-coloured leaves fluttered down from the ginkgo trees, chasséeing in lazy, acrobatic loops, as though animated by Walt Disney. I resented every awning under which I was forced to follow Aunt Margo, every second spent in yet another shop smelling of fusty dust. My private plans had included repeatedly wandering in and out of the lobby of the Brill

Building, one-time home of the Songwriting Factory, to meditate on Burt Bacharach, and then doing the helicopter trip again, though admittedly it was getting difficult to hide the expenditure from Alan, as this one would be my seventh.

It was surprising that Aunt Margo had ever agreed to this expedition at all, as she was generally ashamed to be seen with me. My unruly hair, my strange fashionless garments, the startling sweaters and Fifties' pedal-pushers, though unremarkable here in the Village, were nevertheless outré in Aunt Margo's manicured, matching-accessory social circles. In this regard, Alan had not helped matters along by laboriously explaining how I'm kitted out by jumble sales and Oxfam. But in an antique store somewhere in the West Village, I watched a little game being played out before me, and understood why she had embraced with alacrity Alan's suggestion that I accompany her.

'Now, I don't want same-day delivery,' Aunt Margo was giving instructions in her loud, flat, deaf voice. 'The study has to be cleared out, and anyway, my nephew won't need it just yet. It's a homecoming gift.'

The object of these remarks was a hulking great kneehole desk in carefully distressed reproduction rosewood.

'Good taste is so important, wouldn't you say?' she continued, handing over her credit card. 'To surround oneself with the decorative! Unfortunately, my nephew does not have enough of that at present, and I know he misses it. He tells me so.'

I was generally turning up my nose at the whole lot of them – Aunt Margo, the desk, the young man, who seemed to be upholstered in the same velvet as a nearby chaise longue – when my eye caught sight of her thin fingers gripping the back of a bentwood chair while her card was being swiped. And I noticed a tell-tale return of colour to the knuckles when the sales slip came chugging through the machine, accepted.

My assumptions went chugging through a validation check of their own. So this wasn't just a petty scam designed to needle Annie. This gift was important to her. Could it be that Alan was all she had? At home, Aunt Margo talked loudly of well-connected friends, but now that I came to think of it, we had never seen hide nor hair of them. Maybe her dislike of me was not a willed condition, but one of those pernicious jealousies that gnaw. Perhaps the very mention of me gave her pain. I thought of that gallery of dead faces on her flocked wall, and of Alan, who was never coming home to sit at that monstrosity of a desk, and it was with better grace that I sat out the remainder of this transaction, and followed on for the rest of the morning from shop to shop, gamely registering cracked china jugs and rows of chipped Bakelite radio casings, most of which could have come off Old Ollie's rag and bone cart.

Over the course of this expedition I learned to look for reading matter as the best distraction, and when we reached our final curio shop of the morning, I found a laminated collection of old magazine adverts for radios and record players – Philco, RCA Victor, photographs of doting families sitting round their Radiograms in the 1960s. On the edge of my vision I could see the proprietor, obviously a longtime acquaintance of Aunt Margo, and whose name, I gathered, was Larry.

'Of course, two ninety-five is a little more than the price of your usual purchase, but you can see . . .'

As he ran on in this time-honoured vein, my attention was swept away by an ad inviting parents to give their children the benefit of music's 'true colours': 'Their delicate ears can pick out the true colors; buy this FM radio, and let them hear the green fields of Debussy, the sunset hues of Bizet.'

I was rereading this extraordinary assumption of childhood synaesthesia, when a phrase of Larry's loomed across these thoughts like something cold blocking the sun.

'. . . sepia, as you see. Truly quaint. See this charming photo of the Queen of the May. Though the later pictures are of less interest to you, I'm sure you'll agree that the entire collection is a worthy purchase.'

On 'Queen of the May' I spun round, and there it was in his finicky hands. Even as my blood ebbed, and my heart thudded in a ribcage that was hollow, I was thinking that this was inevitable. Of course it was; it had the same, mad inescapability that had clawed me into the events of the summer of 1965.

On legs made of water, I crossed to the empire chair on which Aunt Margo's bone-thin figure was propped, her leathery hand reaching out for the album.

'May I?' I intervened.

Without benefit of reply, I took the object from Larry's hands, and my last doubt vanished. It really was Mrs Clitheroe's photograph album. I found myself raising it to my face and breathing in the leather; in spite of everything, it still smelled like heaven, aristocratically impervious to the pounding that its corners had taken and the smears across its face. Larry may have been speaking, or Aunt Margo; I talked straight across them.

'I know this album. It belonged to a friend of mine. I've known it all my life.'

'Well, isn't that a coincidence, now!' oozed Larry. 'Of course, I recognized this was English. And I guess you're from England too, right?'

'Right.' I raised it again to my nose and thirty-five years fell away. 'How did it come to be here, do you know?'

'You mean the United States?'

'No, I know that. I mean your particular shop.'

'Well, I guess a house clearance; some elderly lady passed away maybe.' He caught himself up and glanced apologetically at Aunt Margo. 'I can make enquiries with the dealer I bought it from. You staying in town long?'

'It's OK, I know whose house it came from.' *A hundred bucks apiece from a dealer off Bleeker*, the great-nephew had said. He'd *told* me. Was that why I'd finally given in when Aunt Margo mentioned where she was heading? I opened the album to a bookmark that Larry had slipped between its pages. Queen Nell smiled at me, her cheeks dimpled in an expression so similar to Jenny Clitheroe's that my heart turned over and I couldn't trust myself to speak. The very pretty girl on Nell's right was last year's queen perhaps, standing in awkward posed profile, arms and legs oddly displaced like an Egyptian frieze, in the act of lowering a crown of blossom onto Nell's bobbed hair. My mind saw Dorothea in our garden shed, and smelled the grass cuttings and creosote. I could taste the fresh air of the 1960s, the confidence and energy.

The pages slipped and I found myself looking at Jenny Clitheroe herself, seated at someone's piano. This was a glossy black and white print, professional quality, reportage. Why? How? I had no idea, but miraculously I knew what she was playing, must have known all those years ago: the Moody Blues' 'Go Now'. There she was, hair flying, slim fingers stroking out the R&B, the chords throbbing, chords as rich and blue as her smoky voice, as her eyes, those remembered irises of blue-lace agate – her eyes! Oh, look at her, my God, the expression in the eyes, narrowed, shining. Something I'd had no way of understanding at the age of ten – no wonder I'd loved this woman, she exuded heat, there was a force field around her; this is the most sensual creature I've ever seen.

In my current state of permanent arousal, this vicarious understanding of the look in her eyes, responding to the excitement of her throbbing R&B, caught me unawares, sent a long, visceral flush rippling white-hot through my body. Astounded, I swung sharply round and hid my own eyes from Larry and Aunt Margo.

'Well, Larry, thank you for finding it.' Her harsh tones grated across my chaotic thoughts.

'You're welcome.'

'And now, if you don't mind, I'll leave a deposit and drop by later with the balance. Is that all right with you?'

'Oh please!' I cried, reaching for my own wallet. 'I wouldn't think of it! Of course you must let me.'

'But why would you do that? I should think I can pay for my own portraits.'

I paused, the first hint of disquiet just beginning to nibble at the edges of my mind.

'Aunt Margo, I would really like to take this home. The owner's name was Jenny Clitheroe, and she died when I was ten. I never quite forgot the loss of her. This album is woven into my own life almost as much as Jenny's.'

But Aunt Margo had turned away. She couldn't hear what people were saying when she turned away. Which is why she'd done it. I side-stepped her and started again.

'Aunt Margo, the owner was a Mrs Clitheroe. When I was small . . .'

She flicked a glove at me dismissively. 'Well, of course you can have all those contemporary photos, that are not *decorative*. I don't have any use for them, only the ones of a picturesque and antique nature.' A long fingernail flicked at the corners of Nell's picture, where it was slotted into its neat cuts in the page. 'Just look! I can slip every photo out and put the entire book to new use. My pressed flowers would look so sweet in here.'

'Aunt Margo.' I stopped. She was fidgeting in her handbag, unfolding five-dollar bills from a thin roll. Larry had taken on the waxwork-dummy look of a stranger caught up in someone else's dispute.

'Please, I'm sorry to sound so emotional about this, but you see, Mrs Clitheroe died. She was murdered. And during all the trauma, this photograph album came to mean the world to me. It personified her. Almost embodied her. It mustn't be dismembered.'

I'd raised my voice on that final phrase, which alone penetrated Aunt Margo's protective deafness. She caught my last, inept, word. 'Dismember' was not a welcome description of her activities in the pursuit of Good Taste. Her voice slammed across the frowzy atmosphere of the store.

'You could never have known any one of the people in the antique photographs,' she pointed out. 'So how can they be of value to you?'

She creaked from the chair and folded a bundle of bills into Larry's reluctant palm, the money rustling like pages of the spider's web glassine.

'And you never once showed an interest in my own vintage portraits, so why am I supposed to believe you would take care of these? I know you – pop songs, that's all you care for!'

'Perhaps,' put in Larry, looking frightened when both women turned to him, 'perhaps as this is a family matter, your husband, ma'am,' (to me), 'will be the best adjudicator?' He gave us a pallid smile.

Aunt Margo ignored this remark, but it gave me pause. Alan. Yes, of course. I must get hold of him. He would explain; he was the one person she would listen to.

*   *   *

The long ride uptown to Aunt Margo's apartment was sickening, the cab lurching in the traffic, full of the smell of its own plasticky seats. Aunt Margo sat back with an acrid air of triumph, so that my own mind swung between the upheaval of its own emotions and a sort of horrified pity for her. The sight of Jenny's image had warped me – I was a raw child of ten again, who had just lost her heroine. One photograph after another resurrected itself from my memory, while the chords of 'Go Now' haunted me, their descending A flat major scale in perpetual motion, descending for ever in my head with the mad logic of an Escher staircase.

'I often think I should have followed my cousin Mabel to New York, Annie. I would have been less out of place there, less of an oddity.'

Yes, you were an exoticism in our conservative village. I understand that now.

'Always remember that it's not comfortable being out of the ordinary; people are scared of the unconventional. But in a city like New York my sort gets overlooked in all the colour and noise. I should have been happier there.'

We pulled up outside the apartment. I paid the hefty fare, as Aunt Margo expected me to. I told her goodbye, but shrank from the routine peck on the cheek. Shouldn't have done that; shouldn't have antagonized her further. Standing uncertainly on the sidewalk. What now? Just get hold of Alan, ask him to talk to her. Before we left home, he'd rented a new mobile phone, one that could roam across the US. The only drawback was that I'd never thought to ask him for the number. OK, well, I'd better get on and find him in person, then. Hail another cab.

'Would you take me to the convention centre, please.'

'You mean the Javits Center?'

Not a propitious start. Had Alan mentioned where this conference was being held? Doubtless. But was I listening?

'It's a medical convention,' I explained to the driver. 'Do you know of one in town?'

'New York's full of conventions, lady, always. You certain yours ain't at one of the hotels? There's a lot held in the big hotels – the Sheratons, the Marriott Marquis, the . . .'

As he continued the roll-call, I decided with growing certainty that Alan's conference wasn't at one of the hotels – if it were, that's where we'd be staying, because that is how my husband does things. And if the particular hotel were full, he'd still manage to get a room, and someone else would sleep in the stairwell.

'What's the Javits Center?' I asked.

'Conventions.'

'Let's try it.'

We pulled away from the kerb, and headed back across town. The low sun glittered on the windscreen, silver-plating the shop windows, bleaching out colour, distorting perspective.

'Where is it?'

'Right across town. Eleventh Avenue. Takes up three blocks in the West 30s.'

Miles, then. Miles of city traffic.

Alan *will* get this sorted, I admonished myself as we drove through the crowded streets, but only if you present the case calmly. Alan's severest censure of anybody was that they were 'out of control'. Treat this anxiety as though it were stage fright: deep breaths and into the warm-up exercises I teach my students.

'Do re mi,' I sang softly, rising up the scale, 'fa so la ti do.'

'You say something?'

'Nope.'

'Sorry, thought you did.'

I abandoned that, and stared disconsolately out of the window. Clusters of DON'T signs bristled from a single pole: DON'T HONK, NO LEFT TURN, NO RIGHT TURN, NO TRUCKS, DON'T EVEN *THINK* OF PARKING HERE.

An outdoor-pursuits store had a sign in the window: NOW IS THE DISCOUNT OFF OUR WINTER TENT. Nice one.

The Moody Blues left me, and instead something else haunted my head, 'MacArthur Park' – '. . . someone left the cake out in the rain . . . all the sweet green icing flowing down'. The genius of its self-pitying image drips across my unstable thoughts. Why? And suddenly I saw myself in Horace and Doris Frobisher's garden, holding between my bitten fingers Jenny Clitheroe's green ink, my tears dissolving her words.

As we ground to another halt, I caught a kerbside monologue from one teenage girl to another: 'And this party was like *so weird*. And all night I was like – hey, this is so *weird*, and he was like – weird? *Why* is it weird? And I was like . . .'

I wound up the window. I bet I could out-weird you, my dear. 'Ruby Tuesday'.

The Stones had released it in January 1967, as the flip side of 'Let's Spend the Night Together'. I'd weathered this surprisingly well. I had long accepted that although the song was inside my head, I nevertheless hadn't composed it, so that its sudden exterior existence didn't dash any hopes of mine. It was more like the long-heralded arrival of some rare and beautiful event, like a solar eclipse or the bloom of a once-in-a-lifetime tropical flower. Right over the top, admittedly, but I was still only eleven, and believed that the Beatles and Stones were the highest form of evolved life. Anyway, the release of 'Ruby Tuesday' hadn't given me anything like the jolt I'd got when I first heard the Beatles' *Abbey Road* album, with the

240

track 'She Came in Through the Bathroom Window'.

My story had electrified Daniel. In our pokey little flat in Notting Hill, he had executed his impressions of it in acrylic on canvas stretched across a plywood frame and stuck about with kapok, until the whole suggested some preternatural avian shape, like an upsoaring anthology of words and colour. He called it 'Painting Songs into Being', and sold it to a gallery in the East End for five hundred pounds. A decade later, one of the Cork Street galleries would pay ten thousand for it on the secondary market, and bring Daniel's name to the attention of the chattering classes. And now it was in the Hayward, part of his Retrospective. And next summer it would be here, at the Guggenheim, where it would take up permanent residence. The magnet of New York, pulling us all.

I fidgeted in the taxi, *longing* to get my hands on the photograph album, aching to rustle through its glassine and stroke the matt petal-texture of its pages. And to review the cavalcade of those images that had been contemporary when I last saw them, but which would be history now. The 1960s. An age of lost innocence. Perhaps *the* age of lost innocence, rejection of so many mores, when the establishment lost its immunity for all time. I was just eight when the BBC broadcast *That Was The Week That Was*, calling Macmillan's government 'yesterday's men'. The war generation had come into its own. And that excitement, that sense of liberation, was unique to them – the previous generation would never have believed it, and mine would take it for granted.

So I suppose if you had to choose a year for a couple of ten-year-olds to play havoc with the investigations of an authoritative police officer, 1965 was as good as any.

24

My ideas of the Jacob K. Javits Convention Center,
vague though they were, had run along classroom
lines, with bells ringing, and crowds filing out of lecture
theatres, from which line I could grab my husband.
What I actually found was a vast hall under an arty criss-
cross strutted roof, and banners everywhere.

'Welcome to the ACN – New York Update',
screamed one, which meant nothing to me. Other
banners and arrows offered me REGISTRATION and
EXHIBITORS and POSTER SESSIONS. Around me milled the
conference-goers, with their name badges and canvas
bags lumpy with books. Unthinkable to interrupt their
earnest progress and ask for help. There were also
some posters set on easels.

'PLAN TO ATTEND' said one of them, 'Tuesday 9:15
a.m.: How to Reduce Your Tax and Avoid Accidental
Disinheritance'.

Damn, I was at the wrong convention. Damn. I
stepped back and careened into a thin, bearded man in
a yarmulke.

'Excuse me!'

'Oh, I'm so sorry!'

To his left I could see another easel.

'Thursday 7:30 a.m.: Seminar – Facets of the Nicotinic Receptor'.

A distant memory from my medical school days came whispering down the years. And on a nearby notice board: AMERICAN COLLEGE OF NEUROLOGY – NEW YORK UPDATE.

Neurology – that was it! I wasn't at the wrong convention.

There was an overall thrust in the direction of some escalators. I followed.

'See your badge, ma'am?'

'Actually, I'm just looking for my husband.'

'You can't come in if you're not registered.'

I was afraid of that. 'Do you know how I can get a message to someone here?'

'You tried the Message Center?'

I looked gormlessly around me.

'Down the hall.'

'Thank you.'

'You're welcome.'

I passed a lot more escalators and announcement posters, and the only thing that became clear to me was that there were seminars being held in meeting rooms all over New York, and my husband could be absolutely anywhere in the city.

Another banner. MESSAGE CENTER. Tables with stubby pencils and forms.

IF YOUR NAME APPEARS ON THE MONITOR,
PLEASE RETRIEVE YOUR MESSAGE FROM
PERSONNEL BEHIND THE MESSAGE
CENTER COUNTER.

Two   computer   screens,   on   which   surnames

continually scrolled: 'A–L' said the sign on the first; 'M–Z' the second.

This was no good. Suddenly I remembered the mobile. Of course. The sensible place to leave a message was his mobile phone. But who would have his new number? His secretary in England, Emma. I looked at my watch. 12.14. At home it was 5.14 p.m. Emma wouldn't leave before 5.30. I couldn't remember her direct line, but if I dialled Alan's, I would get his voicemail, and the message always told me I could reach Emma by pressing the star key.

'Excuse me. Is there a phone nearby?'

'Up those stairs.'

'Thanks.'

'You're welcome.'

Up the stairs were two banks of phones – some seated booths and a standing cluster round a column. And a queue.

There's time enough, don't fret. I checked my watch. 12.16. 12.17. Nobody moved. 12.19. I tried and failed to gather the courage to tell the people in front of me that this was an emergency. 12.21. One phone became free; the queue nudged forward.

An emergency? In my head I heard my own voice explaining the truth: I'm trying to stop something happening that will flood me with pain every single time I think about it for the rest of my life. No, what I'm trying to stop is a desecration – the final indignity to someone remarkable whose murder was a sin. I pictured Aunt Margo's fingers plucking the photographs out of their lovingly cut slots.

OK, I told myself. Say you can't prevent her, and this time tomorrow every picture in the album has been stripped out. With Alan's eventual support, couldn't they all be restored later? But when I envisaged the album, I saw a treasure trove full of tucked-in notes, Mrs Clitheroe's delicate pressed flowers, letters, mementoes — the *obiter dicta* of her life. Aunt Margo would bin the lot, of course she would, associating them with me. Tear them up, probably, along with a couple of dozen photographs. She would paste her own pressed flowers all over the beautiful Edwardian pages. And she would start as soon as she could.

12.22. One of the standing phones was suddenly free. I was there.

Gleaming chrome with bulky metal keys and a flock of instruction plaques. A ribbon of words across the LED display: 'Please swipe your credit card.' Credit card out of wallet. Swipe it. The message continued: 'Please swipe your credit card.' Oh come *on*! I polished the black strip, checked the diagram on the phone, swiped it left, right, upside down. 'Please swipe your credit card.'

Damn it and sod it!

Now what?

A coin slot: US COINS ONLY. I feed in a fistful and dial. I get a recorded voice. *That number is invalid.* I notice the lever labelled COIN RETURN, push at it and am rewarded by the sound of a jackpot. Now what?

INTERNATIONAL CALL OPERATOR, says one of the plaques: DIAL 01 + COUNTRY CODE + NUMBER. A human voice, which is the best I've managed to come up with so far.

'AT&T long-distance operator. What is the number you're calling?'

'It's to the UK. My credit card doesn't seem to be working, but I have some change . . .' I scrabbled at the coins in the tray, '. . . about two dollars in quarters and dimes.'

'Do you have an AT&T card?'

'No. Can't I get even a minute to England with two dollars?'

'Sure. Dial 011 then 44, then the number without the leading zero.'

'I tried that, and it didn't work.'

'Dial first, then feed in the coins when you connect.'

'OK, I'll try again.'

'Thank you for calling AT&T.'

I put the phone down and dial. I'm not given a chance to feed any coins in. *That number is invalid*, says the voice. *That number is invalid*.

'No it bloody isn't!' I shout back. The queue behind me shuffles uneasily. Out of the corner of my eye I catch sight of my watch. 12.26.

Away from home, Alan never dials a call direct; he uses a freephone number and the call is billed later. His card has been propped against one of the bedside lamps all week, and in my head I can hear the tune the keypad plays as he taps the digits in.

Well, toll-free numbers begin 1-800. I close my eyes and behind the darkness I watch a grainy image form on the back of my eyelids. 'Come on!' I tell myself. 'You can do party tricks with numbers, so put it to some use! Start by visualizing the colours; 1-800 is cold blues and earth colours – what's next?'

'Excuse me, ma'am.'

I jump, and the keys jiggle.

'If you're not gonna use the phone, I'd like to make a call.'

'Sorry, but I'm trying to remember the number.'

'If I could just . . .'

'I'm sorry, but this is an emergency. Please.'

He steps reluctantly aside, but he's taken with him my developing image of Alan's card. I waste a minute or so chafing. Then I hear a ballad singing itself in my head: 'Autumn Leaves'. Johnny Mercer. The phone number is the colour of autumn. I can hear beech woods crisp with bronze sixes;

rich, mulchy eights. Birches and their golden fives.

'Autumn Leaves' . . .

I've got it. 1-800-868-5566.

The voice that trills in my ear is British; relief and comfort seep through my bones. The voice of home. This is something deep in the human psyche.

I look at my watch. 12.31. At home it's 5.31 p.m.

The chirpy sound of the British double-ringing tone. Then: 'You're through to the voicemail of Dr Alan Muller. I will be out of the office . . .'

I press the star key to get Emma. Pause, then Emma comes on the line, and I'm so relieved tears course down my cheeks.

'Emma! This is Annie, Alan's wife. I know this must sound peculiar, but . . .'

'. . . not at my desk, but if you leave a message after the . . .'

'NO!'

Behind me, respectable figures strung with plastic name badges shuffle and huff.

'Oh please no!'

I slam the phone back into the cradle, whiplashing its metal cord, and thump my hand against the chrome, rattling its silly grinning metal teeth. A male voice appears at my ear, a voice full of uniform.

'This phone is property of the phone company, ma'am. And there is a line behind you waiting to use it!'

The switchboard! I can try Alan's company switchboard. I grab the receiver again, and attempt to feed in the digits once more.

'Ma'am,' says the uniform, 'you have been ten minutes trying different numbers and not getting through. We would really appreciate it if you would go sort out your difficulties and let someone else in line make their call!'

'Please!' I plead, trying to tap numbers in at the same time, which I can't, because I've never been able to do two things at once. 'I have to phone the UK before they close for business!'

His voice is messing it all up, dragging hostile colours across the palette – fat figure threes waddle in with their rusty reds. Swaggering green sevens. *Think keyboard patterns, instead!* What did my fingers do last time? OK. I've got it.

'You're through to the voicemail of Dr . . .'

At the end of his message, Alan always tells the caller to press 0 to return to the switchboard. I press 0.

'American BioTechnologies, good evening. Christine speaking, how may . . .'

Oh, for God's sake! 'This is Dr Muller's wife. I want Emma Dobson. Have I missed her?'

'Oh, hello, Mrs Muller. This is Christine. We have met, actually.'

'*Have I missed Emma?*'

'By about two minutes, Mrs Muller.'

'Damn and sod!'

'You can catch her in the morning. She's usually in by 8.30.'

'In fact, I'm trying to get hold of anyone who might know my husband's cellphone number. I know this sounds silly, but . . .'

'Well, I can give you the number, Mrs Muller.'

'No, he's changed it. This one . . .'

'I've got all the medical directors' numbers, up to date. Hold on. Here we are. It's . . .'

I don't carry pens, I don't carry paper and I'm far too shaken to start memorizing more bloody numbers. But I have make-up, and there's the perforated metal casing around this godforsaken phone.

'Sorry, Christine, could you start again?'

The soft brown of my eyebrow pencil gives out after the first six digits. I get the last ones down by ruining my lipstick just milliseconds before the uniform reappears.

'Ma'am, you cannot do this! You cannot deface this property!'

'Thank you, Christine. Bye.'

Now dial the new number. Don't listen to the man in the uniform. A ringing tone.

'Alan Muller.'

'*Alan?*'

'Annie?'

'Oh God, oh God, Alan! I'm here. I'm in the Javits Center.'

'What's happened?'

'No, it isn't that kind of emergency. Nobody's ill. But please, please will you come over?'

'Where are you?'

'God knows! There are phones and plate-glass, you can look down on hundreds of exhibition stands . . .'

'I'm at the Message Center.'

'Well, if you go up some stairs you'll find a uniformed official tugging at the sleeve of a woman in candy stripes . . .'

'Jesus, Annie!'

Within seconds Alan was at my elbow. I put down the phone and my eyes absorbed the look on his face. I ran a hand distractedly through my hair, and several grips went pinging across the floor.

'So what's the problem?'

'Look, it won't sound much. But it is.'

'OK, shoot.'

'You'll have to bear with me.' I screwed my fists into a ball, digging my bitten nails into the palms as though squeezing the words out. 'Listen. Do you remember my telling you that when Babette and I were ten, there was a series of murders in our village?'

'Sure.'

249

'It's about that, sort of.'

In the event, I managed to give him a fairly coherent account.

'I can't let her tear the album apart like that,' I finished up. 'It will literally break my heart. I think . . . I think there's a great deal of jealousy, Alan. I think she resents me to the point of malice.'

If Alan were to dismiss the whole thing, I wasn't sure what I would do. But he didn't; he didn't even correct my use of 'literally'.

'You want me to talk to her?'

'Please.'

'OK, I'll call her up.' Alan made a gesture at my hair. 'Annie, could you try to look a little more . . . in control?'

He had a point. For the first time since I'd joined that phone queue, the conference around me made itself felt, the businesslike buzz, the air of collective composure. I could guess how I appeared in my odd-ball clothes, the crazed look in my eyes, my hair windswept so that it resembled something you'd stuff a mattress with.

'Alan, hi!'

'Ah, Dr Stanowitz. Catch up with you later.'

Alan fished a comb from his pocket, and indicated the restrooms.

Re-emerging, I found my husband in conversation with a tall, tanned figure in a business suit. I fretted quietly at Alan's side while this acquaintance kept letting his eyes slip across to me. The name badge identified him as 'I. Eggman'. The Walrus lives on.

'My wife, Annie,' Alan finally admitted.

'Pleased to meet you, Annie.'

'Would you excuse me a moment?' Alan ushered me to one side with a hand under my elbow.

'Did you get hold of Aunt Margo?'

'No. Will you please calm down! I got Ellie.' Ellie was the 'housekeeper', which conjures images of Mrs

Danvers but actually meant the daily help – there was only one Mrs Danvers in that apartment. 'I left a message for her to call me.'

'Right.'

'It's the best I can do.'

'Yes. Thank you.' And then, 'Did Ellie say where she was?'

'Shopping.'

'Shopping.'

'Well, that's good, isn't it? Means she isn't destroying photo albums.'

'No, she didn't take the album home. She left a deposit with the shop, to pick it up later.'

'So why don't you go back there now and buy it? Tell the guy it's a present from me.'

'Can you lend me some money? My credit card won't swipe.'

'How much?'

'Three hundred.'

'*Three hundred bucks?*'

'Fifty, then, for cabs.'

He flicked through his wallet. 'Thirty. The store can imprint your card.' And then, 'Look, Aunt Margo *will* return my call.'

'But won't you be in lectures or whatever with your phone switched off?'

'I'll be out by four thirty. Annie, this is the best I can do!'

'I know. Thanks. I'll be going.'

When you are in love with someone else, I reminded myself, it is all too easy . . . Alan had not belittled my story, but got straight onto the case. What more could he do? Well, he could nip out of his meeting every half hour and try Aunt Margo's number again. That's what Daniel would do for me, I thought, and hated myself for it. And so will Alan perhaps, I said aloud. Perhaps he will do exactly that.

* * *

Like many people with strong synaesthesia, I don't cope well with 3-D problems, telling left from right, following maps, folding ironing boards and deckchairs, finding my way around. Not until I was slamming the door and sliding across the cab seat did I realize that I'd never noted the name of the street off Bleeker, and couldn't remember which end it was. I asked the driver to drop me at Washington Square, hoping that I could retrace our earlier steps. This time, my sense of direction led me into Chelsea before I realized I was wrong, and when, eventually, I did get back to Larry's shop, it was from random foraging.

'Hello, again.'

'Well, hi!'

'Has Miss Muller been back? I'm rather hoping to forestall her. My husband would like to buy that photograph album as a surprise. Am I too late?'

'Oh, well. That's a shame, now.'

Damn. Damn everything. She's beaten me to it.

'Miss Muller phoned a half hour ago to say she'd be back this afternoon, and not to let anybody else make the purchase.' His smile was strained. 'I am *so* sorry, but you see, I can't go against her wishes. Miss Muller is such an old customer . . . I mean *regular* customer, of course.'

'Of course. Well, I'll explain to my husband. Maybe we can find something else for her.'

Larry didn't add that I was welcome to look around the store for a suitable gift; he hadn't believed a word I'd said.

It is my hair that people remember me by. Wrap it in a scarf, and wash off the make-up so that my white-lashed features retreat into the hinterland of my face (and change out of my candy stripes), and only my best friend would recognize me.

I was back. I loitered on the street until some other customers entered the shop. OK *now*. In through the electronic whoop of the door.

There was no sign of Larry. I could see a family browsing through some 1970s retro junk, under the guidance of a young man in a cravat. After a brief exchange – 'Need any help, ma'am?' 'No thanks, just looking!' – he left me to myself. *Mustn't* rush it. Aunt Margo and I had seen Larry put the album tenderly into the drawer of a desk, a fancy French affair with marquetry and clawed feet. Clearly it was his work desk; little piles of receipts sat on its leather inlay, squashed by crystal paperweights. Would Larry lock his desk drawers? Above my head tinkled a dozen chandeliers. I feigned interest in them.

Mustn't rush and bungle it, but on the other hand mustn't dither; either these customers would make a purchase, and the cravat man would be over here to process it, or they wouldn't, and he'd turn his attention to me. Pull the drawer gently and don't hesitate, even if it creaks. NOW.

The drawer flowed out as though on oiled rails. He was a decent carpenter, whoever made this desk. Open, and then shut.

'Be back later!' I called lazily in my best American accent. I was out through the door and onto the sidewalk, with Mrs Clitheroe's photograph album under my black sloppy joe.

'Good of you to come downtown,' said the male partner of the duo, whose name was Kaplan. 'We'd've gladly met you at your hotel.'

'Thanks, but this is fine,' Alan replied. To Alan, the idea of police officers turning up at our hotel was unthinkable, though personally I would have felt more secure if they had – to search our room and find it innocent. There was also something in me that would

have been interested to see this heavily built policeman, in his NYPD blue, perching on the edge of a
dressing table. Here in the precinct, Alan was sitting
back in the chair beside me, amid the serried ranks of
filing cabinets and walls of battleship grey, stretching
out his long legs in their formal suit and tasselled
brogues with all the apparent confidence of an owner-
occupier. But these were police officers and, like me,
they would have noticed the taut skin around his jaw-
line, the way he kept clearing his throat, the tiny tic that
danced in the muscle of Alan's cheek.

Guttural accents from outside the door. 'I told ya,
Joe! You pay me the seven fifty you owe, and I'm back
on your case!'

'But it's a fuckin' frame, man! I can't fight a frame
without a fuckin' lawyer!'

'And I ain't a fuckin' charity! Pay me the seven fifty
and you got me back on your side.'

Kaplan shut the door on the voices, which turned
their volume down, but didn't shut them up completely. Alan's eyes focused on infinity. Anathema to
him, all of it. That jumping muscle was a mani-
festation of Alan's skin crawling.

'You understand, sir, that we do have to pursue this.
The owner's story is that your wife and the other lady,
your aunt you say, had a dispute. It seems that your
wife here felt she had a claim on the album because
she knew it years ago in England, and your aunt was
set on keeping it for herself and chopping it about.'

'My understanding,' corrected Alan, 'is that there
was no question of chopping it about. My aunt only
wanted to remove some old photos. And I had already
agreed to talk her out of doing even that.'

'Agreed? Agreed to who?'

Alan hesitated – had he been wrong-footed? I
thought it was time to chip in.

'I contacted my husband, officer, and he immediately

offered to sort it out. Miss Muller would have listened to his advice – to be frank, she hangs on my husband's every word.' Alan shifted infinitesimally in the hard little seat. 'So you see, I had no motive, no reason to commit a crime in order to keep the album from her.'

'Exactly,' added Alan.

'Yet you did return to the store, ma'am, and tried to buy it yourself.'

We paused. You should never hesitate during interrogation.

I said, 'That was my husband's suggestion, hoping to forestall any embarrassment. Nothing more.'

'Meanwhile Miss Muller had already called up the store and instructed them not to let you have it.'

Alan glanced at me; he hadn't known about that bit.

'Is that accurate?' probed officer Kaplan.

'My husband hadn't yet talked to her. We were in no doubt that the problem would vanish the moment he got her on the phone,' I improvised. I knew I shouldn't volunteer anything, but I added, more to convince Alan than anything else, 'You are very welcome to search my things at the hotel, if you wish.'

He wouldn't *like* it, but it might convince him.

'Thank you, ma'am, but for the present we're just trying to sort out the details.'

Throughout our conversation, Kaplan's colleague hadn't moved. She leaned elegantly against the wall, dark-complexioned, Hispanic, and very striking. Alan hadn't once turned his head for a furtive glance, and I wondered whether he was actually in too deep a state of revulsion even to notice her. Kaplan continued.

'I wonder, ma'am, whether you'd mind filling in some of the background for me.'

'By all means.'

'This album, the proprietor of the store told us you said there was a murder behind the story. Would you mind telling me about that?'

Larry must have told them that I'd talked emotionally about never getting over the loss of Mrs Clitheroe, and how the album was woven into my life. These police officers probably believed that if I recounted the story I'd break down in tears and make myself vulnerable. The trouble was, they were probably right.

'In 1965, a neighbour of ours, a Mrs Clitheroe, was found murdered in her house. We lived in a quiet village, very ordinary and dull, so this was rather traumatic for everyone.'

'And the album?'

'It was hers. We – the children, I mean – used to visit Mrs Clitheroe, and we would sometimes look through it.'

'Police get the killer?'

'They got a confession, but he never came to trial.'

'Why was that?'

I cleared my throat. On the other side of the door, a voice screamed: 'I don't *do* crack, you hear me? You fuckin' hear me, you fuckin' assholes? I do *not* do crack!'

'He died,' I said, 'in a police station. Hanged himself.'

My voice fractured, and Alan intercepted with 'I don't see how this is relevant. Can we move back to the present situation?'

'Sure. In fact, I think that's all for today. I'll just ask you to wait for the commotion to die down,' indicating the screamer, 'and you can go home momentarily.'

We both scrambled to our feet, looking surprised.

Alan said with deliberation, 'No doubt you have considered that the object was easily portable and therefore not problematic for any casual thief to steal?'

He had never learned to deal comfortably with leave-taking, nor to cope well with the social aspects of what he called 'unstructured situations'. There was always a danger that Alan would corner himself into making a summing-up speech.

'Yes, sir,' responded Kaplan, 'but not easily *visible* to a casual thief, inside the closed drawer of the owner's desk.'

Outside, the hullabaloo had moved on. Distant protestations could be heard ringing through a corridor in the background somewhere.

'OK, looks like it's safe for you folks to leave.'

'Thank you,' I said to them, in general valediction.

'You're welcome,' said Kaplan, holding the door open for us.

Alan gave a goodbye nod.

'Oh, before you go,' Kaplan casually sidestepped so that he was astride the threshold. 'I believe Officer Olivares has just one question.'

Alan looked quizzically around him for an Officer Olivares, so I'd been right.

'Could you tell me,' she asked, 'what were the contents of the package you handed in at the FedEx office of your hotel yesterday afternoon?'

My throat dried.

'The delivery address,' she flicked through a notepad, 'was given as 15 Walpole Road, Ealing, London W5 5ML, United Kingdom. Package weighed six pounds and was marked up as "Documents – no commercial value".' She looked up from her notebook. ' "Origin, UK".'

I knew that my face blanched and then flamed. Had the police intercepted it? Was Mrs Clitheroe's photograph album sitting on a police officer's desk on the other side of the wall? If so, they'd got me, no matter what. Bluff it! said my head. Bluff the pair of them.

'Manuscripts,' I said. 'From the Music Exchange, and the Library and Museum of the Performing Arts at Lincoln Center. I'm a musician.'

' "Origin, UK"?', she quoted again.

'Yes. Well, you see, it was British music, mostly. Couldn't get hold of it at home for love nor money.'

257

'Six pounds of British music. Well, I'm glad New York was helpful in that respect.'

'Yes. Thank you.'

'You're welcome.'

Kaplan let us out of the door, and Alan and I walked through the hallway and out into the crackling light of the afternoon, both of us looking directly ahead.

In the taxi back to the hotel, I glanced sideways at Alan's jaw-line, the unhealthy patches of grey where the blood had ebbed. Several times I opened my mouth to frame some species of apology, but I knew that anything I said would sound worse than silence, so I shut up and we rode uptown through the choked traffic without a single word to each other.

THE PAST

25

The passing of August into September presaged a sea change – it meant Back to School. Every year, as the long summer holiday ebbed away from us like a retreating tide, my parents would unlock the empty Victorian buildings and prepare them for the influx that would shortly rip through their ponderous calm. I sometimes went along too, depending on how bored I was, which in turn depended on whether Babette was out somewhere with Auntie Rene. On this particular morning, the day after Mrs Clitheroe's funeral, neither of us could work up any enthusiasm for moping about the village by ourselves; after some indecisive toing and froing, we trailed along with my parents on the explicit promise that we wouldn't go haring round the echoing classrooms like a couple of hooligans, or make nuisances of ourselves to the piano tuner.

It was the piano tuner who swung the balance for us. Mr Micklewhite, a Muningstock man, came every September – though as soon as the radiators were turned on, the piano would meander out of tune again, so that he would invariably have to return at Christmas. Mr Micklewhite had been blind from birth, and tapped his way efficiently through his benighted world with a white cane and highly developed sense of hearing, though he was deaf to my advocacy about getting a guide dog. He lived with his sister, who kept him conventionally dressed and barbered, but his movements were gauche and his eyes wobbled. With my predilection for people on the margins of Muningstock society, I loved and admired him. I'd once coerced Babette into an experiment in which we tapped our way to school with blindfolds and the longest sticks we could muster out of the woods. Yelled at by passers-by, we were finally unblinded by a furious motorist who left skid marks across Mountnessing Road.

The boys called Mr Micklewhite Blind Pugh, which I knew was rude, and also Mick the Stick, which I didn't, and which I innocently repeated once at home, under the impression that it belonged to the same school of nicknames as my father's legendary friends from his homeland – Jones the Post and Evans the Milk.

On this September morning, Babette and I were making ourselves useful by carrying my father's photographs, bound for the walls of the assembly hall. Babette was entrusted with colour prints of our matchbox model on its pedestal of glory inside the New York City pavilion of the World's Fair, while I loped along beside her toting a black and white snap of my father standing next to Mayor Wagner, orating. It was another warm, late-summer day, but because of my sudden focus on school, I sensed tangs of autumn. Neighbours' gardens wore an end of season look, the roses blowsy, overblown. We passed the Mortons', in whose

260

chapped driveway the man of the house proudly buffed his E-type Jag. All the surrounding gardens were enriched by the frothy blossom of the Mortons' Russian vine, which had snaked its way out of their inchoate jungle with designs on throttling the entire neighbourhood; heavy swags of vine lolled complacently across trees, gutters and telegraph wires, like conquering heroes sated from looting the dead.

We had just passed Melena Watson's bungalow when a car pulled up abruptly and the occupants floundered out with much slamming of doors, jackets flapping like bats. The car was a Morris Minor.

'Hello, Horace, Doris!' exclaimed my mother.

'Dai, Myrtle – well met!' Horace strode at them, breathy and dishevelled. His hair seemed to be having a Brylcreem crisis; coppery auburn strands stuck up at improbable angles like pick-a-sticks. 'Actually, this is extremely fortuitous.'

'We're in a bit of a rush this morning,' responded my father hurriedly, anxious to get into school before Mr Micklewhite turned up. He was not a patient individual, and had been known to stand in the front gardens of tardy piano owners, swearing a blue streak and rapping his white stick against the paintwork of their front doors.

'It will just take a minute. It's . . . I'm sorry to say it's necessary, Dai.'

My parents looked at him quizzically. Horace indicated his wife, whose aristocratic features wrinkled apologetically as she drew my parents to one side. When they turned their attention to her, Uncle Horace turned his to Babette, always his favourite, giving us a hearty 'Well, hello, girls' that was suspicious in the extreme, and launching into an ill-prepared monologue about the Harvest Festival. Babette and I leaned away from him, angling towards the other three like ships' figureheads. Odd dribbles of their conversation reached us in counterpoint to Horace's ruthless prattle.

'. . . to the police . . .' I heard Auntie Doris say, '. . . that it was he who killed her . . .'

My father said something, but it was submerged beneath Uncle Horace's talk of wheatsheaves.

'. . . his own shoelaces . . .' said Doris.

'Oh Doris, no!' My mother. 'This is terrible!'

Killed her? So this must be Old Ollie. But *shoelaces*?

'. . . corn dollies around the altar, and tins of baked beans forming a cross . . .'

'. . . whether he was in custody.'

Custardy?

'. . . on jelly and cup-cakes provided by the Mothers' Union.'

'. . . couldn't live with the guilt . . .'

'But to hang himself!'

Hot and cold, I broke away from Uncle Horace and threw myself into the conspiratorial knot.

'*Is Old Ollie dead?*'

They stopped talking.

'Is it Old Ollie that's dead? Is it?' My fault, of course. My fault, my fault.

'Annie.' This was my father.

'She said about the murder and he hanged himself!'

'Annie-*fach*!'

'Annie, dear . . .' Auntie Doris.

'*OLD OLLIE'S DEAD!*'

'You'd better take her home, Myrtle.'

'Home?! I've a full day's work to get through in school. Annie, be quiet, stop this squealing!'

'*O-llie!*'

'Well, at least get her indoors *somewhere*.'

'Behave yourself! I've never heard such a noise!'

I wasn't actually frog-marched to school, but I was swept along, squawking like a toucan, in a maternal grip that wasn't as concerned as it

262

might have been about the distribution of my eczema.

'You promised Daddy and me that you'd stop letting your imagination run away with you.'

'She said Ollie's hanged himself!'

'You shouldn't be listening in on grown-ups' conversations.'

And so it went. In the dwindling distance, I could hear the Frobishers taking solemn leave of my father, Horace's light frame shuffling distractedly from foot to foot while contriving to maintain his hearty mannerisms, Doris's ebony hank of hair flopping from its well-bred restraints, and her jacket collar tucked in all wrong. She was stooping down to talk to Babette with a level gaze and light touch that abruptly put me in mind of Mrs Clitheroe.

I quietened somewhat once my mother had unlocked the school, and we were through the little porch and into the vacant corridor with its quelling air of melancholy, its untenanted coat pegs, the bare fuzz of its notice board, the indelible prints of tiny hands on its paintwork of institutional green. Ollie once said that that colour had a special name; it was called ganggreen. The thought of Ollie set me off again.

My mother, who even I could see had been rendered pale and unsettled by the Frobishers' tidings, was trying her own brand of distraction technique on me, demanding that I redirect my energies towards the piano; it needed to be disrobed of its dustsheet for a start, and unlidded. I could begin by fetching the key from the staffroom cupboard. I was refusing to co-operate when the door opened to my father and, thankfully, Babette.

'Myrtle, you can hear the girl crying from the Breeden Road!'

'And that's my fault, is it?'

'Well, can't you find something to take her mind off it?'

'And what do you suggest, Dai? She's your daughter, too.'

Babette, recognizing that this sort of parental volleying can go on indefinitely, decided to break the cycle.

'Sir,' she began, this being school, 'can we go upstairs and unlock your office and throw the windows open to give the place an airing?'

He turned gratefully to her. 'A good idea, Babette. Annie – you can get my office key from the staffroom cupboard and go upstairs with Babette.'

My mother fished from her handbag the key to the cupboard itself, the key of keys, and handed it over. 'And don't lose it,' she told me.

'And when you get up there, Annie-*fach*, don't take anything off my desk, or mess about with the inkwell. Are you listening?'

'Yes, sir.'

'Babette, you can bring me down the building maintenance ledger from the middle desk drawer.'

'Yes, sir. Come on, Annie.'

We were across the ringing wooden floor and out through a door at the back of the hall into a dim vestibule smelling hotly of lino. Other doors led variously into the staff lavatory, the staffroom itself and outside to a walled garden. A tight staircase with tiny, triangular treads corkscrewed upwards to my father's office, whose ceiling sloped under the eaves. As the door to the hall closed behind us, I started on Babette.

'Did you hear anything?'

'Why was you going on about Old Ollie? It weren't him, Annie.'

'What were they saying?'

'It was about the police station, and someone being dead.'

'Killed himself.'

'But I didn't hear who. They was whispering.'

'Then you don't know it wasn't Ollie!'

'It wouldn't of, Annie. He wouldn't be up the police station.'

'But someone's dead who was accused of the murder.'

'Hung himself with his own shoelaces.'

I stopped midstream and considered this. 'No, Babette. They wouldn't work.'

'Yes they would. Lorraine's friend's dad did it with shoelaces when he went bust and they couldn't pay their hire purchase.'

'Shoelaces?'

'Lorraine's friend's dad's neck was all cut in where he'd hung from them, Lorraine said.'

I stood, appalled, while Babette composedly took the key from my loose fist and opened up the cupboard in the staffroom with its row upon row of keys, hooked and tinkling, and labelled by my mother's neat hand.

'Annie, you know what?'

'What?'

'When Mr Micklewhite gets here to tune the piano, I bet he'll know who it was did hisself in. He always knows everythink – it's probably 'cos he's had his ears trained.'

We scaled the dingy staircase and unlocked my father's office door. Inside was even hotter and smelled of nothing so much as prolonged absence.

'I'll get that book for sir, and if Mr Micklewhite has turned up, we'll both go back down.'

She yanked open the casement window to the fresh air, and collected from my father's desk a red exercise book with 'Maintenance Ledger' printed across the cover. Hearing her small feet tippety-tipping down the stairs, I wandered dissatisfied over to the window.

Across the Breeden Road, agricultural land stretched to the horizon: hedges and fields; a spinney;

fields and hedges. The farmland was ploughed and harrowed into alternating ribbons of coffee and chocolate that looped back on themselves at the edges. September. I had known this view all my life. Standing here now, I could visualize the flavescence of coming autumn; the landscape turning to that rich mix of muted tones that resembled my mother's best tweeds. I could hear school in midterm, the assembly hall ringing with dinnertime. And out of nowhere came my first recognition that this was not for ever; this time next year I would be on my way to secondary school, never again to stand for morning assembly in that chalk-dusty hall with its pitch roof and oak floor, its high windows and railed gallery, with Daddy playing the piano and Mummy standing at the gallery steps.

My reverie was interrupted by a cry, like a ghostly voice from the empty landscape.

'U or ah! U or ah!'

I stopped breathing. Silence. Then I heard it again, a sorrowful ululation from beyond the harrowed fields, as though howling down the wind from a cold nether-world of true rags and bones.

'*BABETTE!*'

I was across my father's office, out of the door and onto the stairs. Halfway down, I tripped heavily, and thumped on my bottom from stair to stair onto the lino below.

'Babette!'

A door slammed. 'Annie, what you done?!'

'I heard Old Ollie. He was moaning like a ghost. Oh Babette, he's haunting me.'

'What?'

'In the fields upstairs. It's because of me and the toga in Mrs Clitheroe's bathroom window,' I ranted, for-getting that Babette still knew nothing of the toga and the bathroom window, forgetting that Dorothea had

266

stopped me telling her. 'And now he's dead and he's haunting me!'

I had picked myself up and was scrabbling slippily at the stairs, getting nowhere, like a hamster on a wheel.

'He's *not* dead! Listen, I been talking to Mr Micklewhite. It weren't nothing to do with Old Ollie, it was Mr Clitheroe. He's hung hisself.'

That stopped me. I could hear the piano now, one single struck note, B flat or thereabouts, tolling bell-like through the assembly hall. I heard the same note struck again, and then the *wa-wa* of Mr Micklewhite bending it in and out of pitch.

'It was Mr Clitheroe, Annie,' she said again, 'he's done hisself in up the nick.'

I stared at Babette, and pointed woozily upwards, in a gesture meant to indicate my father's office window, or the fields, or the ferryman across the River Styx, perhaps. 'But I *heard* Ollie, Babette.'

'So? You can hear me, but it don't mean I've kicked the bucket!'

I continued to look baffled.

'It's Wednesday,' Babette went on, 'and he's out with his horse and cart.'

We each seemed to be unable to understand a word the other said. In an effort to break the deadlock, Babette reopened the door behind her. 'Let's go and talk to Mr Micklewhite,' she advised. 'He can tell you what he told me.'

I followed her, rubbing my behind, which was more than conventionally sore, as I'd landed with a wallop on a particularly scaly patch of eczema. There was Mr Micklewhite in one of his ungainly stances, like a propped up Penny-for-the-Guy in front of our stripped piano, much of its wooden casing having been peeled off and inclined against a radiator. His head was cocked towards the vibrating strings like the dog on His Master's Voice. Babette, always more discreet than I, tiptoed in his direction, so it was only my own footsteps that were intrusive enough to wind him up.

'Annie Cradock!' he roared in instant recognition. 'How many times have I told you not to come clodhopping about in here when I'm working?'

'Sorry, Mr Micklewhite.'

'Stamping up and down like a baby elephant – I can't hear myself think.'

The angry *twang* of B natural above middle C.

'Mr Micklewhite, we know we're not supposed to disturb you, but please may I ask you something?'

He turned in my general direction, his flickery eyes blatting at the wall beyond my left shoulder. These castigations were a ritual to be plugged away at before we could go ahead with the most benign query – why there were more piano strings than notes, how the hammers achieved that diddy bounce, what made him be born blind, and wouldn't he rather have a nice guide dog, a golden Labrador, for instance.

'What I wondered, Mr Micklewhite . . . Babette just told me you know about this person who killed himself up the police station. *In* the police station,' I corrected myself, blocking a hole he might otherwise have darted through. Expecting to enter the next phase of sarcasm, I was not ready for his reply:

'Good riddance to bad rubbish!' accompanied by a violent mime of spitting across the floor.

Shocked, I followed the imaginary gob to its imaginary landing place, sizzling on the pitted oak floorboards.

'What rubbish, Mr Micklewhite?'

'Babette Lucas!' he snapped. 'You already bin here once, bothering the life out of me about it. *You* tell her.'

'It was Mr Clitheroe, Annie,' Babette repeated dutifully.

'And good riddance!' declared Mr Micklewhite again. 'That's what the whole village is saying. Best thing he could've done, hung himself.'

'But why?' It wasn't so much horrific as unimaginable. Leonard Clitheroe wasn't a man of despair; he was an abrupt, angry sort of person, positively barking with life.

'It was guilt, girl. Couldn't live with himself after what he done to his poor wife.'

'You mean, he killed Mrs Clitheroe?'

'Confessed to it. Killed her with the cleaver she kept in the kitchen for chopping up sheep's heads for his tea.'

Pool of blood and brains. Skull to a pulp with a meat-axe.

'He made out they'd been burgled, so as the coppers would think it was them gyppos again, like the caravan robbery.'

'Like that Saturday night over the travellers' camp,' Babette annotated for me, as though she'd been appointed as a sort of amanuensis.

'I've known Mrs Clitheroe ever since they moved up Bluebell Crescent,' he continued. 'Tuned that Bechstein upright of hers spring and autumn. She was a lady. There's not a decent-minded man in Muningstock wouldn't've strung her killer up with his own hands, and that's the truth. There isn't a decent man that isn't glad the swine spared them the trouble.'

He bonged the keyboard with thick, spatulate fingers that didn't look as though they belonged to a pianist, though I knew he was even better than Mrs Clitheroe. Then an irritable wrench to C natural. The note whined.

'A lady like that done in for money. Money!'

'But she didn't have any money,' I objected. 'They were always rowing about it.'

'He took insurance out on her life, the mingy sod.

Got her to innocently sign her name to it, never knowing that it was her own death warrant.'

'I didn't know you could kill a person and get paid for it,' I said pitifully. 'And anyway, the police think Old Ollie did it, because Mrs Maxwell said she saw him climbing in Mrs Clitheroe's bathroom window.'

'Gina Maxwell!' snorted Mr Micklewhite, in exactly the same tone that Uncle Frank had used that night in the garden. 'Gina Maxwell's as thick as pig shit. *I'd* be more bloody use as an eyewitness than she would.'

'Yes,' I conceded, 'but she *did* tell the police and they arrested Old Ollie!'

'Nah, they never believed it was the gyppo, girl, just took him in for a bit, to check it out. And then they found out about the insurance, and picked up Leonard for questioning.'

I thought of the scene in Bon Marché, the tight whispering of those women.

'They arrested him?'

'Now that time it *should* have been arrest; if the coppers'd had any sense they'd've locked him up and thrown away the key. But that stupid bald sod that's in charge let him go home. Well I ask you, *let him go home!*' The last statement was underlined by another gesture of gobbing over the floor, which I interpreted as fair comment on DI Lilliput.

'So why was Mr Clitheroe in the police station committing suicide?'

Babette once more. 'He give hisself up yesterday, Annie, after the funeral.'

'That's right. And when they left him alone in the nick, he took his braces off and hung hisself from the light fitting.'

Braces? I leapt upon the inconsistency with all the energy of an investigating officer detecting a crack in an alibi. 'But Auntie Doris said shoelaces! She said!'

270

'Shoelaces, braces, what's it matter? He's a goner, Annie. Hanging was too good for him.'

Why did everything keep going back to hanging? 'I loved Jenny Clitheroe. I wish they'd hang him.' I could see Leonard in my mind's eye – stiff-jointed, angry, thumping a hand on the seaside donkey mural in Mrs Maxwell's malodorous room. 'Someone was in my lounge yesterday, frigging around with that photo album, and I want to know if they saw something they weren't meant to, and I want to know what they've told the police . . .'

As Mr Micklewhite's piano strings tolled and warped, my thoughts slid in and out of tune in their wake. I could see Mrs Maxwell leaning on the door-jamb of Mrs Clitheroe's French windows, watching the scene with Uncle Horace. Babette's words again: 'She'll tell him. And when she does, he'll kill her.'

Mr Micklewhite had stopped donging at the keyboard. He straightened up and looked intently at where he thought I was. 'Well, you asked me,' he summed up, 'and I reckon you got your money's worth. Now scoot off, the pair of yous, and leave me in peace.'

'Yes, Mr Micklewhite.'

'Thank you, Mr Micklewhite.'

'And when I say scoot, I mean right out of my way. I don't want yous two clattering down them stairs like you was doing a while back.'

With a promise not to fall down any more stairs within his hearing, we scooted as far as we could without running up against my parents, who would have issued similar instructions.

A country school, we were blessed with several acres of ground, some of it wooded, though with each succeeding year, the woods were thinned out and impelled back towards the perimeter in an effort to limit the capers that went on in them, though the only caper I'd ever got up to in the woods was to cry over the tiny lollipop-stick crosses that marked the passing of yet another school gerbil.

The greenery that Babette and I now threw ourselves onto was different from the threadbare playing field of July, with its sports day bunting and patches of acid yellow. Unshorn as yet, the grass had perked up during its convalescence, and dandelions twinkled in its depths. Babette and I rolled on it, pulled it up by the roots, and practised whistling through the blades.

Mr Clitheroe had killed Mrs Clitheroe and taken his own life by hanging from a shoelace. It was just too unlikely. They were only words. Meanwhile, Old Ollie wasn't dead and wasn't in prison, and the bad conscience that had intermittently discoloured my waking hours like a sickly orange cast gently dispersed in the verdant air. And the bathroom window wouldn't matter any more. Surely Lilliput could never want me again now, with the murder solved and the photo album back in his possession via that Judas, Lorraine.

'We should of bought our tennis rackets,' Babette pointed out. They'd been languishing in our bedrooms since the frenzy of Wimbledon fortnight.

'We could get a ball, though,' I reasoned, 'from the sports cupboard. You've still got the other key.'

It was an attractive concept, knocking a ball about over this expanse of meadow. We got up and crept back to the staffroom via the assembly hall ('Just on an errand for sir, Mr Micklewhite!'). Back out again with the appropriate key, we were soon down the corridor and into the infants' cloakroom, inside whose secure walls the sports cupboard was locked for the holidays. Amid the cloakroom's titchy basins, the rows of tiny pegs on the wall at dwarf height and the stack of infants' chairs, I loomed, gangling. I could see myself at five years old, hurrying in from the winter play-ground to hold my frozen hands, the colour of road-kill, under these hot taps. And I could *hear* the pain ringing through my raw skin as the heat penetrated.

'Tennis balls?' suggested Babette from the open cupboard, her voice echoing inside the clangy doors. 'Or the netball?'

'The netball would be nice,' I decided, and then caught the whiff of a pile of fragrant plimsolls. 'Hang on a minute . . . don't shut the doors.'

I pulled one of the shoes from the shelf, starting an avalanche. As plimsolls bounced and rolled around our feet, I fished about me, setting them rightways up like someone rescuing overturned turtles. Then I rooted through the wriggly heap for a reasonable specimen without too many knots and snarls to its bootlaces, and started tugging on them with my bitten fingers.

'What you doing? You'll have Mr Micklewhite at us about the noise.'

'I just want to see . . .'

When you don't have fingernails, it is painful to fiddle with knotted strings. My nail beds were raw and inflamed. 'I'm trying to get a lace out.'

Babette scanned the spreading puddle of rubber and canvas. 'This one's all right.' She fastidiously tweaked a white lace from its eyelets. 'What do you want it for?'

'I want to see how somebody can hang themselves with one.'

'Oh, *Annie!*'

Unravelled, the bootlace looked innocent enough, its ends shiny as though dipped into cream.

'I don't see how Mr Clitheroe could've,' I explained.

'Well, you're not tying one round my neck, Annie Cradock!'

'Of course not! Who do you think I am – Dorothea?'

With the shoelace draped casually around my own neck, I dragged the stack of infants' chairs across the floor to the door we'd entered through. This was tall, teacher-sized, and the interlocked baby-chairs gave me a platform just high enough to set the top of my head level with the huge metal damper that bulged from the lintel with its jutting metal V, like some hideous prosthesis.

'Annie, what you doing?'

'It's all right, I'm only . . .'

I hopped onto the stack and deliberately gave it a wobble. Good; the chairs would be stable enough to bear my weight until I came to kick them away. I held up the lace from the plimsoll and it hung from my fingers like a trickle of dirty milk. Admittedly it was longer than in my mind's eye, but long enough? I pushed at the door, which glided heavily to a close, a credit to its damper. Then I pushed the chair stack right up against it, took my final position on top, and looped one end of the shoelace through the metal V above me. I tugged to make sure it was secure, and then looked at each of the dangling ends in turn to consider which one a suicide would choose for looping round his neck.

'Annie Cradock, don't you dare!'

If this were the start of a reef knot, you'd choose the right-hand end. I did, and lassoed it round my neck with a gawky wave of one arm, all elbow and fist. The shoelace slithered straight off the metal V, and I was left with the thing dangling free once more from my fingers.

'If you don't get down, Annie, I'm going to tell.'

'I'm only . . .'

I tried again, but this time kept a tight hold on both ends. The result was surprisingly tight against my windpipe. But wouldn't you have to run it *twice* round the neck? Otherwise, when the chair was kicked away, surely it would snap. And Mr Clitheroe was a big man, tall.

'Annie! You come down right now or I'm going to tell sir!'

But the lace was too short for a second circuit round the neck, it couldn't be done, not if the intention was to leave sufficient length left over to suspend yourself from some makeshift pivot. Just once round the neck, then. Well, it would never hold, I could prove it, and then we'd *know* the story was all rubbish.

'I'm going to fetch your dad, Annie. I got to.'

My improvised gallows wasn't the only door out of the infants' cloakroom; there was another that led into the playground. Babette's steady steps sounded through the room, out the door, and across the tarmac. Barely registering that I was alone, I ruminated on the comparative virtues of those reef knots, half-hitches and sheepshanks with which I was reluctantly proficient, courtesy of the Brownies, and eventually concluded that as Mr Clitheroe was never in the Brownies, the experiment would be more authentic with a granny knot. Not very comfortable this, I found, so I was now in a hurry to get the whole thing over. Which was just as well, because I had somehow unbalanced the chairs, and in slow motion the column was disintegrating beneath me. I felt the support slip from under my feet and scrabbled at the disappearing base. The lace tightened against my throat.

Adult feet thundered across the playground and my parents plunged through the door. My father ran at me. With a Welshman's instinct, he had doubled over for a rugby tackle, headbutting me in the midriff in mid-sweep. The shoelace did hold, contrary to my predictions; it bit into the damper at its zenith and into my windpipe at its knotted apogee.

'DAI, YOU'RE STRANGLING HER!'

Slung over his back, pounding with my fists and

gurgling, I caught sight of Babette in the doorway. I was scandalized. Every other shock of the morning – Old Ollie's ghostly cries, Leonard Clitheroe killing his wife and hanging himself, this unexpected paternal strangulation – they all vanished as the implication of Babette's betrayal ground its way through the tissues of my heart. This was the first time ever that one of us had snitched on the other. It was beyond belief.

'Babette,' I croaked as my mother unstrung me. 'I'm never going to forgive you!' I was painfully aware that I had made this same threat in past arguments. In fact everything I could possibly say had already been said before, with only temporary sincerity, and I had nothing but a devalued currency with which to express my shattered emotions. 'I'm never talking to you again, Babette!'

I shook myself free of my father, threw open the door, and staggered blindly out of the cloakroom. My mother stormed after me like the Furies, and I was dragged dismally home, stricken and mortified, my thoughts broken and poisoned and pulverized. As we emerged from Rainbird Lane, an aged horse and cart growled past us, and the operatic notes of its owner's string of vowels, 'U or ah,' belted with gusto through the air above Mountnessing Road.

26

I was in a lot of trouble. I was already in trouble for throwing a tantrum on the Breeden Road in front of the Frobishers, let alone slamming out of school and lurching home bawling like a banshee, and drawing the alarmed attention of one housewife after another throughout our clamorous progress across Muningstock.

My mother sent me up to my bedroom and then stamped about crossly downstairs while I howled on the distal side of the bedroom door. Lunch came and went – a sandwich that she slammed onto my chest of drawers with dire warnings about the consequences if it went uneaten. It went uneaten. The day waned. By teatime, I had a face the colour of a mauled steak, my breathing was in spasm, and my wet, blue eyes glowed out of bloodshot whites, eerie and iridescent.

'Annie-*fach*,' ventured my father, sitting on the edge of the bed where I sullenly hiccuped, 'you have to learn to control yourself. You must take an intelligent interest in the consequences of these impulsive actions.'

'There we-weren't any con-con-con . . .'

'Only because Babette behaved like a true friend and saved you from yourself.'

Babette's name fell on my misery, and lay there, smarting.

'You would have killed yourself, Annie – dead on a slab in the mortuary of Epping General. And think what you'd be missing next week with a new school term!'

Ignoring my mumbles about how I'd rather be dead anyway and nobody loved me, he led my prayers ('Our f-father who-who-who . . .') and I was put to bed while it was still daylight, to meditate on the implications of being dead and missing school.

The triangular chink where the curtains didn't quite meet showed a shining mackerel sky; time passed and the west was smeared across with mother-of-pearl, opalescent, a lugubrious gleam in its borrowed light. Being in bed by daylight brought to mind not so much the recent summer, but earlier childhood, comfort and a peace of mind that seemed to have slipped from my life irrevocably like the brake suddenly falling away from previously sedate machinery on a fairground ride.

The following morning. Thursday. True to their beliefs about childrearing, my parents attempted to greet the day as though the previous one were wiped from living memory, though my mother was finding this more of a strain than my father, whose natural buoyancy came into its own in this sort of crisis. Mummy boiled eggs and slapped butter on toast with her eyes always focused a few degrees off anyone else's, like Mr Micklewhite.

One event did brighten up the restrained doom of the breakfast table. The postman arrived with a delivery – Muningstock's postal strike was over! It was a hefty mound, and as my parents slit envelopes and

278

exclaimed and tutted, a postcard slid from the heap. It was Daddy's from America. I registered the New York skyline, light spangling off the water to explode like flashbulbs off the interlocking geometric shapes of lower Manhattan. It was a glorious picture, and my first thought was to take it round to Mrs Clitheroe until reality came back at me like a cattle prod. It went on and on, this nightmare, on and on.

Today I had chores. I was to troop around Muningstock on an expedition for my mother. She was setting up a school display called 'What goes on in our village?' to comprise a specimens table and wall displays, inspired by all our local crafts. Photographs of Percy Maxwell's dahlias, for example; a woolly piece of work from Mrs Watson's knitting machine; a blob of tarmac from the travellers' tarmac business. Thank God Dorothea had gone home, or she'd have suggested a pile of blood-soaked corpses.

I put off going to the Maxwells' to pick up the dahlia photos. It wasn't only Mrs Maxwell that I didn't want to see – with a night's sleep between me and the news, I was more inclined to believe the story about Mr Clitheroe killing himself, and I had a dread of being inside Mrs Maxwell's mucky bungalow to picture him angrily bashing that dent into the donkey on the mural. I was unable to keep my mind from it. I saw superimposed images: Leonard Clitheroe's long, ungainly body swinging in the police station with his face distorted like the gargoyles over the porch of St Matthew's; the whisperers in Bon Marché; my prickly sense of unease that he was being hunted down. I moped along Mountnessing Road on my bicycle, trying to stitch together the odd rags of fact into a story that I could understand. But whichever way up I tried them, they looked exactly like everything else I ever tried to stitch – all the edges were rucked, and you could see daylight through the seams.

My parents went off to school again – something about felling the lime trees before autumn turned the playground into a slimy lime-slide. Spoilsports as ever, my parents. Meanwhile, I cycled round Muningstock, with a promise to take the saddle-bagged trophies into school as soon as I'd completed my rounds. It was a hot day, humid and airless. The sky to the east was black with cloud, from which hung long, straggly threads – rain pouring onto Wittle.

Scooting back along the Breeden Road, pinging my yellow, butterfly-painted bell. Part of the road was being re-tarmacked and I could smell the warmth of it up ahead. I slowed, and hopped off the bike, ready to walk it along the pavement. And there was Rupert.

So the police hadn't sent him to borstal for shoplifting then, not yet anyway. He didn't see me at first; his head was turned towards the hedge, at which he was directing whistling noises. Trying to tempt some unsuspecting animal out of the greenery, perhaps, in order to torment the poor thing. It was only when he gave this up and turned back to the road that he saw me. A sneer sidled slowly across his hairless upper lip.

'You!'

'Hello, Rupert.'

'Out on our little kiddie's tricycle, are we? Mummy and Daddy let us out on our own?'

'It isn't a tricycle, Rupert, it's got two wheels.'

'Ha!'

The tarmac smelled to me of summer – dog days, blue and friendly. Pity there was Rupert to spoil it.

'The police are fucking useless, as predicted. They never caught my schoolmate over that gypsy's murder.'

'Didn't they, Rupert?'

'We're planning another one, together this time, him and me. A couple of pensioners, for practice. A pair of old prunes, one foot in the grave already. Just giving them an extra shove. We've recced the place and now it's the planning stage. Split-second timing. Creep in the back door. Masks on our faces. Balaclava helmets. Frighten them half to death before we start in with the knife. It's the knife work that I'm looking forward to, feeling that blade slip between the ribs. Shocked you, have I?'

Without really meaning to, I rolled my eyes to Heaven. I tried to remember what Babette had said about him in Bon Marché. She'd always thought he was a – what?

'Looks like we'll both be licensed to kill in record time, him and me. MI5's lost loads of spies lately to the Ruskies. There's a double agent in action somewhere high up, a traitor in the corridors of power. So they're recruiting young men like us, enterprising, fearless. Not set in our ways, you see. These middle-aged codgers, they're squeamish about killing when it's someone in authority. Not us, though. We don't give a toss. We're the new generation.'

'Not me, Rupert. I'm off.'

I bumped my bike over a ridge of glutinous new tarmac, and scooted off down Breeden Road. I could coast all the way from there to the pond, sailing past the hedgerows, the soft swish of the wheels, the taste of the breeze that blew my hair behind me like a stream. It tasted of freedom.

By mid-morning, my anthropological artefacts included a jar of Mrs Jarvis's jam, from Melena Watson's mother a knitted 'sports sock' (and judging by the length, the sportsman in question was a Harlem Globetrotter), and something in a sardine tin from old Miss Miles. She claimed to be a hundred and four, and to have Martians living in her rabbit hutch. I had no intention of opening that tin for a look.

Into Bluebell Crescent. There was number sixteen. I noticed the grass strip round the side of the bungalow, unkempt, frayed. I remembered hearing that Percy Maxwell had offered to mow it, and Mr Clitheroe had rudely told him to mind his own business. The sight of this neglect was somehow more terrible now that Leonard Clitheroe was dead. And the jar of dahlias was gone from the wall. I leaned my bike against Mrs Maxwell's gate and started up the crazy-paving path, through the ebullient primary colours of the garden, round the side of the bungalow to the back door. Mrs Maxwell was lying across the top of the path, her feet towards me.

She could have been sunbathing. She could, yet I knew she wasn't. It was extraordinary, this knowledge, it was there before I had consciously taken in the scene, absorbed the visual clues. I just *knew*, and it made things happen to me that were horrible. My chest hurt, and I wet my knickers.

The foreshortened view didn't show me Mrs Maxwell's head until I was further up the path. She looked dumped, like something the coalman would leave; half a hundredweight of nutty slack. When I did see her head, nausea hit me like a punch to the throat. I was desperately sick, bent double and heaving. Next to her head lay Percy's garden spade.

When I reached our house I fell against the kitchen door.

'MUMMY!'

Of course it was locked. Remembering that Mummy and Daddy were at school caused me to retch again. Spittle dangled from my teeth in yellow threads. I made a move to the flower pots where the key was hidden, but I knew I couldn't enter the empty house; the thought terrified me. I scooted back round the side and through the front garden.

The path to Babette's house was no less sinister than ours, but I torpedoed down it to their back door. This, too, was locked. No, they couldn't be out, they couldn't! And even if Auntie Rene and Babette were, what about Lorraine and Uncle Arthur? I hammered on the door.

'LET ME IN! UNCLE ARTHUR, AUNTIE RENE!'

I knew I wasn't safe – the murderer could have stalked me, could be waiting round the side of the house, and I'd be trapped here in the back garden. I knew I ought to start screaming – it would not only deter him, but might even recruit help – but knowing I ought to scream was like knowing I ought to sprout wings and fly. My throat was stuck, my voice locked. The certainty that the murderer was hiding round the front of Babette's house made me heave again, though there was nothing left to show for it but the disgusting sensation of my stomach inverting, and the further scraping of my tortured throat.

Sickness had sent me reeling a few steps down the side path, and when my eyes ceased streaming, I could see the corner of the house. It was clear. Nobody crouched there. I inched forward and the vista widened. Run! I thought I couldn't, but I did. Driven on by sharp lashes of panic, I ran the length of the path, across the Lucases' front garden, and out through their gates into Mountnessing Road. In a shrieking caterwaul of brakes and horn, Uncle Horace's Morris Minor skittered sideways across the greensward, and screamed all the way up to the top of our own driveway, with my mother's beloved wrought-iron gates buckled across its bonnet.

I surveyed this further horror with a degree of dissociation. I watched the gates as they were torn, screaming, from their hinges; saw them clunk off the bonnet of the car onto the concrete of our drive, and lie there twitching like the severed hand in the travellers' camp. The driver's door thrummed – Horace's fists hammering inside. He eventually gave up, and emerged through the passenger door at an unusual angle.

'Sorry, Uncle Horace,' I mumbled.

After a brief, stunned lull he turned his empurpled face on me, his eyes mad with the particular agony of a habitually mild man who was now totally beyond control of his temper.

'You!' he spluttered. 'You moronic . . . cretinous . . .'

Auntie Doris came running out of their drive with secateurs in her hand. 'All right, Horace, I'll handle this.'

'Did you SEE? Did you SEE what the stupid child did?'

Suddenly I wasn't scared any more. In the midst of the wreckage, I was no longer alone with a lurking murderer and my mind pictures of Mrs Maxwell's spade-clobbered head. And if Uncle Horace was himself homicidal, at least this was a style of adult response to my misdemeanours that I was familiar with. Auntie Doris had hurried over to me, but now took an involuntary step back. I knew how I smelled.

'Heavens, you've been tremendously sick, haven't you?' she pointed out, reviewing my splattered frock. 'Why did you run into the road, Annie?'

'I want Mummy and Daddy,' I managed to say, which involved breathing on her, at which she flinched. 'They've gone in to school.'

'You're in a terrible mess. Why did you run out of the Lucases' like that?'

'I want Mummy!'

'We'll telephone the school for you.'

'*Telephone?* I'll say we'll telephone!' shouted her husband, driving a fist already sore from grappling at the driver's door against the heavily scored brickwork of one gateless post.

'Horace! Look at the state she's in – she shot out of Frank and Irene's like a bat out of hell.'

'Get witnesses, Doris! Knock on doors! I want signed statements from anyone who saw this imbecilic . . . gormless . . . feeble-minded . . .'

'*I* saw what happened. Look, I think we ought to get the child indoors.'

Doris led me gently up the drive, edging gingerly around the frazzled Morris and the crimped and sagging acanthus scrolls that were formerly my mother's gates, and then up the path to the back door. I scrabbled for the key, Horace muttering and wiping his eyes. His hands were actually bleeding, I saw now; he drove them frantically through his Brylcreem, which created haemorrhaging highlights that trickled onto his forehead and ears.

'When I telephone the school, Annie,' Doris was saying, looking about for somewhere to rest the bulky secateurs she still carried, 'I'll have to tell your parents how the accident happened. I'll have to let them know that you're in this terrible state.'

'I've wet my knickers, Auntie Doris,' I explained.

'So I see.'

'And I was sick.'

'But who were you running away from?'

'I saw something.'

'In the Lucases'?'

'Mrs Maxwell's dead. She's on the garden path.'

Auntie Doris stood absolutely still. I didn't elaborate. 'I want Mummy and Daddy!' I reminded them.

'Gina,' she said at last.

'Mmm,' I whimpered.

'Tell me.'

'She's been bashed,' I explained. 'Her head's all . . . all . . .' But no, I wasn't going into that.

285

'Horace,' said Auntie Doris levelly, and they looked at each other. She turned back to me. 'Why were you round at Mrs Maxwell's, Annie?'

'I'm going to ring up Mummy and Daddy now.'

'No, no – I'll do it, I promise. It's better if I do.' Another glance passed between husband and wife. 'What on earth do I tell them?'

'Not over the telephone.'

'No,' she agreed. 'Horace, I think you should nip out for a moment.'

'Where?' And then, 'Oh. Yes, I see.'

'Just to . . . to check things over. See if there's anything . . .'

'Anything to be done.'

'I think so. Of course, if you can't bear the idea, I could go myself while you ring the Cradocks.'

'Oh, my dear, no! We'll have to put a call through to DI Lilliput, too.'

'Yes. Yes. I'll get on to Dai and Myrtle first.'

Uncle Horace slipped away leaving us together, my head now ringing with the word 'Lilliput'. That Mrs Maxwell with her head bashed in would trigger Lilliput hadn't previously occurred to me. I sobbed.

'Annie, will you stay in the kitchen a minute while I ring up the school?'

Not on your Nellie would I stay, but it was never put to the test; the shocked atmosphere of the kitchen was suddenly discharged by a babble from the front garden, out of which soared skyward a sharp and plangent lament. My mother had found her gates. I hurtled through the house and out of the front door, helter-skelter, nearly knocking her off her feet, and then proceeded to rage and blub incomprehensibly into the folds of her skirt.

I was given a bath in front of an invited audience – Auntie Doris. Luckily the men weren't also there

286

having a gawp; now that my father had arrived, Horace was no longer alone with the burden of responsibility and the two had gone off together to check my story about a corpse in the Maxwells' garden, and to put their call through to a stunned police force who would, for a moment or two, treat the report as a tasteless hoax. Meanwhile, my mother and Doris turned taps and upped plugs, scrubbed me and lathered me, in hushed tones and total disengagement more in keeping with a post-mortem laying out. My mother kept shaking her head. 'If the child is right and Gina's really dead on her garden path, it must be some sort of accident!'

'Dai and Horace will be back shortly. They'll settle it.'

'I mean, Leonard's dead! How many murderers can there be in the village?'

'It's a nightmare, Myrtle.'

Both the heat and humdrum familiarity of the bath soothed me. The bathroom window was damp with soap-scented steam and a softened light sifted through the frosted glass, webbing the fabric of the tub. I ran a glissando across the water, shaking diamonds into it. Looking up, I saw that Auntie Doris's green eyes were wet with tears. I remembered her crying about Mrs Clitheroe that morning on her own garden path. But crying now for Mrs Maxwell??

With her ebony hair in a tumble, the hieratic features softened and that authoritarian manner muted by shock and tears, Auntie Doris didn't look her usual self at all. In fact she looked, never mind Frank Lucas's habitual disparaging remarks, she looked beautiful. My mother's voice was ragged with bewilderment.

'I cannot make sense of it,' she was saying. 'Granted, Gina was no angel.'

'You can say that again.'

'Everybody knows how spiteful she could be.'

'Indeed.'

287

'Though I suppose I shouldn't talk like that about the poor woman now. *Nil nisi bonum de mortuis.*'

The hair wash was to be next; my mother turned on the shower attachment. I yelped. She distractedly twiddled the hot and cold taps. 'But who could Gina have offended so badly that they went for her with a spade?'

Auntie Doris sat back on her heels and wiped damp strands of black hair from her forehead. 'I feel as though Muningstock were defaced. I know how melodramatic that must sound, but I mean what I say. I feel as though the village has been literally disfigured. Everything I've loved since we got away from Dagenham . . . I was so good, Myrtle, I never once held it against Horace when he took the job in Dagenham but I hated the place, and so, when we came out here to the country, well, of course, it wasn't Cambridge, but I'd accepted that life was never going to be like that again. When he was eventually demobbed it was clear that the ambition had gone out of him. Burma, you see. But when we left Dagenham for Muningstock it seemed like a fresh beginning. And now I feel as though our country lanes, our hearth and home, have been . . .' she paused, searching for the word, 'as though they have been cicatrized. I can't believe the village will ever again be what it was to me.'

'Oh Doris, my dear.'

'I understand now all that imagery in Macbeth, the blood that won't wash off. There's something about murder that's indelible.'

Her face crumpled, and my mother reached out as she would to a pupil at school, enfolding Doris in her wet arms. I had never seen a grown-up weep. I hadn't known that such wells of feeling persisted into adulthood. The discovery was not comfortable.

I turned the water off.

'There there,' said my mother, patting. 'It's always

the strong ones who feel it most. You mustn't break, my dear. Muningstock is relying on you. There's little enough community spirit, and without your leadership, knocking on doors and bringing people together, where will Muningstock find redemption?'

The word fell oddly into the commonplaces of this Dunkirk-spirit speech. Doris sobbed.

'I shouldn't have said that about *nil nisi bonum* just now,' continued my mother. 'There's enough hypocrisy in the world, Heaven knows, and you never have been part of that, you and Horace. Let's not pretend that either of us is sorry Gina's dead. We're not going to miss her. It's Percy we should weep for. And of course poor, dear Jenny.'

At Jenny's name, Doris sobbed again. 'Oh Myrtle, don't talk about hypocrites. As though Horace and I were saints. It's so far from the truth. You'd be horrified . . .'

'Doris, we're none of us blameless.'

'Blameless?! If you just knew! But, dear God, I suppose it will all come out now. Jenny was—'

'Shush. Don't do this. There's something that people do to themselves when they're shocked and frightened; they let it undermine their belief in their own worth. This evil has wrought enough damage, Doris. Don't compound that by letting it work its poison on you. Be kind to yourself; take whatever comforts you can find.'

'Gina—'

'—is dead,' finished my mother. 'Whatever her sins, they're for the Lord's judgement now, not ours.'

Doris began to quieten. She tugged a generous length of toilet tissue from the roll behind her and trumpeted comprehensively into it. My mother dabbed at their clothes with a towel.

'Thank you, Myrtle. I've stopped now, I think. I'll be all right.'

289

In my soap-sudded isolation, I heard again my mother's plaintive question: 'Who could Gina have offended so badly that they went for her with a spade?' Old Ollie, I thought, that's who. I knew, now. In those terrible seconds when I'd turned away from Mrs Maxwell's shattered head, its peroxide blond clotted and glutinous, I'd registered the tiny comfort of catching sight of an old friend: Ollie, horseless and cartless, was at the top of Bluebell Crescent, looking over his shoulder and clambering over the chickenwire that gave onto the fields.

27

No-one was misguided enough to try to send me to
bed. I sat in the front room, enveloped in my mother's
candlewick dressing gown (since Lorraine deprived us
of Mrs Clitheroe's photograph album I'd shunned my
Viyella), with the television and a hot, milky drink,
like a convalescent. Half an hour of this in the increas-
ingly torpid heat and I was dripping. *Watch with
Mother* was on, and I did, though we were continually
interrupted by the telephone – Muningstock people
with condolences for our trouble, plus a question or
two asking was it really Mrs Maxwell? And what with
Mr Clitheroe being dead and everything, did my
mother think there was some mistake about him being
the killer? There were also three calls from the press;
two were the local papers, but the third wasn't – it was
the *Daily Express*.

The storm wouldn't come. Even I, normally impervious to weather until it saturated my socks, was
aware of something heavy going on in the atmosphere,
something ponderous and unwanted. And as though

this were a cue for the arrival of a tempest of any sort, there was a knock at the door and there was DI Lilliput.

He had WPC Swan with him again. Through the thud of my heart, I could hear their voices in the hall asking my father whether they could have a chat with him first 'out of hearing of the kiddie', to establish what Daddy had found 'when you, sir, and Mr Frobisher checked out the scene of crime'. My mother stayed with me in the sitting room where *Tales of the Riverbank* rolled on, though I'd lost the plot the moment I'd heard the police.

It's strange how accurately we can monitor the progress of a distant interview we can't properly hear; I knew when the discussion was drawing to a close and they were about to wrench me away from whatever vestigial comfort I'd been deriving from the riverbank's Rag, Tag and Bobtail. Outside, the first brief splatter of rain had turned to hail, hammering the dark pigment of my mother's roses into the concrete drive so that tomorrow we would find squiggled magenta shapes dancing round the edges, like Auntie Doris's indelible stains of blood.

'Well now, Annie,' Lilliput began, 'I hear you've had a bit of a shock.'

'A bit,' I conceded.

'It must have scared you, too.'

'Mmm.'

'Are you still scared now?'

I most certainly was, but I wasn't telling *him*. His eyes watched me. WPC Swan smiled. There was a notebook in her hand and a pencil; she was going to write down everything I said. I sank into my mother's voluminous candlewick until my head barely protruded over the collar, like a withdrawing tortoise.

'You're an intelligent girl, Annie, so you can

understand when I say that everyone in Muningstock will be a good deal less scared when we've got this culprit, and you can help that process by answering my questions. I think you know that makes sense.'

I heard a degree of complacency in this, and aimed at it. 'It hasn't helped so far, has it? People are still being murdered.'

'Annie-*fach*.' A gentle remonstrance from my father.

'And that's despite all the help you've given the police?'

That remark hung rather heavily in the air. My parents couldn't quite translate it into something they should object to, and of course I wasn't up to any clever riposte. Lilliput let the silence echo a while. The phone rang. My mother got up with apologetic gestures, and it was soon clear that the caller was a stranger.

'Yes, we did know the deceased,' she was saying patiently, 'as you call her. But I really don't wish . . .'

'Mrs Cradock?'

'Excuse me a moment, please,' she said into the phone, and turned to DI Lilliput.

'Mrs Cradock, is that the press?'

'Yes, Inspector.'

'May I?' He took the heavy black receiver from her hand and boomed down it. 'Detective Inspector Lilliput here, CID. Exactly. The police will be issuing a statement in due course. Meanwhile, I'll thank you not to harass innocent persons.' There was a pause. 'All in good time,' he said and replaced the receiver definitively in its cradle. My mother's eyes sparkled.

'Oh, thank you so much, Mr Lilliput. They are such a nuisance, but one doesn't like to be abrupt.'

'This won't have stopped the others. Unless you are expecting a call, I suggest you take the phone off the hook.'

'*Really?*' queried my mother, shocked. 'Isn't that illegal?'

'It is not, Mrs Cradock.'

She gingerly lifted the receiver once more and placed it on the window sill. The remainder of the interview was carried out against a background of electronic noise generated by our local exchange, issuing from the mouthpiece in tones of escalating hysteria.

'Now then, Annie,' resumed Lilliput. 'You went into Bluebell Crescent on an errand for your mother – is that right?'

'That's right.'

'Can you tell me what it was about?'

'Mr Maxwell's dahlias.'

'Yes? How was that?'

'He had some photos of them winning prizes and I was going to take them for our school display.'

'I see. And were you expecting to meet Mr Maxwell when you went round to the bungalow?'

'No, 'cos they'd stopped being on strike.'

'Come again?'

My mother explained. 'Percy Maxwell is a sorter at the post office, Mr Lilliput. During the strike he was home a great deal, but they're all back at work now.'

'Thank you, Mrs Cradock, that's very clear. But would you mind if Annie herself tried to answer all the questions? It's to get us into a flow, so to speak.'

'Oh, certainly. I didn't realize.'

'So, Annie,' he continued, 'was this visit to Bluebell Crescent the first errand today?'

'No.'

'What was?'

'After breakfast I cycled round to Mrs Jarvis's for a jam-jar. I mean a jar of jam.'

'And after that?'

'Mrs Watson's.'

'What did you pick up there?'

'A gi-normous sock. And then Miss Miles.'

'A busy morning for you. And then?'

'Then I went round Mrs Maxwell's.'

'Did anyone say hello to you on your way there?'

'No. Well, I saw Rupert, Farmer Lawrence's nephew, in Breeden Road. But he doesn't count.'

'Anyone else?'

'No.'

'Sure?'

'There wasn't anyone.'

He had placed me now in Bluebell Crescent. I was aware of mugginess, heavy air. I was conscious of a dread related to the Clitheroes' bungalow, and the Maxwells' donkey mural.

'Was Mrs Maxwell's gate open or shut when you reached it?'

'Open. I leaned my bike against it.' A belated thought, 'Daddy . . .?'

'It's all right, Annie-*fach*, I wheeled it home.'

'And then you started up the path.'

'Started. Yes.'

'Do you wear a watch, Annie?'

'No.'

'So you don't know what time it was that you arrived?'

'Not really.' I'd twice been given watches and lost them.

'Never mind. You turned in at her gate and you saw – can you describe it?'

What I saw. There were earwigs, hundreds of them, seething over the crazy paving and Mrs Maxwell's Terylene mini dress. Percy ran a military campaign against earwigs on his dahlias, spraying them with every insecticide he could legally buy, and a few others he'd conjured from an alchemical mix of household cleaners. This earwig infestation, on his

295

path and on his wife, was like overspill from some more profound corruption.

'I saw Mrs Maxwell.'

'Was there anything lying close to her?'

'Mr Maxwell's spade he digs with, for his dahlias.'

'Can you tell me where it was?'

'Next to . . . next to . . .'

'Her head, Annie?'

'Mmm.'

'I wonder whether you might have touched Mrs Maxwell at all, or the spade perhaps. If I'd been you, I probably would have.'

The spade. That first upsurge of nausea had racked me; I'd staggered from its impact. My foot had knocked the handle of the spade and sent it spinning round. When the vomiting stopped, I saw that I'd been sick right across the handle and much of the shaft. Within the second wave I'd got the head of the spade, the paving beside Mrs Maxwell's head, and a largish splash across her bare arm. Dribbling and horrified, I had wiped my mouth on the skirt of her dress before I realized what I was doing.

'I fell over the spade.'

'Could you draw it into this picture?'

Lilliput took from his pocket a notebook with another of his domestic sketch-plans, including the outline of a person. I added the spade lying athwart the path, pointing towards that unspeakable head. Lilliput appraised it.

'Thank you,' he said at last. 'Did you touch anything else, do you remember?'

'I was sick. That touched lots of things.'

'Yes, we know about that. But you yourself?'

'I only touched her arm so as to wipe the sick off it.'

'But you see, someone did move Mrs Maxwell.'

'Well, it wasn't me!' It rankled, the insinuation that I'd

been there at the scene of a murder, dragging a corpse about.

'Annie-*fach*, nobody's telling you off, dear. We only need to understand what happened.'

'I didn't do anything except be sick and wipe her and fall over the spade!'

'Did you notice any sign that another person had been there?'

Any *sign*? Well, she probably hadn't slammed herself over the head. I goggled at him.

'I mean, do you remember anything like a footprint? Or some item lying there that might have been dropped? Or . . .'

'There were smeary marks on the crazy paving. Like a smudgy hand with blood on it, and another one.'

'Can you draw their position on the diagram?'

I took up the pencil again, and did my best to indicate where the handprint had been, plus another splodge that might, I decoded with hindsight, have been a knee; someone bending over the body, after they had . . .

Lilliput turned to a fresh page in his notebook and asked me to sketch the prints. I scribbled some random blobs for him, though coming from me, they inevitably looked more like paw prints.

WPC Swan was rubbing inky stuff onto one of her own hands. Now she smudged it onto a piece of paper. 'Annie, try to picture this lying on Mrs Maxwell's path. Is my blue pattern bigger or smaller than the red one you saw?'

It was no good. Everything about that path was distorted in my memory, looming and retreating like a fever dream. Not that I would have told the police even had I remembered. In case the hand in question was Ollie's.

Lilliput turned to my father. 'Did you notice, sir?'

'Well,' he answered hesitantly, 'it was difficult to

make out anything on the ground next to Gina. I mean, because of the, um, where Annie . . .'

'Yes,' agreed Lilliput, 'that's what we found, too.'

WPC Swan was rubbing cream into her inky hand out of a tiny pot from her pocket. Did she do this often, then?

'It's horrible, feeling sick, isn't it?' she said with her pretty smile, wiping her fingers with a tissue. 'I think it's worse than anything else. I'd rather suffer from toothache.'

'Unfortunately, it's Annie's little weakness,' put in my mother, thereby expunging the small comfort of this well-meant remark. 'Annie vomits at the drop of a hat, don't you, dear?'

'She'll soon toughen up when she gets to medical school,' asserted my father, cheerfully. Lilliput broke through this.

'Did you see anybody while you were in Bluebell Crescent? Anyone at all?'

'No. I already told you.'

'But I'd like you to think back, Annie. Picture the scene in your mind. Bluebell Crescent wasn't in silence, was it? Did any car drive past you? Did you pick up the sound of a footstep, a distant voice?'

Nobody's footfall in Bluebell Crescent, and no sign of life except for Old Ollie legging it over the fence. I considered this. Where had he been when I first turned into Bluebell Crescent? In my mind I saw the loop of the road, the chalet bungalows with their low walls angled next to one another like the stones of an archway. And at the top, where the keystone would be, an open gap where the blond stubble of the fields shone beyond a short stretch of wire fence. Old Ollie was climbing over this wire as I staggered out of Mrs Maxwell's gate, so either he'd walked past me while I was throwing up over the corpse and the murder weapon – which he hadn't, I'd have noticed anything human, I'd probably have clung to him – or he had been hiding. And if he was hiding, it was because he'd seen me cycling up.

Well, if Ollie was afraid that I'd give him away, I wouldn't. He hadn't snitched on me when he'd seen me in Bluebell Crescent that dinnertime when I'd climbed in Mrs Clitheroe's window, and I didn't blame him for what he'd done to Mrs Maxwell, not after what she'd done to him, telling the police he was Mrs Clitheroe's killer, and also telling Mr Clitheroe about the conversation she'd snooped on, so that he'd killed my lovely Mrs Clitheroe.

'Annie?'

'I heard some children making a noise near the pub. There wasn't anyone else. There was nobody, not a single person, especially in Bluebell Crescent!'

Lilliput was looking at me, one of his X-ray looks. WPC Swan's pencil ceased its scratching across her pad. She said gently, 'If you did see someone, and you tell us, it doesn't mean we'll lock them up for the murder, Annie. It only means we need to talk to them to find out whether *they* witnessed anything.'

'I didn't! There wasn't anybody there!'

Lilliput scrutinized me a little more, and then packed away the notebook with our sketches. There was a moment when I thought this heralded his departure, but the sweetness was shortlived.

'Well now, Annie. I expect you'll be relieved to take a break from Mrs Maxwell's for a moment. As you know, hers is not the only killing we've had in the village; there were the two men connected with the travellers' camp, one a traveller himself and the other an East Ender who did business with them. And there was Mrs Clitheroe. These crimes can't all be independent of one another, they're not coincidence. There must be some sort of link running from one to another, and it's my job to find it. As part of that process I need to clear up all the little odds and ends so that we can understand everything that went on. Does that make sense, Annie?'

'I suppose.'

'I'd like to take you back once more to Mrs Clitheroe's bungalow.' He put a hand in another pocket. 'There's one particular point that I think only you can clear up for me.'

I watched him over the top of the candlewick collar. What now?

'Forgive my interrupting, Inspector,' said my mother, 'but may I just ask . . .?'

'Yes, Mrs Cradock?'

'You see, we've known Jenny and Leonard for many years. And Gina, too, of course. But, well, knowing that he can never come to trial makes everything worse, and I wondered whether you could tell us. Leonard did confess to killing Jenny, didn't he?'

'Leonard Clitheroe came to the police station for the express purpose of making a full statement to that effect, which he did.'

'I see. Yes, that is what we heard. The Frobishers told us. It seems so . . . so . . .'

'Myrtle, dear.' My father reached out lightly and touched her on the arm. There was a pause in which she blew her nose.

'Mrs Cradock, I will also tell you in confidence that there were some inconsistencies.'

'I'm not sure . . .'

'Do you remember the last time we met, I was talking to Annie about Mrs Clitheroe's photographs? The album had been stolen from her bungalow but eventually came to light. She had used it not only for photos but also for keeping mementoes, letters and notes – almost like a scrapbook, really. We found jottings on a little pad slipped inside. Mrs Clitheroe had been making lists, like an inventory of items to worry about, and one of these included a memo saying "Warn Leonard" with question marks, and a couple of scribbled lines that were obviously the draft of a note to her husband telling him that she was frightened of something. The tone wasn't consistent with her being afraid of the man she was addressing.'

'I don't quite understand, Inspector.'

'Neither do we, unfortunately. But the police didn't close the file on Mrs Clitheroe's murder with her husband's suicide, Mrs Cradock.'

'Oh,' said my mother.

'Oh,' said my father.

'Well, thank you. I won't interrupt again.' And she gestured expansively towards me, as though handing me over to Lilliput's care.

'Now then, Annie,' he continued. 'Do you remember that a few days before Mrs Clitheroe died – Monday morning last week – you were in her bungalow and she was playing jazz on the piano?'

Where had he got this from? Oh please, not Babette! Did her betrayal extend to this? I felt sick again.

'Mrs Clitheroe was playing to you when Mr and Mrs Frobisher came in. Mrs Clitheroe told them that you had been upset that morning by something you had seen in the travellers' camp.'

Horace and Doris!

Then Lilliput opened his fist, and in the palm was the gold signet ring with its chip of diamond that I had dropped that morning in Mrs Clitheroe's bungalow. *Th-wack!!*

'You look to me as though you recognize this, Annie.'

'I don't!'

'No? Mr Frobisher distinctly remembers: you were sitting on Mrs Clitheroe's piano stool where she'd been improvising some boogie-woogie music. And when Mr Frobisher gave you both the news that the police had found someone murdered – this was the second murder, Annie – you became agitated, and Mrs Clitheroe explained that you had witnessed something frightening over at the travellers' camp that very morning.'

Was there anything he hadn't been told? Horace and Doris must have been gabbing away twenty to the dozen.

'I was just upset because I'd been on the back of Old Ollie's rag and bone cart talking to the dog, and he went off with me by accident, and I ended up at the camp, and I was afraid he'd be cross.'

'The back of Ollie's rag and bone cart?' repeated my father, unable to contain himself.

'It was only 'cos of the dog.'

'Mr Lilliput,' put in my mother, 'please tell us that you're not suggesting Annie stole that ring.'

'There's no question of theft, Mrs Cradock. I believe that Annie found the ring in the travellers' camp under circumstances that caused her distress, and that she took it to Mrs Clitheroe for advice.'

'Well, Annie?'

'I never saw it before!'

'Annie-*fach*, you heard Mr Lilliput – nobody's accusing you. But if that ring is a clue, the police need to know everything they can about it.'

'Shall I tell you what I believe happened? I think you were in the camp when some men came and attacked one of the travellers. I think this ring came loose from them during the scuffle, and you picked it up and took it to Mrs Clitheroe because you were frightened. Now, you know I can't check this with Mrs Clitheroe, so I'm asking you. The point is, Annie, I believe you're the only witness who can help us put the finger on some very bad men.'

Machete Mickey. *Machete* Mickey. I knew, quite suddenly. Reviewed in the educational context of my own home, away from the exotic hurly-burly of the travellers' camp, I knew where I'd seen that word before – in my children's encyclopedia of the world. Machetes were what you used for hacking down forests. So this machete man was rampaging around Muningstock with his sarcastic mate, killing East Enders and chopping the hands off anyone who gave their governor grief. And here was this policeman, demanding that I grass them up.

'It wasn't me!' I spelled out, pitching my voice loud enough to be heard by any passing East End crook. 'I was just upset because of being on Ollie's cart.'

'I think there were two of them, Annie. Perhaps they mentioned another man, the one they'd killed earlier in the day. Is that what frightened you so badly?'

'I never heard any men!'

'Annie-*fach* . . .'

'You're our prime witness, Annie. We need your help to put these criminals behind bars.'

'I never heard the men! They weren't even there!'

'But Mr Frobisher's already told us you saw something . . .'

'At least I know why Mr Clitheroe killed Mrs Clitheroe, which *you* don't. It was because she was going to leave him, and go all lovey-dovey with Uncle Horace – and Mrs Maxwell saw them, so she told him, so he killed her!'

In the utter silence that greeted this outburst, I could almost *see* my audience trying to sort through my pronouns. The sky beyond our net curtains was torched by lightning.

'Horace Frobisher?' asked Lilliput eventually.

'Mmm.' It wasn't as sweet as it should have been, this victory. Something wasn't quite right about the response.

'And exactly when was this lovey-dovey conversation, Annie?'

'Well, when I said it was lovey-dovey . . .'

'I asked *when*?'

'That day.'

'The same Monday?'

'Mmm.'

'Where?'

'There.'

'In front of you?'

'Not on purpose.'

'What does that mean?'

'They didn't know about me.'

'Why?'

'I'd left, then gone back to look for something.'
Remembering that it was the damn ring, I pulled
myself up. 'I'd dropped my hankie.'

'Where was *Mrs* Frobisher?'

'Gone to the toilet!'

'How were they talking – quietly? In whispers?'

'Not whispering, just quiet.'

'So he was asking Mrs Clitheroe to go away with
him?'

'No!'

'Whispering behind Mrs Frobisher's back? Is that
why you're covering for them?'

'You're wrong! He didn't even want it!'

'Right, so Mrs Clitheroe wanted it and he said "no".'

'You don't know anything! It was only Uncle Horace
saying he knew she wanted to leave Mr Clitheroe, he
knew she did, but she'd got to understand he couldn't
let Doris be hurt, because she's his wife!'

On the periphery of my chaotic world, I heard my
mother's painful moan. I saw my father squash his
hand on his face. I saw my mother cover her eyes.

'So where was Mrs Maxwell?'

'The French windows.'

'Doing what?'

'Nothing. Snooping.'

'And Horace Frobisher saw her?'

'I don't know.'

'Did Horace Frobisher see her?'

'Yes!'

'He knew she'd heard the conversation?'

'YES YES YES YES YES YES YES!'

Lilliput spun round to my father. 'Mr Cradock, when you checked the body, did Frobisher seem reluctant to let you join him?'

'Well, I have to say that he did rather. But, Inspector . . .'

'How did he appear?'

'Shaken. But, of course, there was his car accident.'

'When you were at the crime scene, was it possible that he could have tampered with anything?'

'NO!' This was terrible. Whatever had I done? The questions flew, flap, flap, flap, like birds of prey, beaks and claws. WPC Swan's pencil scratched inexorably, like a desperate rodent.

'NO!'

'Be quiet, Annie!'

'It wasn't Uncle Horace!'

'Mrs Cradock, perhaps it would be more appropriate if your husband and I continued our discussion back in the kitchen.'

He and WPC Swan rose, followed by my father, looking stunned. I was panic-stricken.

'You think Uncle Horace did Mrs Maxwell in with a spade for telling on him to Mr Clitheroe!' I spluttered. 'Well, you're wrong, because I saw who it was, I saw them sneaking out of Bluebell Crescent over that wire fence into the fields, and they'd been hiding, and it wasn't Uncle Horace!'

This time, there was almost no break in his stride. 'Who?' Lilliput blasted at me.

'Annie-*fach*, are you making this up? Inspector . . .'

'Mr Cradock, I'll take my Bible oath she's not. We suspected earlier that Annie was covering up for someone. She was suspiciously insistent that there wasn't a soul about.'

'So, who, Annie?'

I sank back into the dressing gown. 'I'm not going to say.' The concept of not saying had felt like a real possibility while I was yelling, but now I could see its flaws.

'WHO?'

'It wasn't Uncle Horace,' I mumbled. Well, the police couldn't wring it out of me. They couldn't hurt me, or lock me up, or take me away from home for refusing to say. Home. I glimpsed the life I'd lead with my parents while I was doing all this refusing, and ice closed around my heart.

'If you think you saw the person who murdered Mrs Maxwell, you have to tell Mr Lilliput. It's a matter of right and wrong, Annie.'

'You will tell him this minute, my girl!'

'I can't,' I mewed pitifully.

'Don't you "can't" me, young lady.'

'Mrs Cradock, this may not be necessary. Let's think about it. Annie saw this individual under suspicious circumstances, and it's somebody she is intent on protecting. There can't be so many people in the village who fit the bill.'

My parents looked at each other.

'Someone Annie is fond of,' continued Lilliput, ruthlessly. 'An individual she would trust, even believing that they'd committed this murder.'

'Ollie,' said my mother.

'Ollie?'

'Our rag and bone man.'

'He knows who Ollie is, Myrtle.'

'I see.' Lilliput turned to me and smiled. 'Climbing

over the wire fence, you said. Into the fields?'

'It wasn't Ollie!'

'Of course. Those fields would take him straight across to the travellers' camp. Doesn't that make sense?'

The voice that answered Lilliput wasn't mine, or my parents', or the quietly scribbling WPC Swan's. It was as unexpected as the hailstorm outside. The voice was Babette's.

'It couldn't of. Not Old Ollie.'

'Babette!'

'Good grief!'

'Heavens above, child! Wherever did you spring from?'

Babette! Her porcelain face, her curls aglow like one of Charles Dickens's stainless little heroines. Having dropped into the fraught atmosphere of the sitting room like an exploding bomb, Babette now took her place placidly on the hearthrug. 'I heard Annie shouting earlier, so I come round. I been here ages in the kitchen.'

'Unfortunately, dear . . .' My mother was out of her chair, extending a shepherding hand. 'We're plumb in the middle of talking to the police.'

But Babette wasn't budging. 'Then Annie said she wasn't going to tell, and you was all saying it was Old Ollie, so I had to speak up.'

'Speak up?'

'Annie couldn't of seen Ollie when you all said, 'cos Uncle Arthur and me was round the travellers' camp all morning and Ollie was there.'

Oh no he wasn't. Babette was looking directly at me – talking to the adults, but looking directly at me. Lying her head off.

'What do you mean, Babette?'

'We was round there 'cos of Uncle Arthur talking to one of the gyppos about a bit of business. And Ollie was about all the time.'

'*All* the time?' Lilliput.

'Yeah. I was a bit bored so I kept watching. I'll say so to whoever you want. I'll write it down and swear if you like.'

'Inspector, we'd better explain – Babette is an extraordinarily truthful little girl.'

Oh yes? Straight at me, her eyes never wavered.

'And this uncle – will he swear too?'

Babette gave a shrug that was momentous even by her standards. 'Dunno. He never sees anythink when he's jawing. But I bet the other travellers'll tell you Ollie was there all the time.'

'Yes,' said Lilliput grimly, 'I bet they will.'

Catching his tone, my mother said uncertainly, 'Inspector, just in case Babette happens to be, well, mistaken, you can still pursue this lead. I'm sure someone in Bluebell Crescent will have noticed him.'

'They're not very good noticers in Bluebell Crescent, Mrs Cradock.' He got to his feet.

'Still, you'll know whose fingerprints to look for, evidence at the scene and so on.'

'Your daughter threw up over them. Anyway, thank you for your help, but I think we'll be going now.'

'Oh! Well, if you're sure that's all, I'll show you out.'

My parents got to their feet rather heavily.

'Goodbye, Annie.' WPC Swan. 'Bye, Babette.'

'Bye.'

The police followed my parents out of the room. Babette and I could hear desultory conversation going on in the hall. Outside, the hail had started again, great pellets of it raining down. Lilliput and WPC Swan were going to get stoned on their way down our drive.

Babette turned to me in an offhand sort of way. 'You all right?'

'Mmm,' I replied. 'I'm all right.'

'Yeah?'

'Yeah.' There was no need to hide behind the candlewick any more. I shrugged it away. Suddenly it felt very odd being in a nightie in the middle of the morning, when I could be up and about.

'It was a bit horrible, though,' I admitted. 'Earlier.'

'Thought so.'

'I don't mean earlier with *them*. Earlier with the . . . when I . . .'

'Yeah, I know. It must have been.'

Babette hopped into an armchair and sank into it, cross-legged and compact, like something you could fold away. We heard the front door open, and the change in timbre of the voices as they stepped outside.

'D'you know for certain it was him that did it, Annie – Ollie?'

'Must be. He must have been hiding or I'd have seen him soon as I went in Bluebell Crescent. And then he was climbing the fence all sort of furtive, without his horse and cart.'

'Still, he could've just been around and saw Mrs Maxwell dead, and then run off 'cos of the trouble he got last time.'

I gave this some thought. 'So, do you think it was Uncle Horace, then?'

'Don't know.' She added, 'And Lilliput don't know, either. You was clever, getting him confused like that.'

'Mmm.'

'The travellers'll say Ollie was up the camp all that time.'

'An alibi, yes.'

'And Doris has had time to sort Horace out. You was clever being sick everywhere, too. I wouldn't of thought of that myself.'

'No. Well, it was a bit messy.'

'Did the trick, though. Whichever of them it was.'

'Oh yes, it did the trick.'

The front door closed and we heard my parents'

footsteps approaching. Then a new cry hollered across from the road. 'Mrs Cradock?' I heard the words 'wrought iron', and the sound of my parents darting back out of the front door.

'There's something I never told you,' said Babette, her voice dropping to a whisper. 'You know Lorraine and me was round Mrs Clitheroe's that day you was up the airport?'

'That's when Lorraine stole the photograph album in the first place,' I reminded her. Golly, Lorraine had only done it to demonstrate that you didn't have to be a trained secret agent to steal things, and therefore Rupert's stories were a load of porkies. All for Rupert!

'Well, her and me was going through the album like I always do, and Lorraine found this letter.'

'What letter?'

'This love letter Mrs Clitheroe was writing. Tucked in between the photo of Nell and Albert's wedding at St Olave's church, June 1925.'

'Oh.'

'Lorraine didn't show it to me then; she only mentioned it after the funeral. The letter weren't finished. It only said "I'm not safe, and I'm going away."'

'Not safe 'cos of Mr Clitheroe, you mean?'

'It didn't say. Just "My darling, by the time you read this, I'll be gone." And then about how she wasn't safe.'

'Oh.'

'And Lorraine put it back where she got it from. D'you reckon Lilliput might have copped a look after he got the photo album back?'

I considered this. 'I don't think so.' I recalled his reaction to my various bombshells. 'I don't think he's ever seen any love letter from Mrs Clitheroe.'

'All in all, Lilliput ain't had a lot of luck, has he?' pointed out Babette comfortably.

Outside, the hailstorm had paused again. A

shadowy figure paced between our gateposts with a steel rule, from right to left. My father appeared to be doing some measurement of his own in the other direction, left to right. Heel to toe. My mother supervised.

'Babette.'

'Yeah?'

'There's something I never told you, either.'

I chronicled the facts quite smartly, considering, and led her through my house-breaking via the bathroom window, and that strange and lovely ruby-red song that had materialized, fully formed and perfect in my mind on Tuesday afternoon while I was painting Mrs Clitheroe. None of which caused Babette to bat an eyelid.

After a respectful silence, she asked, 'What d'you reckon your mum and dad'll do?'

'They'll probably think I got it wrong about Ollie,' I decided. 'Like I was shocked or something. Anyway, Mummy's all upset about her gates.'

'Come round mine, then?'

'Might do. I'll go and get dressed.'

I abandoned the candlewick in a heap and went upstairs. A car could be heard revving in Mountnessing Road. The police. They wouldn't be back, I decided, not for me. By the time I'd got into a clean pair of knickers and a newly ironed frock, Lilliput and WPC Swan barely existed on the fringes of my mind. There was that postcard of my father's – I hadn't even shown it to Babette yet, and there was probably some sort of game we could play around it. Pretend the Beatles had sent it from Shea Stadium, something like that. These things only needed a bit of imagination.

311

THE PRESENT

28

Spring. Four months since we got home from New York, and my immigration visa has come through, so I'm entitled to enter the United States as a resident alien, *pace* David Bowie. Alan did, of course, accept the job.

Swept by the current, I organize our move and at this rate I will end up there by default. Alan and I have negotiated a compromise; our home will be in Westchester but I will rent a studio in the city to teach in. Initially, until I build up what Alan calls 'a solid client base', there will be what he calls 'a serious shortfall between my income and expenditure'. So I'll be subsidized. By the time I settle into a studio it will be June, the start of the students' mass exodus from the city, but never mind; Frank Sinatra had a song about New York in June. And that's when Daniel will be at the Guggenheim for his Retrospective. With my Ruby Tuesday sculpture.

Suddenly there's a valedictory feel to workaday life. I phone everyone I've ever known and book farewell suppers, at which they immediately invite themselves to New York for our first week. I peruse the TV schedules and won't go out if Babette's sister Mandy is on, though given the nature of her success, she's on the screen as often in the States as in Ealing. My home itself begins to recede from me, though that might only be the influence of the black-cab driver Alan and I hailed in the West End last Saturday night, who protested 'Ealing? Ealing? I don't go that far on me holidays!'

And I see Daniel, once a week, at the flat in Butler's Wharf; and every time I do I decide that I'm no more capable of moving to New York and leaving him, than of writing a box-office hit to rival Andrew Lloyd Webber.

Sunday, Walpole Park with Alan. Crocuses and March winds, and what Daniel would call 'a Wordsworth of daffodils'. Puffy clouds scud across the sky like time-lapse photography. We have been to a matinee at the Questors theatre, and now we're watching our scruffy mongrel Benny wheel across the park in a state of transcendental, depersonalized bliss that puts me in mind of Timothy Leary.

We are talking about Benny in an attempt to skid away from a row that has been bounding heavily towards us all afternoon like some sinister special effect from a sci-fi movie. Alan has been trying to persuade me to sell my vintage synthesizers, which I'd started buying secondhand and cheap during my days of writing horror music for the Flintstones. Admittedly, shipping them to New York will be a major task, but as I keep reminding him, his biotech company will be paying.

'I've looked into this, Annie. Your model of Mellotron will fetch five thousand dollars. I guess people break them up for spare parts.'

'No, Alan. The market's there because people make music on them! The Mellotron is the only reason I still get the occasional commission – it isn't that I'm talented, it's just that I'm versatile.'

The sound was warmer in the old days. When the first digital synthesizers arrived in the Eighties, they were brighter, sharper, but cold. It was music with the edges pared by a steel knife.

'Run this past me again, Annie. We're keeping five thousand dollars' worth of stone-age machinery while you accept one commission every two years and waste your time teaching for peanuts.'

This is when we stop, and agree to talk about Benny instead. There's no argument about whether to ship or sell Benny; his range of sound effects is limited, and there can't be much of a market for breaking him up for spare parts.

Alan has been wondering whether I might like to get a second dog once we're settled in Westchester. I hadn't thought about it, but apparently Alan has – something along the lines of a German shepherd or a sheltie. An Afghan hound. A schnauzer, perhaps.

'You mean a puppy?'

'Well, I thought so.'

'I'd adore a puppy, but I can't really take one to the studio every day. He'll scamper up the back of the piano when I'm not looking, and eat through the strings and hammers. He'll electrocute himself chewing cables.'

'You'd take the puppy to the studio?'

'Well, I'll be taking Benny.'

'That isn't so, Annie, a puppy doesn't have to be delinquent. Dogs in the States are crate trained. He'll be fine! You can leave Benny home with him.'

'Alan, is this important?'

'No-o-o. Not at all. I thought maybe if we had two dogs they'd be company for you.'

I looked at him. 'You thought they'd be company for me while I leave them at home and go to the studio?'

Alan shrugged, and that was the end of the conversation. But on Friday evening we returned to Benny again.

It had been a long day at drama school, so when I got home I'd made straight for the gym. Where I promptly fell off the power jogger. I've done this before. When running on the treadmill, I don't travel light; I have various monitors plus headphones all plugged into both me and the equipment. Thus wired up like Muffin the Mule, I work out to a background of rock music, loud enough to be called a foreground. Unfortunately, my brain interprets this as meaning that the music is propelling the treadmill. Mostly, this aberration can be treated as nothing worse than a metaphor; it's like relativity – no-one really cares whether the train is leaving Waterloo or Waterloo is leaving the train, until one of the two comes to a halt in a hurry, and the standing passengers suddenly find themselves tap-dancing. Similarly, I'm fine until I decide to change the CD; I unplug myself from the music and, because I believe the music was powering the jogger, I stand still. Though not for long.

Anyway, I was now home, soaking my sore, chipped bones in a very English bubble bath. I had a cup of tea, a P. G. Wodehouse story, and Vaughan Williams's *A London Symphony* on the hi-fi. The P. G. Wodehouse was about an American in the States who employed an English butler called Blizzard.

When I hear Alan come in, I turn down Vaughan Williams with the remote. Alan walks through into the bedroom and calls a laconic 'hi'. I hear closet doors being opened, and drawers, and then the sound of him phoning Henley-on-Thames, home of his present Head of Data Management, who presumably has also just got in through the door. I know it's Henley and not, for example, New York, because I recognize the tune that the phone's keypad plays when he taps in the number. It's not a bad tune; I've heard worse win the Eurovision Song Contest.

From the varying degrees of muffle on Alan's voice, I gather that he's carrying on this conversation while changing out of his suit, time being money. It won't be a brief call; at a cocktail party, I'd once overheard a colleague of his say 'Trying to get Alan Muller off the phone is like trying to get a terrier off your trouser leg.'

'If we don't lock the database before March Thirty-one,' Alan is saying now, through what I think is a sweatshirt being pulled over his head, 'how are we gonna have the efficacy results for April Two?'

Benny was fast asleep, slumped against the bathroom radiator, with his name tag dangling against the hot metal. This meant that as soon as he moved, the disc would fall back against his neck, and he'd hop about. It regularly happened to me when my gold chain heated up in the sauna.

'Correct, Kelvin. The CDP has this down as the go/no-go decision for phase three.'

I wiggled the hot tap with my toes, and a gorgeous wave of warmth rippled through the water, around and between my thighs. This time I didn't cover myself up; my good-looking husband was not an unwelcome sight when he finally appeared in the doorway.

'Darling, when we're in Westchester, may I have an English butler called Blizzard?'

'They still haven't locked the fucking database,' he informed me. 'Some reconciliation problem. So the phase three will start late.'

'Oh I am sorry,' I said. 'But you won't be there. Can't you let someone else do the worrying?'

'Sure. How's that student who went for the *Showboat* audition?'

'No luck,' I said. 'She didn't get a call-back.'

'But you won't be there,' said Alan. 'Can't you let someone else do the worrying?'

OK, touché. Alan disappeared again. I heard him walk through to the kitchen. In an open-plan space you get to hear the sounds of the house, and this was the fridge, a bottle of wine being uncorked, and a glass poured. Clink, a second glass. A better connoisseur would have had a crack at guessing the grape and the vineyard. After a while, he returned to the bathroom with both glasses.

'I'm sorry, Alan,' I told him. 'I didn't mean to say it like that.'

'Forget it.' He handed me the wine, nearly tripping on Benny's tail, which made him look down. Benny was still fast asleep. 'I guess he's pretty cute.'

'Yep,' I agreed, 'he's pretty cute.'

'There's a look about him, like . . . I don't know . . .'

'Perky?' I suggested. Not that he was perky at the moment, he was comatose, but when Benny was awake there was a jauntiness about the set of his ears, and the brawny eyepatch. Hair bristled across his flat head like a scouring pad. I thought of Alan's imagined Afghan hound, and how it would feel to stroke your fingers through the silky coat. Turn Benny upside down and you could sand floors with him.

'Will you think I'm crazy,' asked Alan, 'if I suggest something?'

'Depends what it is,' I replied, without conspicuous originality.

'Say we were to tell people that Benny was in show-business in London? Just, well, I don't know . . . like they use him for commercials and movies.'

I laughed and blew bubbles across the bath at him. 'Alan, if we tell anyone Benny's expertly trained for the rigorous discipline of film sets, they'll be a bit surprised when neither of us can get him down

317

off the sofa without hauling him bodily by the tail.'

'Yeah, that's true,' he agreed, and sipped. 'Doubt if we'll get through the rest of this Montrachet. There's still five bottles unopened.'

Another scale for measuring our remaining time in London. Shorter than the start up for a phase three clinical trial. Less time than five bottles of Montrachet.

'You know, we could say Benny was kind of a model. For still pictures.'

'Why?'

'No real reason. He just looks the part.'

'Why, Alan?'

But he was gone again, and after a moment I heard him calling a New York number on the cordless phone.

My inner peace, so hard earned, was evaporating like a puddle in the sauna. I took a mouthful of the Montrachet, aware that my palate could only just distinguish it from the cheapest white in our local Safeway, and on some days not from the cheapest red, and turned the hi-fi volume back up again, disregarding the New York call. I tried to sink into the slow movement of the Vaughan Williams, but tonight it sounded like a confectioner's picnic, no more nourishment than a meringue. When Alan finished talking to New York, he came back to the bathroom.

'Thanks for that blast of music, Annie. Ringels thought I'd put him on hold.'

'You've never explained who Ringels is.'

'That why you drowned him out just now?'

'Alan, why do you want to pass off my dog as Lassie?'

'Your dog? I thought he was our dog.'

'Our dog. Whatever.'

'You mean I'm not the father, and this is how I find out?'

'I don't want the jokes. Please just tell me.'

'Nothing to tell. Come on, Annie, back off!'

'Tell me why!' I demanded, as though I were a Boomtown Rat.

He put down the wine glass on the basin. 'OK. This job in the States, we'll be meeting people and entertaining – you agreed to this – members of the board, these guys from venture capital companies. That's my job, Annie.'

'What the bloody hell does this have to do with the dog?'

'Nothing! I told you, it was just a passing thought.'

'*What was?*'

'These people have dogs as part of their lifestyle. We just may want to explain why ours is a scruffy mutt!'

'So we *tell* them why! He was a cruelty case.'

'OK. I know that.'

'Chained up in a shed in the dark and beaten with a chain!'

'I said OK. *OK* – right?'

'No it isn't all right! And how about me?'

'*What?*'

'Not glamorous, dropped out of med. school in the hippie years, teaching for peanuts. How will you explain *me* away in Westchester?'

And we were incandescent. The row went skyward, instantly, like vertical take-off. It was like E. M. Forster's description of every human quarrel – inevitable at the time and incredible afterwards. We screamed at each other, charge and countercharge, my career, his career, my status – all this in a bathroom, so the shouting ricocheted off the tiles and echoed across the neighbouring houses so they must have suspected murder, or at least a cathouse brawl.

After an infinity of this, Alan slammed out, his progress through the house marked by violent upheavals, doors thrown open, drawers thrown shut, clothes and papers slung into cases. The echoing thud of the front door. Then came more remote, inhuman sounds – the electrical hum of garage doors, and then Alan's car, a ragged edge to the revving as he shot out of the drive. Eloquent, all of it. There couldn't have been a single household within our postcode that had failed to follow the plot.

By the time I was able to stop crying, my jaw and ribs ached, and migraine splintered my vision with ziggurats like a Cubist portrait. Hiccuping and virtually blind, I coaxed Benny, the *casus belli*, from under the bed, and went in search of my Migraleve tablets, but these seemed to have been packed away in the crates for shipping, along with every other analgesic in the house. This should have been impossible, and was yet another indictment of my housekeeping skills. I eventually lay down to a white night shot through with pain, in which every word of Alan's clanged inside my head like someone wielding a croquet mallet. The next morning I phoned Babette.

29

A bright, blowy Saturday afternoon in early March, and Babette and I are sitting in my kitchen with Arvo Pärt's *Cantus in Memory of Benjamin Britten*, which happens to be playing on Classic FM. I turn the volume down, so that Babette and I can hear her younger child Sophie, who is ten, playing a sad Scott Joplin rag on the piano in my studio. Its aching, yellow melancholy drifts into the kitchen to mingle with the shivering echoes of the tolling bell from the *Cantus*, and the beneficent aroma of coffee.

The last time Sophie was let loose in my studio was December, a month after Alan and I returned from New York. We had a wonderful time improvising music for the Harry Potter stories, 'Muggle music' she called it, with choir effects and luscious strings and most of all the pitch-bend wheel – wiggle it and the music wobbles in and out of key, like Mr Micklewhite. And while we were thus engaged, Alan was across the courtyard in the house, grossing out the men in Babette's family by discoursing on cancer of the prostate.

Their son Iain has a provisional place at medical school, so Alan, using a system of lateral thinking that seems to work well enough for postulates you can put a dollar sign in front of, judged that he'd enjoy having a real doctor to discuss medicine with man to man. Interestingly, when Alan got onto surgical removal of the testicles, Iain passed out.

This time Sophie is in the studio without me, which is causing her mother serious concern. 'You know what happened when Nigel took his eyes off her that time in the dentist's.'

'Oh come on, Babette, that was ages ago!'

'Exactly. She was smaller then and couldn't reach as far. Limited the damage.'

'But we can hear her. If the Scott Joplin stops, I promise I'll scoot across the courtyard and stop her tearing the internal wiring out of the Korg Triton.'

'What's a Korg Triton when it's at home?'

'Synthesizer. Alan bought it for me for Christmas; a state-of-the-art workstation sampler. It's for all the commissions I'm suddenly going to get. We'll go and ogle it, if you like – brushed aluminium, touch-view panel, for all I know it does intergalactic travel and you can zap Klingons with it.'

Babette was already out of her chair and across to the kitchen door. 'And you've left my daughter in there without a chaperone?'

'But we can *hear* what she's up to. Calm down!'

Reluctantly, Babette let go of the door handle.

'There's no harm she can do. On the contrary, Sophie could record some of her compositions on it and get Alan off my back. Anyway, I want to talk to you.'

'Yes, I thought you might. Bad row, was it?'

'Bad enough.'

'That why Alan's not here?'

322

'Yep. Stormed out of the house last night and hasn't returned.'

'This is about Daniel, I take it.'

'No. No, that's still . . . up in the air.' I heard my voice catch. 'Finish your coffee first.'

I had phoned her this morning with what I'd hoped sounded like a casual invitation to come over for lunch (having promised to provide only deli food and not attempt to cook anything). As I'd opened the front door to them, Sophie had taken one look at me and cried from the street, 'What happened to your eyes, has someone socked you? *Who* socked you – *who, who*?' so that our neighbours would now assume that Alan finished off the evening with a couple of left hooks. But for Babette this wasn't the first time in her life that she'd seen me with puffy eyes.

'Oh Annie!' she'd said in apprehension at the front door. 'You haven't lost Benny, have you?' A long time she's known me.

'Finish your coffee first,' I said again.

Babette sat back down at the table, and returned to what she was doing before this exchange – leafing through Mrs Clitheroe's photograph album. There was a crackle as she turned over a sheet of the spider's web glassine to reveal a black and white photograph in high gloss. 1964. I saw a dinner and dance, the men in dinner jackets, the women in dresses two inches above the knee, heavy eyes, back-combed hair. Every now and then throughout the album, sheets of the spider's web glassine had been inserted back to front, so that instead of protecting the pictures, the high relief had imprinted itself on the photographic surfaces. It had happened to this one. Leonard Clitheroe bared his teeth at the camera through the feathery mesh of etched spider's web, like ripples in a pond. And there was his lovely wife next to him. Her cheeks were dimpled in the familiar smile, but the eyes had a faraway expression that suggested that a lesser woman would have been drooping with boredom.

'Every picture tells a story,' said Babette. 'I wish you'd shown me this before. We were round here not long after you got back from New York.'

'I remember,' I said. 'Muggle music.'

'Sorry?'

'Doesn't matter. Alan was here at the time. We're pretending the album doesn't exist, he and I. The police interview never took place. You know what he's like.'

'You still might have told me, though, Annie, one of the times you've been on the phone sobbing about Daniel. You must have had it here for months.'

'It didn't occur to me that you'd be interested.'

'Well, it might have done. The way I remember, it was me that used to look through Mrs Clitheroe's album. You were always playing the piano.'

Having invited Babette over for comfort and unquestioning support in the wake of last night's row, I was stung disproportionately.

'That isn't quite fair. I got to know the album inside out; I had more than enough to do with it during the murders.' A reflex self-justification, from living with Alan.

'Not on your own, Annie. *With me*. I still think you should have told me you'd found it.'

'Yes, I didn't think.'

'No. Well, I expect you've got a lot on your plate.'

I turned away and fiddled with the coffee percolator. That anybody else living had the remotest claim to interest in Jenny Clitheroe had not crossed my mind for one single, fleeting second. From the corner of my eye, I noticed the sunlight catch Babette's auburn hair, recently reshaped from the long bob she'd worn for years. The few streaks of grey sparkled against her dark eyes. Resentment, already triggered by being made to feel selfish and guilty, prickled even deeper.

'Any road,' she continued, 'I can still hardly believe it's here at all. You say you found it in a bric-a-brac shop in New York of all places?'

'Not so odd, actually. Mrs Clitheroe's cousin lived in Brooklyn, you've probably forgotten that. They always kept in touch, and Jenny didn't have any other close relatives. Well, the cousin died recently, and everything was sold off.'

'But Leonard's estate should have inherited it, surely? I know you can't profit from a crime, but he was never tried.'

'I expect Mrs Clitheroe would have arranged to keep the album in the family, don't you? And remember, we do know she made a will — when she left me the Bechstein.'

'So she did. I hadn't forgotten how much she loved you.'

As intended, the fight went out of me. 'Anyway, *thank God* I happened to be in the shop when the album turned up. I mean, just supposing Alan and I had walked into Aunt Margo's apartment one day and Jenny's mother Nell was looking down at me from the wall, and there were the torn remains of the album . . .'

Babette smiled. 'But it didn't happen, did it?' she pointed out in the tones she would have used to Sophie. 'And life's hard enough without making up things that never happened.'

She reopened the album, and was slowly turning its pages. 'What does Aunt Margo think? Does she know?'

'That I stole it? Alan didn't give me away, but yes, she's been on the phone screaming hellfire. If I do go to the States with Alan, I'll have that to contend with as well.'

'As well,' echoed Babette thoughtfully. Then something in the album caught her eye. 'Wasn't that a peony from Mrs Clitheroe's wedding bouquet?'

I looked at the deadened petals, bereft now of their pigment.

'Looks sad, doesn't it,' continued Babette, 'when you think how marrying him was the death of her.'

The death of her. Then I heard Dorothea: 'I know lots of Nells and Nellies, and every one of them's dead.' They weren't quite all dead then, back in 1965. But they were certainly dead now – like most of the faces in the album, like Babette's parents and my own. And now I was leaving my home and the only man I'd ever loved.

My state of mind this morning was clearly unstable. Grief and fear overwhelmed me. Panic caught my throat, crept up from behind and throttled me like a mugger. I turned away from Babette and lowered my face to the album. The dead looked back at me. I said the first thing that came into my head.

'Do you remember the New York World's Fair? It was where Dad took our matchbox model.'

'Of course I remember.'

'Did I ever tell you it was actually a bit of a fiasco?'

'Yeah?'

'Alan told me. Apparently there was bitter in-fighting. New York's mayor, Mayor Wagner, appointed someone called Robert Moses as president to oversee the planning and design. He'd been in charge of New York's slum clearance programme, which was a total shambles, so this was the simplest way to haul him off it. Unfortunately, Robert Moses was also a self-acclaimed philistine, who publicly despised the arts and architecture. At his appointment, half the team involved went ballistic and resigned, while commentators howled and foamed at the mouth and chewed the carpets.'

'But presumably it was a commercial success.'

'Not really, no. Those vast expositions were out of date by the mid-Sixties. Most countries didn't even bother to sponsor a pavilion. That's why Dad thought up a matchbox model suitable for the New York City pavilion. Great Britain didn't even have one.'

'I never knew that.'

Having firmly planted ourselves back in 1965, we returned nostalgically to the photograph album.

'Do you know, I don't think I've ever told Sophie about the murders. I can't think why – you know how she laps up anything bloodthirsty.'

'I wonder whether DI Lilliput still remembers us?' I said.

'The poor bloke doesn't remember anybody any more; he died just before Christmas.'

'How would you know that?'

'There was an obituary in *The Times*. Jim Lilliput, his name was. He made Chief Constable.'

'I didn't know that either.'

'No. Well.'

No need for her to say it; if I don't ever open a paper, it's always going to be difficult for me to keep up with the news.

'I can't really remember how the pair of us came to be running around Essex with this album in the first place. How did we come to pinch it from Mrs Clitheroe's anyway?'

'*We* didn't pinch it, Babette! You and Lorraine pinched it and saddled me with the consequences.'

'Lorraine?'

'You really don't remember, do you?'

'I never recall the same sort of details you do. I remember Lilliput, and being frightened, and getting chucked off a bus with Dorothea. I remember it never seemed to worry us much that we might be distracting them from Mrs Clitheroe's murder inquiry.'

Across the courtyard, Sophie had now moved on from the earlier melancholy, and was having a crack at the 'Maple Leaf Rag'. She'd started at a fair lick and was accelerating hard. At this rate, I'd be interested to see how far she got towards the finishing post before she either slowed down or her fingers came flying off and wrapped it up on their own.

Babette was wriggling something from behind another black and white picture. Wartime. 'With Mabel at the Anderson shelter, 14 Olive Road.' And tucked behind it, a sixpenny concert programme, a tiny thing you could slip into a pocket without folding. As she did so, a couple of loose photographs fluttered to the floor.

'Chester Gaumont,' read Babette. 'Sunday Concert. I always did find some amazing stuff in here.'

It was autographed by the conductor of the Liverpool Philharmonic – 'Jenny, I'm glad you liked the concert. Enjoy the colours of your music.'

'Colours?' queried Babette. Then 'Chester?'

'That's what it says. September, 1944.'

'That's odd.'

'Why?'

'Well, Mrs Clitheroe had never been up that way, don't you remember? She used to joke about how she'd married a northerner, yet she'd never been north of the home counties.'

'Perhaps Leonard got the autograph for her.'

'It says "I'm glad you liked the concert".'

'Oh yes.'

'A mystery.'

The Liverpool Phil had played an uplifting, wartime programme, including the '*Eine Kleine Nachtmusik*' and the overture from Wagner's *Tannhäuser*. Pretty much the same programme that was playing in Berlin, no doubt.

'I suppose,' I continued, 'it would be daft of me to ask whether you remember how Lorraine found an unfinished letter in here? From when you and she pinched the album in the first place? I remember your saying that Lorraine had been looking through the album, and found the beginnings of a letter Mrs Clitheroe was writing.'

'Why, is it still in here?'

'No. According to you, Lorraine found a love letter that began "My darling" and went on to say that she was leaving home because she didn't feel safe. Anyway, I looked for it. But there's nothing like that in here.'

'Perhaps this New York cousin took it out.'

'I get the impression that the album wasn't much opened in New York.'

'Lilliput then. The police got it back from us eventually, didn't they?'

'Yes, Lorraine posted it to them.'

'Lorraine *again*! God, it's all coming back. You know, if you'd asked me yesterday, I'd have said Lorraine wasn't even in Muningstock during the murders.'

'She was going to keep it for us, and she betrayed her promise. I was distraught. Do you think Lorraine might remember now? I mean, about the letter?'

'Doubt it. Why were you looking?'

'I don't know. Yes, I do. In case there was something else in it, to confirm that it really was her husband she was scared of.'

'Why? I remember him as though it was yesterday. He was horrible. Always shouting at her. He used to knock her about, too.'

'Yes, I know.'

'And he left a signed confession, and then hung himself.'

'I could always phone Lorraine and ask her if she remembers the exact words. She wouldn't mind, would she? I mean, she'd recollect who I am?'

'Annie, what's this all about? A letter in an old photo album belonging to a lady we knew when we were ten. Why?'

'It's been haunting me, Babette. When Gina Maxwell was killed, Lilliput told my mother that the police hadn't closed the file on Mrs Clitheroe, meaning they never really believed Leonard was responsible. And the Maxwell murder was never solved. Which was pretty much my fault, destroying the evidence. It's been preying on my mind.'

'Since when?'

'Since we landed in New York. First it was Dad, this awful feeling of guilt eating at me for letting him down. I kept seeing his face the night I told him I'd chucked medical school. Then Mrs Clitheroe. But the fact is that I've always felt a link with her, Babette, a synaesthetic sort of thing. I've often had a strong sense of her presence.'

'That's the first I've heard of it.'

'Actually no, it isn't. I realize you've never believed me about hearing "Ruby Tuesday" in my head the day of her funeral, but . . .'

'Even if I did accept the way you interpreted that, it was 1965, Annie, and you were ten years old. I haven't heard you worrying about her murder in the meantime.'

'I think it's to do with New York. It was always Mrs Clitheroe I associated with New York; she had a remarkable gift for bringing places to life. All the time Alan and I were in Manhattan, I couldn't look at a skyscraper without seeing and hearing her.'

'Annie, you've been to New York loads of times, including with me, remember? You never went on like this then. You want to know what I think? I think you're hiding behind it. I'm not going to mince words. Somebody's got to talk to you straight, Annie, and if not your oldest friend, then who? You've got some major life decisions to face: this mega move to New York, your marital difficulties, your feelings for Daniel – it's a classic life crisis. I think you're trying to push

330

it all away from you by getting worked up about some-thing else. This is you in denial.'

'Oh, please, not the jargon. Life crisis! Denial! *Hate* that. *Hate* that.'

'Of course you do. We all want to think our troubles are unique. But think about it: you're having an affair, sleeping with another man, telling your husband lies. Yet instead of any of the normal guilty feelings we'd expect from you, here you are agonizing over Mrs Clitheroe's murder when you were ten years old. Anybody would say the same thing, Annie – you're substituting a more comfortable sort of guilt, one you don't actually have to confront because it's literally dead and gone.'

'Perhaps I can't feel guilty about something that feels so right!'

'If I'm not allowed jargon, you're not allowed song lyrics.'

'That wasn't—'

'Look, why don't you tell me about this row with Alan? It's why you asked me round in the first place.'

'Just because I haven't been boring everyone to death about the murders for several decades, doesn't mean they haven't nagged at my conscience, Babette! I think it's perfectly natural that they should. Childhood traumas are a damn sight more mega than any decision about living in Westchester, and we were up to our necks in that one from the first morning Lorraine purloined this album from Bluebell Crescent.'

'Afternoon.'

'What?'

'Not morning, afternoon. I told you, it's all coming back. Uncle Arthur decided to tell Mum Lorraine was pregnant, and the balloon went up. Lorraine dragged me away from the kerfuffle, and as there was nowhere else to escape to, we went back round Bluebell Crescent. We'd already been in Mrs Clitheroe's earlier, browsing through the album, but it was on the second visit that Lorraine got the brilliant idea of nicking it. Annie, you've got to stop telling yourself the past is your own private—'

'Twice? Lorraine had her hands on it twice?'

'What?'

'Lorraine had access to this album in the morning, and then removed it from Bluebell Crescent in the afternoon?'

'What?'

'Is that what you're saying?'

'Yes! *Why?*'

'The letter!'

'What?'

'That's what happened to the letter! Obviously.'

'Look, Annie, shouldn't we be worrying about your husband storming out of the house eighteen hours ago and not coming back home?'

I picked up the displaced photographs from the floor.

'Henderson's Sliding Doors Picnic, 1955.' I'd kept the pictures all these years, and intended to reinstate them in their album just as soon as I'd made up my mind whether they should go before or after the other two Henderson pictures, that Lilliput himself must have returned to the album after they fell out of my knickers in August 1965.

30

Benny was lying at my feet. Actually he was lying *on* my feet, under the table well away from any danger of Sophie. I'd filled Babette in about the row. Now she continued as though following the canine cast to my thoughts.

'Alan's silly remarks about the dog – wasn't that just his own insecurity? After all, this new job is a great deal to take on. And it's, what, six years now since he's worked in the States?'

'Eight.'

'Well then.'

'Alan is a hard-driven, ambitious man. Fair enough. But you see, stated without frills, he hasn't a scrap of respect for what I do. Alan doesn't see teaching as worthwhile, and of course it doesn't pay as well as other work that he thinks I should be doing instead, never mind that I wouldn't get it even if I wanted it, which I absolutely don't.'

'Whatever Alan's feelings, if you go to New York, *can* you teach?'

'Some, yes.'

'But you won't have a job at a drama school.'

'Doubt it.'

'So – what?'

'Well, I suppose I'll mostly coach private students for auditions on Broadway. Who knows? In London, people come to a vocal coach for a dozen reasons. Several of my students are busy career people who use singing to improve their presentation skills or to release stress and I coach a number of foreign students who use it to help their English pronunciation. I also have women from cultures where women are supposed to be seen but not heard, and now they're in England they want to find a voice. It's liberation, Babette – opening up your lungs and letting your voice soar! One of my regulars is a teenager with autism, and I have a young woman with MS who belts out Gloria Gaynor's "I Will Survive" from a wheelchair.' I stopped, belatedly remembering that Babette, too, was a teacher, an excellent and successful one.

'I'm sorry, you know all about how fulfilling teaching can be.'

'Before this departmental headship I did. Now I spend most of my time doing admin., and I can assure you *that's* about as fulfilling as restocking the shelves in Sainsbury's. But look, suppose you do find that you're mostly coaching for auditions, could you manage it over there?'

'Yes, I've checked it out.'

'So you'd be confident enough to teach in New York.'

'Auditioning's the same whether it's Broadway or Timbuktu. And I've done my homework regarding all the peripheral knowledge I'll need. For example, singers have to build up a repertoire – well, I can advise them where in New York they can find interesting old collections of ballads on vinyl and where they can pick up sheet music that's out of print. I've made a list of professional copyists who'll transpose a song for them, or even transcribe it directly off a recording. All that sort of thing.'

'Did you enjoy doing the research?'

'How do you mean?'

'It sounds to me like you enjoyed it. As if something in you *was* enthusiastic, hoping that you *would* go to New York.'

I looked at her.

'That's how it sounds to me,' she repeated.

Like an emanation from Mrs Clitheroe's mysterious concert programme, Classic FM was now playing the overture to *Tannhäuser*.

'Dad loved this,' I said, rubbing some warmth into my arms, which had come up in gooseflesh. 'You realize, he felt precisely the same way about my teaching as Alan does. I was a foul disappointment to him.'

'Yet your dad was a brilliant teacher himself, and he believed in it as a vocation.'

'I was born the day after Einstein died and Dad always hoped I'd take up the torch. He used to dream of Nobel prizes, and then I abandoned medical school for love of a popular music that he despised.'

I thought of my sixth form and the couple of years I'd managed at St Mary's; the great featureless waste of facts and theories and practical techniques, stretching across my days and weeks like a desert of stodge and glue and quicksand. 'I was bored to death. And hated the sight of blood. It was about the worst profession I could have gone for.'

'But it was never your own choice. Your dad wouldn't take no for an answer.'

'It's a common enough problem; I wasn't alone in my intake at St Mary's. There are two professions that otherwise loving parents impel totally unsuitable

335

children into – the priesthood, and medicine.'

December 1975. The Dean's office. 'Pop music,' he'd kept repeating tonelessly throughout the interview, eyeing me as though I were an unexpected fungal infection in a previously healthy passage.

My mother had accepted the news with more resignation than anger. She'd mentioned Daniel's name just once, and I, rendered inflammable by guilt, had railed at her for it, for trying to scapegoat this wonderful man she hardly knew, for failing to credit me with enough initiative to make my own life decisions. For failing. Then suddenly all the passion, the desire to wound, whistled out of me like air from a slashed tyre, because my father hadn't shouted back. He had sat down, covered his face with his hands and cried.

I'd walked the eight miles to Brentwood station. Cold night, moonless; few cars passed me, though I passed them, stationary in their owners' drives, coated with ice like huge, plump, crystallized fruit. I'd arrived home in Notting Hill petrified with cold, and desolate. Daniel had put me into a hot bath and poured brandy into me, but I went down with a severe case of flu that lasted across Christmas. It was Daniel who phoned my mother, over what by then was virtually my dead body, and therefore didn't contravene the injunction. Did I mean to spare my parents further worry? Or was I punishing them? (You'll be sorry when I'm dead.) And for what?

My father's face breaking down in tears haunted me; he stalked through my fever dreams, and hovered in sleep-emergent visions. And when I was forty, and he died, this was the only image in my head, the picture I could not banish while the crematorium curtains were closing, and my expensive, imported male voice choir was singing 'All Through the Night' in my father's woodnotes wild, 'Ar Hyd y Nos'.

*   *   *

Now, here in my Ealing kitchen, as Wagner's music died away, Babette and I expected to hear Sophie's ragtime re-establish itself. Instead there was silence. Babette rose from her chair in alarm, and was already across to the door when a reassuring plink-a-plonk started up again. I thought how proud both my parents had been of Babette. They didn't live to see her get the departmental headship, but she was already teaching biology to A level in a respected Surrey school. She had been out of the country when they died, my mother and then Dad; her husband Nigel was in Washington for a year with the World Bank before he came home to the European Bank in the City, and Babette was appointed Head of Sciences at one of the country's largest secondary schools.

'Your dad liked Alan, didn't he?'

'God, yes. He thought that marrying Alan was the only sensible thing I'd done in twenty years. He died shortly afterwards. It felt like the *nunc dimittis*: "Lord, letteth now Thy servant depart in peace."'

'And Alan was a New Yorker. So, being you, I suppose you saw him as New York incarnate. *And* you'd just lost your mum. *And* Nigel and I were three thousand miles away.'

'And I went headlong at something without thinking.'

'Ah, well. There's a first time for everything.' Babette turned idly back to the photograph album. 'And just in case you didn't have enough problems, there's Daniel.'

'Perhaps it was always inevitable, the way Daniel and I feel about each other . . . Perhaps the divorce was only a temporary separation; another phase of our life together, in a way.'

'Mmm. Only while this temporary separation was going on, Daniel happened to increase his responsibilities to the tune of one boy and one girl.'

'I'm not neglecting that consideration, Babette. I haven't asked him to leave home.'

'But you're happy breaking up your own marriage.'

'Half the time I am. The other half I think it would be better for all concerned if I stayed with Alan but continued to see Daniel on the quiet whenever we can contrive something . . .' My voice trailed off. It didn't sound good, spoken aloud. Actually, I was surprised at just how bad it sounded.

'Look, Annie, you don't need me to tell you you're skating on thin ice. Alan isn't the sort to mess about with. He won't share his possessions.'

'I am not one of—'

'And what about Daniel? Can you really see him leading a double life? Lying and cheating at home?'

I smarted at that. 'Naturally it's extremely distasteful to both of us, Babette, but that is unfortunately the situation we're in.'

'But can you see him doing it for long? Open-hearted Daniel? Betraying someone who trusts him?'

'We've no choice.'

'Annie, some men can manage it, but they're the type who can readily tell lies to themselves. You know Daniel isn't like that.'

'Please, Babette.'

'And how long do you think Alan's going to put up with it all?'

'Please, I'm at the end of my tether. I really do *not* want to hear this.'

'Then why did you ask me over?'

I sat for a while gathering my composure. When eventually I looked up, Babette had put the kettle on, and was making me tea.

'Look, one thing at a time. I don't think you should go to the States like this,' she said simply. 'Alan's bullied you into it.'

'So I should leave him. Of course,' I added with a

338

jolt, 'we're assuming that Alan hasn't already left *me*. You should have been here last night.'

'First things first. You can insist on living in Manhattan. It's not businesslike to rent a place to teach from, Annie. You'll be downgrading your life's work to a subsidized hobby. And anyway, you *love* Manhattan. You've been driving us all potty with the place since you were ten.'

'Alan will never consent to live in the city.'

'I think that depends on how you put your ultimatum.'

'New York or quits?'

'That's what I'd do.'

I was quiet for a moment. 'Babette, the truth is that no matter which side of the world I'm on, I don't think I'm strong enough to stay away from Daniel, never mind whether it's right or wrong or insane. I shall be coming home to see you and Nigel, naturally, and . . .'

'Nigel and I can't help you there, I'm afraid; you won't be coming home to England to see either of us, because we'll be in Washington. Nigel's going back to DC for two years. He signed the contract on Thursday and we're moving in August. So when you're living in New York you'll have a bolthole. Any time you want. We'll be just an hour away by plane. I'll keep the spare room made up.'

The kitchen swam. 'But you can't! I mean – your school here, your science department! You can't possibly go back to the States!'

'Don't you worry about me, I'm flexible, and I've got a Green Card. There's an adult numeracy programme they need someone to head up – I've wanted something like that for years. Listen to me, Annie. It's not only Daniel who isn't cut out for a long-term secret affair. You'll get yourself into a right old pickle, telling lies. You always did, and it always ended in tears.'

*   *   *

Neither of us said anything else. After a bit, Babette left the kitchen and walked across the courtyard to the studio door. 'Sophie, lovey, we're just about Scott-Joplined out! Pack it in, please.'

I heard the initial notes of a complaining whine, followed by her mother's rapid steps across the pine floor of the studio and the sound of a piano lid being firmly shut. Sophie continued to argue as they came back over to the house.

'You've got grade five exams coming up,' Babette was reminding her, 'and we haven't heard you do any of the pieces. I'm sure Auntie Annie would *love* to hear how well you play them.'

'As if!' came Sophie's reply.

'I suppose you don't get subjected to this,' said Babette. '"As if!" and "Dream on!" and "No way, José!"'

'I do not say "no way, José", Mum, that is *so* uncool! Anyway, when you were my age, Dad says you used to say "grotty" and "fab". That's the worst thing I've ever heard of!' Sophie turned to me. 'When you were my age,' she asked, 'what was the absolute worst thing you'd ever heard of?'

'The war in Vietnam.'

'Not you, Mum! I'm asking Auntie Annie!'

'Well now,' I said, thinking, *I can give you more than you bargained for*, 'when I was your age, a lady who lived round the corner from us was murdered.' I paused to milk the moment. 'AND,' I added, 'I thought the police had locked up an innocent man for it by mistake, and I believed that I was the only person in the world who could prove that he hadn't done it.'

'Really?' Sophie turned to her mother. 'Is that true?'

'Sophie! Of course it's true.'

'*Murder*, Mum, and you never said?!'

'As a matter of fact, there were *four* murders,' I told her.

'Who was it, then, the murderer?'

'Actually,' I admitted, with a suspicion that this might not be much of a story after all, 'we don't know. The cases were never solved . . .' I petered out.

'Was it like that man on *Crimewatch*?' probed Sophie. 'He broke into this person's house with a pump-action shotgun and it went *kapow-kapow-kapow*. And my brother got this film out on video with two men who robbed a bank and what they did was . . .'

'Come on, lovey!' Babette interrupted. 'Go and play your exam pieces for Auntie Annie, and then we've got to make a move. Uncle Craig's coming round this evening, if you remember, with the express intention of thrashing you and Iain at table tennis.'

'Thrashing *me*? In his dreams!'

Babette turned to me with a gesture of despair. 'If you don't go to New York,' she said, 'can I leave her in London with you?'

THE PAST

31

'So this Mashie Mickey man did in the first bloke.'
   'No, the *second* bloke did in the first bloke . . .'
   'Machete Mickey did in the *second* bloke.'
   Dorothea considered this. 'So the second dead body used to be the same murderer who killed the first dead body.' But this one stumped even Babette.
   It was the last afternoon of the holidays, and we were on the village green, the three of us reunited (as it were), watching the fair being cleared away, the sweet-shop colours of the merry-go-round dismantled, the tents, the stalls. Between and among the caravans and trailers roamed large men with earrings and neckerchiefs, their hands full of scaffold poles, tired fluffy toys, and plastic bags with goldfish-like slices of carrot, wavering inside the distorting water. Everywhere was the whirr of engines.
   Dorothea and family had dropped in last night on their way home from a Girl Guides jamboree weekend in Chelmsford. Horrified at her reappearance, which Babette and I saw as contravening a sort of Cradock

family version of the Geneva Convention, we were now grudgingly accepting that the visit had been a godsend. For the past three days the press had crawled over the village, knocking on every door in Bluebell Crescent until the reticent residents had called the police, and then shifting their field of operations to Mountnessing Road. True, none of them had taken the slightest interest in us – after all, we were children and couldn't know anything – but our parents were getting seriously frazzled and so, of course, *they* took it out on us. Except Uncle Frank, who thumped a reporter on the nose for pestering him for a quote about Gina Maxwell being the salt of the earth.

Well, the journalists would ease up on Muningstock now they'd got their story, now that Annie Cradock had given her alfresco press conference with extensive lurid details, together with photographs of the narrator reliving her discovery on that gruesome garden path, made all the more poignant by her Girl Guide's uniform.

Meanwhile, Lorraine and Uncle Arthur had gone home, but not before Lorraine had got the entire rigmarole sorted out for us by chatting in the village. She was going to be much missed; there would be young men knocking at Auntie Rene's door and getting shouted at for days.

I resumed our tale. 'There was some stolen jewellery. One of the travellers got his hands on it and he knew this man in the East End called the Governor. He owed him something, so he promised this governor the sparklers.'

'The diamond necklace,' Babette corrected.

'That's right. Then another East End crook . . .'

'. . . called Eddie . . .'

'. . . he heard about it, and tried to steal the jewels first by coming down to Muningstock and burgling the traveller's caravan. Except he wasn't very good at being a burglar. The traveller came home and caught him at it, and Eddie killed him with a knife.'

'So who's got the diamonds now?'

'Eddie got the diamonds.'

'Still?'

'No, not *still*. Eddie was murdered. He was number two.'

'*So who killed Eddie?*'

Babette and I exchanged glances. It was no good getting exasperated with us. We were doing our best.

'The Governor's men came out to Muningstock looking for the jewellery,' I continued coolly. 'They were called Sid the Fiddler and Machete Mickey. They came looking for Eddie and found him in bed in his caravan in a layby, and they . . .' I jibbed. Babette took over the narrative.

'They machete'd him. But that was daft because Eddie hadn't even *got* the necklace any more – he'd given it to one of the travellers who was a . . . a . . .'

'A fence,' I put in.

'So Sid and Mickey went over the travellers' camp to get the necklace for their boss. And chopped this fence's hand off.'

Th-wack!!

'And then things started going wrong round Bluebell Crescent. The same day Eddie got killed and Annie heard that bloke getting his hand hacked off by Mickey's machete, Mrs Maxwell came and snooped on Horace Frobisher with Mrs Clitheroe, and heard Mrs Clitheroe say she was leaving him.'

'That's Mr Clitheroe,' I clarified.

'. . . and then Mrs Maxwell told on them. So a couple of days later he killed his wife to stop her.'

'That's Mr Clitheroe,' I clarified again.

'Only he made it look like a burglary gone wrong, so as the coppers would think it was them travellers again.'

344

'And that's what Mrs Maxwell thought, too,' I added, ''cos when she saw me dressed in a sheet climbing through Mrs Clitheroe's bathroom window, she thought it was Old Ollie, because she was shortsighted.'

'And thick and spiteful.'

'Right,' said Dorothea. 'So Leonard Clitheroe murdered Mrs Clitheroe because of what Mrs Maxwell told him. And the police got it wrong anyway, because they thought he killed her for insurance money.'

'That's right.'

'And Mrs Maxwell got the police to arrest Ollie, and when he got out again, Ollie did her in, to serve her right.'

'Well . . .'

'*Or*,' amended Dorothea, '*Horace* did her in, to shut her up about you-know-what.'

'Perhaps.'

'And the police can't get either of them for it.'

'Looks like it.'

'Meanwhile, the police never actually caught Mrs Clitheroe's murderer – Leonard did it all himself, gave himself up, and did himself in.'

'That's right.'

'And the first murderer, this Eddie bloke, the police never arrested him, either.'

'They couldn't. He was dead.'

'And now they can't find the second murderer, this Mickey?'

'Gone to earth, Lorraine said.'

'And they don't even know who the other traveller *is*, the one who got amputated?'

'That's right.' As far as we understood, no witness had come forward waving a handless stump.

'So,' Dorothea summed up looking disgusted, 'what's that slaphead policeman been *doing*?!'

* * *

We wandered about a bit. Over at the waltzer, we parked ourselves on the slatted wooden steps, from which position Babette scanned her surroundings for Melena Watson, Mrs Watson having told us that she was somewhere about. Dorothea looked thoughtfully across at the dodgems, strategies and tactics showing in the whites of her eyes.

'At the World's Fair in New York,' I began, and was talked down. Dorothea cracked a quick lavatorial joke about Flushing Meadows. This wasn't the first such allusion of the day; at Babette's initial mention of Melena, Dorothea had informed us that her friend who was a doctor's daughter said that this was the medical word for poo with blood in it.

'Oy, yous three!' A very male voice bellowed across us. 'The fair's closed. You can't sit there – we're hauling dangerous machinery around.'

'What dangerous machinery?' countered Dorothea. 'We haven't seen anything more dangerous than a goldfish.'

'Oh, we've got a wise guy, 'ave we? Come on, girls, shift. We'll be back next Easter. You can sit here then.'

We dragged ourselves up, and shuffled reluctantly away from the seductive waltzer. As we passed the merry-go-round, I caught sight of one of the Romany men. It was the same traveller who had come up to Old Ollie in the camp when I was on the back of the cart. The sight of him juxtaposed against the merry-go-round triggered another association. Carousel, I thought. Or, more properly, *Carousel*. Rodgers and Hammerstein. Robbery, and a man dead on the blade of a knife. *Th-wack!!*

I had seen Ollie on Saturday evening. Amid the razzle-dazzle excitement of the fairground, there he had been, plus dog, leaning against a trailer.

'Hello, Ollie. Please may I cuddle your dog?'

'Oh, it's you. Wotcha cock!'

346

After a little while I re-emerged, wiping my face down with a handkerchief.

'Ollie?'

'Yes, cock.'

'It was me that found Mrs Maxwell. On her garden path.'

'I knows that a'ready.'

'Yes. Ollie?'

'What is it, cock?'

'Has your dog still got fleas?'

'Wouldn't letcha all over 'im if 'e 'ad. I drowned the buggers.'

'Did you hose him down?'

'Nah, 'e'd've upped and left 'ome. I give him carbolic barfs.'

'Oh. Ollie?'

'Yes, cock.'

'The police asked me if I saw anyone. Up Bluebell Crescent. I didn't, though. I told them, told Mr Lilliput. I didn't see anybody at all.'

The dog was slowly coming to terms with the withdrawal of affection in my customary, and apparently haphazard, way. His owner was rolling a cigarette, licking and relicking the Rizla paper. Tiny tobacco shards sprouted from the end but didn't fall out. Even Dorothea couldn't do that.

'Don'cha worry,' he told me as he twirled the end into a twist. 'There won't be no more, not now.'

'What do you mean?'

'Wot I say. Maxwell's one were just tit for tat, and don't count. It's all over now, cock, there won't be no more.' And then, 'Giddy-up!' he said out of habit to the dog, and the dog, happy to be doing something, anything, trotted after him.

'Know what my dad said?' asked Dorothea.

Babette and I stopped walking, and considered the

broad panoply of things Uncle Norman might have come out with. First thing this morning he'd tripped over some loose board up in our loft, and announced that last week, the thing had half-killed him, twice.

'No idea,' we decided.

'He said, "After all that's happened to young Annie, she'll go even more doolally."'

Babette and I thought about it.

'Well, she hasn't,' was Babette's verdict.

'No,' agreed Dorothea, 'and Dad doesn't even know the half of it – breaking into Mrs Clitheroe's the day she was murdered—'

'*Shhhhhh!*'

'Honestly, Dorothea!'

'Do you want to get her arrested?'

'But I reckon if Dad knew, then he'd be *really* impressed.'

'I think we better get back,' said Babette flatly. 'My mum said I got to sort my satchel out for tomorrow. And Dorothea, your mum and dad'll be wanting to start off for home.'

Here and there across the fairground enormous brown men with tattoos hollered and hammered, but I couldn't see my traveller among them. And no sign, of course, of Ollie.

'It's a bit more complicated than you said,' I told my companions, though I knew their thoughts had moved on now, to parents and home and school tomorrow; though I knew they weren't listening. 'It's not like I'm scared, but I still sort of know. I know *things* I didn't used to. Horrible things.'

As I considered this, the sounds of the fairground started to close in; I could still hear Saturday night's Wurlitzer organ in every trundling wheel, but now I was conscious of the snarl in the machinery, inhuman, subhuman. I was aware of the rifle range. The air was full of violent men swinging club hammers. I made an effort and conjured Mrs Clitheroe's songs, and sang them cheerfully in my head. Looking back across the green with its lurid stalls, its weaponry, its skulking trailers, I had a sudden foresight. I knew how that grass would look tomorrow, after the heavy vehicles had trundled away dragging their ironmongery behind them. The green would be stencilled with the plan of the vanished fair, its erstwhile layout emblazoned in bleached grass, the very texture waxed and unhealthy, like skin held too long underwater, or the bloodless tissue of disembodied fingers hanging from a severed hand.

'Come *on*, Annie!'

I bent down. A young man in jeans stepped past me with a horse's head under each arm. As carefully as my bitten nails would let me, I picked out of the grass the pathetic corpses of several discarded goldfish and slipped them into my pocket. They could be quietly buried tomorrow in the school spinney, I decided. I'd give them their own little lollipop crosses between the gerbils, with the Lord's Prayer and a verse of 'The Day Thou Gavest Lord is Ended'. Satisfied that I'd done my best for the dead, I straightened up, and followed Babette and Dorothea towards Rainbird Lane and the walk home to get ready for school tomorrow.

THE PRESENT

32

I am staying. I am going. I will finish the affair, but stay in London anyway. I am going to New York, but with plans to meet up with Daniel on one side of the Atlantic or the other. Click! The crystals in the kaleidoscope shake into another pattern. Click! and another. I pack, and organize, and change my mind approximately every thirty seconds.

That exchange with Babette has shaken me up. Could she be right? Is there a stark, prosaic explanation for my sense of being haunted by restless ghosts from my childhood? Has my mind cooked it all up to provide me with excuses not to face the crises in my immediate reality? Babette does have a way of presenting your own arguments back at you that knocks the glitter off them. Perhaps the emotional storm of my love affair had sensitized me to memories of other storms, and suddenly our plane touched down and there was the Manhattan skyline, evocative of all that was wonderful and all that was lost, in that summer of 1965.

But what about the near-supernatural advent of the photograph album? Difficult to dismiss that as co-incidence. But think a moment – think how it happened. Just Aunt Margo trawling through some junk in case she could afford it, and Larry pipes up with a comment about 'Queen of the May'. If I hadn't been obsessing about Mrs Clitheroe, if she hadn't been at the front of my mind, would I ever have latched on to it, there in his stuffy store? Of course not. Not a chance. I would have carried on dreamily reading those 1960s adverts with absolutely no inkling that Mrs Clitheroe's album was just a few feet behind me. The thought made me feel faint.

And Aunt Margo would never have gone for it, not at two hundred and ninety-five dollars! I kicked up that fuss, and she wanted to spite me. No, if I hadn't been preoccupied already, I wouldn't have known the album was there, Aunt Margo would have dismissed it out of hand, and I'd never have been any the wiser.

But even if you wrote that one off, you were still stuck with my 'Ruby Tuesday', a case of precognition that couldn't be explained rationally. Except as memory playing false, I suppose. Memory might play false even in smart-alec synaesthetic *savants* like me with our bizarre associations and yawn-inspiring party tricks. Especially in us, perhaps. If you're someone who thinks Wednesday is green, and threes are red and hostile, you might also be prone to thinking you've heard Rolling Stones songs that haven't been written yet. That's what Babette would say, anyway. Not to mention Alan. Just as long as no-one tells the Guggenheim.

Interesting how Babette described Alan as being New York incarnate. She was right, there must have been a time, when we met and married, when that was true. Alan, not Dad and his model of the Empire State

Building, and not Mrs Clitheroe. In an effort to re-organize my various guilts, I decide to ask Babette whether she would like to keep the photograph album herself. But then another face from the past floats into my mind. There is somebody else with a better claim. From inside the knotted logic of another terrible night, I decide to organize a trip to Horace and Doris Frobisher.

Driving from Ealing to Essex, west to east, I eschew the M25 motorway and take the roads my mother would have known when we lived together, the roads we had driven on the way home from London airport. I set off, yawning, before dawn to miss the worst of the rush hour; I drive along singing 'Sentimental Journey' to Aldgate's curdled traffic and blown litter. But, of course, none of this is familiar territory any more, and without knowing it, I am heading north, rubber-necking for non-existent street signs and swivelling the *A to Z* round and round on my lap. I reach the Hackney Marshes before I recognize where I am, and pull up to take stock. Early morning, and the marshes are effaced by a thick roll of wet mist. Legless dog owners bob along in pursuit of their legless, skating dogs which, barking wildly, wheel in great arcs across my field of vision with all the weightlessness and liberty of the seagulls that soar in great circles over-head. I've found the London fogs, I think. Must tell Aunt Margo.

Out of the car to stretch my legs. A man running after his dog shouts a greeting at me in that camaraderie of early morning when lesser beings are still in bed. I wave back and walk on, direction unknown. This mist-whitened landscape reminds me of somewhere. Helsinki Bay. When my marriage to Daniel was on the rocks, I took off with my revue, *Cruising with Miss Swan and Mr Lilliput*, for a tour. After Hong Kong and Japan we did the Nordic countries.

352

I had calculated our outgoings and expenses, me and the two actors, taking into account a trip that Daniel and I had made the previous summer around Greece on five pounds a day. I made a guess that twice that amount would be a generous budget for Scandinavia, so we starved. One late afternoon at the beginning of March, desolate, I'd walked out across the ice of Helsinki Bay at sundown; the long, slow sunset of the north under its glacial sky, the feverish light, the silver birches phosphorescent. And in that vast icescape, I had walked myself to some sense of peace.

'Wiv a ladder and some glasses,' I now sang quietly, 'you could see to 'Ackney Marshes. If it wasn't for the 'ouses in between.'

We used to sing that on our patch of grass behind the Notting Hill flat, when Daniel wasn't elbow-deep in wet clay depictions of Ilkley Moor, and Black Willie wasn't home for him to wind up.

A mother trots past with a child of pre-school age, muffled up like an Inuit, sex indeterminable. I remember my miscarriage and wonder, for perhaps the millionth time, whether the lost baby was a boy or a girl.

'If it's a girl,' I had tried to joke to Daniel when I was first pregnant, 'would we be burdening her with expectations if we named her Virginia? Virginia Woolf?'

'That depends,' he'd replied with smooth cruelty, 'whether she has a right to my name.'

I was forty when I married Alan, and anyway, he didn't want children. All the noise and untidiness. You wouldn't want to add a baby to it.

The air clears. It feels good, clean as a peeled apple. Ideas spawn and sparkle like the furring of dew on the reedbeds. Ideas like: I'm not actually enslaved to anybody, not even Daniel. I can choose whether to

353

continue the career that I love in the West End or on Broadway, on the merits of that consideration alone. *My* choices. For the first time in weeks, I can feel freedom like fresh air flooding my lungs and blood. I know the unsung joys of a sense of proportion.

Ahead of me, what had been a dim and grainy spot of colour now resolves into a family group. Advancing further, I have a better feel for shape and tone: a large man in a canary-coloured sweater, a small woman, tiny by comparison, with a fan of black hair, and someone even smaller beside her, a child. As I gain on them with my long strides, their gusts of laughter are thrown towards me by a breath of wind. The mist rolls low on the grass, waves of a shallow, white sea.

The man in the sweater hunkers down and then rises again holding aloft a scarf, which turns out, as I get nearer, to be a second child. Laughter and squeals reach me across the diminishing distance. A man, his wife, two children. A family like Daniel's. In fact, Daniel even has a canary-coloured sweater, one component of a wardrobe apparently inspired by Liquorice Allsorts.

I stop as though shot.

Daniel?

The family bounces on ahead. I continue forward on legs that are suddenly full of air.

But that isn't possible! It's entirely possible; the Hackney Marshes aren't so far from Butler's Wharf. It's Monday morning – perhaps Daniel brought the family up to the apartment for the weekend. This thought sears through my heart like a heated knife. Daniel, and Sita, the tiny beautiful Sita, ten years my junior, and their children. That will be Leo whom Daniel is throwing into the air; Alice trotting between them. A family. My heart slams at my chest. I watch him double over, and settle a squirming Leo back on the mist-cleared grass. A voice wafts behind them.

'Wayne!' shouts the woman. 'Get back 'ere where we can see you, we don't want you falling in them boggy bits.'

'You hear your mum, Wayne? Or d'you want the back of me 'and?'

Click! The crystals realign. They are young, the man perhaps thirty, wobbling already with beer gut. Those children are toddlers.

Back at the car, I slump against the steering wheel and weep for an hour. Turning back towards Ealing, I know that it will be a long, long time before the pain fades from the image my mind created of Daniel with Sita and Alice at his side, laughing and throwing into the air a whooping Leo.

'I'm acutely aware,' Alan is saying, staring out of the window into our courtyard, his back to me, 'fully aware that part of your feeling for me when we married was a result of the loss of your mother, and the absence of the normally stabilizing influence of your best friend.' He broke off. 'Oh shit, I sound like an Englishman. You notice that? Every day since we had that fight I get more English and you get more American. At this rate, by the time we land at JFK, I'll be Winston Churchill and you'll have turned into fucking Popeye.'

I don't respond, but give him time to collect himself.

'Maybe,' he resumes, 'there was even the fact that I'm a New Yorker. Before you, I never met – I'd never even *heard* of – anybody with your sense of place. But then, I never met anybody who can *hear skyscrapers* or see the blue in the Blues. Leastways, only patients who need adjustment to their anti-psychotic medication!'

Outside, the lucent blue evening is rent by a raucous note that I would like to believe is the first cuckoo of spring, but which is actually a car alarm. Alan, who loathes the intrusion of other people's noise, turns away from the window: car alarms, police sirens, traffic noise and the clamouring colours and sounds of massed human beings going about their business in the flurry of urban life. Manhattan. It's the sound of skyscrapers that Alan thinks I can hear, though of course it's Alan who can hear it; to me it hardly registers except as a comforting backdrop of warm humanity. As he turns, I see that his face is damp.

'I don't ever want you to tell me what has been going on these last weeks. Just don't tell me *ever*. I only want to say, if you're leaving me, I need to know. There's things I have to prepare. I can forget all this, this . . .' A gesture of helplessness. 'But Jesus, Annie, I have to know if you're coming to live in New York. With me,' he adds quickly, as though even here I might look for a loophole. 'I'll live in Manhattan if that's what it takes, but I've got to know.'

The car alarm has stopped now. My words drop into the silence. 'I have nothing to stay in London for, Alan. I don't know how well we can work things out, but I do know I've always been in love with New York, and I can give you my word that there is nothing for me here. Not even Babette now.'

He turns to me. 'What is it you want?'

'What I can't have. When you're naturally very emotional, there's a certain type of life you can't lead because the pain will kill you. That cuts down your choices. Either I'm with you, Alan, or I'm by myself.'

'So. Which?'

'It's time I had a stab at being a grown-up. And that involves sticking to what I've got. I've never done that. I threw away my marriage to Daniel by disappearing off to Finland as soon as there was trouble, when someone more mature might have stuck it out. I'll give this another go.'

356

'Well,' says Alan eventually, 'it isn't the most enthusiastic response a man ever had from his wife.'

'I realize that.'

'But I expected worse.'

'Can you live with it?'

He smiles, rallying at last. 'I guess there's at least as much chance that I can as you can, Annie,' he says.

THE PAST

In Central Park, Daniel is lying across the hot, red-tiled floor of Bethesda Terrace, photographing an unpartnered, ownerless, high-heeled shoe, and heaping happy anathemas on the collective head of what he calls *the throwaway society*.

'But why should any woman throw away one shoe?' I query, meaning that she wouldn't, and his interpretation is up the creek.

'Exactly!' cries Daniel in triumph. 'They're totally insane!'

They're not on their own, if you ask me. Babette and her fiancé Nigel are leaning backwards from the low wall around the fountain, and splashing each other like five-year-olds. Babette never behaved like a five-year-old even when she was five.

'Daniel, you must get a picture of those two. I've never seen anything like it.'

He turns his attention from the shoe, and directs his lens at Babette and Nigel, who are much too far gone to notice him.

A young man in tie-dyes scoots past me with one rollerskate and a ghetto-blaster, which is playing 'I'm Not in Love' by 10CC. Suddenly it is June of last year. Summer term at St Mary's. I can smell formalin and feel the skin of corpses. Deep in there between the spiralling voices, between the multi-tracked choral effects, in the troughs between one sound wave and its harmonic, the music tastes of starched coats and hospital trolleys, and hellish glass jars with the distortions of disease inside, and the Doppler-scream of ambulance sirens that one day soon will call me to my duty like a muezzin, only I shall be useless at it, completely useless, and the patient will die.

The rollerskater sweeps out of my hearing, and after a moment 'I'm Not in Love' is replaced by the white noise of every human voice in Central Park, and suddenly exultation steals through my blood like an afterglow from brandy. For the first time I begin to understand the several enormities that are my new-found life: I shall never have to set foot on the wards again. I'm a musician now — at last, and for the rest of my life. And I'm here in New York!

Daniel is now photographing a bag lady asleep on the grass and when she wakes up she'll thump him, and Babette and Nigel are so utterly soaked from the fountain that you can see through their clothes and we'll probably all be arrested on the subway. The New York summer sun grills my pale Welsh skin. I start to run. I take off my shoes, kicking them free for the next dotty photographer, and I run barefoot up the ornate steps and fly down the full length of the Mall to veer off across the grass, wending between the walkers and joggers and promenaders and dogs, like a jet-powered skier on a slalom, never taking my eyes from the sky-line of South Manhattan that looms larger and larger as I hurl myself towards it: the self-caricature of New York, with its yellow-taxi jams, and scurrying crowds, its vertical acres of concrete and cold metal and sun-spangled glass.

Music flutes through my bones and radiates from me across the heat-hazed city.

'They Can't Take That Away From Me,' sing George and Ira Gershwin above all our voices.

'I'm Alive,' sing the Hollies from the summer of 1965. 'I'm Alive.'

PAST, PRESENT AND FUTURE

33

Alan decided that we'd spend our last night in London at the Savoy, because of its theatrical associations. We'd originally thought of begging a bed for the night from Babette and Nigel, but we decided that a teary goodbye would not be in the best interests of Sophie, so we didn't ask. They'll be in Washington by August, and will come to us then – provided that the Dakota Building is still standing; Dorothea's three teenage daughters are coming in July.

Our flight is at two o'clock, and the airline's chauffeur arrives for us at half past eleven. Unthinkingly, I'd pictured a white stretch limo with secretive windows, as though New York began as soon as we stepped out of the Savoy, but here is a comfortable family saloon with a chatty driver who lives in Ealing, and hardly winces while hauling all my suitcases into the boot. I haven't got Benny in one of them; he's in kennels until next week, when we get the keys to the apartment and he, in his turn, will be crated up for the airline.

We slide out into the Strand, past two theatres where I have students playing lead roles, towards the clotted traffic of Trafalgar Square. It is a glorious April day. We drive up the Mall, the colour of cinnamon, past St James's Park, with its flowering cherry trees and self-important ducks.

Alan seems to think my departure from London should be set to music, so from the Palace onwards there is a background of Melody FM. I find that I'm superstitiously disappointed that nothing on it can be interpreted as a good omen. What did I want? 'New York, New York' perhaps, followed by that song about 'So Good They Named It Twice', then Dylan's 'Positively 4th Street' then Simon and Garfunkel's 'Bleeker Street' then . . .

The car heads west out of London, and in a surprisingly short time we're at Heathrow and pulling into the drive-through check-in. A young woman in red comes to the car window with our boarding passes, the bags are spirited away, and the car deposits us at the upstairs level of Terminal 3 Departures. I think of my first trip to New York: Daniel, Babette, Nigel and I spent five hours sitting on a floor at Heathrow waiting for standby tickets. For the first time ever, it occurs to me that certain luxuries will become part and parcel of my new life – a whole ream of inconveniences eradicated, or ameliorated, or lumbered onto somebody else.

'Goodbye,' I say to the driver. 'Give my regards to Ealing Broadway.'

'Did you practise that?' Alan asks me.

When we arrive in the Virgin Atlantic lounge he wanders about, alarming people by grappling under their chairs to plug our collection of PCs into the mains. Alan has managed to land us both with laptop computers that are incompatible with the inflight power points of every airline in the world, so now he is charging up our batteries – his, so that he can edit clinical development plans on the plane, and mine presumably in case I'm inspired to compose a movie score on my Sibelius software between here and Kennedy airport. Eventually, we take a seat and order a glass of wine.

'In the Seventies,' I inform him, 'when I lived in Notting Hill, Richard Branson lived just round the corner in Denbigh Terrace. Not that I knew it then.'

'Yeah?'

'We were all frequent customers of his Virgin Records shop.' Daniel and I spent many a happy day flat out on the cushions listening to Tangerine Dream, totally stoned.

'Yeah?' says Alan again. He has found a magazine article about aeroengines. The cover requests him not to remove it from the lounge, so the race is on.

'Absolutely,' I tell him. 'I used to walk past the window display and say "You mark my words, one day that lad will have an airline and a knighthood."'

'Yeah?' repeats my husband, deep in his magazine. I wander off to explore.

There's a reproduction sixteenth-century terrestrial globe, with its squashed, misshapen continents – the almost-Africa, and Europe with its Italy cranked back like a broken limb. No Americas, of course; between west and east is a thick meridian like a tailor's seam waiting to be let out when the known world puts on weight. Still niggled by my superstitions, I abandon the globe, with its implication that my new world lies in the realm of '*Here Be Dragons*'.

Speaking of dragons, the photograph album that was so nearly Aunt Margo's was not in my suitcase. I had made that journey to Muningstock after all. The Frobishers still lived there, and still had their wits about them – Horace eighty now, Doris seventy-six. Horace's eyes still sparkled warm and brown, though the Brylcreem had gone because he had lost his auburn hair. I saw, with a shock of recognition, that Doris's eyes were emerald. I could see how she must have been a striking-looking woman when I was a child, tall and aristocratic, with those eyes and her mass of dark hair.

Muningstock hadn't worn as well as they had; when the M25 cut its swathe through the rural outskirts of Brentwood, the developers had cut theirs through the hornbeam and oak spinneys of my childhood. Muningstock soon spilled over into Wittle Massey, and the entire spillage was now a dormitory for commuters whose work was accessible from motorway junctions 25 to 30. This 'mega-Muningstock' still retained some Essex countryside around its straggling edges, though the fields no longer had hedgerows.

But this lament suggests an idyll spoiled; driving down Mountnessing Road, trying to stare directly ahead like a blinkered horse, I had to remind myself that the village of my childhood was an untidy assortment of bungalows, council houses and a few unprepossessing cottages in need of modernization. To anyone less biased than I, this runaway expansion was probably an improvement.

I had phoned first, and was explicit about the delicate nature of my mission, yet Horace and Doris were comfortably together when I arrived, and ushered me into the back garden to enjoy the sunshine. There was a small sunken garden that I remembered, with mossy bricks bearded with grass, and great padded cushions of aubrietia. I sat on the wall, realizing that Jenny Clitheroe must have sat there many times before me.

'So this was her photograph album,' said Horace, as they, too, lowered themselves onto the gnarled brickwork. 'I don't remember it. Do you, Doris?'

'I do, yes. And I was aware that it fascinated the children.'

We were looking at a picture of a wedding group. 'Ellen and Albert married at St Olave's church, June 1925'. The groom beamed in morning dress, and the bride, Nell, given her full Ellen for the occasion, was laughing in a flurry of petals strewn by women in cloche hats. Below the legend, a copperplate hand had added a line from Thomas Hood's poem: 'It was the time of roses, We plucked them as we passed'.

Imagine if none of this had happened, I thought. Imagine if I were in Muningstock to say goodbye to Jenny Clitheroe before I moved to New York. She would have been in her seventies now. If only we could imagine the dead ageing, I wished, as so many other people have wished, it would feel less as though we'd left them behind. Suppose the dead returned, unchanged – would we have anything to say to them? I turned back to the album. Horace and Doris were gazing at Nell. Perhaps they were seeing Jenny in the luminous face.

'That particular picture once had a letter behind it,' I told them. 'A love letter saying that Jenny was so frightened that she was running away. It didn't say more, but then it wasn't finished, at least not on the morning of the day before she was killed.'

I left a pause. Nobody filled it.

'There's no letter in here now. I searched. At first, I concluded that the police held on to it as evidence. But I was trying too hard; the most likely fate of an incomplete letter is that the writer simply finished it and posted it.'

Across the gardens, from the house I was brought up in, effervesced the sound of children. They were interrupted by an adult: 'Emily, get out of the flower bed – those sandals were new last week!'

'Jenny must have taken advantage of our postal

strike. The postboxes were never boarded up; she knew that any letter she posted that day would sit around for an unpredictable length of time in the sorting office. Long enough to cover her packing up and leaving. In the event, she didn't escape in time, and her letter was delivered along with everybody else's on the Thursday after her funeral. Immediately afterwards, somebody went round to Gina Maxwell's bungalow and hit her over the head with her husband's garden spade.'

After a while, Doris spoke. 'Bring Jenny's letter out here, my dear. Annie deserves to read it. She's come a long way.'

I didn't know whether she was referring to my journey from the vast metropolis, or all the years since the murders. Horace got creakily to his feet. We watched him move indoors.

'A very strange kind of marriage, most people would think,' Doris ran a hand through the aubrietia, 'but it's worked for us, you know. There's never been a lie between us, and we have always been the best of friends.'

'I know,' I said.

'Jenny Clitheroe was a remarkable woman. In our different ways we both loved her.'

'I know,' I said again. 'I've understood that for a long time.'

We sat quietly until Horace returned. He came back out to the garden with a folded letter on watermarked Basildon Bond. The sheets crackled as I unfolded them. I read.

My darling,
   By the time you receive this I shall be gone.
   Sounds like a song, doesn't it? Me and my songs.
   I'll be in touch again as soon as I'm away and –

366

safe. Take that word to heart, my dear. Because, where I am now, I am not safe.

I know how you will react to this, you with your education and scepticism. Sceptical even in my arms, loving beneath the upturned bed.

That stopped me for a moment – it had been Frank Lucas's derogatory expression for the Frobishers' oddly chimneyed bungalow. So they *had* known about his ridicule.

Whatever you think of Leonard, he has no actual evil in him. I know you've never believed me about that black eye, but it wasn't meant, just Leonard throwing things about in one of his tempers. He was more shocked than I was when his aim went wrong. And Leonard isn't disposed to recognize evil in anyone he loves. Poor deluded soul, he actually loves Gina Maxwell – and she *is* evil. She is after my blood.

I think I've worked out how things stand between them: it seems that he's always told her they can't go off together because they're short of money – you know my Leonard and money. Well, I caught Gina one day, here, going through the desk. She had our life insurance policies out. And there was a day when one of Percy's cats made a mess on a skirt of Gina's and she took a shovel to it. Oh yes, it's a long way from that to murder, I know. But I *know*. And I'm running away.

Leonard won't follow me, I think. Please God that Gina doesn't. I shall write again when I find my safe haven. In the meantime, you know how much I love you. Let that warm the emptiness of my going.

Your Jenny.

They watched me read, and when I looked up Horace spoke.

'It was a hot morning, muggy, close. We were in for an electric storm. Jenny's letter was the most appalling shock. From the moment we'd heard she was killed, Doris and I had assumed Leonard did it. I myself had sold him that life insurance policy. And then he confessed and killed himself. I knew all about the affair with Gina, of course – Jenny spoke openly about it to me – but *this*! Leonard must have worked out the truth, and couldn't live with it. I suppose he blamed himself. Perhaps he still loved Gina, even. The poor man must have been in hell.'

'We think the police had already half-guessed the truth,' Doris added.

'Yes. Jenny had made some jottings on a little notepad, apparently. Nothing Lilliput could make an arrest on, but enough to convince him that Leonard was innocent. And eventually, a few days after Gina's death, he deduced the entire story, all of it, and came to us. But,' Horace smiled at me, 'without any solid evidence to act upon . . .'

'. . . for which we have you to thank in part, Annie . . .'

'. . . the police were powerless.'

'And the morning the letter arrived?' I prompted him.

'Doris was with me. I told her I was going for a spin in the car to clear my head, but I stormed round to Gina's. I didn't intend to kill her, only to have it out, tell her I was taking the letter to the police. But I lost my temper. Gina knew about . . . our love affair – she'd overheard a conversation between Jenny and me. She started shouting that if she went down, she'd tell everyone, drag my name and Jenny's reputation into the mud. I walked off – we were actually outside in the garden, *anyone* might have heard – but Gina followed me, still chanting her spite, her filthy remarks about Jen. And so . . .' he sighed, and Doris put an arm around him.

'Don't, my dear,' she said gently. 'Don't.'

We sat for a while, Horace gathering his composure. 'I panicked a bit, afterwards,' he said, taking up his story. 'Didn't want to face Doris immediately after what I'd done. Drove around at random. Perhaps I *was* intending to go to the police and confess, I don't know. Anyway, after a while I came to my senses and drove home. In the meantime you, Annie, my dear, had stumbled upon Gina's body. We have always felt dreadful about that. All these years we've wanted to say how sorry we are that I caused you such trauma. When you ran into the road, and then told Doris that Gina was dead, she knew exactly what had happened. We have always understood each other.' He gave her a squeeze. His wife raised a delicate lace handkerchief to his face, and gently wiped his eyes.

'And when I told you both what I'd found,' I said, 'Doris pushed you to return to the bungalow.'

'Yes. Well, I had to make it look as though there were a need to check your story.'

'Maybe. But she was urging you to do some quick clearing up, before DI Lilliput arrived. Unfortunately, my parents came home, and you had to take my father round there with you.'

'It made very little difference, my dear. I found that you had already caused rather a lot of havoc at the scene of the crime.'

'Nowadays, of course,' said Doris, 'with modern forensic techniques and DNA analysis, the police can make a positive identification from the tiniest traces, but in 1965 detectives still needed a clue.' She imbued the word with all the magical expectation of an Agatha Christie.

'Lilliput died recently,' I told them. 'Had you heard?'

369

'Oh yes. He became Chief Constable, Annie. Our joint escapades, yours and ours, didn't ruin his career, thank goodness. Oh yes, we knew that Jim Lilliput was dead. We sent flowers to the funeral. It was the least we could do.'

I let this extraordinary disclosure have the space it deserved before pressing on with what I had to say. In my old garden, one of the children was singing; it was raggedy and didn't rhyme, and I guessed that she was making it up as she went along. Their kitchen door opened to a blast of Capital Radio, and then closed again.

'Memories are funny things,' I told them cheerfully. 'I tend to remember what people say. If a conversation has emotional significance, I can remember it verbatim for years.'

They smiled at me, apparently unsurprised at the mundane turn the conversation was taking, after my unveiling of Horace as a murderer.

'For example, I've never forgotten telling you, Doris, that I'd found Gina Maxwell dead "on the garden path". You asked me what I was doing round at her bungalow. As I got older, that started to puzzle me. You'd seen me come hurtling out of the Lucases' garden into the road; the natural conclusion would have been that I'd *just* found the body, in which case the garden path I'd found her on would have been the Lucases'. Yet you knew where she was.'

No-one interrupted me. My mind's eye saw Doris weeping in our bathroom, talking about the imagery in *Macbeth*, the indelible bloodstains. I ran a hand through the lawless mass of my hair.

'I also remember another conversation. I apologize for this, Horace, but Gina Maxwell wasn't your only eavesdropper. I overheard the same tête-à-tête. Jenny said "If you're going to put a stop to our affair, I'd be grateful if you'd just tell me." And then, "I'm not sure you're actually capable of stopping it, Horace." Of course, Gina assumed that Jenny was talking about an affair with *you*. But she was never very bright. You and Jenny were on friendly terms, but that was all. Jenny was never in love with any man. You were discussing her love affair with your wife. When you brought the letter from the house just now, there was no envelope. You'd left that indoors because it was addressed to Doris. And the story you just gave me about reading it, storming round to Gina's and losing your temper – that was Doris's story.'

A blackbird started up in the nearby hedge. After a while, its tone changed; the musical phrases shortened and darkened. There was an urgency to them.

'Excuse us,' said Horace and Doris together, and rose arthritically from the wall, to scuttle as best they could across the garden. Startled, I heard the clap of hands, followed by a peevish mewing.

'Off with you!' cried Horace. 'Go on home!'

The blackbird's call continued to cluck from the hedge, but angry now, with a terrible exigency. There was a flap of wings. 'Now don't start on *us*, you silly thing,' said Horace crossly. He and Doris ducked the blackbird, and walked back across the grass, to retake their seats on the wall of the sunken garden.

'Sorry about that,' offered Horace. 'We have a nest of beautiful fledglings, but the silly things sit on the lawn looking pathetic while next door's cat stalks them, polishing his knife and fork. Doris and I are determined to save them.'

'But sometimes,' added his wife, 'when we go to the rescue, the mother bird takes *us* for the culprits, and we get dive bombed.'

'Ah well,' sighed Horace. 'It's worth it; there is very little in the world that is more beautiful than the song of the blackbird in an English country garden.'

'Very little,' agreed Doris, and then, as though it

were a continuation of the same thought, 'Jenny was very fond of you, Annie. She always said you were clever.'

'Yes?'

'Horace was with me when the letter arrived. He had an appointment he couldn't afford to miss with an important client. We were always hard up, you know. It was only for an hour, and he made me promise to sit tight until he got back, and we would telephone the police together about Jenny's letter. Horace was going to pretend that the affair had been with him. He has always protected me.' For the first time, her composure slipped a little. 'And I broke my promise.'

'What did you do when you left Bluebell Crescent?'

'Panicked. Flew around the house like a mad thing. Washed the blood off, but I kept thinking I could still see it. I had turned Gina over, you see, desperately hoping she was merely injured. But where she had fallen. Her head. Anyway, I have never needed Horace so badly. Eventually I went outside in the drive to wait for him. I took the secateurs with me, to make it look as though I were gardening. But he didn't arrive home in quite the manner I was expecting.' She smiled. 'You know, that car crash actually steadied my nerves. Isn't that odd? Nevertheless, I remember desperately trying to get you out of the road and indoors, Annie, so as I would have a chance to speak to Horace alone.'

'Yes. I'm sorry about that. I didn't allow you any chance whatsoever.'

'Ah well. We had time to sort ourselves out afterwards. Mr Lilliput knew, nevertheless,' she added. 'He realized which of us was really Jenny's . . .' she hesitated over the word, reminding me that theirs was a different generation, 'Jenny's lover. He worked out the rest from there. But the poor man couldn't prove a thing.'

I said, rising and brushing the aubrietia petals from

my trousers, 'I never could bring myself to feel sorry for Gina Maxwell, even before I had any idea that it was she who killed Jenny Clitheroe. I only ever felt sorry for Percy.'

'And for poor Leonard,' added Doris. 'The last days of his life must have been an utter nightmare.'

I pictured Doris on the morning after Jenny's murder, on the concrete garden path with its pot-holes. 'I loved Jenny Clitheroe. I wish they'd hang him.' Of course, she would remember that, too. The memory must have caused Doris a lot of pain over the years.

'You did have one witness, you know,' I said. 'You remember our rag and bone man? He was in Bluebell Crescent at the time. After his previous brush with the police, Ollie wasn't going to risk hanging around, and legged it out of there in a hurry. No-one saw him, except me. But a little later, he told me that Gina's murder was just tit for tat and didn't count. I'm sure that somehow he knew the truth. Ollie was no fool.'

'He most certainly knew, Annie. I ran full pelt into poor Ollie as he was walking into Bluebell Crescent from Mountnessing Road. Blood on my hands and knees, even.'

'Weren't you worried?'

'About Ollie? He loathed Gina, dear, she'd had it in for him for years. She really was a poisonous creature, you know. That's why Gina gave Mr Lilliput that twaddle about seeing Ollie breaking into Jenny's.'

'Of course! She didn't see me or anybody else climbing in through the window! Just a smokescreen.'

'See *you*, Annie?'

'That's a long story, and it isn't important. I expect Ollie's dead, too,' I said, with a pang.

'Oh, years ago, dear. Before your parents retired and moved away. He was a genuine Romany, you know, for all his cockney-sparrow style of speech; they gave him

373

the full gypsy funeral. A beautiful Indian summer day, I remember. The flowers were spectacular.'

Tears prickled my eyes. Well, of course he was dead – Ollie had been an elderly man when I was ten! But I had frozen him in my memory. And if you're someone whose recall is extraordinarily powerful, and *all* your memories shimmer with colour like a 1960s acid trip, it isn't always easy to comprehend properly the passage of time.

'I was always glad that Jenny was so fond of you, Annie,' Doris was saying. 'It helped to rebalance things a little in your favour. After all,' she glanced at her husband, 'of course, Babette was a lovely child in every way,' Horace smiled at her, 'but sometimes it was hard on you, Annie, that she stole the show quite so often.'

When I'd arrived, and they'd led me through their sitting room into the garden, I'd noticed the collection of photographs on their chimneypiece, including a portrait of Jenny Clitheroe at her best, and a colour picture taken of the Frobishers standing with Babette and me when we were children, outside the church after Sunday school. To an observer unacquainted with the facts, this would be construed as a family group – Doris and I lanky and skinny, Horace and Babette, slight, auburn and dark-eyed, those Italianate eyes so different from the restrained blue of Frank and Irene, his head leaning towards hers, a fatherly hand resting on her delicate shoulder. Of course. A family group.

'And Jenny was right, wasn't she – you have been very clever,' said Horace. 'Thank you for showing us this album.'

'Jenny would have wanted you to take care of it now.' I placed the Moroccan leather very gently into Doris's hands, its deep green glowing in the warmth of the spring afternoon. 'I'm sure of it.'

* * *

After that, we made smalltalk, chiefly about trans-
formations of places I knew and had once loved, after
which they wished me the best of luck in my exciting
new life in what they called the Big Apple, and I took
my leave. But as I started down the path to the gate, I
changed my mind and turned back. Horace and Doris
were still framed in the doorway, and greeted my turn-
around with a further welcoming smile, in case I'd
changed my mind and was inviting myself to the
evening meal. Or moving in.

'This is a silly question,' I said to them, 'but among the
souvenirs in the album you'll find a programme from a
symphony concert. It was at the Chester Gaumont in
1944, when Jenny must have been fifteen. Would you
have any idea what she was doing in Chester?'

They looked vacant, and then turned blankly to each
other.

'Chester,' repeated Doris. 'I'm reasonably certain
Jenny had never been to the north-west in her life. It
was a joke she shared with Leonard, in as much as
they ever shared or joked.'

'Wartime too,' added Horace. 'People didn't get
about much, not to the other side of the country.
Civilians, I mean.'

'No,' I said. 'It couldn't matter less, really. Just one
last, unsolved mystery. But it would be a funny old
world if we understood everything, wouldn't it?'

'An intolerable one,' agreed Horace fervently, and
we smiled our goodbyes again.

In the car on the way home, I played the CD of the
Beatles' *Abbey Road* album – 'She Came in Through
the Bathroom Window', and another track, one that
did no justice to Paul McCartney's genius, the tasteless
and jangly oompah of 'Maxwell's Silver Hammer' –
homicide; the weapon coming down upon an innocent
victim's head.

375

'Now, if you'd just written them both a few years earlier,' I admonished Paul as he and I approached the slip-road onto the M25, 'I could have worked the whole thing out for myself at the time.'

And now I'm here at Heathrow, and it occurs to me that the day will come when Horace and Doris are no longer around, and it is already possible that I've seen Muningstock for the last time. I'm not so sure about the photograph album – it has a habit of periodically upping sticks and finding a new home, like some fickle lover with the gypsy in him, or an upwardly mobile stray cat. I wouldn't be at all surprised if we met again.

When the flight is called, I collect my hand-baggage from the various cupboards and sockets in which my husband has distributed it, and we walk to the gate. Passports again, boarding passes.

'Thank you, madam, thank you, sir. Straight through the door onto the aircraft, please.'

We can now see our plane through the plate-glass, and Alan stops to explain to me how the flight deck of a 747.400 differs from the airbus A340. Looking startlingly like a small boy in Hamley's, he counts the windows in the double row to calculate the location of our seats, the bar and the masseuse.

'She looks like you.'

'You wish,' I tell him, sounding like Sophie.

'She does!' He means Virgin Atlantic's 'flying lady', streaming along the side of the fuselage, all legs and Titian hair. She's waving something in front of her that Alan crossly defines as a handkerchief when I, true to form, assume it's her knickers; but I'm not listening very hard, because the first thing I notice when we stop to take a look at our aircraft is her name – in unambiguous letters below the flying lady is painted 'Ruby Tuesday'.

'Thank you,' I say aloud to the air. 'That will do nicely.'

And Alan, who assumes I'm referring to our seat assignment, kisses me lightly on the cheek and we board.

MUSIC PERMISSIONS

contact: The Blues Heaven Foundation (Founded by Willie Dixon in 1981), 2120 S. Michigan Avenue, Chicago, IL 60616 U.S.A. / Phone (+1) 312 808-1286 www.bluesheaven.com

'MacArthur Park' words & music by Jimmy Webb © 1968 Canopy Music, USA. PolyGram Music Publishing Limited, 47 British Grove, London W4. Used by kind permission of Music Sales Limited. All rights reserved. International copyright secured.

RAINY DAY WOMEN
Jane Yardley

It is 1971 – hippies, hot pants and extraordinary footwear.
Jo and her friend Frankie are fifteen, and they have a
problem. Frankie's American mother, in England against
her will, is determined to move out of the scruffy Essex
village to civilized London. Jo's family would follow them
if only they could sell their great rambling home, The Red
House, but unfortunately, the house is putting up a fight.
It always did have a life of its own, an architectural oddity
built by an 18th century madman to irritate his wife, but
now its sinister goings-on are driving prospective buyers
away. The capable Jo has always coped with her eccentric
family but they're getting worse. Even more disturbing, Jo
and Frankie are convinced that there's been a murder on
the premises.

As the Red House crumbles around them, Jo and Frankie
are determined to get to the bottom of the mystery so the
Starkey family can sell up and start an ordinary life. But
along comes the devastatingly attractive Florian, folk singer
and opportunist, to cause a chaos all of his own. . .

Rainy Day Women is a black comedy in which teenaged
hopes, fears and egomaniacal tunnel vision are played
out against the background of a seriously dysfunctional
family, some of its members deeply loveable – and some
of them not.

COMING SOON FROM DOUBLEDAY

0 385 604688

A DAY IN THE LIFE

A collection of powerful, entertaining and thought-provoking short stories by some of our finest contemporary writers: Kate Atkinson, Eleanor Bailey, Claire Calman, Mavis Cheek, Candida Clark, Rachel Cusk, Stella Duffy, Helen Dunmore, Esther Freud, Joanne Harris, Maggie O'Farrell, Sarah Parkinson, Justine Picardie, Polly Samson, Rachel Seiffert, Joanna Trollope, Salley Vickers and Jane Yardley.

Each of these acclaimed writers has donated an original short story to this exciting anthology. As Cherie Booth says in the foreword to this collection, it is wonderful that so many female authors have united to support the valuable work of Breast Cancer Care, a leading national charity.

At least £1 will be paid to Breast Cancer Care for every book sold.

0 552 77127 9

BLACK SWAN

A SELECTED LIST OF FINE WRITING
AVAILABLE FROM BLACK SWAN

77127 9	A DAY IN THE LIFE		£6.99
77084 1	COOL FOR CATS	Jessica Adams	£6.99
99313 1	OF LOVE AND SHADOWS	Isabel Allende	£7.99
77105 8	NOT THE END OF THE WORLD	Kate Atkinson	£6.99
99860 5	IDIOGLOSSIA	Eleanor Bailey	£6.99
77097 3	I LIKE IT LIKE THAT	Claire Calman	£6.99
99979 2	GATES OF EDEN	Ethan Coen	£7.99
99686 6	BEACH MUSIC	Pat Conroy	£8.99
99767 6	SISTER OF MY HEART	Chitra Banerjee Divakaruni	£6.99
99990 3	A CRYING SHAME	Renate Dorrestein	£6.99
99985 7	DANCING WITH MINNIE THE TWIG	Mogue Doyle	£6.99
77206 2	PEACETIME	Robert Edric	£6.99
99935 0	PEACE LIKE A RIVER	Leif Enger	£6.99
99954 7	SWIFT AS DESIRE	Laura Esquivel	£6.99
77182 1	THE TIGER BY THE RIVER	Ravi Shankar Etteth	£6.99
99898 2	ALL BONES AND LIES	Anne Fine	£6.99
99885 0	COASTLINERS	Joanne Harris	£6.99
77109 0	THE FOURTH HAND	John Irving	£6.99
77005 1	IN THE KINGDOM OF MISTS	Jane Jakeman	£6.99
99867 2	LIKE WATER IN WILD PLACES	Pamela Jooste	£6.99
99977 6	PERSONAL VELOCITY	Rebecca Miller	£6.99
99909 1	LA CUCINA	Lily Prior	£6.99
99645 9	THE WRONG BOY	Willy Russell	£6.99
99952 0	LIFE ISN'T ALL HA HA HEE HEE	Meera Syal	£6.99
99903 2	ARE YOU MY MOTHER?	Louise Voss	£6.99
99780 3	KNOWLEDGE OF ANGELS	Jill Paton Walsh	£6.99
99673 4	DINA'S BOOK	Herbjørg Wassmo	£7.99

All Transworld titles are available by post from:
Bookpost, PO Box 29, Douglas, Isle of Man, IM99 1BQ
Credit cards accepted. Please telephone 01624 836000,
fax 01624 837033, Internet http://www.bookpost.co.uk
or e-mail: bookshop@enterprise.net for details.
Free postage and packing in the UK. Overseas customers: allow
£2 per book (paperbacks) and £3 per book (hardbacks).